W9-CEH-403

"DEAR TOBY."
SHE LEANED IN EVEN CLOSER.

It needed a tougher man than he to resist the invitation.

His mouth came down on hers and he'd have gasped—if he could. He settled for pressing his lips against hers, and taking her passion and sweetness into his soul. He sensed her breath catch and her heart rate speed up as she kissed him back, her mouth opening to his. Before he could taste her tongue, she found his, caressing with her woman's passion and mortal need.

He kissed on, stroking her tongue with his, meeting her need, driving his own higher.

He paused to let her catch her breath. She restarted the kiss, running her hands up and down his back, until she reached under his shirt and her healer's hands caressed his skin.

He almost came there and then. What had happened to his vampire control?

Who cared as long as he held Laura in his arms? No more furtive visits as she slept. She wanted him, desired him, and soon, very soon . . .

The Novels of Rosemary Laurey:

KEEP ME FOREVER

BE MINE FOREVER

KISS ME FOREVER/LOVE ME FOREVER

Anthologies Featuring Rosemary Laurey:

TEXAS BAD BOYS

IMMORTAL BAD BOYS

ROSEMARY
LAUREY

MIDNIGHT
LOVER

ZEBRA BOOKS
Kensington Publishing Corp.
www.kensingtonbooks.com

ZEBRA BOOKS are published by

Kensington Publishing Corp.
850 Third Avenue
New York, NY 10022

Copyright © 2007 by Rosemary Laurey

All rights reserved. No part of this book may be reproduced
in any form or by any means without the prior written consent of the Publisher, excepting brief quotes used in reviews.

If you purchased this book without a cover you should be
aware that this book is stolen property. It was reported as
"unsold and destroyed" to the Publisher and neither the
Author nor the Publisher has received any payment for this
"stripped book."

All Kensington titles, imprints, and distributed lines are
available at special quantity discounts for bulk purchases for
sales promotion, premiums, fund-raising, educational, or
institutional use.

Special book excerpts or customized printings can also
be created to fit specific needs. For details, write or phone
the office of the Kensington Special Sales Manager: Attn.
Special Sales Department. Kensington Publishing Corp., 850
Third Avenue, New York, NY 10022. Phone: 1-800-221-2647.

Zebra and the Z logo Reg. U.S. Pat. & TM Off.

ISBN-13: 978-0-8217-7929-3
ISBN-10: 0-8217-7929-X

First Printing: March 2007
10 9 8 7 6 5 4 3 2 1

Printed in the United States of America

Chapter 1

There was something decidedly sneaky about skulking about the house in the middle of the night, but Toby Wise was hungry.

Really hungry.

Hungry for the sweet warmth of her mortal blood and the glorious scent of her skin.

Too bad his overactive conscience was giving him such a difficult time. He was vampire. He fed off living mortals. He never harmed them and made certain they had no memory of the event. He'd managed quite nicely for the past century and a half or so. Taking mortal blood for sustenance was what vampires did.

Why was Laura Fox any different?

Because she was.

Damn.

He paid her very well, along with the other nurses who took shifts to care for Piet Connor. The seemingly straightforward plan had been to feed off each of them in turn—necessary since in Oregon he lacked the connections to maintain a constant supply of blood bags. His scheme worked brilliantly until Laura Fox arrived.

After a vampire lifetime of detachment from his food

source, Toby Wise had fallen hard and fast. If he had any survival instincts left, he'd replace her. Obviously survival wasn't as high a priority as it used to be. He couldn't bear the thought of not seeing her. He grudged her every day off and had to rein in his predatory urges to feed off her every single night she was in the house.

It had been four days, an extraordinarily long four days, and tonight he would indulge, sate his unruly self on the joy of her blood, delight in her soul, inhale the very essence of her being, satisfy every vampire instinct, and be consumed with guilt again at the end of it all.

Damn and double damn. Why in the name of Abel did she affect him this way?

He wasn't sure he wanted that one answered. He'd seen what happened to his colony fellows: Kit Marlowe, Justin Corvus, and Tom Kyd. One by one, they'd fallen in love and settled into domestic bliss—or at least the nearest vampire equivalent. Yes, they were very content, obviously happy, and delighting in their respective women. Heck, even ice lady Antonia had found herself a worthy mate.

He, Toby Wise, was thrilled for them, but that sort of lifestyle just wasn't his cup of tea. He'd been a loner since he was seven years old, the day his owner had thrown his mother to the ground and dragged a terrified Toby from her arms. Two days later he'd been sold and shipped off to a plantation in the low country of South Carolina. He'd never seen his mother or seven brothers and sisters again.

No, good friends he had aplenty, but close emotional connections were not for him.

On the other side of the smooth teak door, heartbeats measured two mortal lives. The slower pulse marked Piet Connor's grasp on his sadly limited existence. The other was strong, steady, and vibrant: the heartbeat of a healthy young woman. Toby listened; there was no movement inside. He waited, just to be sure, and slowly opened the door.

Laura was dozing in an easy chair across the room. The shaded light on the table beside her cast a pool of light that highlighted the glints in her auburn hair and cast odd shadows on her hands. She'd been reading a magazine when she nodded off and right now it slid over the smooth white fabric of her uniform. Toby crossed the room and caught the magazine before it hit the ground. No point in letting unnecessary noise disturb anyone. As he placed her copy of *Cosmopolitan* on the table, he smiled. Not exactly sedate reading, but much more fun than the tabloids Nurse Watson favored.

Not that Toby felt for efficient, friendly Nurse Watson a hundredth of the desire the mere thought of Laura stirred. A whisper of breath from her slightly parted lips caressed his hand. Her long eyelashes fluttered, brushing her cheeks. Her skin was the color of rich cream and the texture of silk.

He placed his hand on her head, willing her into deeper sleep, resting his fingers on her auburn curls until her breathing changed. Her hair felt different tonight, firmer somehow. Maybe she used one of those sprays or mousses they were always pushing on TV. A pity—he preferred her curls soft and silky so they curled around his fingers.

Yes, all very well, but he could hardly request she pick her shampoo and hair products to suit him! He did, however, permit himself to run his fingers through her hair before tilting her head to one side and loosening the top button to open her collar and expose the smooth, pale column of her neck.

The scent of skin and her firm, steady pulse had him ready. Very ready. His gums itched as his blood hunger rose. Leaning closer, he gently licked over the pulse at the base of her neck and pressed his lips to her skin. He bit carefully and precisely, as only a vampire could, and her blood rose to him. Sweetness, richness, life, and strength flowed from her as he absorbed the sustenance he needed. He drank slowly, very slowly, to prolong the pleasure while taking the least needed.

Her breathing quickened, her body tensed a little as her heartbeat sped. She let out a little sigh and leaned into him.

Talk about temptation!

As he wrapped an arm around her shoulder to hold her steady, he was only too aware of the wondrous warmth of her body, the glorious swell of her breasts and the scent of aroused woman. She was responding to his touch. Never before . . . or had she and he'd refused to acknowledge? He slowed his tasting but kept his lips on her neck, needing the connection, the link with her mortality, relishing the few moments of intimacy. He held her close, reveling in her scent and warmth. He ran a hand over the curve of her breast and down her belly and back, wanting to feel her skin but knowing that would weaken his resolve. As his lips pulled on her blood, her body tensed more, her hips rocked, her breasts pressed against his arm. His mind joined hers, to share the joy he drew from her. Her heartbeat raced, but with pleasure, not fear. He gathered up his own satisfaction and let it wash over her, filling her mind with her own sweetness until she shuddered as a soft climax rippled through her.

He still held her, waiting until her body calmed and her heartbeat settled. Gently he took his lips away and licked the site of his bite. She'd heal fast and never know what she'd given him. He eased his arm away from her shoulders and stood. He dropped a kiss on her forehead, leaving a suggestion that she wake in fifteen minutes and make herself a cup of the mint tea she so enjoyed, before he disappeared into the shadows.

Toby heard Laura go down the hall to the kitchen in precisely fifteen minutes. She'd take her cup back to Piet's room and no doubt have a relaxed and peaceful night.

Which was more than he would.

He was strung tight with restlessness. He really should feed somewhere else next time but he knew he wouldn't. Laura Fox was a drug. A need. He'd keep her close. Protect her.

And right now, he'd better run or fly off some of his restlessness. He was here to work. To sort out the mess of Connor Inc. He might not need as much sleep as a mortal, but he did need his wits about him in the morning. He just hoped he'd have them all intact.

Laura Fox dropped a tea bag into a mug and poured on boiling water. She was thirsty, very thirsty in fact. She hadn't meant to fall asleep—after all, she was paid to watch Mr. Connor and take care of anything he needed—but doze off she had and as a result felt strangely energized and relaxed. Maybe power naps were as helpful as some people claimed. On the other hand, did power naps usually involve wildly erotic dreams about employers? Not that she'd complain. Mr. Toby Wise was pretty much the substance of dreams. Tall, good looking, with a Brit accent smooth enough to melt butter and darned considerate and courteous to boot.

Too damn bad she was committed to poking, prying and investigating him. Why the hell had she ever agreed?

Restored by Laura's unwitting gift, Toby was more than ready to face the morning. Things were going well. The irregular goings-on at Connor Inc. were either dismantled or disposed of. He'd done what Elizabeth Connor Kyd had asked of him, and had the pleasure of living once again on his native soil.

He looked up as the door opened. "The Feds are here?" he asked his secretary. He'd been expecting them but it didn't mean he had to welcome them.

"Yes, Mr. Wise." Sarah Wallace, the middle-aged and wonderfully efficient assistant he'd inherited with the rest of Connor Inc., twitched the corner of her mouth. "I can always stall them."

Not much point, really. He shrugged and grinned. "Send in the clowns!"

She permitted herself a smile. "Would you like an urgent transatlantic call in a few minutes?"

He *would* like a good chin wag with Tom Kyd about this but might as well find out what they wanted, or rather, knew. "Let's hear them out first. But how about you stay and take notes."

"Good idea, Mr. Wise. A witness never hurts, but say as little as possible without a lawyer present."

Good advice. Ms. Wallace was a godsend. As she swiveled on her sensible one-inch heels, he stopped her. "Just a sec. Have they ever been here before?"

Before he'd taken on the running of Connor Inc., he meant, and she understood. "There was one occasion, while Mr. Radcliffe was here."

"What happened?"

"They stayed about ten minutes, left, and never came back. . . ."

They probably were lucky to get out alive and without brain damage, given Laran's monstrous, unethical and hideous methods. If vampires had blood pressure, Toby's would be mounting, but as it was . . . "Let's hope this visit will be as brief." With Sarah present, he couldn't use mind control. He should have thought of that before he asked her to stay but . . .

There were two of them.

He really noticed only one. The younger, shorter, dark-skinned and very definitely female one: Agent Healy, whose slim navy skirt rose enticingly up her legs as she sat in the chair Sarah drew up for her. "Grace Healy" read the little rectangle of card on his desk. The other, Agent Randall Bright, looked anything but bright, but Toby had been around long enough not to let appearances deceive him. Bright was older, with a generous paunch, a florid complexion and large, strong hands.

Foolish mortal! He actually had the nerve to try the hard-squeeze handshake. Toby resisted the temptation to crush a few metatarsals but met grasp with grip, looking Agent Bright in the eye as he smiled and closed his fingers over the man's hand. "To what do I owe the honor of this visit?"

"You replaced Mr. Radcliffe?" Bright asked as he retrieved his slightly compressed hand.

"I did." A brief smile and look of helpful interest seemed in order here.

"You wouldn't know where we could locate him?" Agent Healy asked.

He would. The incinerated remains of Laran Radcliffe were in London—at the bottom of the Serpentine, or was it the Regents Canal? Never mind. She wanted an answer. "He was in England in March. He called Mr. Connor from somewhere in Devon and hasn't been heard of since."

He wouldn't have believed it either. Bright snorted. Healy just raised a perfectly plucked eyebrow. "Nothing?"

"Not a dicky bird!" Too late he remembered "dicky" might offend. It wasn't always easy communicating in his native land. Mind you, things had changed a bit since 1865. The fact that Grace Healy was an FBI agent rather underscored the fact. Back then, she'd have been picking cotton or, if very fortunate, gracing her owner's mattress.

"What about his pay? Bank accounts? 401(k)? He just left all that?"

"Yes. Since we have no record of a next of kin, we set up an escrow account, in case he reappears."

"You think that likely?" Bright asked.

"To be honest, no." Not unless ashes could reanimate.

"What makes you so sure, Mr. Wise?"

Toby turned to Agent Healy. "Because two members of my colony witnessed a witch destroy him" might be pushing credibility a trifle. "Because of the tangle he left behind him."

They obviously hadn't expected him to admit the existence of irregularities quite this early in the conversation. It was most likely a big mistake. But he'd just made it. Toby leaned back, letting his leather chair rock slightly. "When Laran Radcliffe departed, disappeared, absconded, or whatever, Mr. Connor's daughter, Elizabeth, hired me to sort things out."

"And you found . . . ?"

Toby made himself look at her but forbade himself to smile. "I'm not in a position to share details of company finances at this point." Not until he made damn sure Elizabeth's father was in the clear.

Agent Bright leaned over his paunch. "We could subpoena financial records."

"Yes, you could." And would have already if they had enough proof. "Hardly necessary since Connor Inc. is willing to cooperate." Toby smiled. Neither smiled back. "The financial records are in a pig's ear of a mess. We're in the middle of an internal audit. Once that's completed . . ."

"You'll cooperate?" Agent Healy asked.

"Madam," Toby eyed the warm-coffee skin on the slim neck that rose out of the silk blouse. The scent of human flesh promised warm, rich blood. "I am cooperating—as far as I can in the circumstances. In a few weeks we should know the extent of the goings-on." After the auditors went over the sanitized accounts. It had taken Kit, Dixie and himself the better part of four days and no sleep to go over every computer in the company. The FBI agents were welcome to dig and delve to their mortal hearts' content. There was nothing to find.

"Meanwhile, perhaps we should speak to Mr. Connor." Agent Healy leaned forward.

Good luck to them! "You are aware he had a serious stroke."

"So it has been reported."

They doubted? Surely they'd checked hospital records. He shrugged. "I can only reiterate our willingness to cooperate and repeat what I said in my correspondence: Radcliffe's actions were totally unauthorized. Leave a list of what you want, and after I talk to our lawyers . . ."

"We'd rather talk to Mr. Connor."

Toby restrained the scowl. Attractive or not, the woman was as persistent as a rooster on a hen—wrong simile, but accurate. "If you feel it necessary, by all means call his medical team and arrange a convenient time. But I warn you, he is in no physical or mental condition to answer questions. His inability to run the company was the reason Ms. Connor brought me in."

The both stood up. Exact timing perhaps, or did G-men and -women have secret communication?

"We'll be back in touch, Mr. Wise," Bright said and nodded to Agent Healy to leave.

As the door closed behind them, Toby turned to Ms. Wallace. "What did you make of that?"

"Odd," she replied. "I think they came to intimidate and get you sweating, and you played it cool. Congratulations!"

No matter what they did, they'd never get him sweating, but he wasn't sure congratulations were in order.

Toby drove back to the house on Devil's Elbow faster than was judicious on the twisting road, but an odd urgency propelled him: a niggling suspicion that those two FBI agents would arrive at the house and badger Piet Connor. Not that it would do them any good, and it might just prove his point that the man was way beyond answering their questions. On a good day Piet recognized his nurses and Toby. On a bad day . . . Toby shook his head. He had only Elizabeth's word for the vital, intelligent and driven man her father had been before blind ambition and lust for power led him to ally himself with a renegade vampire who'd zapped his mind.

Toby had promised Elizabeth to look after her father and unravel the tangled mess of Connor Inc.

So far he'd dismantled the money laundering. It had necessitated closures and redundancies, but they had been needed to sever the links of Laran's nasty enterprise. And now . . . Toby turned into the drive that led up to the Connors' clifftop house. This part of the country was so different from his native South Carolina—and he relished the difference. Even after almost a century and a half, memories of slavery still had him shuddering.

He eased the car to a stop before the automatic garage doors and pulled inside. Making himself walk at mortal speed, he strode through the house to where Piet Connor sat huddled in a wheelchair in the glazed-in porch. The man spent hours just watching the ocean.

"Hello, Piet," Toby said, bending down to be eye-to-eye with his shriveled body.

A faltering smile followed the light of recognition. "Hello, Toby. Is my Lizzie coming?"

"Soon," Toby replied. She'd promised to fly over for a week at the end of the month. He'd be darn glad to see her—and Tom. Tom Kyd had proved his friendship once again by fixing computer records and helping sort out the mess that had once been a thriving multinational conglomerate.

"I miss Lizzie," Piet Connor muttered. "Must say I'm sorry. Didn't mean . . ." A tear trickled down his cheek as his voice faltered.

Toby wiped away the tear with the pad of his thumb. "Never mind, Piet. She understands." More than the old man would ever realize.

He turned to the nurse in the pastel blue uniform who hovered a few feet way. "Difficult day, Nurse Redding?"

"No more than most," she replied. "Will you sit with him while I fix his dinner?"

"Of course."

"Sure I can't fix you anything?"

"Thank you. I'll get something later." Having plenty of staff did make Piet's care easier, but it seemed they'd all taken on the mission of trying to feed Toby as well. Thank Abel, none of them lived in, or they'd soon notice his nonstandard eating habits.

As Nurse Redding walked out and toward the kitchen, Toby moved Piet's wheelchair closer to the French windows and pulled up a chair beside him. Together they watched the last traces of sunset fade into evening, Piet saying nothing, just grasping Toby's hand, like a child scared of getting lost. Toby glanced sideways at Piet. Maybe he should have invited the FBI here and let them see once and for all that Piet Connor was no longer responsible for Connor Inc. or much else in this world. But there was the risk that the visit would distress him. When Elizabeth came over, they'd have to talk this out. Heck, he might as well call her now, except—he glanced at his watch—London was eight hours ahead. Tom would be home from hunting by now, and they'd be unlikely to welcome interruption just to talk. He'd call later.

Meanwhile, he should ponder the ramifications of today's visit. What exactly did the FBI know, or suspect, about Laran Radcliffe's activities? If they had any notion of the full extent, they'd have arrived with subpoenas, and search and arrest warrants—not that it would have done them much good. Seemed they had suspicions but no proof. It was his job to ensure that no possible proof remained. Laran was history, his activities over and done with for good. Connor Inc. was once more a legitimate business, and he, Toby Wise, was going to see to it.

"Dinner's ready, Mr. Connor!"

How the woman stayed so cheerful intrigued Toby, but mortals were different, and cheerful was better than dour. "Why not bring it out here, Nurse? I'll feed him and you can leave. He'll be fine."

She hesitated. She'd balk totally if she knew she was leaving her frail patient in the hands of a vampire. Toby smiled. "Honestly. We'll be alright. Piet likes listening to the ocean. I'll feed him, and Nurse Fox will be here in an hour or so and she'll ready him for bed."

She hesitated just long enough to satisfy her professional scruples. With three school-age children at home, she more than welcomed getting off early. "If you're sure it's okay. It really would help, and Nurse Fox is always punctual. I've warmed up some nice soup, and there's the vanilla pudding Nurse Watson made yesterday."

A few minutes later, the sound of her Toyota faded in the evening air as she drove down the drive toward the main road, and Toby eased his hand from Piet's and reached for the tray she'd left on the table. He had a strong suspicion that steak and onions or a nice roast chicken was a better choice for a man's dinner than soup and vanilla pap, but since he'd been a blacksmith, not a cook, in his mortal days, it would have to do.

It was sad to see a once-strong man dribble his dinner down his chin. The damage that blasted Laran had caused! Yes, he'd received his comeuppance at Elizabeth's hands, but the harm he'd wrought still lingered. "What made you ally yourself with him, old man?" Toby whispered as he spooned up the pale yellow pudding. "Was it just lust for power, or did he gain sway by force of will?" It was doubtful they'd ever know.

And right now, he, Toby, had better press his energies to deflecting the damn FBI, and bury the riddles of the past. Laran's origins and final motives were a mystery. A lone vampire was an anomaly in Toby's experience. They tended to hang together for support.

Supper over, Toby left the tray in the kitchen and turned to rejoin Piet on the terrace when his mobile rang.

"Toby? I'm sorry to bother you. It's Adela." Piet's ex-wife and Elizabeth's stepmother. "I'm having a bit of trouble."

Indeed. She was house swapping with another witch somewhere near Dark Falls, on the Umpaqua River. She had helped out with Piet, that Toby granted, but he preserved intact his instinctive unease about witches. Elizabeth had proved her honor and her loyalty to the coven; Adela was another matter entirely. "What can I do for you, Adela?"

"Things here are a bit awkward. . . . I need to get away for a few days until everything calms down." She sounded scared, definitely out of character for a mortal who'd faced down Vlad Tepes.

"What happened?"

Her hesitation no doubt underscored her reluctance to ask help from a vampire. "It's the people here," she replied at last. "Gertrude did mention difficulty, but honestly, I've never in my life encountered anything on this scale. First it was flower pots smashed and a rosebush hacked down. Then it was nasty notes on the front door blaming me for dead farm animals. As if I'd go around ripping the throats out of sheep and cows. Ridiculous!" Yes, but frightening too—at least to a lone female mortal in an unfamiliar place. "This was supposed to be a quiet summer and it's turning out vile. I could take the mutterings, the nasty notes and the crossing fingers behind my back, but this afternoon . . ." Her voice tightened in terror. This was not the woman he knew.

"What happened, Adela?"

"I know I'm probably overreacting, but this morning I found all four tires slashed. I've called both service stations in the place and none have replacements. That alone wouldn't have bothered me so much—hell, it's a small town and I doubt they get much call for Italian import tires—but this afternoon I found a note under a rock on the back step: 'Thou shalt not suffer a witch to live.' Quite honestly, Toby, I'm scared."

He didn't blame her. She had to be at her wits' end to apply to a vampire for succor. "The night nurse is due in half an hour or so. I'll come over as soon as she arrives. You can stay here." He just hoped it wouldn't be for long. But a witch hunt in this day and age? Ridiculous!

The minute Laura Fox arrived, Toby was out the door and heading his red Mercedes toward Dark Falls.

Chapter 2

It was heavy dusk by the time Toby reached the outskirts of the small town. Quiet and peaceful, a knot of tourists sitting out on the front porch of the Kountry Kitchen, the town looked like something out of a tourist brochure, until he drove through the town and saw Adela's vandalized car parked beside the little house. She hadn't told the half of it: The slashed tires were just the beginning. The windshield had been smashed and some noxious substance poured all over the bonnet. Someone wanted Adela grounded.

As he parked and walked over to inspect the damage, Toby glimpsed a shadow at the window and a flicker of a curtain. He didn't blame her being cautious. Down at the end of a dirt road, a good hundred meters or more from the nearest neighbor, she should have been safe and unbothered. Instead . . .

"Toby?" She called from the half-open door. "Thank the goddess!"

At the panic in her voice, he crossed the front lawn in seconds and was inside the house, pulling the door closed behind him. "I'm here and you're going to be gone in a jiffy." The change in her was shocking. Gone was the confident, almost defiant woman he'd met a month or so earlier.

She backed away from him and slumped down on a chair. "I feel foolish calling you like an idiot, but afterward, I was so glad I did. This last thing freaked me out."

"The car being vandalized? I saw what they'd done. Tires was just the beginning."

She shook her head. "No, worse than that. I almost upchucked when I saw it on the back porch." She looked pale enough to do just that, right here and now.

"What the hell happened, Adela?" Witch she might be, but she was a terrified woman and needed help.

She shook her head. "Just fifteen minutes ago. I went out to fill up the bird feeders before I left and . . ." She swallowed, and a shudder shook her shoulders. "It was horrible, and heck, they think I'm doing that sort of thing!"

"Doing what, Adela?"

She got herself together with effort. "I can't bear to look at it again. I should have dragged it away and at least buried it but . . ." She stood up. "Look, I need a cup of tea. Mind waiting while I get one? Then we'll go."

Why not? "Go ahead. I'll have a look at what bothered you so." Might give him a clue to the perpetrators. Harassing a defenseless woman—perhaps not totally defenseless, but she was alone—was unacceptable in his book. "Out the back, you said?"

She nodded. "On the path below the back porch steps, look . . ." She met his eyes. "It's nasty, but I suppose blood doesn't bother you quite as much as it does me."

Not usually, but this did. The bloody, mangled remains of a large dog lay on the cracked concrete. It had been dead when dumped. There had been no bleeding, at least not here, but . . . Toby crouched down to look closer. It had been a shaggy, long-limbed sheep dog sort of cross. The throat being ripped out must have killed it. He guessed the leg had been torn off afterward, and at some point, something had ripped open the animal's gut and now flies buzzed over the spilled entrails.

No wonder it turned Adela's stomach. He tamped down the anger at the unknown person who'd dumped this here. And who—or rather what—in the name of Abel had so mangled the creature's carcass?

He noticed the stench right away. Not the sick, sweet smell of a freshly killed corpse, but the rank, foul stench of . . . He had no idea, but it was a definite clue to something. From the corner of his eye he noticed the note tucked under a rock. The message was clear and to the point. "First it kills my hens, then my dog. You called this creature up, witch. You have it coming. We've all had enough." Underneath was the aforementioned Bible verse.

The devil wasn't the only one who could quote scripture for his own purposes. Leaving the dog on the path—he'd bury it later—Toby went back into the house, note in hand. Adela looked up from opening a tin of tea bags. "You saw it?"

He nodded. "And I found this." He handed her the note.

She glanced at it and shook her head. "They blame me for it coming. Hell, I didn't bring it. I've never even seen it."

"Seen what?" Shock made mortals more obtuse than usual.

She snapped the lid back on the tin and dropped a tea bag into a mug before looking straight at him. "You believe mythical creatures can be real?"

"Since I'm one of those mythical creatures, yes."

She let out a dry chuckle. "Should have anticipated

that, shouldn't I?" She shook her head, moved the mug to the side of the stove and pulled out a bentwood chair. "Have a seat. This will take a minute and might just test your ability to suspend disbelief."

That he doubted. He might be young by vampire standards, but he could give her a century and a good bit more. He took the chair. "Go on."

"Have you ever heard of a chupacabra?"

So far she was winning. He shook his head. "What is it?"

She got up as the kettle boiled, and filled the mug. "What I believed to be a mythical creature or the product of a deranged imagination but"—she sat back down, clasping the mug in both hands—"it's a vicious creature. I've done a fair bit of research since the trouble first started. Seems they come from Central America and Mexico. One was supposedly seen in Kalamath Falls a year or so back. They hide out in caves and holes, savage animals, and generally cause mayhem in quiet rural parts."

Was that the rank smell he'd noticed? Perhaps. "And you've seen one here? One killed that dog?"

She sipped the tea and put the mug down. Had to be too hot for a mortal palate. "I haven't seen it to know if it exists, but people 'round here claim to have. And yes, they believe it responsible for the recent killings of animals." She paused, looking at the steaming liquid—mint, by the smell wafting up. "They also"—she looked up, a frown between her eyes—"are convinced it's my familiar."

"What?"

She nodded. "My familiar. No black cats or toads in these parts. I supposedly have a creature I'd never heard of until I came here. They think I brought it with me, or summoned it, and that I send it out to savage livestock!"

If animals were being found in the same condition as

that poor hound, he understood the locals' anxiety, but . . . "Why blame you?"

She shrugged. "Why not? I'm a newcomer and I made the grave mistake of being open about my calling." She picked up the mug and sipped. "I promised Gertrude I'd take care of her house. So far, I've had flower pots smashed, windows broken, shrubs vandalized and now her car is ruined. It's just too . . ." She jumped as the front door bell rang. "Who the hell is that?"

One way to find out. "I'll see. You stay here. If they try any funny tricks with me . . ."

She gave a wry smile. "Thanks."

It was a sheriff's deputy, all official and self-important with his star and gun belt and sweat circles under his arms. Toby rather enjoyed the man's shock at seeing a tall black man instead of a slender white woman.

"What are you doing here? I came to see Mrs. Whyte."

"I'm visiting Mrs. Whyte. She asked me to come after the unsettling incident today."

"Yes, well." He glanced across at the damaged vehicle. "It's about that that I came."

At least the local law were on top of things. "Come in. She's in the kitchen." Toby stood aside as the man ambled over the threshold, hands on his belt. A big mistake, to judge by the look on Adela's face as he walked into the kitchen. She stood, lips tight and eyes hard.

"Officer Johnson," she said, obviously not relieved the law had arrived.

"You had more trouble up here, Mrs. Whyte, I notice. How come you didn't call me?"

Her chin lifted. "I decided not to bother you."

"Major damage, by the look of things. Should have been reported."

"Oh, I don't know about that." Her voice took on a

deceptively casual note, vastly different from a few minutes earlier.

"How come, Mrs. Whyte?" He stood, legs apart, one hand on the butt of his gun.

"Well, Officer, as your colleague said after the broken windows and the shed catching fire, out here it's impossible to keep track of things. I decided you were right and left the insurance to handle it."

Toby's senses went on alert. The local law had brushed off earlier troubles, had it? What now?

"Well, I heard about it. Saul Grady told me about his bird dog being savaged. Valuable dog, it was too."

"Did he tell you where he dumped it, Officer?" Toby asked.

The interruption was patently unwelcome. "That's not what I'm here about. A valuable dog was killed and I was asked to investigate. We all know that Mrs. Whyte brought that creature with her and we've had enough of it." He shifted his hips and drew his shoulders back. "I need you to come downtown with me and answer a few questions, Mrs. Whyte."

Enough was enough! One glance at Adela's rigid shoulders and Toby spoke. "Officer?" The man turned to scowl at him. It was enough. Toby caught and held eye contact. "Officer, there is no need for Mrs. Whyte to accompany you. She is the victim here. Go back and leave her in peace." He nearly added "unless you can do your job and protect her," but no point in overloading a possibly small mind with too much detail.

The man blinked. "Right. I don't need her to accompany me. She's the victim." He blinked again. "I'll see you later," he said and turned toward the front door.

Toby made sure it was wide open for him and watched as he drove away down the dusty road. The antagonistic law disposed of, he returned to the kitchen, where Adela sat, wide-eyed with shock.

"I've heard about vampire hypnotism," she said, her voice definitely wobbling, "but never imagined . . ."

"I did not hypnotize him!" Drat her and her superstition and half-knowledge. "I merely suggested an alternative course of action." Shocked she might be, but still . . . "You didn't want to go with him, did you?"

"Hell, no!" She caught a breath. "Please don't get me wrong. I am utterly appreciative of your intervention, just astounded and amazed." She shuddered. "I didn't fancy a night in the local jail with just Deputy Johnson for company."

"There's something not right here." Even a mortal could have worked that out. "You need to get away fast, in case my suggestion fades and that sweaty oaf of an apology for law enforcement returns." He reached into his pocket for his keys. "Take my car and go to Devil's Elbow. The sooner you're out of here the better."

She actually looked ready to argue but closed her mouth and nodded. "What about you?"

"I don't need a car to get back and I want to look around and see if I can find this mythical creature of yours. If he—it—is what's causing this, he'd best be taken care of."

"I'm not even sure he exists. I haven't seen it."

"I smelled it. There's something there. I'll try to find its trail."

"It's going to be dark in less than an hour."

"I can see in the dark, Adela."

Had to be a mark of her exhaustion and stress that she merely nodded. "I need to pack something."

"Skip it! I think time is of the essence here. Whatever you need we can find or send someone out to buy."

"At least I'm packing a toothbrush." And, he noticed, the bowls and candles from the mantelpiece. Her sacred vessels, no doubt. Oh well, if Tom Kyd could take a witch as his partner, he, Toby, could at least give one shelter. He'd concede she was fast. Fifteen minutes later, she had a zip bag packed and his car keys in her hand.

"Sure you'll be okay?" she asked.

He had to smile. "I imagine I will be. Just be certain that you leave Piet's old study window wide open. I'll fly back through there."

"I see." He hoped she didn't. He much preferred transmogrifying in private. "I'll call the night nurse and tell her you're coming. You know your way around the house. If I have news, I'll tell you in the morning." He followed her to the door. "Just one more thing, a favor if you would." He reached into his pocket for his wallet. "Mind taking this with you? Just leave it on my desk."

She stared. "Okay, but why?"

Some things just had to be spelled out to mortals. "I don't mind leaving clothes behind when I shift, but I don't want to leave my credit cards and license, and if you'd also take my watch"—he pulled the metal band over his hand—"I'd be most obliged."

She shoved both into her handbag and nodded. "Sure you'll be okay?"

"Of course. You need to get away safely. You don't want to be here if that officer decides to come back."

She didn't hang around to disagree.

Once she was gone, he called Laura Fox, the night nurse. He asked her, as a favor, to make sure the largest guest room was ready, adding that he was unlikely to be back much before morning.

That done, Toby went out through the back porch and sniffed the air around the very dead dog.

Laura could not believe her luck. An unexpected overnight visitor was a complication, but the guest rooms were at the other end of the house from her patient's suite and if Mr. Wise was going to be gone all night, she'd be able to have a good snoop around. Assuming she could stifle her conscience.

Why did Dad always put her on the spot? Okay, like any good newspaper man, he was on the lookout for a good story, but really he and his new partner, Axel Radcliffe, were getting obsessed about Piet Connor and his company. First she had to get a job working in the house, then report about Mr. Connor. She soon told them the old man barely knew what day of the week it was half the time. And they'd taken some convincing.

Now it was poke through the desk and pry in the computer for business records. She'd refused outright when her father first broached the idea but found herself agreeing after spooky Axel insisted. She still didn't know why the hell she'd said yes. Whatever Dad thought about the man, Axel gave her the creeps. Yes, he'd bought into the failing local paper and put it back on its feet, but really, the way he persisted about wanting a big scoop about Connor Inc., you'd think he'd bought into the *Washington Post,* not the *Dark Falls Weekly News.*

Still, dammit, she'd agreed. She'd wait until all was quiet and then she'd have a quick sneak and go back home, tell them she'd found nothing at all and hope to heaven they'd shelve the whole ridiculous obsession.

The front door opening an hour or so later yanked Laura from the prickings of her conscience. Damn! If

Mr. Wise was back, that put an end to her sneaking tonight, which was an immense relief.

It wasn't her employer.

"Hello?" a very female voice called.

The visitor. And with her own key. Interesting. Not that it really surprised Laura; a man as attractive as Mr. Wise no doubt had a string of women at his beck and call. Funny, he hadn't come back with this one, though.

"Good evening." Laura stepped into the wide entrance hall, where the woman stood, a bulging overnight bag in her hand. "You must be Adela Whyte. Mr. Wise mentioned you were coming."

"I am. Is Piet asleep? I won't wake him but haven't seen him for a couple of weeks."

Who was she? Old friend of the family? She looked to be forty, maybe even fifty, and seemed stressed. "There's not much change, never is." Would have been easier to insist he was out for the night, but she was planning enough sneakiness for one night. She wasn't adding telling lies to someone's face.

A shadow of anxiety crossed the woman's face. She set her bag on the slate-tiled floor. "Let me go in now; I'd hate to disturb him later. He's still in the little sitting room?"

Laura nodded. "Yes. He likes being moved out to the terrace during the day."

"He always loved the ocean." She held out her hand. "I'm Adela Whyte, Piet's ex-wife—or rather, one of them."

Interesting. "Laura Fox, one of the nursing team, as no doubt you guessed."

"And may the goddess bless you for that. Can't be an easy job for a young woman, coping with a near-helpless old man, and he's not the easiest of patients, I imagine."

Seemed rude to agree, and Laura wasn't too comfortable

being painted as Florence Nightingale when she was planning domestic espionage. "He's old and weak—must be frustrating for him."

The woman laughed. "My dear, he's only three years older than I! But he's taken less care of himself." She crossed the hall and opened Piet's door.

He was lying as Laura had left him: on his back, heavy hands resting on the tightly folded sheet, his head on several pillows and his eyes shut. Only his breathing showed he was not yet asleep. Adela Whyte moved over to the high hospital bed and perched on the edge, wrinkling the blankets. Laura told herself to chill. The woman couldn't stay up all night.

Adela sat in silence for a few seconds. "Piet?" she said at last.

From her vantage point across the bed, Laura saw his eyes open. It took a moment or two for him to focus. "Adela?" he said. "You again?"

"Yes, me again," she replied. "Thought I'd drop by and see how you were."

He didn't reply right off, just stared with only half-comprehending eyes. He didn't seem distressed, just frowned as if searching for recognition or memory in his damaged brain. Then his hand reached out for Adela's. "He hurt Lizzie, didn't he?"

That caught Laura's attention. Perhaps she'd hear something that would keep Dad happy awhile and save her from rummaging though private papers.

Adela sighed. "Lizzie's fine, Piet. Don't worry yourself. She's well and happy and has found herself a good man."

"Toby says she's coming to see me. I want to see her. Tell her I'm sorry." He paused and frowned as if pulling thoughts from the shadows in his mind. "You were right, you know. I should have listened."

Adela patted his hand. "It's okay, Piet. Don't worry yourself. Go to sleep. You want to be as well as you can when she gets here."

He nodded as his lids dropped over his tired eyes. Adela waited a few minutes, then gently withdrew her hand from his grasp. She turned to Laura as she stood up and, with a brief smile and a gesture of her head, indicated she wanted to speak to her outside.

As Laura closed the door behind them, Adela asked, "He's not getting any better, is he?"

Torn between her seemingly genuine concern and uncertainty about the woman's position in the family, Laura hesitated. "Hard to tell, but on the whole, no."

Adela shrugged. In the half light of the dim hall, she looked worn and tired. "It's to be expected, I suppose, but one hopes all the same."

"Can I get you anything?"

"I'll make myself a cup of tea and get to bed. I doubt Toby will be back much before morning."

Good news! Now all she had to do was get Adela off to bed. "I'll make it and bring it up to you if you'd like."

"Thank you, my dear, but I think I need to sit awhile. I'll make my own." Laura followed her into the kitchen. By the way Adela plugged in the electric kettle and found the tea bags and cups, she obviously knew her way around. "Want a cup?" Adela asked Laura.

Why not? "Thanks. I oughtn't stay, but I'll take it back with me."

"Is he showing any improvement at all?" Adela took a second cup from the cabinet and dropped in a tea bag.

Torn between professional discretion and the feeling this woman might know something of previous events, Laura replied, "Not a lot. He talks a great deal about Lizzie. She's your daughter, right?"

"Stepdaughter, but she's a lovely young woman. You've met her?"

"No, she visited a few days before I was hired. I've only worked here a few weeks. Mr. Connor talks about her all the time." She paused. Just how far should she dig for hints? "He seems to be worried about something, often says he's sorry. Could just be confusion but it really seems to bother him. . . ." Heavens, she was being far too obvious.

Adela shrugged. "He and Lizzie had a couple of differences. Fathers and daughters do, you know." Didn't she!

"I suppose so, it just seems to prey on his mind." Sheesh, the woman should tell her to MYOB.

Instead she got up and poured water into both cups and handed one to Laura. "Here you are. I'm going to take mine upstairs. I know where the room is; don't bother yourself. I hope Piet has an easy night."

So did Laura. She still had major misgivings about poking around, but Dad had been so insistent, almost desperate. Seems his new partner was convinced there were underhanded goings-on at Connor Inc. and that details had to be here in the house.

Damn! Still, she'd have a look and hopefully be able to tell him in the morning that there was absolutely nothing and that Axel Radcliffe was barking up the wrong tree.

Chapter 3

The trail was unmistakable. It led, as expected, to the neighbor's land. Toby even found the exact position where the unfortunate dog had been savaged. The scent was stronger here and mingled with the dog's dying terror. He understood the owner's anger at finding his dog mauled to death, but blaming Adela was a bit over the top. And as for sending the Neanderthal deputy over to haul her down for "questioning"—Abel give him patience! Narrow-minded small towns still dotted the map just as they had in his mortal days.

He was not lingering here. The last thing he needed was for said neighbor to accuse him of trespassing. Taking the still-strong scent as his guide, Toby followed it for a couple of miles through the growing dark to the riverbank and what appeared to be the creature's lair among a heap of rocks. The opening was small. Toby sensed a heartbeat—at least of sorts—within. Unwilling to transmogrify small and face the chupacabra in its own territory, Toby decided to wait. Sooner or later the creature would emerge. It would be interesting to encounter another living myth, and Toby had no doubt of his ability to influence it to leave the neighborhood.

Once it was gone, Adela could return and hopefully the town would soon settle down.

He picked a convenient perch in a nearby tree and waited, while the summer night fell around him.

It was almost full dark when he caught the first movement among the rocks. A mortal might well have missed it but not even a mortal could ignore the rank odor. If the locals believed witches dealt in fire and brimstone, small wonder they blamed Adela for this creature.

Vampire senses alert, Toby waited, watching two glittering eyes that peered from the dark recess. In a swift movement that took him by surprise, the creature emerged. Not much surprised Toby after a century and a half, but the chupacabra had him staring.

Abel preserve him! The creature was something out of a nightmare. The face was a prototype for a gargoyle and the body appeared to have been constructed out of spare parts.

It stood up on its hind legs, its short forepaws had massive claws that obviously made up for the lack of arm length, and it was covered all over with wrinkled gray skin that looked scaly and tough. It turned its head from side to side, senses and eyes alert, as it sniffed the air and curled up its upper lip, baring teeth that even impressed a vampire.

No wonder it had ripped that dog's throat out! Any animal smaller than a rhinoceros would come off second-best in a tangle with a chupacabra.

And he, Toby Wise, was going to have to deal with it. A polite request to vacate the vicinity was unlikely to be effective.

Damn and double damn.

Oh, well. No point in dillydallying. As the chupacabra turned and set off across the field, no doubt in search of

more livestock or domestic animals to savage, Toby
dropped from the tree, landing just a couple of meters
in front of it.

The creature paused in its tracks for about three seconds. As Toby decided the thing stank even worse at
close quarters, the chupacabra lunged, vicious teeth
bared, obviously aiming for his throat. Toby thanked
Abel for vampire reflexes as he leapt over the creature
and landed behind it.

It spun around, almost as fast as Toby, but he had it
puzzled. After all, dogs and sheep lacked a vampire's
jumping ability and speed. The delay was only momen-
tary. The chupacabra snarled again and, as Toby moved
in to grab it by the throat, raked his arms with its claws.

The wounds stung, but not enough to slow a vampire.
Toby tightened his grip and, ignoring the hissing and
the slashing claws, lifted it off its feet.

It promptly ripped his trousers and opened a gash in
Toby's thigh, proving its hind claws were every bit as
sharp, and somehow, despite Toby's grasp, it swiveled
its neck and bit his wrist.

Damn! Toby tightened his hold, the creature's choking
gasps echoing in the night. Toby hated killing, despised
needless bloodshed, but this creature could not be permitted to plague the neighborhood.

Maintaining his grasp, he swung the animal around
and slammed it on the ground, bringing his knee down
on its chest and pressing his arm across its throat.

It was several long minutes before the chupacabra
took its last breath.

Once sure it was dead, Toby released his grasp and
stood up. It was now pitch dark, not that that was any
impediment to a vampire. He looked at the limp creature sprawled in the dirt and wondered from which pit

of hell it had emerged. He really should be acclaimed as the savior of Dark Falls, but he'd settle for making life easier for Adela.

He looked around, wondering where to put the creature so its corpse would be conveniently found by the local populace, when he heard distant engines.

Tucking the chupacabra among a clump of bushes, where it was unlikely to be found until he was ready, Toby headed toward the road.

A convoy of assorted cars, jeeps and pickup trucks passed by where Toby hid among the trees. Why? There was nothing up here except Adela's house. They'd already passed the drive to the neighbor who'd dumped the damn dog in her back garden.

They had to be heading for Adela's house. Maybe the deputy did have a good reason for getting her away, which meant he knew, or darn well had an good inkling, what was going on. In fact, damned if he wasn't bringing up the rear.

Fine! Adela was far from harm now and Toby felt like putting a spanner in the works of whatever nastiness the local yokels had in mind.

Stopping only to strip off his pale blue shirt, as it was rather a flag in the dark—perhaps he should start conforming and wear black like any respectable vampire—he tossed the remnants of pale silk into the woods and followed the vanguard.

He should have stripped off his trousers as well. They were navy and good camouflage, not that he needed it in the night—black skin gave its own cover—but the darn chupacabra had ripped his left trouser leg from midthigh to below the knee, and the fabric flapped as he ran. But he wasn't about to stop again; he darn well wasn't letting the marauding locals out of his sight.

He'd been right. They stopped in a cluster in front of Adela's house, headlights shining as they gathered in a knot just beyond the front lawn. There were twelve, perhaps fifteen of them. No, another group of half a dozen piled out of an SUV. There had to be twenty.

What sort of cowards had to mass in such numbers against a lone woman? He had to chuckle. They had no idea whom she had on her side. Twenty to one was about even between mortals and vamps. He stayed in the shadows of the trees; no need to reveal himself when he could hear quite well at a distance.

Seemed there was a bit of disagreement over exactly how to proceed. Good, let the mortals dither and delay. Toby looked around; the ground sloped a little and some of the cars were parked rather carelessly. How considerate of the owners to leave them unlocked. Saved him the bother of breaking in.

He slipped close to the most convenient, opened the door and took the car out of Park. After closing the door carefully, Toby nudged the bumper with his foot.

The resulting crash diverted attention from the main project. Several men gathered around offering advice on how to shift the car off the tree, and ribbing "Ted" on having left the car in Neutral. Ted expressed his disgust at the slander. A couple of them took his part and it looked as if a nice fracas was brewing, until a more focused, and less easily distracted, member of the company reminded them they'd come to "smoke out the damn witch," not fuss over a few dents and scratches.

It was going to be tricky to adhere to colony ethics and desist from harming mortals. Toby could argue these specimens were subhuman, but that point was specious at best. Better toe the line, but the code said nothing about hindering and inconveniencing mortals.

While they had a little fun breaking windows and yelling epithets certain to mortify their mothers, Toby grabbed fistfuls of dirt and grass and blocked up a few exhaust pipes. Crude but likely to irritate. He was pondering the wisdom of smashing a few windshields when a voice rose above the others, suggesting they'd done enough.

It was drowned out by a mob baying for blood. Long-suppressed memories burned in Toby's mind. Horror clamped his gut, but damn! He was vampire! Nothing they did could harm him now. Seemed Adela's apparent absence enraged them. Dear Abel, had they really planned to harm her?

Definitely! Fuel cans were produced, and as Toby crept closer—not much caring at this point if he was seen—a select few doused the front and back porches and the shrubs and door with petrol.

Bastards!

Anger roiled in his mind. Thank Abel Adela had called him. What sort of mortal did this to another? Right, if he knew the answer to that he'd hold the key to world peace. Meanwhile, a gray-haired man who looked like every child's dream grandpa, tossed a lighted match toward the front steps.

The vapor ignited with a loud rush, followed a moment of quiet before the first flames roared, burning through the azaleas and catching the wooden trellis beside the front door. Minutes later, the front door went up in flames and the crowd cheered.

And through it all, the deputy stood apart, watching.

That did it!

While the monsters watched and cheered—Toby half-expected to see them dance around the flames—he ran back to the rocks and pulled out the limp body of the chupacabra.

He was back in minutes, settling the noxious carcass in the driver's seat of the deputy's cruiser. The vehicle would never be the same.

With the mob engrossed in destruction, Toby only needed ten minutes to jam up the remaining exhausts and shove his fist through each windshield.

They wouldn't forget this night in a hurry.

Time to go home.

There was nothing left for him to do. As he paused against a large pickup, tiredness washed over him. He'd better fly rather than try to transmogrify. Would take longer but used less energy.

Ripping off his ruined trousers, he tossed them into the flames. His boxers, shoes and socks he draped over the sheriff's radio aerial just for the hell of it. Toby ran to the open field adjoining Adela's now-burning house. The flames were licking at the windows now; it was only a matter of time before the entire house was engulfed. As he watched, there was an explosion accompanied by yells and screams as her vandalized car blew up.

Definitely the moment to vacate the vicinity.

Summoning his remaining strength, Toby tensed and ran and leaped into the air, propelling himself through the night toward Devil's Elbow.

He hoped Adela had remembered to leave the window open.

Maybe fortune did favor the sneaky and the under-handed. The unexpected guest was asleep (Laura peered round the door to be sure), and Mr. Connor was dozing peacefully. With Mr. Wise not returning until morning, she had several good hours to poke and pry and hope-fully find something to satisfy her father. Once she did, she was quitting. She could not look these people in the face knowing she'd spied on them. She wouldn't have even considered it, but Dad had been close to tears when he begged her. It beat her how he let his new partner pressure him so.

The paper was Dad's bailiwick; she was the one prying on nice people and a fair employer.

She booted up the computer and after a good hour found nothing. E-mail was password protected—nothing unusual in that. Hers was too. Quicken showed nothing more than personal bank accounts. She certainly envied his bank balances, but having a very nice savings account was hardly illegal. There were a couple of locked files, but if they held the dubious secrets Dad was after, she couldn't access them. The files she could open held ordinary-seeming business correspondence and a bunch of IRS tax publications.

Drawing a blank there, she looked at the bookmarks in his Web browser. He seemed to be interested in South Carolina history, but that was hardly the basis for an exposé. She shut the computer down, checking that the keyboard and mouse were left exactly as she'd found them, and went for the desk drawers.

They were virtually empty, probably cleaned out after Mr. Connor's stroke, and there hadn't been time to accumulate the usual clutter. Mr. Wise appeared to have a liking for purple felt-tip pens and often ripped out articles from *Business Week,* but that was that.

Maybe the filing cabinet would have what she needed.

The bottom two drawers were locked. Interesting, but the keys weren't in the desk drawers, and picking locks wasn't part of her training. She had the top one open and was flicking through the files when a sound like a wild gust of wind made her turn around.

Her employer stood in the middle of the carpet, frowning. At her. "What the hell are you doing?" he asked. Her mouth dropped open as he came toward her. "I repeat, Nurse Fox, what exactly do you think you are doing?"

"I . . ." Inventing a plausible lie was beyond her capabilities right now. Hard to think when caught in the wrong by an irate employer. A naked, irate employer. He was tall, very black and even better looking than a couple of her stray fantasies had suggested.

He was also bleeding. "You're hurt."

"Utterly irrelevant, Nurse Fox. Please answer my question." He crossed the carpet and put his hand on her shoulder. Nakedness didn't seem to faze him. She'd be equally cool. After all, she was a nurse. She'd seen plenty of naked men in her job, but not standing upright, inches from her and meeting her eyes in a way that demanded the truth. "What are you looking for?"

Toby watched as the instinct to lie crumbled before his compulsion to tell the truth. "Proof of illegal activity."

Toby hissed. Damn FBI! Planting agents in Piet's house! They didn't miss a trick. "Who sent you?" If it was either of the agents this morning . . .

"Dad, he sent me."

Rather unsubtle! Mortals! He needed to know if "Dad" was an FBI code name but damn, he was worn out and the effort to bend her will this much had him close to dropping. "Indeed. Go back to your patient, Nurse Fox. You'll tell me everything in the morning." He watched as she blinked, her green eyes still confused, and then walked across the room to the door without looking back.

* * *

It wasn't until ten minutes later, as he stood under the shower, Toby realized he'd not removed her memory. Later. He'd do it in the morning. Wasn't much of a worry after all. If she called her field supervisor and reported her quarry had appeared as if by magic in the middle of the room without a stitch of clothing, they'd think she'd been taking funny pills.

Not that Toby was in the habit of wandering around naked in front of employees. Or anyone, come to that. But he was shocked. He liked Nurse Fox. Really liked her. Too darn much for his own good and . . . damn! He'd tasted from an FBI agent. Darn good thing on those occasions he'd held her under glamour. What would the feds do with the knowledge they were investigating a vampire? He'd end up in some nasty experimental bunker somewhere.

He had to be much more careful.

And he was still bleeding. Whatever that chupacabra had in its saliva and claws slowed healing. Thank Abel for the emergency supply of blood in the hidden refrigerator in the bedroom. It took four bags, but finally the scratches healed. Toby hid the empty bags to dispose of later, and went to bed. A couple of hours' rest and he'd be right as rain, and ready to get the full story from the devious and delectable Laura Fox.

Chapter 4

"Sheesh, Toby, let you loose in your native land and mayhem happens."

Call an old friend for advice and support and look what you get. "You're a fine one to talk, Kit Marlowe. Who had half the colony in his sitting room last year for an ethics enquiry?"

"Wasn't over me. That was Justin. Besides, it was a weak point of law anyway. Everyone knew Justin wasn't culpable. Now this business of yours . . ."

"Yes?"

"You're telling me it's a bit complicated and involves mortals."

Too damn many of them. "I'm trying to decide whom to handle first—this FBI lass in my household or the pair breathing down my neck—and what to do about Adela, not forgetting a burnt-out shell of a house and an exploded car." He'd ignore the scars on his thigh and arms for now. Not that they didn't worry him. The last time he'd scarred was after a beating when he was mortal and another man's property. But at least these new ones were fading, if slowly.

"See to the girl. She's right in your pocket, so to speak.

If Adela's pal is anywhere near as practical as she is, she has insurance. Once you get that sorted out, Adela can come and stay with Heather and leave you to hoodwink the FBI." He paused while Toby hoped his phone wasn't tapped. "Want me to come out there, old chap?"

It was a generous offer. "I'll let you know if I need you. I won't ask you to get a safe conduct from Vlad unless we have to. In fact, heck, if I do need backup, I'd better call on him first anyway." No point in treading on toes if he didn't have to. He was already here as a grace-and-favor visitor.

"Yeah! No point in ruffling our Romanian friend's bat wings. Call me if you need me, alright, pal?"

Toby agreed he would and hung up. He did need to call Vlad, he supposed, though how to explain the chupacabra, he had no idea. First, he'd take Kit's advice and see to the girl.

Laura Fox had a rotten night. Her patient slept like a baby while she fretted and paced. Talk about a fiasco! Well, most of it. Getting caught with her hands in her employer's files was darn good reason for dismissal and if she wasn't supremely lucky could get her blacklisted with all the local agencies. There was a lesson here about heeding her own conscience. Seeing Toby Wise in the altogether was the only bright spot in the fiasco, and she'd been too shocked and shaken to fully appreciate the opportunity. More fool her. Trouble was she'd genuinely liked the man. Okay—tell the truth—she had a bit of a crush on him. Attractive, a perfect gentleman through and through, and his smooth voice and lush Brit accent had curled her toes on more than one occasion. Not that now was the time to dwell on the decidedly erotic dreams he'd featured in.

She'd messed up. It was her own doing. She'd explain why she was searching through his private papers and leave and hope he let it go at that.

She was still trying to figure out why she felt this compulsion to tell him everything, when he opened the door.

"How's Piet?"

"He had a good night." She took a step toward Toby. "I need to talk to you."

"Yes." He nodded. "Let's go in the kitchen. No point in waking Piet." He held the door for her and she walked down the hall to the kitchen. "Have a seat." He held a chair for her.

His courtesy made her action seem even sleazier than ever.

She sat, took a deep breath and looked straight into his dark eyes. "Mr. Wise . . ." How the heck was she to start?

He smiled. "You were going to explain what you were doing in my study."

She did. Against all caution and her own sense of discretion, she told the lot. Everything. Her father's depression after her mother died. How he let the paper go until it was on its last legs. The financial backing from a new partner. Her own personal dislike for said partner, and now, her father's near-panicky insistence she take the job here and find "something" so he could write up an exposé of wrongdoings at Connor Inc.

It came out in a rush. Tired, she took another deep breath and listened to the clock on the wall tick away the minutes while she waited to be fired.

Toby Wise frowned. "Interesting. Would you like a cup of coffee, Laura?"

Was he kidding her? Was it a Brit custom to offer coffee before firing employees? "Coffee?"

"Why not? I want to talk to you, and I don't doubt you could use the caffeine after a long night."

She could use a stiff drink more, but she could hardly ask for gin when she was about to be unemployed, and she did have to drive home. "Er . . . thanks."

"Milk, sugar?" he asked as he filled two mugs from the full carafe under the automatic coffeemaker.

"Both, please." He took his black and had to have a throat of steel. She watched his Adam's apple bounce as he swallowed coffee too hot for her to even sip. He set his mug down on the table with a soft thud.

"Laura, don't look so worried. I'm not going to eat you—or sack you, come to that. But I do insist you answer a few questions."

"Okay." Or so she hoped. At least she still had a job. Incredible, really. "What do you want to know?" Whatever it was she would answer truthfully. She couldn't lie to him.

Where to start? He couldn't hold her under mind sway forever but he had to know who was investigating him and why. "Do you work for the FBI, Laura?"

Her green eyes widened. "No!"

That was clear enough and he detected no sign of prevarication in her mind. "Who really sent you to pry, then?"

"Dad." Bore out what she'd said earlier. "He wants a big scoop for his paper."

"What paper is that?"

"The *Dark Falls Weekly News*."

Interesting coincidence. A small, local weekly, no doubt. "Why pick me?"

The skin between her eyebrows creased and she shook her head. "I don't really know. I think it was the new owner leaning on him. He's an odd man." And the mention of him caused her to tense her shoulders. Interesting.

"What's his name?"

"Axel Radcliffe."

By Abel and all his creation! It couldn't be! Too much of a coincidence! But she wasn't lying. He was certain of that and . . . He was losing his hold on her mind. Concentrate. Focus. Get the facts. "When did he buy the paper?"

"About six months back. He offered to buy a half share. If he hadn't, I think it would have folded. Seemed a godsend at the time but now I wonder."

So did he, but on slightly different points. "Where does this Radcliffe chap live?" Investigation was in order.

She scowled. No other word for it. She frowned and bit her lip. "With Dad!" The fact obviously distressed her. "He was staying in a bed-and-breakfast at first, then moved in. It's a big house and I don't live there anymore, but they are never apart. It's creepy. Dad's almost scared to cross him."

It was more than creepy. He had to investigate this and keep Laura as far away as possible. "Were you planning on seeing your father today?"

"No, I was going to call him if I found anything."

Fair enough. "Tell him it wasn't possible. Piet had a restless night and there was a visitor in the house, and I came in late." All true.

"I will." Her eyes were clear and honest. No wonder she'd done such a lousy job of spying. Devious just wasn't in her. "But Dad . . . ?"

"That's okay. I want you to help me find out why this Axel Radcliffe wants to learn about Connor Inc. and me. Tomorrow I'll find something for you to take to keep them satisfied a little while. Won't be much but should keep them off your back for a few days."

Sheer relief shone across her face. "You really mean it?"

"Most certainly, I do. I want to know why he finds

us so fascinating." Not that he couldn't make an educated guess. If the annihilated and unlamented Laran Radcliffe had kin hereabouts, they had trouble.

As if he didn't have enough on his plate already.

"Oh! Thank you!" Laura reached over and grasped his hands. Hers were warm and living and he fought the urge to mesh fingers. Too bad he'd taken her blood; now it sang to him. Talk about sweet temptation.

He let go of his hold on her mind. "Don't worry, Laura. You see to Piet, I'll find something you can take to your father tomorrow." Even if he had to make it up.

Toby had to smile overhearing Laura assure the day nurse that Piet had a "quiet" night. Piet had to be the only member of the household who hadn't gone through menace, shock, fright or unarmed combat in the past twelve hours.

Toby took his phone out onto the terrace and sat gazing at the ocean for several minutes before punching a number into his speed dial. He had no idea what Vlad would do or might expect him to do, but having another Radcliffe in the vicinity was a coincidence that could not be ignored.

"So . . ." Vlad said after Toby finished. He'd left out most of the events of the evening, focusing on what Vlad needed to know. "You're convinced I've another rogue vampire squatting in my territory?"

Having Laran, and now Axel, undetected no doubt stuck in the Lord of Wallachia's craw. "It's a rather incredible coincidence, don't you think? Seems like a similar setup, getting the confidence and gratitude of a mortal and then using him. I plan on going over there and seeing what I can find out."

"Let me know what you discover. If he is a vampire,

I'll send an emissary to him for tribute. Might use that French revenant, Larouselière. He helped over the other Radcliffe, I believe."

He'd shared information. Hadn't exactly rolled up his sleeves or dirtied his hands. "I'll call as soon as I find anything more."

"I'll await your phone call, Wise. Good day."

Adela paled ashen, as only a mortal could, when Toby recounted the unpleasant events of the night. She did manage a rather choked laugh over the chupacabra in the deputy's cruiser. "He must have had a hissy fit when he found it."

"I sincerely hope so. Unfortunately, I didn't stay around to watch. I'd rather like to see the cop car in daylight. I bet it's rather nasty. And I am looking forward to meeting the deputy again."

"You're going back?"

"*We're* going back, just as soon as you have breakfast. As the good friend I am, I'll drive you back home this morning. We'll both express astonishment and horror at finding your house and car destroyed, and who better to explain what happened than the local arm of the law." Sarcastic, but who cared? He smiled. "I will certainly encourage him to make a thorough investigation. A report will be needed for the insurance, of course, and"—he paused and chuckled—"if it does come to an enquiry, the traces of petrol, the tire marks in the road and over the grass, to say nothing of all the footprints, might really catch an arson investigator's eye."

"You're enjoying this, aren't you?" Her tone implied a definite disapproval.

"What I'm enjoying is the prospect of making a venal deputy squirm like a worm on a hook. Instead of

protecting you, he threatened you, then oversaw the
destruction of your home."

"Gertrude's home, actually, and her car." Adela let out
a slow sigh and shook her head. "How am I going to tell
her?"

"Why don't we discover what there is to tell first."
There was the outside chance a freak thunderstorm had
extinguished the blaze. Unlikely but . . .

"Let's set off now; forget breakfast."

No, she needed food. She was mortal, after all. "We
can leave now if you wish, but we'll stop at one of those
fast-food places and get you sustenance. Never actually
had occasion to enter one myself, but I assume you
know how they function."

Most days Laura found the drive home, down the
coast toward Florence, a nice, relaxing transition. Today
it seemed each bend and twist mirrored her confusion.
Her mind raced over the events of the night and the
early morning, and what she did, or did not, feel toward
Toby Wise.

Okay. He was handsome, charming and bedworthy in
the extreme. He was genuinely concerned with Mr.
Connor and considerate of the staff. But darn it, he was
her employer and she'd resolutely shoved her attraction
to the far recesses of her mind. She was not about to fall
for an employer. That way lay misery, a broken heart
and ultimately the need for a new job.

Trouble was, no matter how firm her resolve not to
dwell on Toby's all too apparent merits, her subcon-
scious wasn't getting the message. There had been the
three dreams (she wasn't likely to ever forget a single
one). On three occasions when she'd dozed off during
the still of the night, Toby starred in the colorful images

of her REM sleep. She'd had a few fantasies in her time, but nothing as vivid as these. She'd felt his hands on her shoulders, his lips on her neck, the cool brush of his skin on hers and the blinding ecstasy of his kiss.

Yes, well. Dreams were dreams. All very nice and all that, but they were not the forefront of her worries right now. The events of last night and this morning were going to take all day to sort out.

When she reached Florence, instead of going straight home, she drove down to the river and parked overlooking the harbor. Morning sun glittering on the water should have calmed and relaxed her. It barely registered.

Why in Hades had she caved in to her father's ridiculous suggestion? Because he was scared for his job and she loved him. Simple, stupid and inescapable. The paper had been her father's and her grandfather's passion; too bad Dad's enthusiasm for journalism wasn't matched with business sense. This new partner had bought into the paper for a fair price and kept Dad on as editor, but at what cost?

Her peace of mind, for a start.

And talking of peace of mind, would she ever know any again as long as the image of her employer standing square on the Oriental carpet, stark naked, was seared into her memory?

It was enough to give her brain fever. Heck, her heart rate soared when she was foolish enough to indulge in a glimpse of memory.

Tall, broad-shouldered and narrow-hipped, skin like dark satin, but instead of his usual calm smile, a look of utter outrage on his face.

It was like a twisted dream, but it had happened. She had no business being in Toby's study, and he had every right to wander about his own rooms, naked, in the middle of the night, if he so chose. She'd been the one way out of line.

But his reaction mystified her.

Instead of firing her, Toby listened sympathetically (though how and why she'd spilled her guts quite so completely, she'd never know) and offered to help! How exactly he planned on producing some sort of mythical figures or papers to satisfy Dad beat her, but some deep instinct told her Toby Wise would not let her down.

Damn, the man was bedworthy, honorable, helpful and her boss. What an unsettling combination!

And even more unsettling: Her father's car was parked in her driveway and he was waiting on the small rectangle of concrete that served as her front porch.

As she pulled off the road, he leapt off the porch and grabbed the door handle the minute she stopped. Before she turned the engine off, he had the door open. "You have what I need, Laura? Where is it?" His shaking hand grabbed her arm. "I must have it. Give it to me!"

"Dad! For heaven's sake, let me get out of the car."

He moved just enough for her to get her feet on the ground and stand but kept his hold. "What do you have, Laura?" He peered past her into the car. "Where is it?"

"I don't have anything yet, Dad. I'll try again tomorrow. . . ."

"What do you mean?" His voice rose to a shriek. "You promised! I have to have it!" His lips trembled like a scared child's and his eyes were wet with tears.

On top of last night, this was about all she could take. She shoved the door closed with her hip as he let out the first sob. "Get inside," she insisted, more or less yanking him along.

As he collapsed, sobbing, onto the sofa, she sat beside him, awash with guilt at her irritation. Whatever was going on had him in knots. Sheesh! He hadn't cried like this when Mom died. What possessed him? She kept her arm round his shoulders, handed him a handful of tissues and waited it out. She'd known he was under pressure, but to crack like this . . .

He didn't cry long. He wiped his face and eyes and glared at her. "I counted on you, Laura, and you've let me down. Does my future mean nothing to you?"

"Dad, please listen. I agreed to see what I could find and have not gone back on that. Last night it wasn't possible. It was a disturbed night." For her, if not for her patient. "An unexpected guest arrived in the middle of the night and Mr. Wise asked me to check everything was ready for her. He came in later and between one thing and another it wasn't possible."

"You mean you didn't bother!"

"Did you want me to get caught with my hands in the filing cabinet?"

He paled, shock making his swollen red eyes even larger. "Dear God, no! Don't be utterly stupid, Laura! This has to be secret, you know that. No one must know what you are doing."

But Toby did and . . . She'd get a headache if she tried to work that one out. Between her father going irrational and her ill-used employer being understanding it seemed no one was acting the way she expected.

"Then, Dad, please let me choose the right time for this."

"Axel is not going to be happy."

"Then maybe Axel Radcliffe should do his own dirty work!"

That earned her another glare and he grabbed her wrist. "You don't know what you're talking about. I couldn't manage without Axel. Don't you realize he saved the paper? I need him, Laura, and you're going to help me." Her hand was going numb, and she was majorly irked.

"Right now, Dad"—she stood, pulling her wrist back—"I'm having a cup of coffee, then going down to the Laundromat. I have errands to run, and I plan on sleeping some before going to work tonight."

"You always were selfish! Think of yourself first, don't you?"

Deep breath needed here. "Dad, to find something to keep you and your precious Mr. Radcliffe happy, I need to stay employed. So, take your pick. Do I go into work tonight or not?"

"Now you're being silly. Of course you'll go to work." He stood, still shaking.

"Want a drink, Dad? I've got Coke and can fix tea or coffee."

He shook his head. "No, Laura. I won't stay." He squared his shoulders. "I need to return to the office and let Axel know you failed us."

When did he get so darn expert at making her feel guilty? "Come back in the morning, Dad. I'll have something."

"You promise?"

"I do." Toby had, and she trusted him.

Maybe right now he was concocting some spurious document for her. She couldn't quite figure out why he was helping, but she'd caught his interest in Axel Radcliffe. That was a bit odd too. Perhaps this was a personal vendetta. After all, she wouldn't be working there if Dad and Axel hadn't pushed her to apply for the job. Perhaps she should ask a few questions and do a bit of investigating on her own.

Chapter 5

Yesterday Toby had driven this road, thinking perhaps Adela was overreacting. Now he wondered what exactly awaited them in Dark Falls. He was actually quite curious to hear what tale the deputy had to spin.

"I don't know what to tell Gertrude," Adela said, shaking her head. "I should have called her and told her."

"Best wait until we know for sure. Might not be as bad as it looked last night. It was dark."

She gave a dry chuckle. "Toby, I appreciate your efforts to be tactful but are you really telling me you couldn't see with your vampire sight?"

"I could see, but couldn't foresee how it would burn. Something may be left."

Not much.

The house was a charred shell, the car a heap of black metal. The smell of burned rubber still lingered in the air and the remaining grass and shrubs were trampled underfoot.

"Dear goddess!" Adela said, her voice tight and low with shock. "It's destroyed."

He couldn't argue. "I brought a camera. A few pictures for the insurance will help your friend."

"I bet her insurance papers were in the house."

He smiled. "We can take care of things."

That earned him a sideways look. "Oh! I forgot how you people manage everything." Obviously realizing that sounded snippy, she shrugged. "Sorry, didn't quite mean that the way it came out."

Maybe she hadn't. One never knew with a witch. Not that he'd known that many others. Elizabeth Kyd and old Nora back on the plantation were about it. "Never mind. Do what you, or Gertrude, can. If there's any trouble, the colony is at your service."

"Of two witches?"

"Why not?"

"Thank you," she said, as they walked to the back of the ruin. Here it was even worse. The flames having swept this direction and engulfed two trees and a low hedge that bordered the now-ruined vegetable garden. Astounding what a bunch of clodhopping yahoos could do in a few hours.

What if Adela had been in the house? True, the deputy made an attempt to remove her from the house, but even so . . . "Adela, someone's coming." At her raised eyebrow, he grinned. Couldn't help it. "Up the road. They'll be here in a minute. Want to stay out of sight?"

"Why should I? I've a vampire to defend me."

"Better keep that under your hat. As unfriendly as the locals are, they'll start sharpening stakes."

"Ouch." She smiled back. "Works, does it?"

Best to let mortals think it did. "Let's meet the visitors, shall we?"

They turned the side of the house just as the cruiser pulled up and two deputies got out, one reaching into the boot for a bundle of stakes. Interesting. A coincidence, of course. Toby hoped.

"Toby?" Adela whispered, tension tightening her voice.

He shook his head and grinned and walked up to the deputy, who was standing, back to the house, watching as the deputy reached into the boot again. "Get the lead out, Travers! We haven't got all day."

"Ah! Good morning, Officer!"

The man spun in surprise and welcomed them both with a deep scowl. "You here again?"

"Indeed I am."

"What are you doing here?"

Toby took several steps forward. Might as well invade the man's personal space while he was at it. "I brought Mrs. Whyte back home and . . ."

"What exactly happened?" Adela asked.

"The house burned down last night." He didn't sound exactly concerned.

"So I observed."

Toby held back a smile. Adela sounded positively waspish. And the deputy did not appreciate her attitude. "These things happen. Where were you?"

Adela was not one to be browbeaten. "Fortunately, out of the house."

"Yeah, well, you can't get in there now." He nodded to the deputy. "Travers, get that crime scene tape." The deputy bestowed another frown on them.

"You suspect a crime here, Officer? Surely not arson?" Sarcastic, yes, but justified in the circumstances.

"What are you suggesting?" The man had an impressive repertoire of belligerent facial expressions.

"You mentioned a crime, Deputy, and I have to agree. It's rather odd that the house burned down with no one there."

"Wasn't the local fire department called?" Adela added, obviously getting into deputy-baiting.

"Back here, so far from the road, no one saw anything until it was too late," he lied. "It was pretty burned out before anyone noticed."

Toby resisted the urge to grab the man's mind and force an admission of complicity. There was time. "Unfortunate. But I feel sure we can count on your good offices, to ensure there is no vandalism of the remains." The second deputy paused in unwinding the yellow tape and Toby fancied a flicker of a smirk on his face.

Another fulsome scowl from the first deputy. Perhaps he suspected Toby was taking the mick. "You Australian or what?"

"Neither." Toby met his scowl with a smile and a shake of his head. "I'm from South Carolina but have lived in the U.K. for a few years." Nearly a century and a half, to be accurate. "Perhaps I picked up a bit of an accent."

The man grunted back. "You can't get in either, you know. No one crosses that tape."

"I can't imagine why anyone would want to!" Adela replied, an edge in her voice under the apparent nonchalance. "I'll have to let Gertrude know what happened. I'm sure she'll want to contact you and the local fire chief—for the insurance, of course. I expect they'll send someone down to investigate. At least then we'll know how it all started."

Good for Adela! The belligerence register went up at least five notches.

"We'll see about that."

"I trust you will, Officer." The man had his hand on the butt of his gun. Not that the prospect of a bullet bothered Toby, but Adela was mortal and vulnerable to gunshots. He took her arm. "We might as well get back. You need to contact the owner so she can take care of everything." He couldn't resist a final genial smile at the sad specimen of law enforcement. "I'm sure you'll be contacted."

"He should be damn thankful," Adela muttered between clenched teeth, "that I follow the Wiccan reede of 'Harm to none.' He's a lying bastard!"

"I do sympathize. If I hadn't been hamstrung by our code, I'd have been tempted to sink my teeth in his throat! But"—he paused as he negotiated a sharp bend—"the most pressing need is to contact your friend."

"I have this hideous worry that Gertrude didn't have insurance."

"I wouldn't worry about that."

"And why not? Replacing a house and all your furniture and belongings isn't exactly like buying a new washing machine!"

Mortals did get testy under stress. "If she is uninsured, we contact our mutual acquaintance Mr. Roman."

"Vlad?" She must be the only mortal to know the Lord of Wallachia's traveling name.

"I don't doubt in his vast empire, he has an insurance company or two. If nothing else, he will make sure the arson is investigated."

"Why would he do that?"

"Because one of the conditions of my stay in his territory was I keep watch on you. He will not be pleased at what happened, and he and his clan don't adhere to the strict tenets of our colony."

Took her a minute or two to digest that lump of surprise. "What have I done to merit his concern like that?"

He couldn't hold back the chuckle. "My dear Adela. I would hazard a guess, you're the only mortal who's looked him in the eyes and demanded something of him. Few vampires would even dare that. You did and survived intact. He admires you and respects you. And in addition, Elizabeth, your protégée, destroyed a vampire who invaded his territory and not only ignored all the conventions of hospitality but did active harm that could have rebounded on Vlad's clan. Yes, Adela, Vlad Tepes holds you in high regard."

He heard her swallow. "I'm not entirely sure that's a welcome circumstance."

He understood, being none too relaxed knowing he owed Vlad a favor for his continued sojourn in his territory. "It's a whole lot better than earning his enmity."

She didn't argue with that. "How old and powerful is he?"

"Let's put it this way: If Vlad had found Laran, I doubt he'd have needed magic. Also, he has a nasty reputation for killing slowly."

She shuddered. "Not a person to piss off, right?"

"No, my dear Adela. Definitely not."

They headed back to Devil's Elbow, Adela to contact her friend Gertrude, and Toby intending to head for the office. But as he turned off the road and headed up the drive to the house, he glimpsed two black cars through the trees. Swearing under his breath, he reversed. Fast.

"Adela," he said, letting the engine idle as he stopped. "I have visitors. May I suggest you get out here? There's a path down to the beach. I'll come and get you when the coast is clear." He sensed an argument rising. "Unless you really want to get entangled with the FBI."

"They are still investigating Piet?"

"Unfortunately, yes. At least seeing him might satisfy them that he cannot help them with their enquiries, but who knows what they might make of his ex-wife staying in the house."

She took no more convincing. "Damn, I need to call

Gertrude but . . ." She opened the door. "See you soon—I hope."

He waited, just long enough to be sure she found the path, before proceeding toward the house.

It was a car and a van, both parked askew, blocking the garage door. Toby parked, crossed the drive and nodded at the two drivers propping up their respective front bumpers. "Busy morning, gentlemen?"

"You can't go in there," one answered, reaching out an arm to block Toby's way.

He didn't even pause to argue, just entered one mind, then the second. They could catch grief later. Right now he was feeling less than sympathetic toward law enforcement of all stripes. Toby stepped into the hall, just in time to meet Agent Bright directing two others, carrying a computer and a box of papers.

"Acquiring evidence, Agent Bright? I did agree to hand over whatever you requested."

"No need, Mr. Wise. I have a search warrant and a subpoena for certain documents and your computer and disks." He pulled a paper from his inside pocket and flashed it at Toby.

Faster than Bright could tuck it safely away, Toby took it from him. Ignoring the man's surprise, Toby read. Fast. He looked up at the agent's irate eyes. "Find everything you want?"

Courtesy and helpfulness appeared unwelcome. How times had changed! "Obstruct me and I'll have you arrested!" Bright scowled as he all but elbowed Toby out of the way. He'd have succeeded with a fellow mortal. As it was, with luck he would have a rather sore elbow.

"I have no intention of doing so."

Amy Redding, the current day nurse, came rushing

out. "Oh! Mr. Wise, thank heavens you're back. It's been terrible; I had no idea what to do, and they had papers."

Toby rested his hand on her shoulder. Pity he couldn't will calm on her, but he had too large an audience for that. "Never mind, Nurse Redding. Is Piet alright?"

"Yes, I think so. They pestered him a bit, finally gave up. The poor man. It upset him some but he's settled back. The banging and bumping distracted him a bit, but he'll be fine."

Toby hoped the same could be said for the Duncan Phyfe library table in the study. However, if they scratched it, they did. He could see for himself the slate floor in the hall would never be the same again. "I'll sit with Piet, Nurse Redding. I'm sure you're due for a break. I never expected you'd have to cope with this." His gesture included the dark-suited types scurrying back and forth. One, Toby noticed, carried his printer.

Let the mortals have their fun. They'd find nothing. Tom Kyd was too good for them.

It was almost an hour before they finished moving furniture and confiscating disks and subversive-looking books. Toby considered himself the soul of endurance and patience, but Bright's insistence he sign for, and accept, a receipt almost drove him to the edge.

Granger Fox snapped his cell phone shut. Interesting, and the perfect out from the unpleasantness looming ahead. A suspicious fire on the outskirts of Dark Falls was good enough reason to dash over and see what sort of story he could find. He had a legitimate excuse not to obey the order to return to Axel and report, but the compulsion was too strong.

He could no more disobey than fly.

He drove the remaining distance to the newspaper office and braced himself. He had failed and deserved the coming chastisement.

"She *what*?" Axel's eyes blazed almost red as he glared. "You were told to see she obeyed. Maybe I need to encourage her."

"No!" He wasn't that far gone to let Axel have his hands on Laura. "She'll get what you want. There was coming and going all night. She didn't want to risk getting caught. That wouldn't help, would it?"

Axel's silent shrug implied little concern over any possible awkwardness for Laura. "She'd better get me something tonight, without fail."

"She promised, didn't she? My Laura will come up with something." He so hoped.

"So"—the light in Axel's eyes turned to a feral gleam—"come here, Granger. Take off your shirt."

It was what Granger Fox feared, loathed, dreaded . . . and yearned for as much as air and sunshine. His fingers trembled as he unbuttoned his checked shirt. He pulled it off his arms and, still holding his shirt by the collar, looked up at Axel.

"Your left arm this time, I think."

Taking a deep breath, Granger stepped forward and held out his left arm. A cold hand grabbed his upper arm and yanked him close. He held his breath, bracing for the pain as Axel's fangs scraped skin. Granger winced, almost suppressed the groan and shuddered as Axel sucked hard, pulling at the flesh until the skin tore more and Granger cried out.

He could have screamed, for all the difference it made. Axel fed, taking what he wanted while Granger waited, passive, steadying himself on the desk with his free hand.

Then, as always, through the pain and hurt came a flicker of pleasure, like a match in pitch dark. Granger exhaled as the slender dart of sensation became a raging blaze. For a few, brief moments, he rode the wave of ecstasy, until Axel abruptly pulled his mouth away and Granger was jerked back to the reality of a messy office and an unwritten story.

Axel reached for the dropped shirt and wiped his mouth with it before tossing it to Granger. "Better get dressed. Might shock the populace to find you in your undershirt."

Giddy and lightheaded, Granger sank into the desk chair and reached into a drawer for the tissues he kept for these moments. As Axel slammed the door behind him, Granger held a wodge of tissues to the still-seeping wound. It would soon stop bleeding. It always did. But his arm—heck, both arms, legs and chest were a mass of scars and fading bruises. If he had any sense he'd refuse Axel before the man bled him to death. But that had never happened. Denying Axel was beyond his strength. He needed Axel, dreaded being abandoned, and for him to keep Axel, Laura had to come up to snuff.

What a day! Talk about an insane twenty-four hours. Toby scowled at the phone. He'd had a panic-stricken phone call, faced down a decidedly venal deputy, rescued Adela from a witch hunt, witnessed arson, fought a filthy mythical beast, found the woman he'd developed a tendre for rifling though his filing cabinets, and had his home invaded by the FBI. On top of all that, he had to call Vlad Tepes.

He should be able to manage that. Might even actually get a couple of hours in at the office if he looked lively, not that it really was worth it at this point and—damn! He'd forgotten that Adela was still down on the beach waiting for him to give the all clear.

Still, it was a nice morning. Alright, a nice afternoon. She could wait. She owed him, whereas he was in Vlad's territory.

First, he called the office. Sarah Wallace's "Hello, Mr. Wise's office. May I help you?" was the best reminder of normality he'd had all day.

"Sarah, Toby here. I'm not coming in today. Our friends Healy and Bright were here at the house."

Her snort showed what she thought of the FBI. "They're here right now, grabbing and snatching and waving search warrants and I don't know what. I feel sorry for the cleaning crew this evening. The place is in a shambles."

"Tell maintenance to send in extra teams if needed, and ask everyone there to tidy up their own areas as best they can. Let the marauders take whatever they want. Just be sure they leave the coffeemakers. I don't want a staff revolt tomorrow morning."

Her snort suggested she didn't appreciate levity. "They are taking computers, backup drives, disks. It's ridiculous!"

He agreed and wondered how many months it would take them to realize they were barking up an empty tree. "Let them have their fun. There's nothing there to find. Just do your best to see people don't get too upset."

"I'll do my best. . . ." She would.

"I'll be in early." Maybe even before dawn. Doing his best to convince her to persuade everyone else not to worry. Toby hung up.

Now to explain what was going on (or as much of it as Toby knew or hypothesized) to the Lord of Wallachia.

Chapter 6

Vlad was a darn good listener. Toby made his report as brief as possible but was still pretty involved and based, he realized, on Laura's word and the coincidence of a surname.

It was more than enough for Vlad Tepes.

"I'll send Zeke down to see what's going on. Better an unknown investigate than you, who plan to stay awhile. Zeke can poke and pry and ask nosy questions, then report what's happening." Nothing like seizing the moment. "And just in case he does find an intruder, Larouselière will be on his way too."

Short but seldom sweet, Vlad rang off. Toby was covered now and, with a bit of luck, Vlad would take care of everything, and leave Toby to concentrate on Connor Inc. and the FBI. More than enough for one vampire.

As Toby headed for the beach to give Adela the all clear, he couldn't help wondering how Etienne Larouselière, who seldom left France and never, to Toby's knowledge, ventured beyond Europe, was in obligation to Vlad Tepes.

Not that he didn't have far more pressing things on his mind. Between the FBI, arson, a venal deputy and now a vampire poaching in his borrowed territory, it was just as well he wasn't hampered with mortal limitations.

He'd rather fancied descending the cliff head first, à la Bram Stoker, but, since there was a mother watching three small children digging in the sand, he came down the steps mortal style.

Adela was sitting, perched on rocks on the far side of the beach. "I watched them leave," she said, looking up at the road bridge that spanned high over the inlet. "Looked like a convoy leaving. Did they strip the house?"

"We still have beds and a refrigerator, and I think they left the bathrooms intact."

She shook her head and sighed. "Is Piet okay?"

"Thankfully, he was oblivious to most of it. He started fretting at all the noise and doors banging, but the nurse calmed him down and one good thing: ten minutes attempted conversation and they decided he was no longer a good source of information. I doubt they'll subpoena him anytime soon."

"What about you?"

"I'm not worried. Not now. At least the house is clear. Want to come back and try to sort out your complication?"

"I called Gertrude while I was waiting." Her mobile was still in her hand. "She was shocked and upset, as you'd expect, but it seems she is either very cautious and provident or had a premonition. She put all her papers, house deed, insurance, car titles and everything in a lock box in the bank just before she left and took copies with her. She's contacting them and will fax over any forms I need completed."

"If she wants to come down, she can stay here, if you like." What was one more?

"Toby, you are such a nice man!" She gave him a quick hug. "But better not. If she comes, which I don't think she wants to, I'll find us a B and B or a motel. Gertrude is pretty sensitive to aura and if she noticed you didn't have one, she might just put two and two together. Aside from your need for privacy, I think she has enough stress already without adding a vampire to the mix."

Good point. "You're right." No point in mentioning there would be two vamps in the house. Better keep her in ignorance. "You'll need a car. Want to use the Mercedes?"

"Don't wish to sound ungrateful, but is there anything slightly less conspicuous?"

"Ah! You fancy slipping in and out with as little attention as possible."

"Might be judicious, in the circumstances."

Sensible woman. "We need the van for Piet, but there is a Hummer."

She tilted her head to one side. "Nothing as plebeian as a Bug or a Toyota for a vampire!"

"They'd hardly fit our image, would they?"

"And Hummers do?"

"Hummers are different." And besides, it was Piet's, but at least that got a smile out of her. She was strung out—understandably enough—but strung-out mortals took risks and made mistakes, and right now he wasn't sure he had energy or time to iron out another crimp around him. "When do you want it? It might need petrol."

"I can check that. I can fill it up this evening."

One complication dealt with; now he had to decide what to do with Laura—besides wanting her in his bed.

It didn't bode well to set off for work with a raging headache. Come to that, it didn't bode well to set off for work knowing her employer thought her a thief. Toby Wise had listened to her convoluted tale about her father, but that didn't stifle the sneaking suspicion he was going to do a lot more than "help" her. Why in the name of sanity would he fabricate "evidence"? Was he trying to trap her? And why hadn't she flatly refused Dad from the get-go? Because she was a sucker for a sob story, that was why, and when the sob storyteller was her father . . . Damn! The least she should do was offer to quit the job before she dug herself in any deeper. Dad would rant and wail, but he was asking too much, far, far too much. She was darn lucky Toby hadn't fired her on the spot.

Thinking and driving at the same time made her head ache. Roadwork on 101 delayed her when she'd hoped to actually arrive early and to crown it, after turning off the road and up the curving drive to the house. Just a few yards ahead was a vast, black Town Car. Toby had visitors, unless the local police had raided the budget and gone ostentatious.

Visitors meant Toby would be occupied all evening. Would he forget his promise to help her out?

Zeke Randolph surveyed the sweeping, wooded drive with its strategic glimpses of beach and ocean. Very nice if you liked that sort of thing. He preferred cities. Felt safer in them. But Devil's Elbow seemed okay. Heck, after checking out this tale of another rogue vampire—sheer moonshine, in Zeke's opinion, two in the same decade, let alone the same year, was pushing it a bit—he might even snatch a day or two on the beach.

He eased the sleek nose of the gleaming Town Car round another bend, brushing tree branches. Better take care. Vlad wouldn't gripe about renting an expensive car—he was a believer in impressing the populace—but charges for dents and scratches were another matter.

Wowee! Zeke's first sight of the house impressed, despite his determination to be cool about everything, although he admitted curiosity about meeting a British vampire brother. Turning the car sharply, he sprayed gravel—damn, better watch that—and parked. He reached for his overnight case and headed for the wide open front door.

And all but froze.

The woman from the El—the witch he'd met a few months earlier—was standing in the doorway.

Wasn't often Zeke Randolph was stopped in his tracks, but this woman had just managed it for the second time.

Adela couldn't believe her eyes. She'd stepped out to check on the Hummer Toby had lent her and came face to face with the vampire from Chicago. The one who turned out to be an aide or secretary or whatever he was to Dracula.

She gaped. He stared.

"You!" They practically spoke in unison. Hers was more of a strangled gasp. His, an accusation.

"Yes," she managed with slightly less horror than her earlier monosyllable. "You want to see Toby?" She had no idea what this vamp was doing so far from the Windy City, and preferred not to know.

"He's expecting me."

News to her, but she had quite enough to worry about without adding an extra vamp to the mix. "He's inside, in his study, I think."

"Okay. Where will I find that?"

She was about to show him when the night nurse

pulled up. The front drive was looking like a parking lot. And Zeke—she now remembered his name—was looking at the nurse as if she were good enough to eat, a circumstance that was far too probable to be comfortable.

Adela grabbed his arm. "Let me take you into the study." Over her shoulder, she called, "Piet's out on the terrace, Laura."

Laura paused just inside the double front doors. "I need to talk to Mr. Wise."

"So do I," Zeke said.

"I'm here!" A calm, oh-so-Brit voice announced.

Adela decided Toby could cope with all this while she ran away to get gas and find a spot for quiet meditation and prayer.

He came forward, hand outstretched. "Hello, Zeke. I was expecting you but not quite this early. Brilliant, and thank you for coming."

Zeke grabbed the hand. The subsequent handshake would have crippled a mortal. Zeke grinned. Toby offered a polite smile.

"Glad to come, man! Not often I get a weekend by the ocean, but when Vlad the man says, 'Zeke, get yourself to Oregon!' I get my tail into action." He looked around the wide, slate-floor hall. "Nice place you've got here."

"It is, and it's borrowed. I'm a guest here too." There was just the teeniest bit of aspersion in his words. Adela sympathized. They surely did not need this on top of everything else today.

"Excuse me, Mr. Wise?" Laura, the nurse, hovered on the fringes of Zeke's unmistakable presence.

"Ah! Laura!"

Curious. Very curious. Toby's wide smile and the light in his eyes suggested more than professional interest. Goddess help the girl! Or maybe she already had! After all, Lizzie seemed more than content with her vampire. Meanwhile . . . "Toby, I'm off. Thanks for the keys. I'll gas it up."

"Don't go back there alone."

Came out as an order, but she'd take it as friendly concern. He'd been incredibly supportive through it all so far. "Don't worry. I won't! See you later!"

She didn't exactly run but needed vampire-free space and clear, tension-free air. Adela hoped Laura would be okay but sensed Toby could be depended on.

Toby didn't blame Adela scarpering off fast as the Hummer could carry her. He rather envied her the opportunity, but he had responsibilities, and two were standing at arm's length. "Laura, I have news for you. Not quite what I had in mind but should serve, for a few days at least. Please see to Piet and let Amy Redding leave, and I'll talk to you soon. I've matters to discuss with Mr. Randolph." Who was giving Laura far too much of his attention.

"Call me Zeke," he said, with a decidedly interested smile.

"Good evening," Laura replied, seemingly unimpressed. Good! "Welcome to Oregon. I hope you enjoy your stay, and if you'll excuse me, I must see to my patient."

The look that came Toby's way begged him not to let her down. He wanted to tell her he wouldn't ever, but couldn't while Zeke was within earshot. And damn him for watching as Laura walked away, down the long corridor toward Piet's suite.

"Very nice!" Zeke turned up his mouth in a smug smile.

"She's marked and she's mine!" He snarled it and didn't care. Hospitality be damned. The riot of emotion all but curdling his brain stunned Toby. If Zeke as much as breathed on her . . .

"Hey! It's cool, man." Zeke stepped back and raised both hands in a gesture of submission. "Nothing in it. She's yours. I respect that."

"I trust you will." If he didn't, he'd rip out Zeke's guts and hang him with them.

"Well, man, I'm here and ready to take care of this Radcliffe dude."

Abel help him! Zeke made Toby feel like an alien in his own country, but they had to work together, and if Vlad thought he was the vamp for the job, he'd not question the Lord of Wallachia. "Better come into my study."

Perhaps not the best choice. Zeke stared at the bare desk, the wide-open filing cabinet, books obviously swept off shelves, and a couple of overturned chairs.

"Hey, man! You been broken into?"

"No, just a visit from the FBI!"

"No shit!"

"I rather disagree. In my opinion, it's a pile of shit!"

Zeke threw back his head and laughed. It reminded Toby the lad had only been eighteen when transformed, if gossip were true. "You said it! Why are they on your case?"

Toby put his finger to his lips. Zeke's nod conveyed he understood the room might be bugged. "Have a seat," Toby said, crossing the room and picking up an overturned Sheraton chair and tossing it to Zeke, who caught it deftly, set it upright and sat down, waiting. Toby brought the other over.

"They have some bee in their bonnet that Connor Inc. is/was/has been involved in money laundering. It's my belief that the old CFO, Laran Radcliffe, gave them some false information, no doubt to cause us even more trouble." Toby shook his head. He doubted they'd installed closed-circuit TV, but he was rather getting into the spirit of this. "The man runs off. They keep asking me where he is. As if I'm likely to know! Hell! I've done nothing the past three months but sort out the books and try to make sense of the mess.

"I offer to cooperate. Agree to give them anything they want, and in reply they come barging in here when I'm out, scaring the willies out of the nurse and pestering poor Piet." Another pause for emphasis. "At least now they can't suspect him of conniving to flout any laws. The old chap doesn't know what day it is half the time."

"You said it, man!"

Zeke looked ready to elaborate. No point in risking overkill. "Hold on, Zeke. If you want to smoke, let's go outside."

Had to hand it to him, the lad picked up clues fast. "Oh, man! I thought you Left Coast people were laid-back."

This could get to be fun. "Not when it comes to smoking on an Aubusson. Outside."

"This is something else." Zeke leaned against the balustrade and looked out over the ocean. "And I thought Lake Michigan was big."

"In point of fact, it is. The Pacific happens to be vast."

"You lucked out getting this job."

"Maybe."

Zeke gave him a knowing smile. "Nice house. Cushy job. A bit of excitement from the Feds and a very nice companion. You lucked out, man."

Right! The so-called companion was just around the corner of the house with Piet. In spite of the brisk ocean breeze and Zeke's pungent aftershave, Toby swore he could smell her. Yes, he was losing his grip. A few tastes and he was claiming her! Just would not do. Back to business. "Vlad did not send you here to enjoy the ocean breeze."

"No! What's happening? Another rogue poaching on our territory?"

"I suspect so. I only heard about it this morning, but the circumstances combined with the coincidence of the name was enough to concern me. Vlad, I gather, agrees."

"He told me to find out all I can and report. So?" He shrugged. "Where do I start?"

Unfortunately, with Laura. "I'll get the nurse. She mentioned it to me."

Laura jumped up as Toby entered Piet's screen porch. Elizabeth had added this on, right on the corner where it caught both land and sea breezes. The old man seemed to enjoy it here. Laura was less relaxed.

"Mr. Wise?" she asked, her face pale and taut with worry. "What happened? Amy was saying the FBI had a search warrant and . . ."

He should have known this would happen. "She's right. They had a search warrant and took my computer and armloads of papers." Not that it would do them any good. "In the ensuing chaos and mess, I didn't get together what I promised for you but . . ." He went on fast, seeing her bite her lip and frown. "We have something even better that you can feed your bothersome newspaper man." Better not call him a vampire. "Tell him the Feds took the place apart, so there has to be something going on. Should keep him happy and he can't expect you to find anything when it supposedly is all in the hands of the FBI."

"I'll tell him." She looked Toby right in the eyes.

"Why are you helping me? Why didn't you just fire me and be done with me?"

Not the moment to tell the truth. "Because you are a good nurse and Piet likes you." And I love your blood and spirit. "I believe your story. You were wrong to pry but weren't acting off your own bat but to help your father and . . ." Better pick the fragments of truth carefully here. "You mentioned the name of your father's new partner: Axel Radcliffe. I suspected he might have some connection with our missing CFO."

"Oh! The man who ran off with money."

Toby nodded. "You think Axel Radcliffe is going to do the same? Dad has no money. That was why he sold the interest in the paper and . . ."

Toby touched her shoulder to calm her. It was a bit of a mistake. Feeling her warmth put too many good ideas into his brain. "I'm not sure of anything, Laura." Other than that he wanted her skin under his lips. "But the name caught my attention. It's not particularly common, but not rare either. I've called in a private detective from Chicago to investigate. Would you be willing to tell him all you told me this morning?" Had it only been this morning? Abel! It had been a long day and was nowhere near ending yet.

"The man who arrived just before I did?"

The lout who'd eyed her with hunger and presumption. "Yes. His name is Randolph, Zeke Randolph."

"And he's a detective?" Sort of. Toby nodded. "Okay then, I'll tell him. If you think it will help."

She was as good as her word. Zeke obviously unnerved her, wise woman there, but after Toby brought chairs out from the debris of the study, insisted she sit and sent calming suggestions her way, she told everything, only excluding the details of his mode of attire when he found her rifling through his drawers.

Toby sensed the stress in her and appreciated more than ever her honesty and genuine dilemma. She was worried—scared, even—for her father, angry at the situation he'd placed her in, and broadcasted a whole range of emotions that had Toby wanting to pull her into his arms and tell he'd make it all right.

He was losing it!

Right in the middle of a tangled situation of major proportions, he was falling for a green-eyed mortal. Definitely ill-advised.

Telling Zeke that Laura was marked and owned was an inspiration. The vamp's attitude changed 180 degrees. He questioned her, yes. Some probing questions too, but he was courteous and respectful. Funny how even the most ostensibly street-smart vampires respected the ancient laws. Having Vlad Tepes to answer to no doubt had something to do with it.

Laura left to watch over Piet and was well out of earshot when Zeke turned to Toby, one bushy eyebrow raised. "Think she's telling the truth, the whole truth?"

Knowing darn well he was also under scrutiny here, Toby replied, "Not the whole truth. She left out a minor detail, more out of embarrassment than anything else, I imagine." He filled Zeke in with the precise details of his entry through the window. No point in sharing the events of the evening prior to his awkward and enraged arrival.

He expected the laugh and the wicked, knowing grin. "Man! That must have been some sight." The annoying grin widened. "Was she impressed?"

"I didn't ask! Hardly seemed apropos at the time."

"You Brits miss all the chances with your tight-assed attitude."

Time to steer the conversation back on track. "What do you think about this second Radcliffe? Coincidence or something more?"

Zeke shrugged. "Hard to tell. The boss is taking it seriously. Told me to look around and be careful. That French dude is on his way too."

"Larouselière?"

"Yeah. That was his name. Some sort of expert, right?"

"Yes. Expert in vampire lore, vampire and human history and seduction." And if he as much as smiled at Laura . . . "He's coming here?"

"On his way as we speak. The boss said you know something about these rogue vampires too. Characteristics, habits . . ."

"I was present when Etienne Larouselière briefed us in London over Laran. If this one's the same, they are vicious and predatory. The sort of vampires who give the rest of us a bad name. Origins in South or Central America. They eat mortal food and thus pass easily among them. Are repulsed by silver, and about the only way to kill them is magic." At least that took care of Laran Radcliffe—with side effects, he amended to himself, thinking of Piet's sorry condition.

"Yeah! Vlad mentioned the silver. He's having a few toys made to help if needed. Lucky dude getting to eat. I sure miss having a nice double bacon cheeseburger and fries once in a while. And bring on the ketchup!"

"My hankering is for grits and collards with ham hocks, like my mother used to cook." And he could still smell them even though he barely remembered his mother's face.

Zeke went quiet. Definitely out of character. "You

were sure lucky. I never knew my mother. Grew up in foster homes."

Zeke needed educating about the realities of slavery, but not right now. "Tough luck that."

He shrugged, much more the Zeke Toby knew and slightly mistrusted. "It's the breaks. Some were good. Others the pits, but it's history. Better get busy on this Axel dude. Ever seen him?"

"No, but you've Laura's description and the addresses she gave you. I can give you a map and directions."

"Thanks, man! I'll indulge in a couple of blood bags and set off in a couple of hours. Easier to pry around at night when the pesky mortals are in bed."

"Be careful. We don't exactly know what we are dealing with here." Perhaps he should have mentioned the chupacabra, but he didn't want Adela yanked into this, and what earthly connection could there be?

Zeke grinned. That look must have driven teachers and authorities batty. "Man! Don't worry about me. I'm a big bad vampire dude. No one gets the better of Zeke Randolph!"

Chapter 7

Axel Radcliffe looked down at the inert, but still breathing, Granger Fox. The useless mortal had passed out yet again. Inconvenient if he was weakening. Damn! He needed the man alive. The local excuse for a newspaper was perfect cover for asking questions and poking and prying. And getting that bitch of a daughter involved was an inspiration. Pity she was so useless. Looked as though he'd have to use her to gain entry into the house himself. A threat to rip out her father's throat would no doubt work wonders with her professional scruples. He'd been far, far too patient with these mortals. He'd come to this chilly, rain-washed country to discover what happened to his brother vampire, who'd sent such glowing reports of success and then disappeared without a trace, along with the money he'd supposedly put aside for their benefit.

If Laran had double-crossed them, he would suffer, slowly. If another had harmed Axel's nest brother . . . Axel smiled at the prospect of wreaking slow and painful revenge.

Opening the door, Axel stepped out into the evening. Might as well take a turn around the vicinity and look for his familiar while he was about it. The creature went out hunting last night and hadn't returned. Odd. He might have found shelter in the rocks by the river, or even evicted a fox from its den, but he seldom failed to return.

The phone ringing intruded the vampire's thoughts. Why the hell didn't Granger answer the frigging thing? Because he was still unconscious! Unsure why he bothered, Axel walked back into the house. Glancing at the caller ID, he smiled and picked up the receiver.

"Dad!" Bloody Laura maybe, for once, with something of use.

"Your father is resting." Telling her the man had passed out through loss of blood might distract her from the important issues.

"Oh! Will you tell him I called?"

"No. You will tell me what you planned to say to him."

The bitch had the effrontery to hesitate. He should have taken her blood too and bound her to obedience, but one did have standards and female blood just wasn't the same. "I'd rather speak to him. Ask him to call me, please."

Damn her to misery and despair! "Your father needs your information. Believe me, Laura, if you love him, you will tell me. Now!"

Still the bitch paused! What did he have to do, make her father scream? "Okay, but still ask him to call me, please?"

"Get on with it, Laura."

"There is something going on here. Something major. You and Dad were dead right." Dead might be the word if she didn't get to the point. "The FBI were here with . . ."

"What?" Couldn't be! If she was lying . . .

"The FBI." She spoke slowly as if to a simpleminded mortal. Damn her impudence! "They had a search warrant and took away all the computers, disks, masses of books and papers, practically stripped Mr. Wise's study and went through the library as well."

"What were they looking for?"

"They didn't say." Smart-ass bimbo!

"Try an educated guess."

"Amy Redding, who's here in the day, saw them and said they kept talking about financial records."

"That's all?" He hung up. Shit and bugger! Double bugger! What now? Had the feeble mortal government sussed out Laran's activities? Didn't help him finding out if Laran had run off with the money. But at least a bit of disorder and suspicion among mortals couldn't hurt.

Meanwhile, he had a missing pet to find.

Leaving the doors wide open, Axel Radcliffe, vampire enforcer, set off along the river at a run.

His pet was in none of its usual dens. He ran on beyond the town, past the charred ruins of the witch's house and out into open country. Nothing. Irritated, he turned back, pausing at the still-warm ruins of the house. Pity he'd missed that. Disasters added piquancy to life, and he hadn't watched a witch burn since the Colonial Inquisition left his native land.

Axel slowed to jogging pace and circled the house. Nothing there. Charred rafters, furniture buried under ash and debris. No pickings, not even a dead cat. He did catch the odd trace of his pet down by the river, but that was hardly surprising. It traveled that way frequently.

Irritated, Axel headed for the town. He wasn't hungry. Granger had supplied more than enough to keep him satisfied a couple of days, but Axel felt the urge to bite on an unwilling neck, and it was Friday, after all. There were usually a few sottish yokels drinking away their pathetic paychecks. Cheap alcohol didn't improve the blood, but terror always added piquancy. He missed that. Granger was getting far too resigned. He never resisted these days.

Approaching the town from the south, Axel passed a car repair shop. He stopped midstride and backed up a couple of paces. The scent was strong and unmistakable. His pet was here or had been very recently. Leaping the eight-foot fence, Axel took stock of his surroundings and followed the scent, passing a dozen or so cars in various stages of decay until he reached a locked work shed that was pathetically easy to enter.

Odd that. His pet seldom entered buildings, but the scent led right to a police cruiser. The front seats had been stripped out and lay on the ground along with the carpets and the plastic barrier intended to protect the fat deputy from nasty little felons.

And all carried the scent of his pet.

Which was strongest over to the side. He walked to a heap covered with a tarp and found his pet. Neck broken, tossed among the refuse.

Anger and loss raged through his mind. He brushed aside the question of what puny mortal could destroy his pet. That deputy had some questions to answer!

Axel gathered his pet into his arms. In seconds he was racing toward the town. In minutes he stood outside the police department. Inside the deputy dozed. He woke as Axel kicked down the door.

"Now, see here!" He was on his feet, gun drawn.

Axel was tempted to let him shoot, just to enjoy the look on his face when his victim kept coming closer, gunshot wounds and all, but the noise might bring in other mortals, and much as he was in the mood for a massacre, he hadn't the time.

Shifting his pet over his shoulder, Axel grabbed the

gun and tossed it across the room. "Don't bother to reach for another. I'll just break it, maybe on your head!"

"Now, see here! I'm the law here in Dark Falls and you'd better . . ." His right hand reached for a button under the desk. Axel reached faster and broke three fingers.

As the man sat down clutching his hand and making a laudable attempt not to scream, Axel put his pet on the desk. "What happened? Tell me or I'll rip your cock off and shove it down your throat!"

The man swallowed, perhaps in anticipation. "What are you bringing that thing here for? We got rid of it."

My, my, he was sewing his own shroud. "Indeed. Why?"

"I found it in my cruiser. Some sort of joke. You did it?" Axel didn't deign to reply, just stared. It was sufficient. "Let me tell you, it wasn't funny. Out on a call and I find that in my passenger seat. Stinks to high heaven too. I've had to have the entire inside redone. Filthy smelly thing. Don't know what it is, but it needed to be dead."

That did it! Axel grabbed him by the neck, lifting him out of his chair and squeezing until he went red, purple and finally blue, and the smell of human urine and excrement filled the office.

And the man had the effrontery to call his pet "filthy and smelly."

Axel let him drop with a satisfied smile, gathered his pet into his arms and ran, racing at full speed until he reached the river back where his pet liked to hunt.

Sitting down on the grass, Axel consumed his pet, bite by bite. Power and strength, even dead power and strength, was not to be wasted.

* * *

Her patient was asleep. Toby was working at the other end of the house. The houseguest, Adela, was out for the evening. Even the private detective had driven off into the night in his flashy car. Laura was alone in the quiet of the night and worrying.

She should have spoken to Dad, told creepy Axel to wake him up. Darn, it wasn't late and Dad didn't go to bed early. Something was shifty. Hell! Everything involving Axel was shifty. The pressure he'd put on Dad over this story was nuts and put her in an untenable position. If Toby Wise had been any other employer, he'd have fired her on the spot and no doubt reported her actions to the agency, and bang would have gone any chance of further employment in this part of the state.

Darn it, first thing tomorrow she was going over to the newspaper office and having a good, long talk with her father. He now had his story, and as far as she was concerned that was that.

She had a headache from worry, and it was such a beautiful night.

She went indoors and made herself a cup of mint tea to calm herself and give her the pick-up she needed. Checking first that her patient still slept and his window was open so she'd hear if he called out, Laura took her tea out onto the screened-in porch and sat down in the glider. Sipping the fragrant brew did ease the tension. Good. A few minutes listening to the breakers on the cliffs below and enjoying the ocean breeze did wonders for her threatening headache.

She was about to take her empty mug back inside when Toby Wise appeared silently out of the dark.

"You spoke to your father?"

"Yes, or rather I spoke to Axel Radcliffe." She paused. "You really think he might be a crook?"

He came closer, a dark figure in the dark evening. "Maybe, maybe not, could be just a coincidence with the name, but in the circumstances, it bears investigating."

"You could have just told the FBI." Thinking about it, that made more sense.

Toby shook his head. "I wouldn't fancy setting them on an innocent person." After what Amy Redding told her about this afternoon's invasion, she understood his reluctance. "If Zeke turns up anything, then we can pass it on."

"Thanks again for helping me out."

He smiled, teeth white and rather large in the dark. "You paid me the compliment of confiding in me. I hope it was enough to satisfy your father's curiosity."

It should be! He could make a front-page story out of it! "He'd better be!" She should thank Toby again and go in, but somehow the night wrapped her in peace, and Piet wasn't stirring. "Beautiful here, isn't it?"

"I love it." He walked over to the balustrade and turned to face her. "I've been impressed. I never imagined the West Coast was so beautiful."

"Different from England?"

"Very. I got used to it. I loved some of the countryside, but this is magnificent."

"Isn't England your home?" He sure sounded as if it was.

He shook his head, almost absently. "No. I was born in South Carolina but left years ago."

"You left the sunshine of Myrtle Beach for the rain and drizzle of England?"

"There were far more pressing issues than weather at the time." Escaping slave catchers and a burning desire to be his own man, not another's property, for a start.

The darkness in his tone had her wondering "what

issues?" but seemed more than out of place to ask. Besides, she should check on Piet. She stood, mug in hand.

Toby came closer and put his hand on her shoulder. His fingers felt cool through her uniform. "Don't go yet, Laura, have a seat." She sat. "Rest, Laura, rest. It's been a long and stressful day." That she wouldn't argue with. Her eyes closed.

He'd been feeding off mortals for well over a century. Why the sudden pang of reluctance tonight? Why the overwhelming desire? He wanted her. He yearned for her skin against her lips and her life essence on his tongue. Needed her. Needed to feel her warm skin under his fingers, and her soft hair against his face.

He brushed the hair away from her ear and neck, before stroking the side of her neck until she turned her head away from him, offering the smooth column of her neck. Desire flared through him like a raging burn. He wanted to taste her. His irritated declaration to Zeke had been close to the truth. Laura was his; all that remained was to mark her so that Zeke and every other revenant on the planet would respect his claim—and keep their greasy claws and fangs off her!

Toby brushed his lips up behind her ear, then down to the beating pulse at the base of her neck.

She sighed, soft, low, barely discernible above the sound of the waves on the rocks below, but to his vampire hearing it was clear and sweet, a validation, an entreaty for more, an expression of pleasure, or was he utterly off his roost?

He wasn't sure he cared. Sanity was an irrelevant detail when his mind was filled with Laura, the sweet, mortal scent of her skin, the living pulse beating under his lips and the steady rise and fall of her breasts. Breasts that were warm and soft and nipples that were visible through her uniform. She was aroused. By his kiss on her neck? Was it possible? Yes, if her soft sighs were anything to go by.

He teased the skin over her pulse with the tip of his tongue and she whimpered, stretching back her neck as if asking for more.

Torn between amazement, bewilderment and delight, Toby eased his arm behind her shoulders and, holding her steady, kissed her neck hard and long, sucking her skin and caressing with his tongue. The soft whimper became a moan.

As the moan faded to a sexy sigh, he bit, and a sweet whimper of longing filled the night.

He had to brace himself against the chair with his free arm. By Abel! His mind zapped red and fiery as Laura's mortal blood hit his tongue. Such warmth, richness and sweetness. Such power and life! He drank, taking her lifeblood with an abandon that shocked him. But he needed her and, by the way she reached up in her sleep and grabbed his head, his touch was anything but unwelcome. He didn't understand this. Didn't need to. Didn't need anything but her closeness, her mortal warmth and her sweet, sexy moans that rose in a crescendo as her body tensed and her hips rocked.

He eased sucking. Had to, or he'd leave her weak, but he couldn't take his mouth away. Not yet. Kissing slowly and gently, he held her close, her sighs and whimpers a joy to his ears, letting his lips play on her skin until her body tensed. She let out a cry and shook with a climax. Amazed at the wonder of her, he held her close as the sweet shudders of her climax faded and she lay limp and sated in his arms.

Incredible, impossible, wonderful but oh, so very real! She had climaxed from his vampire kiss. He'd always tried to leave his blood partners relaxed and happy. With his lovers, both mortal and vampire, he'd endeavored to give every satisfaction but never, ever had another blood partner climaxed from a bite alone.

But she wasn't just a blood partner, she was Laura, the woman he'd fancied from the minute she walked in the wide double doors of Piet's house. Laura, who was torn between integrity and her father's needs. The woman who might just have given them a clue to the vampire Radcliffe.

As he stood and kissed her forehead, he vowed to himself that he would protect her and her kin for as long as they lived.

The thought brushed his mind that once he'd have been lynched for daring to kiss her, but times were long changed. Now he was vampire, and no mortal could oppose him.

Yes, vampire! With her mortal lifeblood surging through his body, filled with tenderness, awe and energy, he willed her to wake in a few minutes. Then vaulted the railings that surrounded the terrace, raced along the top of the cliff, swung down it using hand and foot holds and tore across the sands, leaping cartwheels and jumping somersaults high in the air.

He was vampire, fired by her sweetness and mortal blood, he was as good as invincible.

Chapter 8

Zeke was tempted to spit long and hard and add a few choice cuss words for good measure. He was vampire. Vampires didn't get lost but, dammit, he had! After driving for hours on country roads without street lights and seeing far more of the Pacific Ocean by moonlight than one vamp should endure in an eternity, he conceded defeat and headed back to Devil's Elbow. Appropriately named! On the way back he drove through Florence twice and narrowly missed heading for Eugene. And he wasn't going to think about the scrape on the rear fender where he'd grazed a lamppost while reversing.

Either Toby and that mortal woman had given him lousy directions and the wrong damn map, or he was out of his element. Damn! Why the heck didn't they have buses and an El out here? He'd try again in daylight, drag the wiseass Brit vampire with him if need be, get whatever information he could and get his tail back to Chicago on the first flight available.

He'd had a bad feeling about this job from the minute he arrived, and so far his instincts had been right on.

At least he was on the way back. A few blood bags—

pity the little nurse had already been claimed—and he'd be set up to rest awhile and restart in daylight.

With better damn directions.

He passed the signpost for the state park, took the next left and scowled at the rearview mirror when the car following him the past six or seven miles turned close on his tail.

Annoyance that some yokel fancied tailing him dissipated in the realization it was the witch—Vlad's witch, who was seeming ensconced in the Wise household.

The more he thought about it, the worse his skin crawled. Could she be the reason he wandered the countryside like a lost goat? Had she hexed him? Pushing aside his instinctive fear of magic, witchery and voodoo in any form—he was a big, bad, black vampire, after all—he turned his car sharply at the end of the drive, parked and was standing by her car as she turned off the engine.

He did the gentlemanly thing and opened the driver's door.

Her clear, intent eyes met his in the moonlight. She was scared of him. Terrified. Odd when she didn't appear the least spooked by Wise. She was as nervous as she'd been confronting him on the El, and as frightened as when she'd insisted he take her to Vlad, but Zeke knew damn well she'd never admit it, even to herself.

"Good evening, Zeke," she said, standing up on the gravel drive and holding her keys between her fingers like impromptu brass knuckles. Handy perhaps against mortal attackers and rapists, pretty darn useless against a vamp, and she knew it.

"Hi. Never thought to meet you this far from the Loop."

As he closed the door, she stepped a little aside. "I

could say the same, Zeke. A bit out of your element, aren't you?"

"You said it! Too many trees, and fucking Mother Nature!" He shook his head, amazed he was admitting his discomfort to a witch! "Sorry!" His foster mother would have whooped his ass and washed his mouth out with Lifebuoy for cussing to a woman. "It's just this place gives me the willies. It's as if there's something out there."

She gave him a look of total understanding. "It's a clear night around here," she replied. "There's nothing harmful for miles, not now. But go down 101 south of Florence and then inland a bit, and the air is steeped in negative energy."

"Yeah, right! That must be why I got lost!"

Him and his big vampire mouth! Scrutiny wasn't the word for the look she gave him. "You've been driving around there? Near Dark Falls?" Was she worried, really scared or pissed off? Hard to tell.

"Sure!" Shrug it off as none of her mortal business.

Not so easy. She was a witch, wasn't she? "Zeke, I think we need to talk."

Well, well! Earlier she'd all but trembled at the sight of him. Now she wanted a chat. He was tempted to shove a mind thrall her way and send her to bed, but Vlad held her in respect. He'd better not dis her.

He hadn't meant to end up sitting on the terrace watching the moonlight over the ocean, but that's where they were.

He let her start.

She didn't seem too eager.

After a long silence, she said, "Zeke, the last thing I want is to poke my nose in vampire affairs, but it's odd that you have business in Dark Falls."

"I don't. It's near here. I just drove through the damn town half a dozen times trying to get to Wyatt's Bend." Shit! More information than he'd intended to share!

"Wyatt's Bend?" She picked right up on it. Just his luck. "You were close. It's about ten miles or so south of Dark Falls. Nearer the coast. Not much there, though. Just a few houses and a campground."

And a rogue vampire. Maybe. "What's all this trouble and negative energy?" Damn silly expression, in his opinion. "That you've found." Change the subject, Zeke, my man—might learn something.

She let out a tight laugh. "Oh, not much, just a hate crime, threats, arson, and some sort of bizarre and vicious creature." She shook her head and chuckled but didn't sound amused one little bit. "Want to know the details?"

"Yeah."

He listened, stunned, for the next fifteen minutes. No wonder Wise had given her refuge. This place stank! Give him nice dirty crime in a dark back alley any day of the week.

He sat in silence a few minutes, listening to the breakers and trying to figure out what connection, if any, there was between this prejudice—and prejudice it damn well was—and his job of finding a possibly imaginary, trespassing vamp.

None, he decided. It was odd, but weird coincidences happened all the time. Especially when a witch was involved.

"So, what are you doing here? Routine vamp job?"

He should have expected that. "If I told you that, I'd have to kill you." He tried to make a joke of the threat but made sure it was a threat.

Didn't work. "No, you wouldn't, Zeke." She stood up.

Even gave him a smile. "If knowing vampire secrets was a capital crime, I'd have been killed months ago."

And with that line, and a damn good parting shot it was, she wished him pleasant dreams and turned her back. He watched her walk the length of the terrace and into the house.

Gutsy babe, if a little older than he usually went for, and a nice ass. As he watched the light come on in a room upstairs, it struck him that Toby hadn't proclaimed the witch off-limits.

Zeke sat in the night, pondering the wisdom or stupidity of snacking on a witch. He'd just about decided to take the risk, when his host leapt over the railing and took a seat next to him.

"Well," Toby asked, "had any luck?"

Zeke snarled. Bad manners, yes, but his host had lousy timing. Three minutes more and Zeke would have been up the outside of the house and through Adela's open window. Could the tight-assed Brit vampire read minds?

"That bad?" Toby pulled up a chair and sat a couple of feet away. "Nothing there?"

"I never even found 'there'! Drove around in circles all evening. I'm sick of the fucking countryside, and ocean views are overrated."

Toby smiled. Zeke's second-grade teacher would have called it a smirk. "Sorry, nothing's worse than a wasted evening."

Zeke could name a good many worse things, but recognized Toby's attempt at sympathy, not that he needed any. "I'm going back in daylight. I'll find him." And take him out if Vlad said so.

"When you do, I want the chance to talk to him."

Zeke raised an eyebrow. "Feeling friendly?"

Seemed even smooth-talking Brits could scowl. With

a bit of practice the dude might even snarl. "No, Zeke. The reverse. I want ten minutes to find out what the hell he's doing, and how he connects to the mess I have here."

"Just ten minutes, huh?"

"It will suffice."

Zeke refused to acknowledge the shiver slithering down his spine. Seemed Toby was hard-assed as well as tight-assed. Just meant he'd have to find this Radcliffe character first. "Think I'll go back in daylight, after a rest and a nice snack." Slipping into Adela's room still wasn't impossible.

"There's ample blood in the fridge in your room."

Even a streetwise vamp got the implied message. Okay, he'd keep his fangs to himself. "Thanks."

"My pleasure," Toby replied with a tight, self-satisfied smile and little wimpy nod of his head. "You know," he went on, "you might want to take Adela with you, if she can spare the time."

Shit! Could he read minds? "The witch!" Confuse with fake horror. Worked most of the time.

Toby nodded. "Adela knows the area. She also has reason to go back there, and I'd feel happier if she had a big, bad vamp in tow."

"Why?"

Toby told him, answering most of the questions in his head, and a few extras that came leaping out as Toby talked.

"No shit!" Zeke muttered after Toby finished and the only sound was the ocean and some damn owl off in the distance.

"No shit," Toby replied with a twitch of his mouth. "No shit indeed."

"Think there's any connection between them all? I

mean the witch's trouble"—which he already knew about—"this monster thing and the suspect vamp?"

Toby shrugged. "I can't see how. Adela moved out here on a chance. She did a house swap with another witch. The chupacabra? Don't rightly know what it really was. Some sort of minor demon, perhaps. Maybe attracted to the area because of magic. Your guess is as good as mine there. But the connection with this second Radcliffe? That is too much to be a coincidence. Trust me, I'd never have called Vlad if I wasn't darn sure.

"There's too many similarities not to be a connection. You heard Laura. The creature exerts an unusual influence on her father—to the point he appears terrified. And look how he wormed his way into the man's confidence, buying into a wonky company and propping it up." He looked out over the ocean and frowned in the dark.

"What are you planning?"

Toby looked back at him, eyes intent. "Protecting Laura is my priority. Saving her father if possible, for her sake, comes next. I'd hate to see another mortal end up like poor old Piet Connor." He barely paused a beat before asking, "What are your plans?"

"Me? Find out what the hell we're dealing with and report back to my boss."

"And then . . . ?"

"What the hell do you mean?" He was going back to nice mean streets and plenty of good ole carbon monoxide in the air.

"Just wondered if you were any good in a fight."

His sharp laugh hung between them. "Every bit as good as you . . . nigger."

Now Toby laughed. Loud, long and clear. "If that was intended to insult me, you're a century and a half too late, boy! I was called that every day of my life for the first twenty years of it. I'm immune."

Speechless was a brand-new experience. Zeke stared at Toby. "You ain't joshing, are you?"

"No, Zeke, I'm not joshing. If you ever want a lecture about life on a profitable rice plantation, I can give you the grisly details."

He'd just as soon skip that but . . . "How the hell did you get away and when were you transformed?"

"There was a lot of chaos during the war. I went to Charleston on an errand for my owner. There was an English ship on the quay—a blockade runner. If it got through the blockade, it could get out. I stowed on board. Three days out at sea, I was discovered. I'd no idea how far the British Isles were. Would have starved if they hadn't found me but the captain was a fair man and not one to waste good labor. He had me work my passage, then got me a job in the Liverpool docks. My transformation happened years later."

"You call him 'fair' when he was aiding and abetting Southern slave owners?"

"He captained a ship. He ruled that ship. He could have had me tossed overboard. Instead he gave me the very chance I needed. I never bothered to dissect his politics."

Since politics had never been Zeke's strong point, he let it go. He waited for the trade of information—for Toby to ask how *he'd* been transformed.

Instead, Toby stood. "I'm off to sleep, suggest you do too. No way of guessing what we'll end up doing tomorrow."

He would find out in a few hours. Might as well take Toby up on the offer of blood bags. Plenty of them. Something told Zeke he'd be needing his strength.

* * *

Laura sat still as a shadow in the dark. Only about a third made sense, but that third had her horrified. A monster in Dark Falls and Toby killing it. Witches, vampires, talk of slavery and a "war." The only one Toby could have been in was Vietnam, but he wouldn't have fought that from South Carolina, would he? But among all the semi-nonsensical fragments, one thing came through clear. Axel Radcliffe meant harm and since Dad was close to him, her father was at risk.

She had to do something. What? Instinct was to grab the nearest phone and warn Dad, but before she even considered that move, she knew it was useless. Dad all but worshipped the ground the man trod on and besides, Axel now owned most of Dad's newspaper.

No, she had to move carefully, find proof, indisputable, irrefutable proof and then Dad would believe her. How? Latch on to Zeke, the detective? Too obvious, perhaps, but he had asked her for information. Why not ask back?

Seemed he'd done and found nothing tonight. He must have missed the road from Dark Falls to Wyatt's Bend. Perhaps she should offer to navigate for him in the morning, but having her ride shotgun would only bring attention to him. Not that Zeke, tall, black and with a shaved head, wouldn't get plenty of attention on his own.

What a mess! But mess or not, she was darn well going to look out for Dad. The question was, how?

Chapter 9

Sally Preston arrived in good time to take over. Laura helped her bathe and dress Piet and settle him in his favorite chair on the terrace. Then, while Sally fixed him scrambled eggs, Laura made her exit. She couldn't wait to get home, plan her next move and have a long, long talk with Dad. But first . . .

She took a deep breath. She'd made her decision in the turmoil of the night and had to follow through.

Toby was sitting on the terrace with Zeke, both of them talking to Piet, or at least letting the old man feel he was part of their conversation. Some days Piet was pretty much coherent, other times he was lost in his own hazy world. This morning he'd been particularly out of it, which made Toby's efforts especially thoughtful.

Not that he wasn't always. He was a considerate employer. That was the root of the trouble. If he hadn't been, she wouldn't be obsessing about him to the point of featuring him in sexy dreams. Now that she had a story to satisfy Dad, there was no reason for her to stay, apart from getting her emotions whirled and snagged.

No reason at all!

"Excuse me, Mr. Wise." She took a couple of steps

across the stone terrace. The detective looked at her, and Piet lifted his chin and nodded on recognition.

Toby stood and smiled. "Laura?"

Another deep, calming breath needed here. "Sorry to interrupt but I need to speak to you before I leave." Or she'd never get up the guts to again.

"Of course." He excused himself to Piet, exchanged nods with Zeke and stood aside to let Laura walk back into the house.

He opened the door to the seldom-used sitting room. Tactful of him not to use the study. She avoided it whenever possible. Thoughts of that room and Toby in his naked splendor were permanently etched on her memory. "What can I do, Laura?" he asked. "Was the story enough to keep your father happy?"

"I hope so." She looked up into his dark eyes and made herself go on. "Toby, I have to tell you. I'm giving notice. At least a week. Longer if necessary. But I need to go."

"No!" His eyes flashed from interested to alarmed. "Leave? You mean quit your job here?"

"Yes. It's best."

She was utterly and completely wrong! He could compel her to stay. All he needed was a little mind control. He'd taken her blood, he could invade her mind. But along with that power came the certainly that he'd never force her against her will. *If* it was her will.

"Laura, why?" Damned inarticulate but shock wasn't the name for what roiled inside him.

"I have to."

"No, you don't!" This was getting nowhere. They could yes/no all morning. "Laura"—he made himself speak calmly. Hell, he was vampire, wasn't he? "Please, why do you want to leave? If it's another job, I'll meet whatever they're offering."

Wrong move. Her forehead creased and her fists clenched. He'd sensed stress before; now irritation was all too apparent. But she was not walking away from him. Not if he had anything to do with it.

He closed his hand over her elbow. "Sit down and please explain why." That much compulsion he permitted himself as he steered her toward the leather sofa and sat down beside her. "Why, Laura?" he repeated. He had to know.

She gave a long, slow sigh and shook her head. If that didn't wring him out, the look in her eyes did. Why had he ever indulged himself and taken her blood? She was like a drug to his mind and senses.

"I have to."

"Who says so?" Was her father or that damn Radcliffe pressuring her?

"I say so." Did she really sound reluctant or was that wishful thinking?

"Alright," he replied. "You've given me notice and offered to stay until I get a replacement. Fine." A total lie, that last bit, but now she looked relieved and . . . hurt. He was out of his depth here. Better swim on. "May I ask for the courtesy of an explanation?"

"Yes." She conceded, biting her lip and studying the odd abstract painting over the fireplace before running both hands through her hair and turning back to look at him. Was it his imagination or were there tears in her green eyes? "You've been a great employer and I've enjoyed taking care of Piet. I did a lousy thing prying through your private papers and you had every right to sack me on the spot."

He nodded and let her go on. She needed to spew out whatever was bothering her.

"Instead, you helped me out. Didn't really make sense, but I'll be grateful forever and for giving me a story for Dad." That was courtesy of the FBI but he was happy to take the credit. He wasn't happy about much else at this moment. "I took the job to get the story and now I have it. There's no reason for me to stay."

He didn't need to be vampire to know she was lying through her teeth. But why lie? He'd had her blood. He felt her anguish, her reluctance to leave, her deep desire to stay, to be near him! His mind imploded and exploded all at once and the same instant. He'd hankered, hungered, lusted after her and all the while she . . .

Wonderful, incredible and . . . "Laura, that's all past. I didn't fire you on the spot because I suspected you were FBI." And wanted the chance to mind-probe you. "You're not. I helped out because I believed you." He'd darn well have known if she were lying.

"If this is intended to make me feel any better about leaving, it isn't!"

"That wasn't my intention, Laura. I don't want you to leave. Didn't I make that clear?" Go easy. Upsetting her wouldn't help anything.

She looked back up at him. her eyes now clear. "It's better for me to go, Toby. Soon."

"No, it's not!"

"What exactly do you mean?" Snippy wasn't the word.

He was going for broke here and telling the truth—or at least some of it. "I'd like you to stay, Laura, at least for a couple of weeks."

She hesitated. "That's fine. Until you get a replacement."

"Until Zeke sorts out about this Radcliffe chap and then . . ."

"You're really worried about him?"

Damn, trust her to interrupt just when he was getting the main point of it all. "Yes!"

"I know." She gave a little sigh. "I overheard a lot of what you said on the terrace last night."

Dear Father Abel! "You listened?"

"I didn't 'listen.' I overheard. If you talk beneath an open window, what am I supposed to do? Move Piet's bed to another room? Pop my head out of the window and ask you to move? Put cotton wool in my ears? I tried not to hear what you were saying and I missed bits of it but . . ." She frowned hard and shook her head.

"That's why you want to quit?" Even a vamp's brain had trouble making sense of all this. He could just wipe her memory, might just be the easiest all around. But he wouldn't . . .

"No! That's not it!"

He was doing this badly. She was way beyond testy. This was tearing her up and it was up to him to take care of it. If he'd misread her emotions he was in the soup. "Laura." He took her hand in his. She trembled but she made no effort to pull away. Her fingers were long and capable, nails manicured but cut short and unpolished. Working hands. Healing hands. Mortal hands. He might be making a life-wrecking mistake but what the hell! He was dead anyway by some people's reckoning!

"Laura." Her hand was still warm between his. She might just yank it away in the next two seconds. "If you want to quit, fine. I'll write you sterling references, whatever you need to find another job. But once you're no longer an employee, I have a favor to ask . . ." She was listening. Intent. "I want you to go out with me."

"Go out where?"

"You choose. A play, a film—I mean, a movie—a walk on the beach, a drive down the coast. You name it."

Her fingers tightened around his. "You mean date you?"

"Yes." That's what he meant.

She looked gobsmacked. But not irate. More perplexed. "You're serious. You want to date me? Why?"

Damn good question, but she hadn't refused, and her eyes were bright with interest. Hope? Astonishment? He had one second to come up with the right answer. "Have you looked in the mirror lately? Looked into your heart? Peeped into your soul? You're beautiful, Laura, in every way."

She blushed. A real, honest-to-goodness blush that flushed her face and colored her neck a delicious pink as her blood rose. And she smiled. "You really mean it, don't you?"

It was his turn to smile.

He tightened his hold on her hand.

"Okay if I quit right now?" She didn't wait for an answer, just reached out for him with her free hand. He was faster. Drawing her close, wrapping one arm around her shoulder, as he cupped the back of her head with his free hand and covered her mouth with his.

The first kiss was slow, sweet and gentle—lips meeting lips, touch savoring touch as he inhaled the sweetness of her mortality and savored the taste of her lips. His fingers ruffled her hair as the arm around her shoulders drew her closer. He lifted his lips a minute to whisper her name, but she pulled him back and kissed him, opening her lips and teasing the tip of his tongue with hers.

What man, mortal or immortal, could refuse the invitation?

Her kiss brought fire, sweetness and heat. She moved

in closer, wrapping her arms around his shoulder, holding him, pressing herself against him. A wild abandon possessed him. He'd fantasized about kissing her, felt the warmth and the beauty of her climax last night, but to have her willing in his arms had him drunk with desire. He pressed his lips harder on hers and she let out a little sexy whimper as his tongue caressed hers. She was incredible. Wonderful. Meeting his need with desire and his touch with passion. She shifted sideways to press her body over his. Her heart raced and her pulse throbbed against his fingertips as he caressed her neck.

He yearned to taste her again, to feel her richness against his tongue, but it was too early. Too soon. He lifted his mouth, holding her close. He smiled down at her.

She grinned back. "I'm quitting."

"Sure?" What an inadequate reply. But his mind was groggy with passion, happiness and a wild urge to take her clothes off and continue this conversation naked.

Her laugh was deep, earthy and even sexier than her smile. "Did that really happen or am I hallucinating?"

"I assure you, it wasn't an hallucination."

"Good." She drew back a little, but only a little. She was still close enough for the warmth of her skin to touch his soul. "You know this is nuts."

"Why?"

She had to think about that. No doubt her brain was in the same state as his. "I work for you. I mean, I used to. I quit. Right?"

"Laura, your working for me is a mere incidental. I assure you, excellent as the other nurses are, I have no lustful thoughts for them."

She let that sink in. "That's a relief! You mean you have lustful thoughts about me?"

"From the moment you walked in the door. You were

so very professional, and with all one hears about sexual harassment over here in the States . . ."

Her giggle was sexy too. "You know why I really want to quit? I couldn't take it anymore. I was having dreams, about you. Quite fantastic dreams actually, and having 'lustful thoughts' for an employer is most unprofessional."

"Now we can be as unprofessional as we like."

"Yeah!"

She leaned into him, somehow wrapped her leg over his, and he accepted her invitation to unprofessionalism. They needed to talk—there was unsettled business between them, but it could wait. The world could wait while he let her kisses go to his head and the sweet mortal warmth of her body and the delicious feel of her breast under his hand sent his body into overdrive.

He stroked down her back and over the curve of her hip. He wanted her close enough to feel his erection, to know how much he wanted and needed her and . . .

"Toby, sorry to bother you but . . ."

They pulled apart as the door opened, but Laura's leg was still caught over his, and she looked as if she'd had a tumble in the hay. Adela would have to be blind not to notice.

"Sorry!" Her blush pretty much confirmed she wasn't blind and had no doubt registered every little nuance.

"No reason to apologize." What a lie. Toby stood and crossed the room. At least he could draw attention from Laura. "What is it, Adela?" It had better be a matter of life and death.

"There's a delivery, Toby, and apparently only you can sign for it." Her mouth quirked a little as she took in Laura standing and smoothing down her uniform. Damn! Looked like the aftermath of some kinky scene. Well, darn it! It wasn't! He'd just laid his dignity at

Laura's feet and been swept off his own! Lousy cliché, yes, but he couldn't help smiling.

"You need to sign for it, Toby. It's a rather large, sealed box by special delivery." Damn, had to be Larouselière all packed up from Vlad. "I considered faking your signature but . . ."

"Alright, Adela! I'm coming."

"Toby?" Laura stood at his elbow, smiling. "I really need to get home. I'll be back tonight."

"Come back early." He didn't want her to leave but . . .

"I will." She put her hand on his arm, stood on tiptoe and kissed him very chastely on the cheek. "This is insane, you know?"

"I know, but isn't it wonderful?" Heck, he'd not felt this heady and exhilarated since the day he stood on the quayside in Liverpool and knew no one would ever enslave him again.

"Yeah!" Her eyes lit with excitement. For him.

"Take care."

"I will. I'm going to spend an exciting day doing laundry and cleaning the house."

"And I'll spend mine finding out what the FBI have left of Connor Inc." Not that it seemed important right now, but there were employees to consider.

She drove off, taking a slice of his heart with him, but even the ache felt wonderful.

He left himself almost immediately, leaving Adela giving Zeke directions to Wyatt's Bend.

He wished him luck. He wished himself luck. A witch as a houseguest, a rogue vampire in the vicinity, the FBI, falling in love—life in Oregon was nothing if not interesting.

Chapter 10

Adela really hoped Zeke got where he was going. Honestly! You'd think, with all the other powers vampires possessed, they'd have a sense of direction. A directionally impaired vampire. The idea had her grinning. Still, he had managed to follow her to the outskirts of Dark Falls and had taken the right road off toward Wyatt's Bend. If he got lost again, it wasn't her fault.

Turning in the opposite direction, Adela headed up the narrow road toward the charred ruin of Gertrude's house. She didn't really blame Gertrude for refusing, after all, to come down and see the horrid mess that was once her home. Being right on the spot, Adela could easily get the fire department and the police to fill in the forms Gertrude faxed. Adela had even agreed to meet with the insurance adjuster and take him to the house. All perfectly reasonable and fair since the arson occurred during Adela's occupancy.

Why, then, did she have this nagging worry that trouble lurked very close?

Perhaps she was hanging around vampires too much.

She took a couple of dozen photos with the digital camera Toby lent her. From whatever angle you looked, the house was done for. Anger flared toward the mob and the deputy, who stood by and watched. Maybe Gertrude was very wise to not return but to take the insurance and run. Didn't make the offense any less heinous. The venal residents of Dark Falls tempted her to forget the Wiccan maxim of "Do harm to none."

Drat! The overwhelmingly negative energy that swirled around the area was having its influence. She got back in her borrowed Hummer, shoved the camera in the glove compartment and headed for the volunteer fire department on the far side of the town.

"Fill in a form?" The teenage volunteer washing the relic of a fire engine looked as if she'd asked him to swing from the rafters by his toes.

"Yes. It's important." He shrugged and aimed the hose at the right rear wheel. "Is there anyone else here?" Someone with a modicum of intelligence and public duty. "Only Bud out the back."

Bud had one arm but a more than average complement of brains. He took the forms from Adela, scanned them and nodded. "About the fire over near the river."

"The fire in Gertrude Anderson's house!" Why did everyone want to ignore the fact that an old woman was now homeless?

"Miss Anderson? Who taught typing at the high school?"

"Yes!" Could be a lie, but Gertrude had mentioned retiring from teaching.

"Well, I'll be . . ." He shook his head. "That was a bad fire."

"Yes, and I promised her I'd take care of the formalities this end."

"The captain will have to do them." He looked up at Adela. "I'll see that he does."

Seemed there was at least one decent person in this town. "Thank you very much. There's a SASE clipped to the form."

"Good of you. Always helps."

Meant it got mailed back rather than binned, most likely. "Thanks. I need to drop another off with the deputy."

He shook his head. "You'd better give it to one of the lot come in from Eugene. Deputy Johnson got himself murdered last night."

The drive into town helped her get her mind straight. A little. She hadn't liked the deputy. He'd been a bully, lazy and a sad specimen of law enforcement. He'd have locked her up if Toby hadn't intervened with his vampire mind tricks, but **he** didn't deserve to die. Hell, no one did. Well, almost no one. Who in their right mind had killed the deputy? Half the law enforcement of the state would be in on this case.

Half the law enforcement of the state seemed to be milling around Main Street. She counted four marked cars and a couple of vans. Seemed the law had taken over the Kountry Kitchen across the street.

She parked on a side street away from the jammed Main Street. The atmosphere around was heavy with tension, disorder and evil. The last shocked her, but there was no mistaking. Something very bad had happened here. Okay, a man had been murdered, that was bad enough, but the venom, hatred and vicious emotions around her were stifling. She'd hand over the forms to the first deputy she set eyes on and hightail it out of here.

Cops and people waiting to talk to cops filled half the tables in the diner. Adela took an empty seat at the counter, ordered coffee and, catching the aromas wafting from the griddle, added a ham omelet and toast. Toby was a generous host, but he tended to overlook the matter of feeding guests.

"I need to talk to one of the deputies," Adela said to the waitress who poured her coffee. "I know they're busy but it won't take ten minutes. I'd hoped to see the local deputy but . . ."

"Too late there, honey." Adela noticed the name "Judy" embroidered on her uniform pocket as she put two plastic cream containers in the saucer and moved the sugar canister in Adela's direction. "He was killed last night."

"So I heard. I've just been at the fire department. Bud there told me." She gave herself full marks for remembering his name.

It helped. "Bud Drake's my mother's cousin."

"He suggested I talk to one of the other deputies instead, but they all look occupied." And in fairness arson did take second place to murder.

Judy smiled. "I'll have a word with Lance Boynton. He's a good guy. I bet he'll give you ten minutes." She picked up the carafe off the warmer and walked over to replenish coffee cups.

Adela sipped on the hot coffee and looked out across the diner to the street beyond. A large police van pulled up in front of the police office and a body bag was carried out.

A number of officers stood in silence as the dark shape was pushed into the back of the van. As it drove away, they got right back to questioning. Judy, good as her word, took the chance to whisper something to a sandy-haired deputy. They both glanced her way. Adela nodded in recognition and went back to her coffee, hoping this would be over soon.

Judy had just topped up her coffee, and Adela was eyeing the omelet sizzling on the griddle when a quiet voice asked, "Ma'am, if I might have a word."

Great. Two minutes to explain what she needed and the omelet would be ready. "By all means." Taking the envelope with her, she followed him to the table.

A dark-haired man sat there. No, a dark-haired vampire. And she suspected she was the only one in the diner who even had an inkling.

"Deputy," she began, "I'm sorry to interrupt but . . ."

"That's okay, ma'am. Have a seat."

"Thanks. I believe Judy mentioned these forms. I know you're incredibly busy but . . ."

"That's okay, ma'am. Just a minute, if you please. Your name?"

"Adela Whyte." Odd that he wrote it down.

He looked at the vampire. "Can you make a positive identification?"

"Certainly." The creature even smirked. "This is the woman."

She was aware of another deputy standing behind her, and a third opposite.

"Do you have an address in Dark Falls or nearby, Mrs. Whyte?"

"I did but it burned down two nights ago." Terse but that was why she'd come into town after all. If he'd just taken the darn packet, she'd be gone. She wasn't even sure she'd stay to eat. The vampire opposite gave her the willies.

"Oh yes, it was your house that burned."

"That's why I need a police report, for the insurance."

"I see." She was glad he did because she was getting

lost here. "If you'd just come over with us to the deputy's office we can get this straight."

Might actually be better than waiting for them to mail it in. Obviously they were busy. "Okay."

Deputy Boynton and a fair-haired young woman deputy walked across the road with her. They went in the back door—there still was plenty of activity in the front room and Adela had no desire to enter another crime scene.

In the back office, Lance Boynton glanced at the packet, asked for identification and then the nightmare began. An hour and a half later, she'd been fingerprinted, stripped, and searched and was locked in one of the three cells, arrested for the murder of Deputy Johnson.

Adela was angry, scared and upset. So much for civil rights; she'd been refused access to a telephone on the grounds that the only line was in use.

Why had that vampire lied? She had a pretty good guess who he was, and that, unfortunately, told her how he had so much influence with the police.

Trouble was, when she didn't come back, Toby would no doubt think she'd stayed in a B and B after all.

Damn! They had to give her access to a phone eventually. All she needed was one call.

Fortuitous wasn't the word! Axel Radcliffe accepted the thanks from the entire sheriff's department for his speedy identification of the murderer and strolled down the miserable little street to the newspaper office.

Good move fingering the witch. If they were stupid enough to believe a 120-pound woman of her age could throttle a 270-pound man with her bare hands and almost rip his head off, they deserved to be duped.

Couldn't last, but would keep the law happy and the witch off the streets long enough. The one person in this pathetic dead-end town who might pose any sort of risk to him was safely out of the way. Of course, it would be even better to let the deputy's office burn to the ground with her in it, but two arsons in the same week might strike even these yokels as a trifle out of the ordinary. As long as his suggestion to not allow her to use the telephone held strong, there was no way she was getting out of there.

Laura backed out of her driveway and turned right. She could put this off and wax the floor or clean windows, but after the odd conversation she'd overheard last night, she couldn't get over the fact that an intelligent man—two intelligent men, come to that—really believed Axel might be a vampire.

If that was so, Dad was in danger. She had to warn him, although whether he'd listen was another matter.

Forty minutes or so later, she drove down into Dark Falls and almost clipped a police cruiser, parked askew on the corner by the hardware store. What was going on? The street was packed with cop cars and a couple of large vans parked in front of the deputy's office.

She turned right onto a side street, drove down an alley, parked behind the *Dark Falls Weekly News* office and went in by the back entrance.

And right away wished she'd used the front door. When she'd helped Dad on the paper back in high school, they'd made coffee and eaten lunch together in the little back kitchen. Eating anything here now, they'd risk typhoid or food poisoning. She had to shoulder the door into the hallway open. Obviously a seldom-used part of the premises.

Dad used to be so particular. Maybe it was her fault for not dropping by more often, but heck, she had her own house to keep clean.

No point in going all domestic. She had more pressing things on her mind than the state of the kitchen floor. Her priority was to speak to Dad.

The old printing press stood silent. Dad (or, no doubt, Axel) had decided it was more economic to have it printed in Eugene. What had happened to old Bert, who'd manned the press ever since she could remember? Or his assistant, Ted, who'd given her her first kiss during one Christmas party? Off to better jobs, she hoped. Maybe Bert had retired. She wasn't getting waylaid by nostalgia. The very immediate present was her concern. Dad's office was down the dark hallway and off to the right. At least that much hadn't changed. She opened the door. "Dad . . ." she began and broke off. Stunned. Axel was leaning over her father, arms wrapped around his shoulders as if to embrace him! Her stomach did a back somersault as she caught her breath. Utterly robbed of words, Laura froze and gaped as Axel stood up and snarled. No other word for it.

"Don't you knock before entering closed doors?"

That really pissed her off. "I've never before knocked at my father's office door. Why should I start now?" Damn him! He still had both hands on her father's shoulders and was actually whispering in his ear.

"Maybe you should, Laura," her father said.

"You never used to shut the door," she pointed out.

"Things are different now."

No doubt about that! But now was not the time to indulge in shock or hysterics. She'd come to see Dad.

She hadn't really put much stock in the talk of vampires, had taken it to be figurative rather than literal, but seeing Axel snarl, she understood the comparison. The man was positively lethal looking and needed to cut his fingernails.

She smiled. "So I see. I wanted to follow up on my call last night. Sorry I missed you, but I hope you got a story from the message I left with Axel." If he'd passed it on.

"I did, Laura. Not what we'd hoped for but it's enough for now. Local events pushed it to an inside back page."

"What were the FBI looking for?" That was Axel.

"I didn't hear details and they'd all gone by the time I arrived." As if they'd have told her! "But they took the computer, files, disks and pretty much wrecked the place." Besides, she wanted to know what was happening down the street. Now. "What's going on here? I couldn't get through Main Street. How about I take you to lunch, Dad, and you tell me all about it?"

"Can't do lunch, dear." She'd have taken the rebuff more kindly if he hadn't looked at Axel before replying. "Too much happening."

"Surely you'll eat lunch?"

"Your father said no."

She jumped at the vehemence in Axel's voice. Sheesh! She hadn't invited him! "If you're too busy, Dad." She made a point of emphasizing "Dad." "I understand. Things are certainly humming outside. What happened?" Maybe she'd get him outside, alone, and drop a word of caution in his ear.

"The deputy was murdered last night."

She grabbed the edge of the desk to steady herself. "What?" She hadn't much liked Deputy Johnson. She'd been at school with his daughter and sensed he bullied

Jenn and her sisters. But murder! "Any idea why? Or who did it?" Certainly would have knocked anything else off the front page.

"They have already made an arrest." Axel gave a fangy smile. Her imagination was getting away with her.

"That was fast! Who?"

"The witch who lived down by the river. The one who was burned out of her house two nights ago. Adela Whyte, her name is," Axel replied.

"You wouldn't know her, Laura," Dad added. Talk about shock. It was a wonder she was processing anything. "She moved here a few months back."

"I see." A complete lie. She had to make sense of this. "They're sure she killed him?"

"Certainly." Axel as good as gloated. "She was identified."

True, Adela had been out until late last night, but Laura couldn't imagine her killing anyone. "How was he killed?"

"My, my, aren't we curious?" Now the obnoxious creature was patronizing!

"I imagine that will be public knowledge, if it isn't already. I'll read it in the paper, won't I?"

"Laura, that was impertinent!"

How could Dad pick on her? Easily, it seemed. "Dad, a public figure is murdered. Of course I'm curious."

"Strangled." Axel drew out the word as if relishing the idea. "Throttled. The life was squeezed out of him."

Impossible! But saying so would no doubt garner another snide comment. Adela needed help and Toby would be the one to do it. She had to call him the minute she got out of here.

But she wasn't quite ready to give up on her reason for driving over here. Deep breath. "Dad, sorry for interrupting when you're obviously so busy but could we get together another time? Tomorrow, perhaps? Have lunch at the Kountry Kitchen, or we could drive into Florence."

"Why don't you come and eat at our house?" Axel asked. Heck, could Dad never answer for himself? "I'm sure your father would be happy to have you."

It was also *her* home, wasn't it? Her savings had paid for a new roof not that long ago. "I'd like some time with my father. Alone." Heck, might as well say it.

"Laura!" Sharp was not the word for her father's tone. "That was rude of you! Apologize to Axel!"

When the sun rose over the Pacific! Between worry, shock and disgust she was about to lose it. "Dad, what's so unreasonable or rude about wanting to have lunch with my father? If you're busy now, you name the day. I'd just like to talk."

"And what's so secret that you can't say to Axel too?"

Volumes! She shook her head. "With all due respect, you're my father. Axel isn't!" All this was doing was raising her blood pressure and widening the toothy smirk on Axel's pasty face. Someone should tell him black wasn't his color.

"My, my. Testy today, aren't we?"

That finished her.

Another deep, calming breath.

"I'll talk to you later, Dad. Good afternoon, Axel." The whole thing was so creepy. She didn't want to even consider that Dad and Axel were lovers, but why else would Dad act that way?

She went out the front way; once through the filthy back kitchen was more than enough. Barely took in the crowds and cars on Main Street as she turned down a side street to the alley and her car. Something was really wrong, majorly wrong.

She had her key in the lock when Axel appeared, eyes wide and bright and the nastiest grin curling his toothy mouth.

"So, don't want me in your little-girl tête-à-tête with Daddy?"

Why soft-soap it anymore? "No, I don't! I don't trust you. I don't like the way you treat Dad, or your influence over him. You're underhanded, sneaky . . ." She gave up. Why waste time and words? What she really wanted was out of here.

"Sneaky, am I? Underhanded? You asinine, pathetic mortal, you!" Now he looked like a creature from a nightmare. His lips curled to show . . . fangs! He moved toward her, fingers curled like a claw. She backed away but the car was behind her. Her only hope was to dart sideways, but she couldn't move. The hate and viciousness in his eyes had her petrified.

Terror rising cold in her gut, she flinched, waiting for him to strike. He took another step, hissed and then screamed and leapt back. "Bitch!" He wailed as if in pain. "Think yourself clever, do you? You can't wear silver forever. I'll wait and you'll be mine, just. . ."

She didn't wait to hear the rest.

While he snarled at her, his back against the wall, Laura wrenched open the car door and was down the alley at top speed, taking a couple of trash cans on her way.

She had no idea what had just happened, but she wanted to be a long way away from it.

She had no idea where she was going. She just drove as fast and as far as she could, until she finally pulled into a gas station and sat there, shaking and sobbing.

When she got herself together, she noticed the grass

and thistles growing through the concrete and the nettles bordering the boarded-up building. Just as well she'd picked a long-closed gas station. At least here she'd let herself go in private. But now she had to get herself together. Where to start? Adela was in jail, accused of murder. Something was majorly wrong with Dad, and Axel was insane.

She needed help and so did Adela. Laura picked up her cell phone.

The Feds arrived a second time at Connor Inc. about ten minutes before Toby, so he had the dubious pleasure of watching them wreak havoc two days in succession. There were more this time, and they made more mess but left faster.

He was old enough to be grateful for the smallest of mercies.

Thankful he had employees able enough to cope, Toby picked up his U.K.-based phone—expensive but less likely to be monitored than the company one—and called Elizabeth.

"I'm coming over," she said. "I must see Dad."

He bit back the instinctive response, that it wasn't necessary. It no doubt was for her peace of mind, and it was her home, after all. Piet was always glad to see her, even if he forgot her visit twenty-four hours later. And there was the purely selfish thought that Elizabeth might give him a few pointers on how to handle things with Laura.

"Let me know when you land. I'll come and meet you. Your Hummer is still here but Adela's borrowing it right now. Hers had a mishap." The full story could wait.

"She's okay?"

"Oh, yes. Minor flap at the time but everything's quite alright now." Almost.

"She wasn't hurt or anything?"

"Oh, no. She's as right as rain."

Elizabeth rang off. Toby snapped his phone shut. Time to do something constructive with what was left of the day, he supposed.

His other mobile rang. It was Laura. He pressed the green button. "Laura? What's happened?"

"Toby?" Her voice shook through her obvious effort to hide her agitation. "Thank God!"

Her gasp shocked him. "What's the matter?"

"Lots of things, but one I really need your help with. You need to get Adela out of jail."

What? Not that wretched deputy again. "If he dared arrest her . . ."

"He didn't arrest her. One of the other deputies did." She went on, quite concisely given her level of agitation, and filled him in on a tale so incredible it had to be true. "I don't believe for one moment that she killed him. She couldn't. He's taller and heavier, and it's ridiculous, but there are the oddest things going on here."

He didn't doubt it. "Where are you?"

"I don't really know. I just drove away until I found somewhere to stop and think. Toby?" she paused. "You know I mentioned overhearing you and that detective last night."

"Yes, don't worry about it."

"It's not that. You talked about Axel being a vampire. Did you mean that or was it just an expression? After all, vampires aren't real, are they?"

Bless her little cotton socks, she really picked her moments. "They are very rare, Laura. But there have been instances."

"Well, there's something really odd about Axel."

Dear Abel! "Stay away from him, Laura!"

"Don't worry, I will, but I'm worried about Dad. Axel's weird and scary."

What was happening there? Nothing good, by all accounts. "Laura, please, are you safely out of the town?"

"Yeah!"

"Stay where you are and I'll come out to you."

"I don't know where I am! I just drove. Let me think. There's a Super Softee Freeze just before you turn off for Dark Falls. I'll be there."

"Alright Laura, go straight there, please, and wait for me. It might take a little while but I'll be bringing a lawyer with me."

That call over, he tried to call Zeke. Might as well bring in vamp, as well as mortal, reinforcements. No reply. He'd try later. Probably turned off his phone while he snooped and sleuthed.

He had better luck with the company lawyer. "Dave, I need the name of a good criminal lawyer and I need it this afternoon."

Dave Burns gave better than a name. "If it's just getting bail and getting her out, I'll come with you. Before I got smart, I worked as a public defender. I know how to face down police departments who bend the law."

Chapter 11

Adela's map and directions sure helped. Not that Zeke would be in any hurry to admit to anyone that he needed help from a witch, and a white one at that (he had to grin) to find his way around. He reached the house, obviously inhabited but currently empty—not a sound of a mortal heartbeat anywhere. He should have asked that nurse to come with him and invite him in. As it was, he settled for sneaking and peering, skills he'd perfected as a teenager looking for trouble.

One thing he caught right away: the odor of sour vampire, strong, sharp and repulsive. Exactly what Adela had found around her daughter's house. There it had been stale and bad. This was fresh and foul. What sort of creatures lived like this and left such a trail? And how, if they stank like this, could they live among mortals and conceal their nature? Heck, they'd stand out in a gathering of street people.

No doubt about it, the Brit vampire's suspicion was dead on the mark. What now? He should report what he found. He'd been sent to confirm the presence or not of a rogue vamp. What the boss planned, Zeke had no idea but knew darn well the discourtesy wouldn't be ignored. Someone was due to face an irritated Vlad Tepes. Not good—for them.

Might as well pass on the news to vamp central. He opened his cell phone and pressed the first speed dial. Two rings later, Vlad himself answered.

"Zeke?"

"Yes, Boss?"

"Found anything?"

"You bet! I'm at the house right now. No doubt about it. Stinks just like before. Same bloodline, I guess."

"So Wise suggested." Vlad paused. "Larouselière is on his way. Once he wakes, you and Wise need to tell him all you know." Right, the French vamp slept in daylight. Rather showy and nerdy, Zeke always thought, but . . . "I'll be down soon. Just check one more thing. Look for bones, recent graves, in case he's draining mortals."

"Yes, sir."

Fun job but someone had to do it. Zeke put away his phone and looked around. The house stood on several acres of land. They could have an army buried here, except it was so overgrown that even Zeke's town-dweller's eyes could see that there'd been no digging recently. Still, orders were orders. Using his vamp speed, Zeke ran the perimeter of the lot. It was like a damn obstacle race, with trees, roots, green things with spikes on them growing all over the place. He was darn glad he had vampire skin. The wretched vegetation would puncture mortal hide.

He paused to look around. There was an easier way to survey the property. Why hadn't he thought of it sooner? Had to be the country air addling his brain. He ran toward the house. Using the porch railing as leverage, he swung up to the roof and perched along the ridge.

Nice. He could see for miles. Well, a long way at least.

The ground was undisturbed. To the right, the other side of the narrow road, were fields of something or other growing in nice straight rows, and in the distance, through trees, were other roofs. In the other direction was a river.

He was about to jump down when he heard an approaching car. His was nicely hidden but . . . damn! The car turned up the drive and parked itself in front of the garage—the garage Zeke hadn't checked out.

He lay flat on the roof, peering over as the driver stepped out. He was tall, dark-haired and pale. Mortal? No. A vamp. No heartbeat! This had to be his quarry. Strange, the way he stood looking around, sniffing the air. Definitely not a mortal. Besides, there wasn't the least family resemblance between this dude and the sexy little nurse Toby had gotten his fangs into.

The vamp went into the house. Obviously needed no invitation. Zeke waited ten minutes, then cautiously slid down the back of the roof, intending to take off at top speed toward his car.

Just as his feet touched the ground and he straightened, something hit him hard on the back of his head. He stumbled and was pushed down. He opened his eyes but before he could fight back, he screamed as a stake pierced his back, pinning him to the ground.

Adela had made six requests to make a phone call and was about to make her seventh. One every half-hour, according to the clock just visible through the bars if she sat on the end of the hard cot. Ten minutes more and she'd ask again. Until then, Adela forced calming thoughts into her teeming brain.

She'd had plenty of time to order her thoughts and make

vain attempts to make sense of all this. The vampire—she was nine hundred percent sure he was a vampire—had identified her as a murderess. Why? She half-wished she'd outed him, except that would have earned her a cell of the padded variety. Drafty and noisy was better—marginally.

Refusing to let her make a call was odd in the extreme. So was keeping her here instead of taking her down to the jail in Eugene. Unless there really was some funny business going on. But what? She wasn't on top of the list of the late deputy's favorite people but why drag her into this?

She closed her eyes and sat cross-legged on the cot in a valiant effort to compose herself. It was getting harder every minute. She glanced up at the clock. Almost time to make another token request for use of a phone she knew would be denied, when she heard footsteps coming down the hall—multiple footsteps and Deputy Boynton sounding most put out.

"She's charged with murder!"

"Formally charged?"

"Well, no, we're holding her for the time being."

"For the past four hours? Without access to a telephone?" Whomever the unseen voice belonged to, he was her friend.

"Hasn't been four hours. We booked her in at eleven."

"And kept her incommunicado since!"

And then they came into sight. The deputy who'd arrested her, a man she'd never seen before and . . . Toby.

She was across the cell, leaning against the bars as they came into view. Her heart raced when she met Toby's eyes.

Behind him the sheriff and the strange man wrangled on.

"You got here," she said, still suspecting an hallucination. "I couldn't call. They never let me."

"I know. Dave is having a field day over that. I'll get you out of here. Hold on, old thing."

She'd resent that last bit if she wasn't all-out and utterly relieved. She believed him. Vamps got their own way, but how? This wasn't a parking ticket or even a DUI. This was murder, for freaking sakes!

"Deputy, you will unlock her cell. She will leave while you and Lawyer Burns take care of all the formalities."

The deputy stared, gulped, blinked and nodded. "Right away."

Once the door was open, Toby grinned. "Get out the back door. Laura is waiting for you. Leave and don't stop until you're back at Devil's Elbow."

"What about you?"

"I'll take care of things here. You get away, before the rat who accused you senses what's happened."

Good advice. Seemed Toby knew more of what was going on than she did. Even if this did feel like a jail-break, she trusted Toby. This wasn't the first bind he'd saved her from this week, after all. "You'll take care?"

He grinned. "I'm vampire, Adela. I'll be okay and so will Dave. You hurry and make sure Laura gets the hell out of here."

Taking him at his word, she darted down the hallway, leaving the arguing male voices behind.

Laura had the engine running. "Get in the back, under the blanket," she said. "Better if no one sees you."

"Won't argue with that," Adela replied. "And thanks a bunch." She crouched on the floor and pulled the gray blanket over her.

The car took off.

Laura was sweating as she left Dark Falls behind. Toby had been right. This was a flea-brained idea, but since he'd not come up with a better plan, they'd used hers.

And Adela was free.

"Okay?" she called back.

"Fine, and thanks."

Laura suspected that was way off from the truth, but everything was relative and the dirty floor of her backseat was vastly preferable to sitting in a jail cell. "Look, I'm going to stop in about ten minutes and you can come up front." When she did, Laura had several questions that needed answers, or rather suspicions that needed confirmation.

Once she was well clear of Dark Falls, Laura pulled over to the side of the road. "Want to come up front?" Adela didn't wait for a second invitation. The poor woman was a long way from the serene, self-contained guest of the house.

"Sorry about making you ride on the floor, but Toby said to be sure no one saw you leave town. If I'd known what was going to happen, I'd have cleaned the inside of the car."

"If I'd know what was going to happen, I'd have stayed the hell away from Dark Falls!"

"Yes!" Who wouldn't have? "There's a comb in the glove compartment and I brought a sandwich and a couple of drinks. I picked them up while I was waiting for Toby."

"Thanks." She took the drink first and half-drained it before rifling through the glove compartment for the comb. "Thank you so much," she repeated, as she unwrapped the sandwich. "For the food and the rescue."

Laura started the car and headed north. "The rescue was Toby's doing. I just called and told him what had happened."

Adela almost choked on the ham and Swiss on a poppy-seed bun. "You called him? I wondered how he knew to come and get me out, but how did you know?"

Good question. Where to start? They had a good

twenty minutes' drive to Devil's Elbow. "I was in Dark Falls and heard the talk." No need to say exactly who was talking. "Didn't seem likely there were two people burned out of their houses in the past forty-eight hours. So I called Toby."

"Thank you." Adela put a mountain of heartfelt meaning into the two words. "My dear, I am indebted. I was afraid I'd never get out of there alive." She let out a long sigh, leaned back in the seat and closed her eyes. "Thank you."

"You're welcome. Glad I could help." Especially if it meant foiling Axel. But how come he had this sort of influence? Was he really a vampire? And what did he have against Adela? "Why would Axel Radcliffe want you locked up?" Inquisitive, but the question had been nagging her all day.

"I think because I'm a witch."

Good thing they were on one of the rare straight stretches of Highway 101. "A witch!" After last night's conversations, why not?

"Yes, my dear," Adela replied, a note of amusement coming through her tired voice. "A witch, and no, I do not ride a broomstick or have a pointed black hat or naturally green face. I'm a Wiccan. I practice white magic."

"Is that why Axel has it in for you?"

Pause. "Maybe, although I'd never met him in my life before he accused me in the Kountry Kitchen."

This got weirder and scarier by the minute. "Do you think Axel meant you harm? Means others harm?" He'd certainly tried to attack her.

"I do, my dear. I think he is vicious and dangerous. Not just for what he did to me." She paused. "His sort mean little good to anyone but themselves."

Thanks a lot! But wasn't that what she'd figured out

for herself? "I'm really worried about my father. Axel Radcliffe is his partner and now lives with him. He seems to have my father cowed." Adela's long silence wasn't a good sign. On the other hand, did she want soothing platitudes? "I have to go back and talk to him again—once I get you safely to Devil's Elbow," she added when Adela gave a little gasp.

"My dear, may I suggest you tell Toby and ask him to help. I do not think you are strong enough to take on Axel Radcliffe on your own."

Laura agreed but . . . "I have to do something. I'm worried for Dad."

"Tell Toby and young Zeke."

"I hate to bother them." Besides, it was her trouble, not Toby's. He had more than enough already.

"My dear, I don't believe Toby would consider it a 'bother.' Unless I'm completely misreading what's in front of my eyes, Toby Wise has a distinct fondness for you."

The silence and the spreading flush up her face pretty much showed Laura reciprocated. Interesting. Very interesting. "He's a good person, Laura," Adela said. "Unusual in many ways." Like being dead. "But honorable and decent." A few months back she'd never have imagined saying that about a vampire. Knowledge did change one's perspective.

"I know that," Laura replied. "I know."

Adela hoped the silence meant she was considering asking for Toby's help. On her own that vile creature could swallow her. Maybe literally. "Trust Toby, then, and please don't try any individual heroics. True strength lies in knowing when you need the help of others."

Another long silence. She could almost hear the younger woman's mind clicking. Poor girl, she'd had a rough day too, by the sound of things.

"Adela, can I ask you something?"

"Of course."

"Do you think vampires are real?"

So she was beginning to figure it out, was she? Good for her. "I don't just think they are. I know they are." Might as well say it straight.

Laura turned and gaped at her. "Really?"

"Yes, really, dear, and please watch out." There was a particularly sharp bend and a tunnel ahead.

Laura gave her attention, or at least her sight, to the road. As it straightened out, she said, "You're serious." It wasn't a question.

"Yes, I am, my dear. They are not common but they do exist."

"Then Axel really is a vampire!" she half-whispered, as if not wanting it to be true. "Oh, my God!" Her knuckles whitened as she clutched the steering wheel. She turned a stricken face to Adela. "Dad's in the thrall of a vampire! The walking dead! An evil revenant is using him! Sucking his blood!" She was going pale to the point of green.

Adela reached over and held the wheel, just in case. "We don't know all of that. If he is using your father, he needs him and won't really harm him." She hoped. "Toby can't be far behind us. He'll help. He got me out of jail, didn't he?"

Laura conceded the point with a nod and a bite of her lip. "What can he do against a vampire?"

So she'd only twigged about Axel, not the rest of them. Interesting. "You might be surprised." Astounded, most likely! "What made you suspect Axel was a vampire?"

"I didn't. Not really. I overheard Toby and that detective, Zeke, talking last night when Piet's window was open. I thought they'd been drinking; it sounded so preposterous, but now . . ." She shook her head. "It's still preposterous but seems it's true."

"There are more things in heaven and earth, Horatio . . ." Adela quoted.

"Than are dreamt of in your philosophy," Laura capped. "Very apt!" she said with a little smile. "Is that Wiccan philosophy or just the Bard's?"

"Old Will had a line about everything, I think," Adela replied. "But yes, there is so much more in the world for good and evil than most people ever dream."

"Like vampires." Oh, dear! The poor girl was going green again. "Or witches—although you're not evil."

Bless her for that! "Some are. They dabble in the black arts, but I don't and you shouldn't assume all vampires are made in Axel's mold either." There! She'd done her bit for Toby's cause. He could take over now.

After a long silence, Laura said, "I don't know what to do."

Adela knew a cry from the heart when she heard one. At least they were close to home. She would feel happier inside the strong stone walls of Piet's house. "My dear, when we get home, I'm going to make you a cup of tea with a shot of rum in it. You are going to sit in a nice comfortable chair and sip it slowly and relax. I'm going to have a long, long shower and scrub that nasty jail off my skin and out of my hair. Then, with a bit of luck, Toby will be back and you are going to be wise and smart enough to ask him for help."

"Yes, ma'am," Laura replied with a praiseworthy attempt at a smile.

Five minutes later, they turned off the road and up the winding drive. At least the FBI weren't decorating the drive today.

Chapter 12

Didn't take long to snatch the pertinent memories from Dave's brain and send him on his way, unaware of the service he'd rendered. He might wonder why he was driving home from this direction, but Toby left the knowledge that he'd done a minor, but very much appreciated, favor for the acting boss of Connor Inc.

All in all, Toby was pleased with the outcome but still worried about the implications of Adela's engineered arrest. Even given that Axel was unaware Adela was under another vamp's protection, the action was unacceptable. Toby considered it tantamount to a challenge.

He had time to contemplate the next move. While Dave checked to be sure Laura and Adela were off and away, Toby had taken care of the deputy's memories. He might wonder at the used, but now unoccupied, cell but wouldn't connect Adela with his confusion.

A good day's work. Now home, to check on the women.

Adela greeted him with a smile and a hug that made him feel like a conquering hero. Nice of her, and he was truly glad he'd saved her from whatever nasty machinations that Radcliffe specimen had in mind, but she wasn't his first priority.

And she knew it.

"Laura is napping. She was all stressed out and since my calming tisanes are all ashes, I made her some mint tea and added a dash of rum. She needed it."

"Sure you didn't add a few incantations?"

"Of course! I added a relaxing spell. I believe in covering all bases. She needed rest. And Toby, you need to talk to her. I mean *really* talk to her. On the way back, she asked me if I believed vampires were real."

"She overheard Zeke and me last night. She doesn't really understand."

"Undoubtedly, but she deserves to know what's going on, and you, Toby, have a lot of explaining to do!"

He was willing to make allowances—after all, Adela had had a difficult day, but . . . "Dash it all, Adela. She's better off not knowing."

"Since when is ignorance a benefit? Honestly, Toby! She's already aware Axel is a vampire. She's scared witless for her father, and I wouldn't put it past her to go rushing off to defend him."

Neither would he. Damn! "I'll talk to her, tell her to leave it all to me." And Zeke when he finally swanned in.

Adela folded her arms on her chest and tapped her foot. "Think that will take care of everything, do you? Sweet goddess!" She raised her eyes to the high pitched ceiling and sighed loud and long. "This is why I never remarried! Men, dead or revenant, are just too obtuse to be endured. Toby!" She unfolded her arms and stepped close until she was almost nose to nose. "Live up to your name! Get Wise! Laura is head over heels in love with you and she deserves to know what's going on!"

"What?" If he'd had breath it would have stopped. "Adela, she's grateful."

"Grateful, my ass!" The out-of-character profanity shocked him. "She's a nurse. She's a professional. She's hardly going to admit she's lusting after her employer. She's more likely to quit."

"But she has already!"

"My point precisely! Wise up! You're a vampire, for goodness' sake!" On that parting shot, she turned and made for the staircase.

What next? Pausing only to ascertain Nurse Redding hadn't overheard Adela—unlikely through two closed doors and the TV, but it never hurt to be cautious. Toby often questioned how much intellectual satisfaction Piet drew from soap operas and game shows, but today thanked Abel for them. Toby looked in on Laura, sleeping the sleep of the emotionally exhausted and slightly intoxicated. Adela made a good move there but easy enough for her to ladle out advice. How in the name of Abel and all his kindred did you look the woman you love in the eye and say, "Oh, by the way, darling, I'm a vampire"?

Axel looked down at the shriveled heap of rapidly disintegrating vampire. The bastard had taken a satisfyingly drawn-out time to die, but damn his eyes and his maker, he'd refused to his last sentient moment to reveal his name, his origins or his reason to be snooping where he had no business.

Frustrated at the failure, Axel kicked Zeke's thigh and swore as the dessicated flesh and bone crumbled, showering his shoes and pant cuffs with pale dust. Cursing, he shook out his pant legs and brushed off his shoes on the grass. Satisfied they were presentable, he walked away. He had no more use for the moldering vampire. Granger could clean up the remains when he got back.

Taking the route through the woods, Axel ran back toward town. One unexpected pest disposed of; now it was time to take care of the witch.

Toby perched on the arm of the sofa and watched Laura sleep. With each breath, her breasts rose and fell against the blue cotton of her T-shirt. Her lips parted slightly and her long, dark lashes rested against her fair skin. She was mortal, fragile, beautiful, utterly desirable and . . . what? Was Adela right?

There was only one way to be sure.

He waited until she stirred, turning slightly in the confines of the recliner. Her breathing changed. She was close to waking.

"Laura?"

He'd whispered, but her eyelids flicked open and rather groggy green eyes met his. "Toby." Her smile, combined with tousled hair and rumpled clothes, suggested she'd spent a sexy few hours. How appearances deceived. But sexy she was, and . . . "That was some cup of tea. I was out for the count!"

"You needed the rest."

She sat up and looked at her watch. "Heavens! It's that late?"

"Don't worry. I think we need to talk."

She swung her feet to the ground and stood up. "I need to get home and changed and back here." She smoothed her crumpled shirt.

"No need." He'd ignore the raised eyebrows and the look of total disagreement. "Laura, more than anything we need to talk. I called the agency, told them you'd had a family emergency and to send a substitute for the next three to five days."

Very thoughtful of him and very, very presumptuous. She was on her feet and for ten seconds was actually looking down at him. "Why did you do that? I can't take a three-day vacation! I have rent to pay and my car is due for a tune-up!"

He stood and reached out for her hand. His touch soothed, but she resisted the impulse to close her fingers around his. "Laura, what's more important, your father or the car?"

That was fighting dirty. At least he hadn't offered to pay her anyway. "Yes. I do need to talk to you about Dad . . . and the vampire." He didn't bat an eyelid. Shit! It was true! She'd taken a leap into the *X-Files!*

"Let's go down on the beach. It's quiet on a weekday afternoon, and private."

"Okay."

"Need a jacket or sweater?"

"I've got one in the car." If it hadn't ended up filthy on the floor during her mad dash from Dark Falls.

"I'll find one." He took a man's cashmere cardigan from the hall closet. "Come on," he said. "Let's go."

Laura was glad of the warmth of cashmere wrapped around her. A brisk breeze from the ocean ruffled her hair, but the cool afternoon meant they had the beach to themselves. Nice. Perfect. Romantic. But she'd come here to get some questions answered, the first one being: "Is my father in danger?" Toby's hesitation pretty much answered that one. Damn! She should have stayed and not been such a wimp running away when Axel did his Bela Lugosi act.

She stopped and looked at Toby. "So, Axel really is a vampire who means Dad harm?"

"Yes, to the first, as I already told you. To the second, I don't know. If my guess is right, he's more intent on holding power over your father, and influencing and using him, rather than direct harm."

And that was good news? Could be worse. "Think that's why Dad plagued me and nagged about getting something on you or Connor Inc.?" Sort of made sense now. Dad's insistence hadn't been like him at all.

"I do, although what he wanted it for, I'm not sure."

"Supposedly a big exposé." Although the circulation of the *Dark Falls Weekly News* was hardly enough to get national attention. "Beats me why he settled for a little weekly rag."

"Maybe the *Oregonian* or the *Register-Guard* weren't in need of capital."

She couldn't help the smile. "Good point! Doesn't help Dad, though."

Toby quashed the thought that nothing could help her father. What mattered now was to protect her. "Not immediately, but once Zeke returns we intend to put our heads together."

"What can two men do against a vampire?" Now was a good time to tell her it would be two vampires, but . . . "He's nasty. Real mean. He went for me today as I was leaving."

"What?" Fury raged in him at the thought that the vermin had dared. "What did he do?" He grabbed her arms. "Did he hurt you?"

"No, but you are!"

He let go. "Sorry, Laura." He stroked her upper arms where he'd grabbed. "The thought of that reptile daring to hurt you . . ."

"Reptile, is he? Thought he was a vampire." She'd even smiled. Darn! The woman had courage. "He didn't hurt me. Scared me, yes, but . . ."

"What did he do?"

"It was odd. Really strange." She shook her head and started walking again, as if the movement helped her. "Bizarre." She sighed. He took her hand. Her fingers closed over his with all the warmth of her mortality. "I'd left them both in the newspaper office. I was irked at Dad refusing to listen or really talk to me and decided to leave him and go home. I'd parked in the alley behind the office because the main street was packed with police cars.

"I was about to get in my car, when Axel appeared as if from nowhere and lunged for me. I was really scared, thinking he was going to grab me or hit me or attack somehow, then even weirder, he sort of fell back, almost cringing against the wall, muttering at me."

How dare he! But why stop his attack? "What was he muttering?" Could these vamps curse? Cast spells? He went cold to his bones at the thought.

"Bunch of nonsense. Something about I might think I'm clever wearing it but I couldn't wear it forever and he'd get me one of these days. Sounded as if he meant it too."

He didn't doubt it one iota. Something she was wearing? Toby cast his mind back to the summit meeting in Tom Kyd's London house, where Etienne Larouselière had advised about besting Laran Radcliffe. Their weapons had been magic and . . . "Were you wearing silver?"

"Silver?" Her hair ruffled in the ocean breeze as she looked up at him. "Silver?" she repeated as if trying to make sense of his question. "Only my mother's locket. I wear it all the time." She reached into the neck of her T-shirt and pulled out an ornate silver locket on a heavy chain. "It was originally my great-grandmother's. When Mom died it came to me."

He reached out for the locket as it swung on the end of the chain. The metal was warm from her skin. Warm, smooth and had saved her life. Curious, he nicked open the locket with his fingernail. The woman had to be her mother; the resemblance of firm chin and high cheekbones was unmistakable. Laura had also inherited the smile and the gleam of determination in the clear green eyes. The man, presumably Laura's father, lacked the vitality and spark of his wife. Toby dreaded to think what he looked like now, after months of Axel's control and manipulation.

"This locket saved you from whatever Axel planned," he told Laura. "Don't ever take it off." He slipped it back inside her T-shirt. The metal had cooled fast between his fingers, but nestling between her breasts, it would soon warm again.

She went quiet. So quiet he could hear her heartbeat. Hear it speed up. He'd scared her, but he had to warn her. To do otherwise would be criminal.

"So"—she swallowed—"all the stuff about silver, and mirrors and stakes and crosses and holy water is true?" She sounded skeptical, or was it scared?

"The silver is true. As for the rest"—he shrugged— "inventions of a literary hack." Stoker had caused quite a ripple of amusement when a copy of *Dracula* was passed around the colony after it first came out. If the public was gullible enough to swallow that nonsense, vampires were safe from detection.

As long as menaces like the Radcliffes weren't allowed to roam the world.

"How do you know they aren't?" Laura asked.

He wanted to kiss her, not argue, but had to make her

understand the risks and convince her to stay where he could keep her safe. "I know silver protects."

"Okay." She meshed her fingers with his. The touch had him yearning for more of her skin, more of her. "I'll wear my locket. It did the job this morning." Her shudder belied her lighthearted tone.

"And stay here, close to me."

"And leave Dad to that vampire? No way, José!"

He should have anticipated that! "No, Laura, not to abandon your father, but to help us."

"Help whom? And how?"

"Me, Zeke." When he finally strolled back in. "And another friend, Etienne Larouselière, when he arrives this evening." Maybe he should explain the Frenchman right now, but . . .

"What are you, then? A bunch of twenty-first-century Van Helsings?"

Now it was his turn to shudder. "No!"

She actually had the cheek to smile. "Got you on the raw there, did I?"

He should not be feeling lustful while explaining mortal danger, but he was. It would take a much stronger man than he was not to respond to her. "Van Helsing was fiction. I'm not."

"No." Forget a smile, she was now grinning up at him, a very sexy glint in her eyes. "Thank heaven you're not a figment of my imagination, Toby. I'm so glad you're real, and here!" So, by Abel, was he! She stopped walking and turned to him, her grip on his hand tightening. "Can you and Zeke really help Dad, and get rid of Axel?"

"Yes!" He pulled her close, resting his chin on the top of her head, and she leaned into him. His entire body responded to her closeness. He needed her, wanted her, and feared he could never live up to her expectations. Could the three of them take on this second Radcliffe?

"Oh, Toby," she whispered into his chest. The scent of her hair and the wondrous, mortal warmth of her struck a chord in his soul, and he just knew he could take on an entire colony of Radcliffes for her. She had the same effect on him as his first taste of rum aboard that blockade runner. His brain sparked, his thoughts raced and his body was about to betray him utterly.

As close as she was, she'd surely notice.

She had. She looked up at him, her breathing speeding as she whispered, "Toby?" Her lips stayed parted, her breath warm in the cool air, her pulse throbbing at the base of her neck, her heartbeat strong and sure.

It wasn't just his cock responding. His gums itched, and right now that was not what he needed her to see. "Laura," he said, forcing his fangs to remain high. "Laura."

"Dear Toby." She leaned in even closer. Her eyes widened as she felt his erection press against her soft belly but she didn't draw back. She gave a little gasp and her lips parted wider.

It needed a tougher man than he to resist the invitation. His mouth came down on hers and he'd have gasped—if he could. He settled for pressing his lips against hers, and taking her passion and sweetness into his soul. He sensed her breath catch and her heart rate speed up as she kissed him back, her mouth opening to his. Before he could taste her tongue, she found his, caressing with her woman's passion and mortal need.

He drew her even closer, pressing her against him. Her arms enclosed his back until they were chest to chest and knee to knee. She was soft where he was hard and his need burned like a fury.

He kissed on, stroking her tongue with his, meeting her need, driving his own higher.

He paused to let her catch her breath. She restarted the kiss, running her hands up and down his back, until she reached under his shirt and her healer's hands caressed his skin.

He almost came there and then. What had happened to his vampire control?

Who cared as long as he held Laura in his arms? No more furtive visits as she slept. She wanted him, desired him, and soon, very soon . . .

Once they stopped kissing.

Her mouth was warm and sweet and welcoming. He kissed deeper, more deeply than in his dreams, tasting her heat and passion, and offering his. Offering himself, his everything.

"Oh, Toby! Dear Toby." Her voice, muffled by their kiss, was clear and arousing to his enhanced hearing. When he slipped his hand under her T-shirt and cupped the lace that covered her breast, her groan had him shaking.

He pulled back, easing his mouth off hers. "I love you, Laura."

"I know!" Her laugh was sexy, husky and almost lost as he covered her mouth again with his.

He needed her, ached for her, longed for her, and darn, she was in the same condition. She pulled her mouth off his, her chest heaving against his with her ragged breathing. "We shouldn't be doing this here."

"You're right," he replied and swept her into his arms.

Laura couldn't, didn't even try to hold back the gasp. Talk about getting carried away. Her sane self wanted to protest, to insist this was grossly unprofessional, and besides, weren't they here to talk about Dad?

But she didn't.

Not with her brain fogged to blazes by Toby's kisses. Okay, *their* kisses. She'd been no slouch there, but heavens, he could win the kissing Olympics, and lying in his arms, smack dab against his magnificent chest, fitted very nicely into a couple of rather naughty fantasies. Not that she'd ever imagined him striding across the beach with her in his arms or how incredible it would feel with those arms grasping her close. Her body hummed with need. She hadn't felt like this for a man since . . . since never!

She just about gave up trying to think, rested her head against the smooth cotton of his shirt and let the fantasy continue. She expected him to set her on her feet when they reached the cliff and anticipated sliding down his lovely hard body, but he didn't even pause, just walked up the steps, and then started running toward the house.

Chapter 13

Toby didn't make for the front door, but the side one by the kitchen, and then up the seldom-used back stairs two at a time. He crossed the wide landing, nudged open a door with his elbow and slowly set her on the floor.

Laura relished the not insignificant pleasure of sliding her body down his. He was hard and his dark eyes gleamed with need.

He wasn't even breathing fast. Where the heck did he work out? Not that Toby's fitness regime was foremost in her mind.

Or his.

He smiled, teeth white and gleaming, eyes dark and almost feral. His hands were cool on her face as he cradled it in his hands and brushed her lips with his. "Sure about this?"

Damn scruples, professionalism and correctness! Laura stood on tiptoe, reached for his head and pressed her mouth hard on his lips. Sweet heaven on Sunday! With a sigh of anticipation she pressed his lips open and tapped the tip of his tongue.

He responded like a wild thing, curling his tongue over hers, yanking her body against him, and letting out a growl as his tongue plunged deep into her mouth, stirring wild need and desire for another, even more pleasurable, invasion.

She yanked his shirt from his pants and ran her hands over his cool, firm flesh, exploring his back and chest with fingers that had a will of their own. A fingertip brushed the different texture of a nipple. Smiling to herself, Laura teased the tip until it hardened, before pulling up his shirt and drawing the sweet, dark flesh between her lips as she stroked his other nipple to a matching firmness.

"What do you have in mind, woman?" Toby asked, ending with a little groan as she tugged his nipple with her teeth.

"Exactly the same as you!"

"Praise Abel!" he said, tugging her T-shirt out of her jeans and pulling it over her head. "Nice!" His fingers dipped inside the edge of her bra and caressed her breasts, before dipping deeper and finding her nipple. Hers was as hard as his in seconds, and a rush of heat pooled between her legs.

He smiled.

"I want you naked," he said, his voice almost raspy. Her bra fell to the carpet.

She wasn't likely to miss it. "Likewise," she replied, pulling up his shirt. He was gentleman enough to give her a hand.

They were both naked to the waist, but it was still far too much clothing. Laura grabbed at his belt, easing the free end through the loops in his pants. Need made her clumsy, or was her brain so fired with thoughts of sex that her coordination was shot to blazes?

Didn't matter much as he placed his cool hands over hers and released his belt. Then his zipper. Every muscle in his chest and arms rippled like dark satin as he stepped out of his pants, kicked off his shoes and bent to tug off his socks.

Impressive wasn't the word. Just the sight of Toby in tightie whities would set her libido raging, if it wasn't on high power already.

"You are beautiful," Laura whispered, stroking her hands over his chest and down toward the wide elastic waistband. She was feeling utterly shameless and enjoying every second of it.

"You are overdressed!"

Compared with him, yes but . . . "And that's a problem?"

"Not much longer!" Strong male hands grasped her by the waist and swung her around to land on her back on the bed. As she bounced he grabbed the waistband of her jeans and had them unsnapped and unzipped and down her legs before she could catch her breath.

"Hey, wait a minute!" she said as he relieved her of socks and sneakers.

He stood at the foot of the bed, an almost wicked glint in his eyes as he smiled down at her. "Much better!" The mattress dipped as he put one knee on the bed and leaned over her. "By Abel! You are the most beautiful creature I've ever seen."

"Seen a lot of naked women, have you?" A man as hot as Toby no doubt had them lining up to buy tickets.

"I can't remember. Not when I can touch you." Nice line but . . . her mind skittered as he ran a finger between her breasts, over her chest and down over her belly to her pussy.

She whimpered as he stroked and parted the curls over her pussy. She was wet. Heck, she was soaking. "Sure you want this, Laura?"

What a question at this point! "I don't get naked to do crosswords!"

His laugh came from deep in his belly. It was sexy, lighthearted and suggestive, all at the same time. "Good!"

She'd have said something snappy back, but his body was on hers, his thighs parting her legs and his erection pressing hard on her. A gasp was the best she could manage as Toby kissed her.

Something in the far recesses of her mind roared like a rush of air in a tunnel, or the waves against the cliffs below them. She was beyond thought, past reason. She was a wild, sexual woman who needed her man, needed him deep and hard inside her.

A thin flicker of reason or convention muttered this was insanity, sheer foolishness, but it was fast extinguished by her crashing, blinding need.

She could feel him, taste him, smell him. Her hips rocked against him as she arched her back and pressed her mouth onto his and he invaded her with his tongue. In the far distance, she heard sighs and little moans, and closed her eyes to block out everything but the touch and taste of her lover.

When he took his mouth away, she sagged back and muttered, "Wow! Does everyone in England kiss like that?" She'd spent her vacation money on a trip to Cozumel—what a waste.

"No," he replied. "Just me."

She almost forgave the smirk. He was entitled to be self-satisfied. Except they both needed considerably *more* satisfaction.

He half-rolled off her, considerate of him as it did feel good to breathe again, but she missed the press of his flesh on hers. He was an aphrodisiac on legs and . . .

She leaned up and found herself at eye level with his bulging briefs. She couldn't hold back the grin as she licked her lips. Lewd, yes, but oh! What a sight to gladden a needy woman's heart!

Could be a whole lot better, though. Sitting up, she leaned forward and yanked down the elastic of his briefs. And gaped.

He was . . . magnificent, beautiful, hard as polished ebony. Hard for her. With a little gasp she leaned forward and touched the smooth head of his cock with her lips.

Driven by his stifled groan, she circled him with her lips and took him in her mouth. He grabbed her head as she fluttered her tongue around the rim of his cock and teased his frenulum with light swift touches.

She was shameless, uninhibited, outrageous. Never had she been this forward in her life, and she was enjoying every second as she relished the sheer female power of holding his manhood between her teeth.

Toby let out another groan, louder and longer this time as it accompanied a wide sweep of her tongue, and then he pulled back as he eased her head off him. "Enough, Laura. Five more seconds of that and I'll come."

"And that would be bad?" Brazen wasn't in it and it felt so all-around fantastic.

"Yes," he replied. He was naked now. Had his briefs evaporated? "Very bad. Because I intend to make this last until I have you begging for a climax."

"Sounds good."

He wasn't kidding! She hadn't had many occasions where reality surpassed her fantasies, but sheesh, this was one of them. He kissed her, cool lips against her heated ones, his tongue deep in her mouth until she moaned and shifted, needing more, much more than just kisses. Her nipples were hard and aching and her clit throbbed like an extra pulse.

He lifted his mouth off hers and smiled. "Delicious," he whispered. "Where should I kiss you next?"

"My breasts. My nipples are so hard they hurt!"

"I'll kiss them better."

"Better" was the word, except the sheer thrill of his mouth on her nipples did absolutely nothing to assuage her need.

It was so wonderful.

Through her groans, she held onto his head, wanting more but wanting release too. Not caring if she ever came as long as he kissed her like this forever. Her hips rocked of their own volition and her mind fogged with arousal.

Toby eased his mouth off her breasts and said, "I'm going to kiss every inch of your luscious body."

He wasn't a man for idle promises.

She moaned, sighed and groaned, her back arching, toes curling and hips rocking as his incredible lips kissed over her shoulders, down her arms, across her belly, and up and down her legs. She'd never found her ankles an erogenous zone before, never realized how sensitive the backs of her knees were. As for the moan he wrung from her as he kissed the soft skin behind her ear, that echoed in her skull while he covered her belly with soft, fluttery kisses.

She could probably have held out over the nips on her inner thighs, but when he parted her pussy and placed his mouth over her, she literally left the bed, thrashing her hips and legs as he held her tight with his mouth and made her scream.

Shaking and breathless, her voice hoarse, she gasped. "God, Toby! That was wonderful!"

"It's not over yet," he replied, shifting up the mattress to kneel between her still-shaking thighs.

"I can't take any more!" She was sated, worn and drained.

"Oh, yes, you can, my love."

"No! I . . ." she began as he grasped her hips with strong hands, but her protests were lost in a shriek of joy as he lifted her to his cock and drove in deep.

Her mind blanked out. Reasoning, speech, thought were impossible. Her entire being was concentrated on the power of the man thrust deep inside her. She tightened her muscles around him and had the satisfaction of hearing him groan.

But not for long.

Her cries soon blocked his groans and grunts of pleasure. It should be impossible to come again so soon, but she wasn't just climaxing, she was spiraling to new heights, greater pleasure and unbelievable sensation as his cock worked her hard and wondrously, driving her to a level of sexual joy she'd have thought impossible.

She came again and again in a wild crescendo of orgasms that had her screaming and begging him to stop, to give her more, to keep on forever and ever. Time, the room, her worries were lost in a wild tempest of sensation, joy and utter satiation.

She was still whimpering with happiness when Toby leaned over her and kissed her neck. The touch set her off again.

And set him off.

With one final, mighty thrust, he came. She felt his joy, his release and his satisfaction but was too limp and too worn to do more than smile at him and gasp. "Incredible!"

"My love, you are," he replied, leaning over her and still hard inside her. "More incredible than I'd ever imagined."

He sounded hoarse too.

Something niggled at the back of her mind, but she was too relaxed and limp to think. Wasn't every day she had sex like that! Wasn't ever she'd had sex like that, to be precise. Except her mind was too woozy and content to care anything for precision.

"Toby?" she whispered but couldn't remember what it was she had to ask him.

"Hush," he said as she felt him ease out of her. The mattress shifted as he stood and bent over her, brushing aside her damp hair to kiss her forehead. "I wore you out, my love. Sleep. We can talk later. For now, rest. Your nursing shift is covered and you are safe here. Sleep."

She took the suggestion.

Toby watched as her eyes closed and her breathing altered. She was fast asleep and would be for hours. Probably until morning. He'd laid on a heavy suggestion.

He hated to leave her but lying beside her to watch her awaken was a pleasure that would have to wait. He had a rogue vampire to deal with, a visiting vampire about to rouse, a witch in the house, and he hoped to Abel Zeke was back. He needed to know what he'd discovered. Maybe with Zeke's discoveries, Etienne's input and Adela's help they'd dispose of the menace for Vlad. Elizabeth's skills had vanquished Laran, and hadn't Adela been her teacher?

"Oh, Toby!"

Damn! Had Adela been lying in wait? "What can I do for you, Adela?"

"You'd better call our Romanian friend in Chicago. Soon."

"What happened?"

"Nothing that I'm aware of, but he called an hour or so ago. I told him a white lie that you were out. He called back half an hour ago, very insistent that you call the instant you got in and asked me if I knew where Zeke had gone."

"Zeke?"

"Yes, seemed a bit wound up. He also demanded to know what I was doing answering your phone—that was the first time he called."

"What did you tell him?"

"That you'd offered hospitality when my house burned down. Didn't see adding any extraneous details. Besides, I got the impression my abode was an irrelevancy."

"Isn't Zeke back?"

"Not yet."

Damn the vamp! He should be here to cope with his irascible maker. Still, Toby had more sense than to antagonize the most powerful vampire on the North American continent and his host to all vampire intents and purposes. "I'll call him. Adela . . ."

She smiled. Hell, she grinned as if anticipating his request. "Yes?"

"Laura needs to stay here a few days, until things are settled. She didn't stop to pack, and her clothes are a bit . . . rumpled. Could you lend her something?"

"Of course. Lucky I did a bit of shopping yesterday."

True, most of Adela's clothes were ashes. "You can spare something?"

"Of course. Might not be exactly what she'd choose but it will do." She paused, giving him a long, steady stare. "You did tell her about yourself, didn't you?"

Damn! Why couldn't she keep her nose out of his affairs? "She understands that Axel is a vampire and very dangerous. She's worried about her father, but I convinced her that it was in Axel's interest to keep him safe and well."

"So you chickened out of telling her the truth!"

"It wasn't the time!" *If it was any of her business.*

"No?" The woman never gave up. "Walk on the beach nearly an hour, spend the afternoon in close proximity and the opportunity never arose?"

"Damn it, Adela!" *Was this what happened when you took a witch into your house?*

She shook her head, then astounded him by kissing his cheek. "She loves you, Toby. She has a right to know what you are as well as who you are."

"Think it's easy to tell her, do you?" He was snarling but it didn't appear to perturb her one iota.

"Of course not, but, Toby, think! If she believes what you told her about Axel, she accepts the existence of vampires. If she's staying in this house with you, Zeke, when he reappears, and the other one downstairs"—how the hell did she know about Larouselière?—"don't you think she might catch on? Better you tell her than someone else."

Knowing Adela was right irritated him even more. "Look, Adela, I'm obliged for your help lending Laura clothes. I need to see what Vlad is harping on about."

With what he hoped was vampire dignity, Toby went downstairs and into his study.

Adela shook her head at his back. Seemed a century and a half or more of living didn't add anything to male comprehension. If Toby wasn't careful, Laura would discover his nature by chance, or from an unguarded comment, and then he *would* have fences to mend.

Adela tapped gently on the door, then opened it quietly, hoping to leave the pile of clothes and slip out unnoticed. Laura was awake and looking contented. Extraordinarily contented. Good for Toby, if only he'd saved a little energy for full disclosure, though. "Sorry, did I wake you?"

"No, I was just dozing."

"Toby mentioned you'd come away without packing and asked me to lend you something to wear. I hope it fits. We can go shopping in Eugene tomorrow if you need more." At least that would get her out of the way during the vampire summit meeting that seemed to be brewing. Adela had heard all about Etienne Larouselière from Elizabeth. His presence meant serious doo-doo.

"Thanks." Laura sat up, pulling the bedclothes up to her chin, but nothing could disguise the look of total relaxation on her face.

The girl needed time to herself. Adela set the pile of folded clothes on the chest of drawers. "I hope they fit. You're thinner than I am but the waist is elastic. Do you need anything else? A cup of tea?" The truth? Full disclosure?

Laura shook her head. "No thanks." Then frowned. "There's just one thing. You know Toby well, right?"

"I've known him for a few months. My stepdaughter married one of his old friends." Very, very old, as it happened.

Laura's brow creased as she pondered that one. Adela was tempted to make a hasty exit before she was asked questions Toby should be answering. Drat him! "I see," Laura said, obviously pondering the connection. "Is that why Toby came over to work here?"

This was pretty safe ground. "Yes. Elizabeth wanted someone to manage things after Piet was taken ill. Everything was in a mess after his former partner absconded." That was all common knowledge, after all.

"Odd that Mr. Connor's former partner had the same last name as the vampire who bought into Dad's newspaper."

And Toby really thought he could pull the wool over her eyes? Men could be so thick! Adela took a deep breath. She was no doubt pissing off a vampire here but . . . "Draw your own conclusions there, Laura."

"I did and I think I'm losing it. I only half-believe the tale about Axel being a vampire, but now you're saying there are—were—two of them?" Her eyes widened with shock. "What if Dad ends up like Mr. Connor?"

Definitely Toby's province, but since he'd fallen down on the job . . . "How long has Axel been with your father?"

"Five, six months."

Thank the goddess! "Laran was with Piet nearly six years. His influence was much longer." Plus Piet was a greedy, ambitious bastard in his former personality.

"I see."

That Adela truly doubted, but the girl did deserve the truth. "Look here, my dear. We'd be lying to say there wasn't danger to your father, but trust in Toby and Zeke to handle this. They've also brought in another vampire expert."

"Is the world full of vampires and vampire hunters and I've just been too wrapped up in myself to notice?"

"I think they make sure no one notices."

"I see."

Not really, she didn't. "Then I suggest you pin Toby to the sticking point and ask him what's really going on."

Chapter 14

"Vlad? Toby Wise here."

"What happened to Zeke?"

So much for cordial and conversational. A testy Dracula was not what he needed right now. "He's due back anytime. He went over to Dark Falls to investigate Axel Radcliffe. Want me to ask him to call?" Surely Zeke reported in at intervals.

"Zeke is dead."

"What?" Stupid response. As his creator, Vlad would know. "When?" Much better question.

"About six p.m. our time."

A quick bit of mental arithmetic put that slap in the middle of Adela's rescue. "What can we do?"

"Join in avenging him! Is the Frenchman there?"

"Yes, but not stirring yet."

The hiss expressed clear frustration. "He will be by the time I get there."

"When can we expect you?"

"I'm leaving as soon as I hang up."

Good. Vlad's power could only help. In the distance, Toby heard a faint click—Etienne emerging from his packing case, presumably. "How many are you bringing with you?"

"Two of my best warriors." How like Vlad to use that expression! "When the frog awakens, find out how we can take this creature alive."

That Toby already knew. "Assuming he is of the same bloodline as Laran, his only weaknesses are to silver and magic."

Pause. "You know this for a fact?"

If it was anyone other than Vlad Tepes, he'd take umbrage at that. "I was present at the meeting at Tom's house when Gwyltha consulted Etienne."

"Ah, yes. That outcome was most satisfactory. A pity Tom Kyd's little ghoul witch isn't available to us."

Vlad was lucky neither Tom nor Elizabeth had heard that comment. It was a toss-up who'd take the most insult. "Adela Whyte is here."

"Ah! Yes. An intriguing mortal but her powers, I understand, are second to the little ghoul's." If he didn't know better, he'd have sworn Vlad sighed. "But since my wish is to capture, not annihilate, perhaps she will do."

"There's a complication, a limit to how much she can, or should, help us. She needs to leave the area as soon as possible." On a return flight on Vlad's plane would be a brilliant idea.

"Indeed? Why?"

Toby explained.

"Then she has reason to want vengeance. I need her powers."

Someone should explain to Vlad that mortals were not put on the planet for his convenience. Not that Toby fancied taking on the job! "You can talk to her when you get here, Vlad." And he'd warn Adela. She had endured quite enough the past couple of days. She might not be up to subduing rogue vampires, if she reconciled that with "Harm to none."

Toby snapped his phone shut and turned to greet Etienne. As always the Frenchman was perfectly groomed, clothes unrumpled, even after hours in a box, dark hair precisely coiffed, and the customary irritating smile plastered all over his handsome face.

Annoying enough, but it was the sight of Laura positively gaping at the frog that set Toby off. "When did you wake up?"

"Mon ami, it is dusk," Etienne replied. "Why would I not wake?"

Laura goggled at Etienne, her eyes all but popping out of her head. What was so fascinating about him floored Toby. Yes, he had just oozed out of a packing case, but that did not explain why the frog felt entitled to ogle Laura as if she were a juicy hothouse peach in winter.

"Weren't you asleep, Laura?" Toby knew darn well he'd put a glamour on her not thirty minutes ago. She should be out for the count for hours. Was he losing his touch?

"Yes." She managed, but only just, to drag her eyes off Etienne. "Adela lent me some clothes and . . ." Her attention was back on Larouselière.

Before she came out with the question that obviously hovered on her lips, the door opened again. By Abel! It was like Piccadilly Circus in here.

"Laura, did the clothes work?" Adela began, then in the space of about four seconds, her sharp eyes took in Etienne, his traveling box, and Laura's obvious confusion. "Ah!" she said, crossing the carpet to Etienne. How the heck did he draw women like a magnet? "You must be Etienne Larouselière. My stepdaughter, Elizabeth Connor Kyd, mentioned you." She held out her hand, which Etienne kissed.

"Enchanté, madame. I remember your daughter, la petite goule. A woman of power and courage. To meet her mother is indeed an honor."

If vampires puked, Toby would have ruined the carpet by now. "Look here, Adela . . ."

She fixed him with a very odd look. "I suppose you didn't have the conversation I urged."

Now she was nagging him! What happened to mortals being scared of vampires?

"I've been a trifle busy with one thing and another."

Her mouth quirked. "So I noticed. Toby, I'm giving you ten minutes. Explain fast!" Ultimatum delivered, Etienne was rewarded with a smile. "Welcome to Oregon. Let me take you on the cliffs and show you the beauty of the Pacific before darkness falls completely. Toby needs a few minutes with Laura."

Larouselière raised a perfectly shaped eyebrow at Toby. "Bon chance, mon ami." To Adela he bestowed a smile. "With delight, dear lady. You honor me."

The door had barely closed behind them when Laura asked, "What that heck was that about? And why was that man crawling out of the packing case?"

Ten minutes, Adela said? Ten *days* wouldn't be enough. "It's a bit complicated, Laura."

"Wouldn't 'weird' be a better word? That was the box that was delivered earlier today. Was he looking for something, and how come you didn't introduce me?"

"Have a seat." Would give him another thirty seconds to think. If he was lucky.

She sat beside him on the leather sofa. The fabric of her borrowed shell suit crackled as she moved. The bright sheen of the pink fabric had his fingers itching to stroke her arms and legs. He clenched his fists but allowed himself to rest his arm on the sofa back. Close but not touching.

She turned to him, eyes intent. "Well?"

"Well" was the last word to describe the situation or how he felt right now. "Apologies for not introducing you to Larouselière. I was a bit distracted. I'll remedy that when he gets back."

Good start. She nodded. "Okay. I'm a bit distracted myself." And gave a naughty grin. "Was he really in that box?"

"Yes. Um . . ." Better get going before she asked a harder question. "It's complicated. I need you to listen, and, Laura, however incredible this sounds, I swear it's the gospel truth." Would she be smiling so when he finished? If Vlad wasn't a few hours away, he'd have more time but he didn't and the longer he procrastinated . . .

"What's wrong, Toby?"

"Nothing's wrong. Just complicated and hard to explain, and Adela was right—I should have told you this earlier."

"Told me what?" She edged away a little. "Are you married?"

"Heavens, no!" She looked relieved. Not for long. "Remember I told you Axel was a vampire and you worked out that Laran had been one too."

"Sure." A mortal would take a deep breath here. He didn't need mortal props. Did he? "Just one thing," she went on. "If they are vampires, how come Axel can wander about in daylight?"

"Many vampires aren't affected by sunlight. It's a Hollywood myth." Better plow on while she digested that. "Thing is, Laura, Axel isn't the only vampire around here in Oregon right now." At that, her eyes widened. Horror? Disbelief? He wished he knew. Or did he?

"You mean the place is teeming with them. I have been unobservant!"

Sarcasm was not a good sign. "Not teeming. Just a few, but they are not like Axel. Most vamps make great effort to go unnoticed."

"Really? Like invisible?"

"No, just to blend in with mortals so we can live in peace."

She missed the slip of the tongue. "Oh, come off it, Toby. You're seriously trying to tell me there are vampires all around and no one notices?"

"It's when people notice we have trouble. That's why Axel is such a menace, apart from the harm to your father. His outrageous actions will draw attention to himself and to the rest of us."

She wasn't drunk. She wasn't dreaming and Toby didn't appear delusional but . . . "Hold on a minute here," Laura said, amazed how steady her voice was. "You're telling me there really are other vampires around here? Who?"

"Etienne, for a start, but he is of a bloodline that cannot tolerate daylight. That's why he travels in an lightproof box."

Ridiculous, impossible, except she had watched him emerge and stretch as if confined in a tight space. "Why did he come here?"

"To help. He is a student of vampire lore."

A vampire consultant! And why did Toby keep saying "we" and "the rest of us"? "Anyone else I know? Adela?" Surely not; she was so normal, given she was supposed to be a witch.

"Good heavens, no!" He sounded mildly shocked. "Look here, Laura! One thing you must believe. I love you! Utterly and totally. I want you. I need you. I will protect you and take care of you. You need never be afraid of me. I will never harm you. You have my oath. My word."

She was more irked than afraid. Maybe the fear would come later. What she was thinking was incredible, but no more incredible than half the things she'd heard, seen or witnessed in the past couple of days. She took a deep breath. "Who else is a vampire, Toby?" She had to hear it from his lips. She'd no doubt pass out with shock, but he had to confirm or refute.

"There's three more, maybe four coming soon. They're going to make sure your father and Dark Falls are safe."

She was getting ready to shake him. Either her imagination had gone berserk, or he was waffling. Maybe both. She thought back to their incredible lovemaking and ran her fingers over the mark on her neck and felt her body throb in response. That was no ordinary hickey. "What about you, Toby? Are you a vampire?" Sweet heaven on Sunday! She'd said it! Time for men in white coats to barge through the door.

He looked as if he were headed for the tumbrels. "Yes."

Something inside her snarled in shock. It wasn't possible. Was it? How could he be? "A vampire?" she whispered, her voice tight with shock. She'd have noticed, wouldn't she? How? This was Toby who'd said he loved her. Who had made love to her. She reached out and grasped his hand. How come she hadn't noticed how cool his skin was earlier? She had a lot of how-comes.

He muttered something unintelligible and held her at arm's length. "You don't understand what's involved, Laura."

He was right there. "What woman does when she gets

involved with a man? I need a week to sort out all my questions and will be lucky to get five minutes, but, Toby, I take your word you mean me no harm. Let's go from there."

"You're not worried? Afraid what's going to happen? Scared about what I might do to you?"

"Yes to all three, and I'll most likely have hysterics in a little while, but right now I'm holding you and your bloodsucking buddies to the promise to get Axel off Dad's back!" Or should that be neck? She stifled a nervous giggle.

Toby stared at the mortal he loved. The scent of her skin filled his awareness, stirring memories of their lovemaking and the incredible taste of her living blood. She was Laura. She was a wonder, a joy, a magnificent being, and she'd matter-of-factly accepted he was revenant. "Do you have any idea of the ramifications involved in our relationship?"

"None at all." He darn well had. Okay, he was in Vlad's territory and he was noted for his relaxed ways when it came to mortals, but Toby hadn't withdrawn from his home colony, and Gwyltha, his leader, had very definite ideas. "But I assume you will enlighten me."

If he didn't darken her life in the process. "Laura, I'm asking a lot of you. There won't be time to explain what I need to. You'll have to take a great deal on trust in the next few hours."

"Toby, you've put a lot of faith in me the past few days. The least I can do is return the trust."

She had no idea what she was agreeing to, but he wouldn't fail her. "I knew there was a reason I loved you, Laura. The first day you walked in the house I wanted you."

She grinned. "That's good. I had the hots for you too.

That's why I almost hated Dad for insisting I poke and pry. It seemed so sleazy."

"It brought us together. If I hadn't caught you, you'd still be putting on your frightfully professional nurse act, instead of showing me what a wild, sexy woman you are."

She leaned into him. "Think we'll have time for an encore?"

"We'll make time." He pulled her to him. She fitted against his body as if they'd been made to belong together. Her vitality warmed his soul. Her incredible, easy acceptance astounded him, but he was not about to question it. Not yet. Once they were through this snarl, they'd have all the time in the world. They'd have eternity together.

Apart from the awkward little detail of her mortality.

"I'm going back downtown," Axel called to Granger, who was washing dishes. "You may wait up for me."

The man nodded. He was getting too subservient to be interesting anymore, but his veins were handy and he had been useful in getting the confidence of the pathetic little town. Granger Fox and his trivial little news sheet had saved him a lot of energy when it came to glamouring and compelling mortals.

Not that he was much closer to finding his lost brother in blood. That Laran had stolen a small fortune, as the FBI investigation implied, was perfectly understandable, but that he'd not paid the tribute to the clan was unacceptable. Awkward too, for both of them, but as long as Axel remained here in Oregon, no one from the clan could touch him.

All he had to do was entrench himself nicely and he

was secure for eternity. There was only one person in the town with power to thwart his plans. And she would soon be neutralized.

Witches! He'd scared the first one away and what happened? Another appeared and sterner measures were necessary. She should have been burned, as befitted a witch, if the stupid deputy hadn't let silly scruples get in the way. Tonight the deputy's office would burn too. This time Axel would perform the office himself.

It would be a satisfying evening.

The deputy stared at Axel as if he'd been speaking in tongues. "There's no one back there." He angled his head to the single cell. "We've had too much doing with Sam's death to even bother with minor offenses."

"And the woman you arrested for his murder?"

The blank look sparked fury. Not pausing to ready him, Axel mind-probed, ignoring the man's spasm of pain as Axel scoured his brain. The deputy collapsed to the floor as Axel released him. This was war! His mind had been cleared, all memory of the staged arrest gone and so, as Axel rushed back to the cells, was the witch.

Was she this powerful? Never! No mortal woman had this sort of strength. This interference, coupled with the intruder he had extinguished this morning, meant invasion. He threw back his head and howled. It wasn't possible! Intolerable! Not after these months of setting up this town as his personal fief!

Axel strode back to the office just as the incompetent deputy was struggling to his feet. He'd hit his head, and a trickle of blood oozed down his cheek. Why not? Let the man serve some use. Axel grabbed him by the shirt and tore the collar to expose his neck. Before the fool even grasped what lay ahead, Axel dug his fangs in and drank. He sucked until long after the struggles ceased. If there was any life left as the body dropped to the floor, it was irrelevant. Power surged as Axel reared his head and licked his lips before wiping his mouth on the back of his hand.

Power surging through him, he raced down Main Street and headed for home and a quiet spot to ponder the conundrum of who'd taken the witch, and why?

Chapter 15

"What happens next, Toby?" Laura asked.

Very, very good question. "We wait for the vampires I expect to arrive, and then we put our heads together."

"Okay," Laura replied in a tone that implied it really wasn't at all. "Let me get this straight, we'll have five or six vampires in the house, plus myself and Adela. Ever thought that might disturb Piet? Get noticed by the substitute nurse?"

"Yes, of course!" Did she think he had no sense? "It's going to be tricky."

She was sexy even when she rolled her eyes at him. "More like impossible!"

She had a lot to learn about vampires.

"Not impossible, Laura, just difficult. We excel at difficult."

He excelled at *being* difficult! Laura sighed. "And between now and then? What about my father tomorrow? What about Adela? Think they won't notice she isn't locked up anymore?"

"We took care of all that. The deputy won't remember anything about her."

"What about the rest of the people who were in the

Kountry Kitchen? To say nothing of Axel, who will certainly remember? Even vampires can't manage mass hypnosis. Can they?"

"It's not hypnosis! It's . . ." He broke off. "I can't explain. You'll have to trust me."

"When you don't trust me?"

His dark eyes flashed. So she'd pissed him off. He grabbed both arms, pulling her close so they were eye to eye since she stood on tiptoe to meet his glare. "Listen up and get this straight, Laura. I do trust you. I trust you with my nature. I trust you with my being and my existence. What I'm not free to do is tell you about others of my kind. I'll share my secrets but not theirs."

Fair enough, but it beat her how hypnotizing or whatever it was, wasn't harming others but . . . she was facing a rather irate vampire. She should be terrified, shouldn't she? "Toby, you're going to leave bruises."

"Sorry!" He dropped his grasp and pushed up her sleeve to examine her arms. "Didn't meant to, love." He kissed the red mark on her forearm and she felt it deep in her pussy.

"Oh, my!"

He grinned before very carefully and deliberately kissing her other arm. "Feel better?"

"Yes, Toby, and I'll feel a whole lot better when this is over and Dad's safe. Can't we just fetch him and bring him here?"

She could tell he was considering this by the look in his eyes and the crease between his brows. "We could try, love, but I think he might refuse to leave Axel. They will have bonded."

Now it was her turn to frown. "By 'bonded' you mean with blood?"

"Yes and maybe more. I don't know. We often mix

blood and sex, but frequently take blood alone. For some vampires the two are inexorably mixed."

Now she did want to puke. Dad and Axel! "Oh, God! I hope not!"

"If you want to know, we can ask Etienne. He's a vampire expert. He's studied the different bloodlines. It was his knowledge helped us overcome Laran."

"I'm not sure I want to know these details. Unless it helps get Dad out from under Axel." Oh, dear, she hadn't said that, had she?

Not that Toby seemed to pick up on it. He was alert to something else. Listening. "A car's coming. They must be here!"

He was out the door and across the hall in moments. Laura tagged right behind. Might as well get a glimpse of these uber-vampires.

Etienne and Adela joined them at the front door. Distant beams of light through the trees showed an approaching car until a wide sweep of headlights followed the curve and a car pulled up right next to Laura's Toyota.

Toby crossed the short distance to open the driver's door and a young woman got out.

Etienne muttered, "C'est madame la goule!"

Adela raced across the drive. "Lizzie!" she called, and the two women hugged wildly. "How wonderful!"

Laura hung back. She guessed this was Piet's daughter. He'd mumbled her name so many times, she'd attained a mythical presence in Laura's mind and now she stood in the light from the front door, tall, blond and beautiful. Just the sort of person you don't want to meet disheveled and wearing borrowed clothes.

"Toby!" Elizabeth said, hugging him.

"Wasn't expecting you this soon," he replied. "We've had a few complications."

"I know," she replied. "Vlad called Gwyltha and said he'd sent Zeke down here. Gwyltha called me and here I am. Just as well, as there's bad weather in Chicago and all flights are grounded."

"We were expecting Vlad tonight."

"Not unless he really can control the weather."

Was this good or bad news? Laura had no idea, but Toby seemed worried, so she might as well be. Was this woman another vampire? And who the heck was Gwyltha?

Etienne didn't have any hesitation; he bowed to Elizabeth and kissed her hand. "Once again we meet, madame goule. I heard word of your astounding success in Devon. My felicitations."

"Thank you, Etienne. It was your knowledge helped us. Let's hope we're as successful this time."

That left everyone silent a few seconds. Put Laura in mind of her long-dead grandmother's claims of angels passing overhead.

Then Elizabeth noticed Laura standing on the step. "I'm Elizabeth Kyd," she said, coming forward, hand outstretched.

"Laura Fox."

"Great to meet you!"

"Let's get indoors." That was Adela shepherding them through the front door. "I think we need to talk." She called to the men standing on the drive. "Toby and Etienne, please bring in Lizzie's things." She turned back to Lizzie. "Did you bring food? There's precious little in the house."

"I've a cooler full. I stocked up in Eugene." Elizabeth paused in the wide entrance hall. "Before we do anything else, I want to see Dad. Then we'll catch up on what's happening."

The two men—okay, vampires—came through the door, Toby carrying a suitcase and Etienne clutching a large ice chest.

"We've a slight problem, Lizzie," Toby said. "Adela's in your room."

She shrugged. "Never mind. We'll share. It's got two beds. Just take my stuff up. After I see Dad, let's all meet in my sitting room. Nice and quiet and, believe me, we have a lot to hash out."

Elizabeth sat by her father's chair and held his hand. As always, she had to fight back the tears.

"That you, Lizzie?" he asked, his voice that of an octogenarian, not a once-able man in his early sixties.

"Yes, Dad, it's me. Just came to see you."

"You're a good girl, Lizzie. A good girl. I told him not to hurt you."

Much good it had done! But that was over and taken care of. She and Heather had recovered; it was Dad who bore the permanent injury. "Never mind, Dad." She reached over and wiped the drool from his mouth and made a silent oath that she'd do whatever she could to save Laura's father from the same sad end.

That another vicious rogue vampire had appeared was incredible, but if Vlad Tepes believed it, she could. He'd given her only the sketchiest information, promising full disclosure when they met. She wasn't waiting. She wanted to know everything, and as soon as possible.

She stayed while the nurse (another new one) readied Dad for the night, and sat by him until he slept.

Then she headed upstairs.

She really needed time to meditate and compose herself. That would have to wait.

Her small sitting room was crowded. Had to be the egos of the two vamps that took up so much space. Adela and the nurse, Laura, certainly didn't. Interesting gathering: two vamps, two mortals and now a ghoul, sort of straddling the two worlds.

True to type, Etienne stood, offering his seat, with a smile that must work on some women. It worked on Antonia once upon a time, after all, and she was no pushover.

Shaking her head, Elizabeth declined his offer and took a seat on the sofa beside Laura. The woman looked way out of her depth. Proved she had brains. Giving her a nervous smile, Laura scooted over to make room.

"Thanks." Elizabeth returned the smile. "Feeling out of your depth?"

"I stepped off the edge hours ago. I'm staying afloat, buoyed up with fear and worry."

Understandable. Elizabeth reached out for her hand and gave it a squeeze. "Okay, Toby and everyone, how about you tell me what's going on?"

It took a while.

There were a few interruptions.

"Dear God! Axel left Mr. Connor the way he is?" Laura whispered, her voice tight with horror. "He did that?"

"Not Axel," Elizabeth said. "Laran, a vampire we think is his kin."

"He destroyed your father."

Didn't take much to follow her line of thinking. "Yes, but Laura"—Elizabeth reached out, taking both her hands in hers—"Laran and my father were together for over six years. How long has Axel been with your father?"

"Six months." She let out a sigh that might have been relief. "Does that mean Dad will be okay?"

Now should have been Toby's time to jump in, if the apparent bond between them was as strong as she sensed. The long, pregnant pause suggested it wasn't. Damn! The woman was tense with worry. "To be honest, we don't know." Toby should be saying this, not her. "Logically, with less influence and less time, he should be safer. We'll pin our hopes on that."

"Right." She sounded less than satisfied.

"Laura," Toby said, speaking up at long last, "there's a lot we don't know."

"We know that your Laran and Dad's Axel have the same last name. They both wormed their way into someone's confidence, took over their businesses and tried very hard to alienate them from their only daughters." She paused and went on. "You agree they are vampires, although both you and Etienne keep insisting they are 'not your sort of vampire.'" Sheesh, she even had Toby's accent down pat. "Zeke, who it seems is not just a private detective after all, went missing after going over to Dad's house to investigate, and this other vampire, Vlad, who's delayed, believes Zeke is dead. Presumably killed by Axel. Doesn't exactly leave me feeling good about Dad."

Laura was strung out. Perfectly understandable in the circumstances but something seemed wrong, unstable here. Elizabeth sympathized with Laura. Her father's existence was at stake here. "I don't blame you, Laura," she said, "and, to be blunt, you're right to be worried. We're dealing with evil here. But we have a couple of vamps on our side. More once Vlad and his cohorts arrive. Plus, I'm here, and Adela."

"He's already had Adela arrested for murder. Might be best—"

"What?" Elizabeth couldn't help interrupting Laura. "Adela, is this true? What happened?"

Between them, Laura and Adela explained.

"And," Toby added, "given the control he has, or rather had, of the local deputy, I don't doubt he instigated the burning of Adela's house."

"What happened at Adela's house?"

Another round of explanations. Things got more complicated by the minute. But at least this time, Elizabeth knew her own name and was in full command of her faculties. Last time she'd sat on a vampire council, she'd still been suffering from the lingering effects of Laran's attack. Now her mind was free and buoyed with the confidence of knowing she had destroyed the vicious creature who'd turned her and Heather into ghouls. Unfortunately, everyone, including Vlad, who just happened not to be here right now, seemed convinced she could do a repeat performance. She wished she shared their confidence.

Elizabeth stood and crossed the room to stand in front of the long window. No one said a word as she watched the white horses among the gray water, and listened to the distant roar of the surf on the beach below.

"I'm not sure I can do it again," she said. "Last time I had backup."

No one argued with that.

Adela said, "Lizzie, my dear, for what it's worth, I will add what power I can to yours."

"Wait a minute!" It was Laura, her voice tight and getting a little high-pitched. "I'm missing something here, okay? So Axel is a vampire and you think he engineered Adela's house fire, killed the sheriff and fingered Adela for it. And, unless I'm way off base, you think he killed Zeke, who, to be honest, looked as if he could take care of himself. And that was before anyone mentioned he was a vampire. And to crown it all, this apparent monster is living in the house with my father!" Her voice rose higher. "Something has to be done! You can talk it over all night if you want to. I'm going to warn Dad."

At least that got Toby over to Laura's side, where he should have been all along. "Listen, Laura," he said, "I will do everything I can to protect your father, and I think I can say the same for everyone in this room, but we're dealing with a force far greater than you could ever overcome. It will take all our combined strength to render him harmless."

"And in the meantime, my father is stuck in his power."

Toby took both her hands in his and looked her in the eyes. "Laura, my love, do you really believe your father will leave Axel on the strength of your word alone?"

Good question. Very accurate point, but it slammed the poor woman a massive whammy. She visibly sagged—into Toby, Elizabeth couldn't help noticing. Looked as though another good old boy from the colony was ensnared. Did either of them realize it yet?

Laura was silent several seconds while her face drained of color as she recognized the horrid truth of Toby's words. Elizabeth's heart tightened in sympathy. How would she have coped, knowing in advance the full extent of Laran's power over her father?

Shaking her head and taking a deep breath, Laura replied, "He wouldn't believe a damn word. He thinks the sun rises and sets with Axel."

"Mademoiselle Laura," Etienne said, stepping forward. Elizabeth had wondered how long it would be before he chimed in. "If I may advise you."

As if anything would stop him. Sheesh, she had to

agree with Tom Kyd, Etienne was full of it. Knew his stuff, yes, but brimming over with ego.

"What?" Laura asked, looking him in the eye while closing her hand over Toby's, an action she didn't think anyone in the room missed. "What do you know about Axel and Dad?"

"Little about your father, mademoiselle, but I know more than anyone about Axel Radcliffe and his bloodline. I am indeed an expert."

Adela stifled a snort at that. Elizabeth had forgotten she'd not encountered Etienne before. Laura just lifted her eyebrows and gave a decidedly skeptical look. "How did you get to be such an expert, Mr. Larouselière?"

"Centuries of assiduous study, mademoiselle. Since I left mortality behind, I have devoted much of my time and my mind to studying the many facets of immortality and especially the nature of my fellow vampires."

"I see." Perhaps she did, but the glance she gave Toby all but said aloud, "Is this guy for real?"

"Etienne helped us dispose of Laran," Toby said. "His knowledge and Elizabeth's skills did the job. I'm sure that's why Vlad and Gwyltha asked her to help now."

"Just a minute. Vlad is the person who is delayed, right? Who's Gwyltha and what, with all due respect, can Elizabeth do against a vampire?"

"She did him in, love. Fixed his wagon. Had him cash in his chips." Toby smiled. "Don't let her mild-mannered appearance fool you. She took him on and took care of him."

"I had help."

"Ah! Madame goule, you are too modest." Etienne raised his hands in a very Gallic gesture. "You annihilated him."

"Etienne's right, Lizzie," Adela added. "Never belittle your skills. We need them."

Poor Laura was looking more confused by the minute. "Hold on again! Why do I feel I'm three weeks behind the rest of you? And why"—Laura looked straight at her—"does Etienne call you 'madame goule'?"

Elizabeth turned to Laura. "To answer your first question, because Toby did a lousy job of explaining things before tossing you in this mess head-first."

"Hey, hold on a minute . . ." Toby began.

She ignored that little interruption. "And second, Etienne calls me 'madame goule' because I am—a ghoul." Poor Laura looked as if she was torn between upchucking and fainting. She glared at Toby instead. He deserved it.

"Why do I feel there's a whole lot more you haven't told me?" Laura asked. "Damn it all! Vampires, ghouls, next thing we'll have Dracula knocking on the front door."

The silence lasted so long, legions of angels had to be passing overhead.

Adela spoke first, moving from her perch on the window seat to sit beside Laura. "My dear, you have been pitched into a whole other world. In my opinion, Toby should have told you much, much more. But you can have that out with him later. Right now we need to tell you as much as we can and as much as you need to know to cope with the current situation."

"Okay." Laura took another deep breath, treated Toby to a rather impressive frown, then looked back at Elizabeth. "What does it mean, that you're a ghoul?"

Now it was Elizabeth's turn to take a long, deep, steadying breath. She'd never put this into words. Before the truth had come in dribs and drabs. Now she had to face it all. And ghouls did get dry mouths and sweaty palms, and she wasn't even thinking about the cold prickles down her spine.

She needed Tom here. Needed his support and love and she . . . was damn well just going to have to cope. Alone.

"Laura, I'm a ghoul because Laran Radcliffe, who we think is some sort of blood kin to Axel, attacked my sister, Heather, Adela's daughter, and myself. He imposed his will and mind on us so savagely, we didn't know where we were or what day it was. We didn't even know our own names or who we were.

"We were rescued, literally, off the streets of Chicago by another vampire—the Vlad Tepes or Mr. Roman the others have mentioned—the one who's been delayed. And I might as well tell you, he actually is Dracula but uses a traveling name when in the U.S. He introduced us to Toby's colony, and there I met Tom Kyd and went back to the U.K. with him and some of the others who live there.

"To cut a long, long story short, I finally found out who I was. It took ages and was in fits and starts and disjointed fragments as my memories came back, but meanwhile Laran was trying to find me and kill me once and for all. With Etienne's help"—might as well nod and acknowledge his part—"we learned Laran's weaknesses and I was able to destroy him. When I did, Heather and I got our minds back, but unfortunately, my father was left as you see him now."

"Killing Laran destroyed your father's mind?"

"I thought so at first, but now I think Laran had already done that. He replaced my father's mind with his." Poor woman looked ready to drop. "I meant what I said earlier, Laran controlled my father for years. Axel has only had a few months with yours. I really think there's hope he'll be unharmed."

"How did you destroy him?" She looked at Etienne. "What do you know about them that makes Axel vulnerable? Aren't vampires immortal?"

"We are immortal, unless destroyed," Toby said. "We all have weaknesses, our own personal Achilles' heels according to our bloodlines. Etienne"—he nodded toward the blond vampire who inclined his head in acknowledgement—"has made a study of vampires everywhere. He helped identify Laran's weaknesses, and now he's here, he'll help take care of Axel."

"But if this Laran and Axel are of the same bloodline, aren't their weaknesses the same?"

"They are," Etienne agreed with a little bow.

"Then why come all this way? Why not just call or send an e-mail?"

Smart woman! Elizabeth had been wondering precisely that. It didn't exactly make sense. What was Etienne up to?

Chapter 16

Toby rolled his eyes as Etienne bowed. Sheesh, the man belonged in the Middle Ages, which, after all, was when he'd been transformed.

"Mademoiselle Laura, I came not only to help as I may with this predicament, but on a commission for the esteemed Mr. Roman."

"Really?" Toby asked, drawing out the vowels and raising a dark eyebrow. "You're working for Vlad?"

Laura exhaled slowly. She'd have to be unconscious not to pick up the tension between the two men—okay, two vampires.

Etienne inclined his head. "I am."

The two of them would have played "stare me out" if Adela hadn't spoken after several pregnant seconds. "And is your commission for Mr. Roman relevant to our current worries, and Laura's apparent, very justified concerns for her father?"

The look on his face had Laura wishing she had a camera. He obviously wasn't big on soliciting female input. "I'd like to know that too."

"While we're at it," Toby said, "I'll admit to curiosity. Anything special you'd care to mention, Larouselière?

Just in passing, like? Something, perhaps, we ought to be aware of?"

Toby spoke as smoothly and easily as ever, but no one could miss the undertone of irritation. And more. Laura bet there were a gazillion shades of vampire nuance that were lost to her. Elizabeth seemed almost amused. Maybe she understood what was going on. Adela just sat back and rested her hands in her lap.

"Larouselière?" Toby repeated, adding a definite edge in his voice.

Uh-oh! Something was going on. Would be nice to know exactly what. Besides, all this sidetracked helping Dad. It was on the tip of Laura's tongue to make that point aloud when Etienne spoke.

"He wanted me here to examine this intruder. One unsanctioned vampire is intolerable to him. A second, totally insupportable. He wants to know their origins and reasons for trespassing. His request, madame goule—and when he arrives I am sure he will make it himself—is that you not incinerate the intruder this time."

What! Laura's jaw sagged as she stared from Etienne to Elizabeth. Both seemed perfectly calm, as if he'd asked her to please not park on the grass, to be careful not to slam a door. "You incinerated a vampire?" She had to ask. If it was bad etiquette, tough. "Burned him up? Cremated him? How?"

"Magic." Elizabeth gave a little shrug and an even smaller smile. "As I said, I'm a witch. We use magic. I had help, a local coven and . . . another. I harnessed the energy of the full moon and it was close to the solstice."

"And you're going to use magic against Axel?" Sounded utterly ludicrous, but if everyone else treated this seriously, who was she to pick holes in the idea?

"If needed, yes." She glanced at Etienne. "Any idea

what Vlad has in mind? He asked me to come, pretty much bludgeoned me into it with a guilt trip over Dad, but if he wants Axel alive . . .”

"Yes," Toby said, jumping in as Elizabeth paused. "Since you seem to be privy to Vlad's plans, would you care to let us know what he has in mind?"

Etienne raised his hands and shoulders in a wide gesture. "I know what I am told: to be ready to interrogate the creature and record everything."

"There's got to be more to it than that! You didn't come all the way from France just to talk to Axel Radcliffe!" Rude, yes, but, honestly, did he think they were that dumb?

"I tend to share Laura's doubt," Toby said. "Perhaps full disclosure would go a long way to settling our mutual unease."

"Toby, mon ami, what do you think?" The pained expression on Etienne's face was close to a work of art.

"I think you're here to feather your own nest in some way, Larouselière. You seldom leave France. Crossing the Channel is as big a performance as flying to the moon. Yet you blithely cross the Atlantic and the whole North American continent on the off chance of a chat!"

"Okay, Etienne, what really did bring you here?" Elizabeth asked.

Adela added, "This should be interesting."

Maybe, but Etienne looked angry and Laura suspected a pissed-off vampire might be tricky. She scooted a little closer to Toby. Not that she needed looking after or anything but . . .

Emotions flashed across the French vampire's face: anger, irritation, confusion, doubt even. Interesting. "Very well," he said, after a few moments of silence. "It is no secret." With another shrug—he had to practice them—he stretched his legs out in front of him. "I am here for research. After the destruction of the pestilent vampire"—he inclined his head toward Elizabeth—"I was curious about his bloodline and spent several weeks studying all I had about his lineage and uncovered an interesting but improbable legend.

"It may be just that—legend, myth—but several of my sources made the same mentions. So, when Vlad did me the honor of enlisting my assistance, I asked a favor in return: to have time, a few minutes, to examine and analyze and determine if indeed the myths and tales were true."

"Are you getting him before or after Vlad is finished with him?" Toby asked, a hint of amusement in his voice.

"Before. I need him sentient and coherent."

The charming smile added such a menace to his words that if Laura hadn't known how hideous and foul Axel was, she'd almost feel sorry for him. As it was . . . "Do me a favor, Etienne, don't leave him standing."

"He won't be, Laura, I promise you that," Toby said. "And talking about this creature, what's so fascinating that you came all this way to confirm?"

"It is *incroyable!* You would not believe it. I barely did but so many accounts would insist it is so." He did like the sound of his voice. Laura for one was getting tired of it but . . . "Seems these vampires, a small and powerful clan, make use of familiars: strange beasts that they protect and nurture, then use to attack. This I wish to confirm or refute."

Adela sat up, her shoulders tight. Laura caught her breath. Toby gave a dry laugh. "Etienne, old chap, you should have called me first. I could have saved you all the bother of getting shipped over here in your coffin."

"Indeed?"

"Definitely 'indeed,'" Adela said. "The 'familiar' wouldn't be called a chupacabra, would it?"

His blue eyes lit up with interest and amazement. "You have studied the myths too?"

"Didn't need to study them. I had one in the neighborhood. Toby killed it."

Nice to see Etienne could be rendered speechless. He was utterly mute for several seconds as he stared from Adela to Toby. "This is true?"

"Yes, old man, it is." Toby then proceeded to share what was, quite literally, a blow-by-blow account of his encounter with the creature. And that had to have been the same evening that . . .

"*Mon Dieu!* So it did exist but is dead. If only I could have seen this."

"Count yourself lucky you didn't!" Toby replied.

"If only I could have seen the corpse." He did rather go on.

"You could try looking in the deputy's cruiser, but with everything else that's happened in Dark Falls, who knows where it might be," Adela said. That led to filling Etienne in with everything else that had happened in the past couple of days.

"You think this Radcliffe is responsible for all this?"

Three of them answered in the same breath. "Yes!"

Elizabeth let out a dry laugh. "Seems the sooner we rid the continent of this one, the better off the world will be and"—she stood—"with that thought in mind, I'll be back in a jiffy."

She went into the bedroom next door, returning moments later with a velvet roll, which she unwrapped. "I thought I'd have trouble getting these through airport security, but they were in my checked luggage." She unrolled the velvet and a pile of silver chains spilled onto the coffee table. "These kept Laran at bay. No reason to suppose they won't work just as well on this specimen."

In minutes, Toby had heavy chains fastened round Laura's neck and wrists. They were intricate, ornate silver and all different. They hung cold against her skin until they warmed. "If it repels vampires, how come you can handle it?" she asked.

"Different bloodlines react in varying ways. Axel cannot venture near silver."

"Of course! This morning!" Was it only a few hours ago? Was this what happened when you skipped breakfast?

"What?" Elizabeth asked and everyone else looked downright interested.

"I told Toby. Right behind the newspaper office, Axel made a lunge for me and then reared back muttering how I couldn't wear it all the time. I had this little chain on." She reached under the heavy one for the fine chain and locket. "Damn him! I can and will wear silver every minute of the day and night."

"I think we're all going to," Adela added. "And I think Elizabeth and I need to confer, after she gets some rest. We have demanding times ahead."

"I will avail myself of the local hospitality." Etienne stood. "You have a preference for my return?" he asked Toby.

"Leave the study window open. You'll be safe enough there. You can lock it when you get back."

"Thank you. I hope and trust our Romanian friend will be here when I awaken."

"Your guess is as good as mine, but if he isn't, we need to put our heads together. That menace did enough harm yesterday; he can't be allowed to continue."

"Perhaps we should reconnoiter?"

"Good idea. I'll meet you down on the beach after you feed. In an hour?"

"Two, mon ami. Some things must not be hastened."

"Fair enough. Just keep away from the house and its inhabitants."

"Of course. I would not so presume."

With another bow, definitely overly dramatic this time, he turned to the open window, levered himself onto the sill and leaped, apparently into thin air.

Laura gave a gasp. "This is going to take some getting used to."

"Good luck!" Elizabeth said. "Every time Tom hops off the window sill or climbs down the roof it gives me the willies. Beats me why they can't go out the front door like most people."

"It's called 'style.'" Toby grinned.

"I call it nerve-racking," Elizabeth said. "Look." She came close to Laura. "I know you're sick about your father, but we're your best chance. Adela and I will do what we can. And by the time Vlad and his entourage get here, you'll have several vamps on your side. We'll rescue him and fix Axel's wagon." She gave her a quick hug. "I won't tell you not to worry, but at least try to get some sleep. It'll be a long night tomorrow."

"Yeah, and I've got to drive home."

"No, you are not!" Toby grabbed her arm. "Stay here. I want you safe."

"And I'm safer here than at home?" Okay, surrounded by a couple of vampires, she no doubt was, but his attitude irked. They'd shared incredible sex. He'd been fantastic over Dad—and her own behavior—but he hadn't bought her. Or did he think he had? Damn!

"Drat it, Laura! You know you are! You're staying here and that's that!"

"I am, am I?"

"Laura," Elizabeth said, "please stay. After all that's happened today there is a good chance Axel is out to get you, if only to use you as leverage with your father. But I have to admit"—she shook her head at Toby—"I thought Tom Kyd was the most overbearing vampire on the planet. You, Toby, have him bested. Lighten up and try asking instead of ordering. I bet Laura will stay if you say 'please.'"

"And while you're at it," Adela added, "do what I've been on at you about all day. Find a nice quiet spot and have a long talk."

"Any more commands, ladies?"

"I think that should do for now." Elizabeth smiled. "Get your questions ready, Laura. You've a lot to learn."

That was the understatement of the year, but with both of them on her side . . . "Yes, this vampire stuff is weird. Mind you, Etienne will be back in a couple of hours, if Toby can't help out . . ."

Toby actually growled. "I can answer anything you want, Laura." His grip on her arm loosened and he took her hand. "Let's go find somewhere where we won't be interrupted."

"She has failed you." Axel glared at Granger. "She needs a stern reminder of her obligations. I've given into your whimpering demands to spare her for too long. Your daughter needs bringing to heel."

"Leave her alone, Axel." There was still defiance in the man. Fascinating, but it wouldn't be there much longer. Once he enslaved Laura, Granger would comply. Utterly.

"But, no, my dear Granger. Remember our pact? I take care of the debts. You and your family take care of me. Your useless daughter failed."

"Was it her fault the FBI took everything? Doesn't that prove there is a story there? That's what you wanted, isn't it?"

"I needed proof. Not absence of proof."

As Granger started with worry, Axel smiled. Crossing the room, he closed his hand over his arm, pulling him to him as his other hand pushed up the mortal's shirtsleeve. His arm was covered with bruises and unhealed bites. There wasn't much use left in him. He would have to take over the daughter if he stayed much longer.

He met Granger's eyes, feeding a little fear into his brain, smiling as he heard the mortal's heartbeat race. "Call her, Granger. Pick up the telephone and tell her you need to speak to her."

Pathetic. Even as his mouth formed his refusal and his head shook to deny him, Granger reached for the phone at his belt, flipped open the cover and pressed speed dial. It rang several times, then, as the bitch's cheerful message started, he snapped the phone shut.

"Why," Axel asked with infinite patience, "did you do that?"

"She's not there!"

"Call back and leave a message. Say you need to see her immediately."'

"I don't! And I won't! She's out!"

"Call her on her cell phone. I don't care what you say, or how many puny lies you tell. I want her here. Now!"

Mortals! If it weren't for their blood, who'd bother with them? A pet was far better company, and the demise of his pet was the fault of a damned mortal. The measly deputy had paid for that offense, and the other idiot, for letting the witch go. Damn! She was another detail he needed to eliminate. This had been a frustrating day.

Hand shaking, shoulders twitching, Granger punched another number into the phone. "She's at work. I shouldn't call her."

Axel just glared and then smiled at the ringing tone. "Convince her, Granger. Convince her." It was just fascinating how easy it was to get mortals to act against their feeble beliefs and ethics. Best of all was the taste of their misery and despair.

Granger would come through, Axel had no doubt of it. Perhaps the day wasn't destined to be fruitless after all.

Chapter 17

"Want a glass of wine, love?" When Laura shook her head, Toby asked, "A cup of tea?"

"I'm tempted to say yes to the wine, but I want a clear head. You're not getting me relaxed and then trying the seduction game on me. I have questions."

"I know, and Adela's right, I should have told you more. How about a cup of tea, lots of answers to questions and then seduction?" Of course she might be so narked she'd walk away. Abel, no!

"Okay, Toby."

She was one perceptive mortal. "Fine, love. What is it? Tea?"

"Lemonade. There's a pitcher in the fridge. And if I am staying here tonight, I need something to eat."

"Better check the kitchen. Between Adela and Elizabeth there has to be something there. And whatever Piet eats."

Laura had never seen the fridge, or the freezer, so full. She couldn't face the effort of actually cooking something. Even opening a can of soup sounded like work. A sandwich was about the limit of her energy right now. Fast and easy, all the sooner to be able to pelt Toby with her questions.

She fixed a ham sandwich, letting Toby deflect Nurse Redding's curiosity when she put her head round the door. Nurse Redding retreated back to Piet's room, but not before casting disapproving frowns in their direction.

"If she can't accept you as a fixture in this house, she'll have to go," Toby said as he reached for a glass and held it under the ice dispenser. "I suppose you want the customary American glass, full of ice."

"Yes, I do, thanks, and wasn't that a quick switch of subject? You don't know for sure I'll be staying. I never agreed."

He smiled, not quite meeting her eyes as he reached for the pitcher of lemonade and filled the glass. "Here you are, love, and don't argue the obvious."

"That's not obvious!"

"No? I have a proposition, but it can wait. I wouldn't put it past dear Nurse Redding to be listening through the wall, a wine glass to her ear."

What a picture. "I'm almost ready." Putting the sandwich on a plate and grabbing a yogurt from the fridge and an apple out of the bowl on the countertop, she went out the door Toby held for her and almost by instinct headed upstairs to his bedroom, or what she'd assumed earlier was his room.

"Do you sleep here?" she asked as he closed the door behind them and she looked around at the long windows and the wide, modern bed with its pale, wooden headboard and matching side tables. "Not in a coffin?" By the look on his face, sleeping wasn't foremost in his mind. Nor in hers, she sort of acknowledged, but first he owed her answers.

She got the first one fast, almost before she sat down on the easy chair by the open window.

"Never have fancied the coffin idea," Toby said, as he took the matching chair opposite and stretched out his legs. "A bit gruesome, in my opinion. Larouselière does, but most of us view that as a bit of Gallic flamboyance."

"Most of us?"

He nodded. "Our mutual enemy, Etienne, Vlad, and myself are not the only vampires on the planet."

She'd more or less figured that out on her own. "How many are there? Hundreds? Thousands?" She wasn't entirely sure she wanted to know the answer but . . .

"Etienne could give you a more accurate answer than I could. He's studied and cataloged the vampire population, or at least some of it. I've personally met somewhere between two and three dozen. Vlad's colony is reputed to number in the scores, maybe even hundreds. Mine is small. Etienne's, I'm not sure. He's a bit cagey about that."

She set the plate down and looked at the sandwich. For a moment, she wasn't as hungry as she had been. "You don't eat food?"

Obviously a touchy question. He raised an eyebrow, gave a funny quirky smile and shrugged. "I don't eat as I did when mortal, if that's your question. But I do feed."

This was the point that put her off her own food. "You drink blood?" Just saying it made her stomach wobble. "Really?"

"I do. Does that repulse you?"

"I'm not sure." Who was she kidding? The thought made her want to barf. "Isn't it a bit gross?" Tactless maybe, but he seemed unfazed.

"At first it horrified me but soon the hunger took care of any qualms."

Made sense. Sort of. Now came the question she

wasn't sure she wanted answering. "Where do you get it?" She just couldn't see careful, considerate, even gentlemanly Toby ripping out throats. Oh, God! Surely not!

"Don't look so horrified. I don't kill. Never have. We don't."

"Axel does."

"He is a monster. Insane. Perverted. He doesn't merit the name of vampire."

"Stories and movies have vampires killing."

"Mere fiction! Rubbish. Think of the attention Axel has drawn onto Dark Falls the past two days. Aside from the immorality of it, it's foolish. If we all acted like that there would be witch hunts, stakings, burnings."

Good point but . . . "You still haven't told me how you get blood." She was more than wondering about earlier today, and what about the wild dreams she'd had on more than one occasion?

"We have ways. Blood bags, many of us have business interests in private blood banks. Also during lovemaking." She thought so. "And sometimes from an unconscious, sleeping donor."

Yes. "Go on. Any particular donor?"

"There has only been one since I came to Oregon."

Her mouth went dry. Not the sort of dryness that lemonade eased. Her stomach tightened. "How many times?"

He went very, very still. The only sounds in the room were the distant surf and whirl of the overhead fan. "From you, Laura. Four times, not counting this afternoon."

"They weren't just dreams, were they?"

Now he smiled. Just a slight curve of the corners of his mouth as his eyes widened and darkened. "Were they good dreams?"

Blood rushed to her face. "Let's put it this way, I

was beginning to think I was obsessing over you. They were . . . vivid."

"In a pleasant way?"

Was he fishing for compliments or what?

"Best I ever had."

The smile became a grin that lit up his eyes and sent a warm thrill right through her. He reached over and rested his hand on her knee. "That was only a shadow, Laura."

"Pretty colorful for a shadow. And what about this afternoon?"

"That, my dear, was my best effort at seduction."

"Your best is pretty damn good." Too blunt, perhaps? She didn't think so. Not by the way he chuckled.

"If you'll let me, I'll promise you 'damn good' for as long as you want."

Wonderful thought but . . . She reached for the lemonade and took a long, slow drink, watching him over the rim of the glass. He was lovely. Sexy. Considerate. And dead! She set down the glass.

"What's the matter, Laura?"

He was too darn good at reading her. "I think it's called total culture shock combined with hormonal overload."

Sometimes bluntness wasn't the best policy. Or was it? "I can definitely help with the latter, and for the former, I think familiarity helps."

"You mean if I hang around you and Etienne, vampires will seem quite commonplace?"

His dark eyebrows lifted. "You can omit the hanging around Larouselière. I'll give you all the exposure to vampire culture you'll ever need."

Despite stalwart efforts to suppress it, the giggle

slipped out. Toby was jealous! "Don't worry. He's not my sort at all."

Toby walked around the table and perched on the edge. If she breathed deeply their knees would touch. "Who is your sort?"

She took a deep breath. "Who do you think?" She had a hundred more questions but they'd still be there later and right now . . . She smiled at Toby and reached out her hand.

His fingers closed over hers, his skin cool. Duh! Hardly surprising. He raised her hand to his mouth and kissed her knuckles. She probably shouldn't smile and ogle him so shamelessly but with a slow ripple of pleasure radiating from her fingertips to her toes, not responding seemed pointless and stupid and ridiculous and an utter waste of a spring night and a luscious man.

Toby stood, keeping hold of her hand, and she moved with him. They were so close that their knees touched and as he drew her hand up to his lips again, she leaned into him, wanting to feel his hard chest against her body, needing to rest her head on his shoulder and feel his arms around her. Not that she was likely to want to stop there.

Tomorrow was likely to be one big mess laced with worry. For now . . .

She lifted her face and smiled.

His mouth came down, his lips cool and confident. His hands on her arms, sure and gentle as he drew her close. His lips touched hers as he held her close, his arms wrapping her in his strength as her mouth opened to his. She let out a little sigh at the rightness of his touch and kissed him back, her tongue finding his with a gentle caress. He responded, deepening his kiss, pulling her even closer so his erection pressed into the softness of her belly as his lips stirred a heat and need within her. A need that kissing alone would never satisfy.

With a frantic whimper, she reached between them with one hand and fumbled with his shirt buttons. She wanted to feel his skin, run her hand over his firm flesh and nestle her face into the soft sprinkling of hair on his chest.

She'd managed enough buttons to ease her finger inside his shirt. His quiet laugh was encouragement to slip a couple more buttons so her palm rested on the soft cotton of his T-shirt.

It wasn't enough; she wanted him skin to skin, something, judging by his hand under her blouse, that he was aiming for as fast as she was. He did a better job at unsnapping her bra than she did trying to yank his shirt out from his pants.

Getting his belt off could only help. She'd half-managed it, when the strains of the *Pink Panther* theme echoed in the room.

"What's that?" Toby asked, lifting his lips.

It took her a few seconds to register. "My cell phone." Why now? And where was it? Sitting in the bag she only half-remembered bringing up.

She was tempted to let it go to voice mail but something made her slip out of Toby's embrace and to dig for the jingling phone. One glance at the readout and she already regretted not ignoring it.

"It's Dad," she said. Why had he chosen this moment to call? And why had she fished the darn phone out instead of letting it ring? She had to answer it now.

Toby obviously agreed. "See what he wants."

She didn't want to know. All she wanted this minute was Toby, but she had no choice. Who knew what was going on down in Dark Falls?

"Laura! Thank God! I've been trying all day to get you. You're not at home."

"No, Dad. I'm at Devil's Elbow. What's the matter?"

"You said this was your day off."

"It was." Why was she feeling so defensive? Having just half-ripped off Toby's shirt might have something to do with it. "I had to come in. Change of plans. These things happen, Dad." Like Toby taking her free hand and staying close. How could she talk to her father when her body was humming with desire?

"I need you and couldn't find you. What have you been doing?"

Not a question to answer truthfully. Not now or ever. "Dad, what's so urgent? Are you okay?"

"Yes, I am, but no thanks to you! You've let me down, Laura, and I depended on you."

She couldn't hold back the sigh. They were right back in the same spot. Mind you, after what she'd learned about Axel today, it all made more sense. "Dad, I'm sorry I couldn't get the information you asked for. It just isn't here." And if it were, she darn well wouldn't hand it over.

"Laura, you aren't listening to me. I have to have something. Axel needs it."

"Then he'd better come and get it!" Oops! Bad move that. Trust her big mouth.

"You don't want that, Laura, you really don't."

She wouldn't argue with that but . . . she glanced at Toby, obviously intent and . . . listening? Why not? If vamps could fly, no doubt they had bionic hearing as well.

"Are you listening, Laura?"

Most of the time. "Sorry, Dad, things are busy here." And a kiss on the back of her neck was a definite distraction.

"I still don't understand what you are doing there."

"The FBI visit spooked one of the nurses, so I'm covering for her." She stifled the pang at lying to her father. It was for a good cause. "Look, Dad, I'll see what I can get for you. It's not easy." But hadn't Toby promised some red herrings? Maybe even minus computers and all, he'd concoct enough to keep Axel quiet until they rescued Dad. "Are you sure you're okay?" Not that he was going to say no if Axel was listening in.

"Of course I am! I don't know why you keep harping on about it. I'm fine! Just sorely disappointed in you, Laura. A father expects his daughter to come through for him."

"I will, Dad." She'd rescue him from Axel's sway. "Bye, Dad. Take care."

She thought she heard a snort as he rang off. What now?

"Toby . . ." she began.

"I heard it all." So she had been right. "He's getting pressure. No doubt about it. The minute Vlad gets here, we're going in."

Sounded like a SWAT mission. Vampire SWAT. Bring in the big fangs.

The giggle was pure nerves. So was the tightening of her hand in his. "He sounded so desperate," she said, looking up at Toby's dark eyes.

"One more day," he promised, "and we'll have this taken care of."

How could she not believe him? He'd come through before and would again. Toby kept his word and she trusted him. Utterly. Tomorrow they had a gazillion issues to sort out, but tonight she had the promise of his body.

She stood on tiptoe and kissed him, just a soft gentle kiss, a brush of her lips on his, until he responded, pulling her against him, opening her mouth and deepening the kiss until, with a whimper of pleasure, she molded her body into his. This was so perfect. Toby was so perfect.

Tonight was for her. For him, and tomorrow they'd save their little corner of the world.

He broke the kiss. Brushing her hair off her forehead, he said, "This is going to be wonderful, Laura, I promise. As wonderful as you are. As brilliant as the day and as sweet as eternity. I love you."

She had her lips parted to reply, when he whisked her off the ground. She gave a gasp, clinging to his arm as he carried her across the room and laid her on his bed.

Chapter 18

There was something she meant to say, but as Toby eased his hands over her breasts, sensations muffled her brain. Talk about a fast worker! Seconds ago she wore a T-shirt and a bra; now she was naked from the waist up.

Happily naked. Delighted to be naked as Toby's incredible hands cupped and stroked her breasts. Thrilled to be naked as he teased her nipples with his fingertips until they almost ached with pleasure.

She did manage to ask, "Where did my clothes get to?"

He just grinned. "What the hell do you need them for? You're wearing too much as it is."

Not much longer. In moments he had her jeans unsnapped and down her legs, and somehow her underwear went with them. Shoes and hose seemed to have evaporated. "How the heck do you do that so fast?"

"Old vampire trick."

Must also be an "old vampire trick" to plant a line of soft butterfly kisses all the way down her ribcage to her navel. And back up. For almost five seconds, she was vaguely disappointed he hadn't proceeded lower, but when his lips reached the swell of her left breast and covered every millimeter of it with kisses before closing his lips over her nipple, she decided not to complain. Better to use her energies smoothing her hands over his short, cropped hair and stroking the dark satin skin on his strong shoulders.

Her entire body responded to his shower of kisses: Her skin tingled, her shoulders arched, her hips rocked, and between her legs a wild flash of heat had her yearning for more. For Toby deep inside her.

And he was obviously going to keep her waiting.

Not that she'd complain. Yet. Not when he was treating the right breast to the same slow loving while his finger made absolutely certain her left nipple never had the chance to forget the utter pleasure of his touch.

Until he lifted his head and moved his hands off her and met her eyes. "Does that please you, my love?"

"Please" seemed woefully inadequate, but right now considering synonyms seemed a dire waste of brainpower.

A silly smirk was much less effort. "It'll do for a start!"

"Do? For a start?" His eyes darkened and his lovely wide mouth twitched. "Woman, for a mortal you have a lot of cheek."

"Two of them!" She grinned, pointing to them with a fingertip. "One, two."

Laura gasped as he flipped her over, and dropped a quick kiss on each butt cheek. "Three, four," he said, stroking them, his touch igniting nerve endings she never knew she possessed.

"Toby!" she managed, with a bit of a squeak, as she got her breath back. "What are you doing?"

"Admiring your delicious posterior." His hands slid up the small of her back to her shoulders and down. "Magnificent. And all mine."

If he was going all possessive on her, she had a thing

or two to say. "How come," she said, leaning up on her elbow and looking over her shoulder at him, "I'm naked and you're still fully dressed?"

"Your wonderful body distracted me."

"I'd enjoy a bit of distraction. How about it?"

His eyes glittered. His mouth spread in a grin as he leaned forward and trailed his fingertips over her butt and down the back of her thigh. "Okay."

By the time she turned around completely and sat up, he was naked. "How the hell do you do that?"

"I'm a vampire. We move fast when we want to."

No kidding.

She was all but dizzy at the speed he operated. Not that she'd complain. Not when naked Toby was every bit as incredible as she remembered. No doubt she had a silly grin on her face, and who cared? He was fantastic: not incredibly tall or fantastically broad-shouldered but his body was smooth and firm as polished mahogany. And every bit as hard. Especially his most prominent part. Hard. Erect. Beautiful.

She wriggled down to the end of the bed and smiled at his lovely cock. Looking up at him and meeting his eyes, she reached out and gently eased her finger down the side of his erection.

His slow grunt was all the encouragement she needed.

Shifting so she was sitting on the end of the bed, she rested her hands on his thighs. Relishing the firm muscle beneath her fingers, she leaned forward and dropped a kiss on the end of his cock.

Her lips sensed his excitement. Heart thumping, she circled the head of his cock with her lips. Her entire body thrilled at the power between her lips and the power in her lips. Easing her mouth lower, she caressed him with her tongue. Her heart raced, her stomach clenched and arousal coursed through her to pool between her legs.

This was so wondrous! So incredible and so, so right! Now became an endless cycle of utter delight as she caressed him with her tongue and lips and reveled in her feminine power. He might be vampire, fast, strong and mighty, but she held him between her lips. He was vulnerable. He made himself vulnerable to her and was obviously, very obviously, enjoying every second.

As her mind focused on his wonderful cock, her body shuddered and a lassitude almost amounting to weakness washed through her. She was aware of his hands on her head, the strength of his thighs under her hands and the glorious sense of utter sexiness, but she wanted more: Toby.

As if sensing her need, Toby eased her head away. "By Abel! I love you. After all these years, I found you, Laura." He bent down and kissed her. He moved faster than she could follow and the next moment she was on the bed, lying on her back, Toby settled between her legs as he nuzzled her belly.

"It unnerves me when you move that fast."

He looked up, a slow, sexy smile curving his mouth. "Sorry, love. I'll go slowly from now on."

Now he almost killed her with gentleness. His lips and hands played her body, driving her arousal to fever pitch. She was sweating with need, shaking with passion as he kissed every inch of her skin, lifting her ankle to run his mouth down the back of her leg, leaning over her to tease her nipples with his tongue and licking the base of her neck until she squirmed.

Just as she was muttering she couldn't take any more, that she needed him deep inside, he slid down the bed, parted her pussy and rested his lips on her moist inner flesh.

She almost flew off the bed. Her body sang as his lips teased and his tongue caressed. She heard whimpers and little cries as if from somewhere beyond her consciousness but she was past thinking, past speaking. All her body knew was sensation: vast, wide spirals of joy, immense waves of pleasure that engulfed her body and her reason.

The little cries became shouts as her passion grew, rushing higher in a wild torrent of need, happiness and emotion that led to a triumphant scream as her climax broke.

As her body roared at the peak, Toby moved. In an instant, he was inside her, his need and desire adding to hers, driving her back to another peak and another, until her mind faded out into a wild sea of pleasure, emotion and sexual exhaustion.

She was panting, sweat running off her breasts and down between her shoulder blades, as she gasped and her pulse beat loudly in her ears.

Her body sagged into the mattress as her pleasure eased. Toby slipped out of her and kissed her hard on the mouth, his tongue entering her as fiercely as his cock had moments earlier.

She was too worn to do anything but feel: to float on sensation and lose herself in the delight of his lips. He covered her face and neck with kisses, leaving her languorous and sated. She sighed, smiling at the ceiling, at Toby and the world.

"My love," he whispered and kissed the base of her neck.

As his mouth closed over her pulse point, wild ripples of pleasure radiated out from the flesh under his lips.

She shivered, sighed and arched her shoulders, seeking to join completely with her lover. She let out a little cry as his fangs pierced her skin, then yelled to the ceiling as utter and total joy engulfed her.

She was floating on a tide of pleasure, resting on a great cloud of happiness as her mind stirred again, drawing her body up into another great crashing climax that left her light-headed but utterly sated.

She couldn't talk. Thought was beyond her, so she wrapped her arms around her lover and sagged her spent body into his strength and enfolding arms.

Toby looked down at the sleeping mortal in his arms and knew he was lost. All he wanted to do for the next few days, weeks, months was stay in bed with Laura and make love to her, to watch her sleep and feel the soft brush of her mortal breath on his arm and the steady throb of her heartbeat under his hand.

Unfortunately, in a few short hours, he had to join forces with Vlad and his minions and hunt a rogue vampire. The prospect did not appeal right now.

But . . . taking care of Axel Radcliffe would free Laura's father from Axel's compulsion. Anything that eased her mind or freed her from worry was a worthwhile endeavor, by Toby's reckoning. Besides, he was curious what information, if any, Vlad could extract from Axel re Laran's money-laundering ventures.

If they had missed a thread or link somewhere in the cleanup of Laran's affairs, better they find it now than leave it for the darn FBI to stumble on.

And that was another problem—what the heck to do about them? The company lawyers assured him all was under control, and he knew there was nothing left on the computers or files to implicate anyone living. But what if there were undiscovered links or trials? Vlad would get them out of Axel.

Over the years, Vlad Tepes and his many aliases had built up a reputation for ruthlessness bordering on viciousness. Toby was only too aware of the pain Vlad had inflicted on Toby's friend Justin, slithering in and wheedling his lover, Gwyltha, away from him. Not that Justin wasn't content and happy now with his Stella, but he'd had over a hundred years of heartache in between.

On the other hand, Vlad's creations and colony members viewed him with respect tinged with affection. There had been no trace of fear or cringing in Zeke's attitude.

Zeke! Toby shook his head. He didn't doubt Vlad's claim that Zeke was dead. As his creator he'd sense his extinction, but how? Zeke was a vampire, and a streetwise one at that. Any creature to overcome him would have to be strong indeed. And there was the nasty little nag that since Zeke was his guest, Vlad might hold him, Toby, responsible.

Damn! At the first hint of that, he'd have Elizabeth or Adela get Laura right away. She was not getting tainted with his misfortune. Alright! No point in meeting trouble halfway. Odds were it would never come to that, but just in case, he'd slip a word to Adela and Elizabeth in the morning. He knew better than mention it to Laura. He'd seen and heard how other women reacted. Let Laura know there was a threat to Toby, she'd be taking on Vlad and his entire colony single-handedly. He'd take care of everything if and when that snag occurred.

Meanwhile, he relaxed beside Laura, inhaling the perfume of her skin and soaking in the warmth of her mortal existence. He longed to bind her to him, to make her his forever, but she was a living, breathing young woman. Death had no part in her existence, for years and decades to come.

He did not doubt for a minute that he loved Laura. That she loved him back was a hope fed by her sleepy loving words, but that life and death separated them was as sure as the rising of the sun, or his uneasy conviction that trouble lay ahead.

Toby eased out of bed, being careful not to disturb Laura. Mortals needed rest. After pulling on his clothes, he walked downstairs, noting the heartbeats in the rooms as he passed. He had a couple of things to do downstairs and might as well get on with them while he waited for Etienne to return from his prowl. He'd be back in the next couple hours, to be safe in his darn box before morning. They'd have time and it mightn't be a bad idea to work out a few things before Vlad and his lot arrived.

Toby was halfway down the main stairs when he caught the sound of a car—no, cars—coming up the drive. Vlad? As the cars approached, Toby focused his hearing. Heartbeats! Mortals? Approaching the house at . . . he glanced at the wall clock in the hall . . . just after three a.m.

Looking through the glass panels by the door, he recognized the first car as it rounded the final bend. Damned FBI again!

At least this time they weren't taking him by surprise. He flung the door open and watched as both cars pulled up and a bevy of enthusiastic agents piled out.

Toby almost wished they would take a potshot at him silhouetted against the open doorway. Would be decidedly satisfying to observe their shock at seeing bullets pass through him and leaving him standing. Discretion and the need to blend in with mortals rather put paid to such theatrical notions.

"Can I help you, gentlemen?" Toby asked. The hint of sarcasm was a complimentary extra.

Seemed Agents Healy and Bright never slept. They led the others into the house and presented Toby with yet another search warrant.

If he'd been mortal, he'd no doubt have sighed. As it was, he shrugged. Unless they planned on carting away furniture and fittings, there wasn't much left to take.

They fanned out over the entry hall, filling it with their dark suits. Even at this hour of the morning they all wore ties—except Agent Healy, who still wore the regulation dark business suit and pastel shirt. Mortals did have such a tendency to be boring and very worrisome. "You forgot something?" Toby asked. Not that he really cared.

"We'd like another look at the office, please," Agent Bright said.

Now he got it; they were suffering from insomnia and decided to toddle on down and wake everyone up. If it had only been Bright and Healy, he'd have thrown a glamour on them and worried about it later. Unfortunately, he doubted he could influence five minds at once. Bugger!

Adela stood on the landing upstairs. Not Laura, good. Maybe this time his sleep compulsion had worked. He wouldn't count on it, though.

"What's happening, Toby?" Adela asked.

"The FBI are back."

She came down the rest of the stairs almost at a run. "Honestly! Haven't you people caused enough disturbance for one lifetime?"

"We have our job to do, ma'am," Healy replied. "Just ensuring we have everything."

"Want the carpets and furniture this time, do you?" Improvident, yes, but Healy was rousing Toby's fury.

"Let them take them, Toby," Adela said. "Just don't let them disturb Piet again. I'll go sit with him and I darn well hope they don't make enough noise to wake Elizabeth. She's out cold after all this travel."

"A new member of household staff?" Healy asked.

"No, Piet's daughter. She flew in from England last night, worried about her father." Adela did imperious well. She was a witch, after all. "All this upheaval is most distressing to a man in his state of health."

It was also distressing to a vampire in his second century. "I'm sure they'll create no more chaos than absolutely necessary, Adela." Abel, forgive him the sarcasm but this was beyond reason.

Her raised eyebrows and twisted quirk of her mouth suggested something falling short of total confidence. She swept through them and headed for Piet's room, just as the nurse appeared. Adela drew the woman back with her.

At least one concern was taken care of. Now all he had to worry about was Laura, Elizabeth and the FBI finding he had everything back up on a remote server. Tom Kyd had promised it was impossible to detect. Toby sincerely hoped so.

Thank Abel, Larouselière was out of the way. If he'd just stay away until this fiasco was taken care of, Toby might even welcome him back into the house. Or maybe not. The frog had better not cast as much as a flicker of an eyelash in Laura's direction.

"Mr. Wise, we're going to look over your study again."

"Go ahead!" As if they needed his permission, but no point in arguing. Let them get done and get out.

He didn't even bother following them into the room but waited at the foot of the stairs, ignoring the thumps and sounds of books falling off the shelves. What the hell was going on? There was virtually nothing left after their last imprecation.

"Come in here a minute please, Mr. Wise," one of the black suits called.

The man had said "please," after all, so Toby went in. "Yes?"

"This box here "—Bright pointed at Etienne's traveling coffin—"new? A delivery you received today?"

"Yes."

"Interesting shipping manifest." Healy held the paper in her hand.

"Really?" What did it say, "one potted vampire"?

"I think we'd better take it with us."

Toby had his lips parted to object but kept the words back, sensing this was intended as a provocation. Designed to make him resist. To give them fuel for whatever they were trying to concoct. He met Bright's beady eyes and shrugged. "Go on, just don't expect me to help you lift it." No doubt Larouselière would throw a Gallic tantrum when he returned, but they'd find him somewhere to sleep. In a house this big there had to be a lightproof wardrobe or storage space.

The pregnant pause pretty much confirmed Toby's suspicions. The black suits looked at one another. At Bright's nod, a couple of them took each end and almost dropped it. Toby barely managed not to smile. The other two, including Healy, added their efforts and carted it out while Bright handed him a receipt.

They were halfway across the entrance hall when Laura and Elizabeth came down. Laura had pulled on clothes, but her hair was tousled and her lips deliciously swollen. She looked like a well-loved woman.

Luckily for them, none of the agents cast her as much

as a glance. They were too busy hauling an empty coffin out the front door.

"What's happening?" Elizabeth asked.

"Toby?" Laura came to stand beside him.

"We had the dubious pleasure of a return visit from the FBI," he replied as she meshed her fingers with his.

"How's Dad?" Elizabeth asked.

"Adela's with him. I don't think they disturbed him— this time."

"They'd better not have!" Giving the departing agents a frown that would have withered lesser mortals, she darted back toward Piet's room.

"Why are they taking that?" Laura asked as the last two stepped over the threshold and headed for the van.

"Necessary for our investigation, ma'am," Bright replied with a self-satisfied smirk. "Thank you for your cooperation, Mr. Wise. It will be noted."

With Laura beside him, Toby restrained himself from muttering the response that sprung to mind. He settled for slamming the heavy door. "They're gone. Let's get back to bed."

"Why did you leave?"

Adela reappearing saved him from that question.

"Thank heaven Piet didn't wake," Adela said, "but that wretched nurse is threatening to quit."

"I hope you convinced her to stay until morning," Toby said.

"She'll stay," Laura said. "No one around here pays as much as Toby does."

"I'll talk to her again in the morning." Elizabeth shook her head. "She's a bit excitable. She might not be any loss."

"Right now, Piet needs as little change in routine as possible," Adela pointed out.

"It's all settled now." Or so Toby hoped. "They've gone." At least for now.

"Did they find anything else this time?" Elizabeth asked. "The study is pretty much stripped."

"Only Larouselière's empty coffin. We'll have to make some temporary provision for him when he gets back. You know the house best, Elizabeth, where—"

"Etienne's coffin?" Adela interrupted. "They took that? This is terrible!"

"We'll manage, Adela," Elizabeth replied, her hand on her stepmother's arm. "There's the wine cellar downstairs. We can make space there for him when he gets back. Take down a mattress and bedclothes. It's—"

"You don't understand!" Adela was pale and shaking. "He's in it!"

"What?" Toby regretted the shout. It scared Adela and no doubt would bring Nurse Fussy out of her lair. "He went out to hunt. It's not yet anywhere near dawn."

"He came back a couple hours ago. I couldn't sleep and was sitting out on the terrace and saw him. We talked for a while." "Talk" had better be the limit of their interaction. "He said he was weary from travel and was going to retire early to rest on his good French soil so as to be at full strength to join in the attack tomorrow."

"You're sure of this?"

"That's what he said. I didn't follow him to tuck him in, but he went into the study."

No wonder two mortals had been unable to lift the "empty" box.

Something had to be done and fast, before the bloody Feds found a dozing vampire. If they roused Larouselière, "bloody" would be the right adjective!

Chapter 19

Laura understood how Alice felt, once down the rabbit hole. Looking from Toby—still sexy enough to make her mouth water—to Adela and Elizabeth, she felt right out of the loop, but one thing was pretty clear through all the mess. "Hadn't someone better go after them? Do something? If you want to keep vampires secret, leaving one in the hands of the Feds is hardly a bright idea."

"I'll go." She hadn't expected rich girl Elizabeth to jump in. Maybe she'd misjudged her.

"No, you won't! Tom would have my hide if anything happened to you." That was just like Toby.

Smart woman! She all but ignored that little interruption. "I can run fast enough to overtake them. Distract them and—"

"And then what? You'll be drained from the run and the damn Feds will have a ghoul and a vampire!" Did Toby have to be quite so snappy? Okay, he was worried but . . . "We'll both go."

Elizabeth nodded. "Okay. Better get a move on, then, or they'll be back in Eugene unloading him."

"Do you have any sort of plan?" Adela asked. "You

can hardly run them down and demand they give Etienne back."

"I'll get ahead of them, slow down enough to be seen, and run in front and cause them to swerve. With a bit of luck they'll hit something or each other. There won't be much traffic about at this hour of the morning, unlikely to be any other witnesses. Then Toby can get the box out and release Etienne. If we move fast enough, we can be gone before they realize what happened and they'll be left with an empty box."

"Better take the damn coffin too! Dawn's not that far away," Toby said.

"Don't you think they might notice it's gone?" Adela asked. "Better leave them with an empty box. And better get a move on. Etienne is stirring."

Toby and Elizabeth all but gaped at her, Toby looking stunned, Elizabeth shocked. It was obvious to Laura she was missing something here.

"Adela, you didn't!" Elizabeth said, in a scandalized voice.

"What I did or did not do is irrelevant!" she snapped back. "Better get going!"

"Right!" Toby's tone suggested it was anything but. It would be so nice to know what was really going on. "We both go. Elizabeth, get dressed and then we go."

"No! I need food more. Besides, a woman running around in nightwear is sure to distract them nicely."

Toby paused, as if weighing her decision, or perhaps his ability to alter it, and nodded. "Good point." He turned to Adela. "Follow us with the Hummer. I bet they've gone south on 101 to take 126 into Eugene. You meet us coming back."

"And please bring some meat, Adela. I'm grabbing something right now but it won't hold me for long."

As Adela agreed, Elizabeth raced back to the kitchen.

"I'll get the Hummer out," Toby said, zipping upstairs in a blur of speed and coming down moments later with his keys in his hand. Seemed he barely registered Laura's presence. Fair enough. That way they wouldn't argue.

Laura followed Adela and Elizabeth into the kitchen and almost wished she hadn't. She was just in time to see Elizabeth chomping down the last half of a very large raw steak. "Sorry," Elizabeth muttered through bloody lips, as she reached for a packet of chicken breasts. "Nothing dainty about the way I eat, but I need the strength. I'm going to burn it up fast."

Who was Laura Fox, nurse, to argue? What did she know about ghouls?

"Coming with me?" Adela asked.

"Yes!"

"Thought so." She had a wonderful, crooked smile. "You fill up the cooler." She indicated a small one on the countertop. "Pack as much as you can in it. Once Lizzie and Toby are off, we'll follow. He can't say much once you're there."

"Easier to ask forgiveness than consent, right?"

Adela grinned. Elizabeth laughed through a chicken breast.

She'd finished the entire packet in moments! What was her digestive system like?

"Ready, Elizabeth?" Toby asked from the door. "We can't let them get too far ahead."

"Ready." She chewed down the last chicken breast and tossed the plastic tray in the trash.

They were both out the door in seconds, moving in a blur. Laura couldn't hold back a gasp. They'd disappeared!

"A bit unnerving, isn't it?" Adela said, by her side. "I knew her as a little girl who was scared of climbing down the cliff path and now . . ." She shook her head.

"What's going on?" Damn! It was Nurse Redding, her beady eyes agog.

"Just getting settled after that awful intrusion," Adela replied faster than Laura could think. "Terrible, wasn't it? I think they pick their times on purpose to make the most disruption. So wonderful that you're here, to make sure Piet isn't disturbed." She was walking back toward his room, sweeping the nurse with her.

Laura shut the front door quite noisily and nipped back into the kitchen. She was closing the fridge after packing three chickens and a couple of plastic bags of pork chops in the cooler when Adela reappeared.

"If only Toby had put one of his vampire compulsions on the woman, I'd be a lot less worried, but we can't hang around. I'll bring the Hummer around the side."

Vampire compulsions? They weren't a Hollywood invention? Was that why she'd slept so soundly? How much else hadn't Toby told her? Okay, they hadn't had much time to talk, but if they had time for wild, sweaty sex, surely a short conversation wasn't asking too much.

She'd have that out with him. Later.

Laura grabbed the cooler and was out the back door, just as Adela pulled the Hummer around. She drove slowly and carefully until they were away from the house, then sped up a little. Once they hit the road she put her foot down. "Doubt we'll catch up with Toby and Lizzie but we can't be that far behind."

Her matter-of-fact acceptance of the fantastic left Laura dry-mouthed for a minute. "How fast can they run?" She asked after a lot of swallowing.

"I doubt anyone has ever timed a vampire—or a ghoul, for that matter—but faster than I'd feel comfortable driving on this road."

"I hope they're okay."

"My dear," Adela replied, slowing a little as she

negotiated a particularly sharp bend, "if it's a case of vampires and mortals, don't waste energy worrying about the vampires."

"Elizabeth isn't a vampire."

"True, but she can hold her own."

That Laura had observed. "If vampires are as strong as they seem and can put on compulsions like you said, why the hell didn't Toby just get rid of the darn Feds the first time they came around?"

"They seem to have this thing about fitting in among mortals and not drawing any sort of attention to themselves."

The splutter was entirely involuntary. "Running FBI cars off the road and snatching Etienne will hardly go unnoticed."

"True, but one of their own is threatened. The gloves go off then. Like Vlad knowing Zeke was killed. There is going to be one big vamp showdown very soon. You might want to take a little holiday until the steam and dust clear."

"With Dad in danger from that leech Axel? And Toby caught up in it? You must be kidding!"

"Good woman." Adela glanced at her, then looked right back at the curving road ahead. She seemed about to add something but grimaced. "Trouble! I sense it. Etienne is hurt."

How did she know? Was there something between Adela and Etienne? Was that what the odd looks earlier implied? "What happened?"

Elizabeth threw back her head as the night swallowed her laugh. It felt marvelous!—the wind in her face, the trees and road signs rushing past in a blur as she ran beside Toby. And kept up with him. Okay, if he took off and flew, she'd be left behind, but right now they were neck and neck. Keeping up with Toby didn't carry quite the same thrill as keeping up with Tom, but in the absence of the vampire she loved, it would do. Might as well enjoy it while she could. Tomorrow promised trouble.

Might be smart to hire an ambulance and take Dad and a nurse off on a short holiday. In fact, the more she thought about it, the more brilliant it seemed. She'd like to take Laura with her. She wanted to get to know her better but figured the odds of Laura leaving Toby right now were up there with snow in August.

At least she'd get Dad out of the way. Perhaps a nice few days up at Crater Lake or . . .

The sound of tearing metal, shouts and gunshots took care of any wondering about possible vacation spots.

Toby sped. It took all she had to keep up, but she managed. A white blur came barreling down the road toward them.

"Larouselière!" Toby called.

She'd concede vamps had the edge on vision. She'd never have recognized the white blur. The white, bloody blur, she realized, as they all slowed to something approaching sprinter's speed. It was Etienne, racing toward them and looking none the better for several bullet holes in his chest and blood all over his face and shoulders.

Recognizing them, he slowed. "My friends, I regret but I am weakened," he said, as Toby ran forward and caught him. "I fear they pursue me."

"Not for long," Toby replied. "They can't follow what they can't see. Give me a hand," he added to Elizabeth. "Let's get him off the road."

He was weakened. Half a dozen bullets will do that, even to a vampire, but with Toby taking his weight, Etienne moving as best he could, and Elizabeth leading, they got him off the road and into the trees. It was precarious but better than taking the other side of the road, down the cliffs.

Etienne sagged onto the ground. Okay, vamps were usually pale but in the moonlight he looked bad. At least he was unlikely to die, even if one wound was dangerously near his heart.

He smiled up at her. "Forgive my state, madame goule. I would not appear like this if not pressed."

Fair enough, and with luck there might be a blanket or two in the Hummer. "Don't sweat it, Etienne. We'd better worry first about getting you back."

"Right," Toby said, "you run back to Adela, Elizabeth. There's a side road we passed a mile or so back. Have her wait there. No point in her getting closer. I'll get Larouselière there if I have to carry him."

She took off, slower this time, to conserve strength. She passed the side road she'd not even noticed earlier, and in a few minutes, the Hummer came beetling toward her. She slowed to almost mortal pace and Adela stopped.

"What's happening?" she asked, leaning out of the window.

"Let me get in and I'll explain." Laura was in the passenger seat—hardly surprising. Elizabeth hadn't thought she'd take meekly to being ordered to stay behind. "Okay"—she leaned forward from her perch on the backseat—"Etienne is free. Looks as though he broke out. He's hurt. Toby's with him. There's a narrow lane to the left in a couple of miles. Turn off there."

"How hurt is he?" Adela asked.

"Bloody, several bullet wounds. If he were mortal, he'd be down, if not dead. He'll heal, given time."

"Should we get him to a doctor?" Laura asked, then answered her own question. "We can't, can we?"

"No, dear," Adela replied. "No need. They heal themselves given enough time."

"Do you have any blankets in back?" Lizzie asked. "We'll need them."

"He's suffering from shock, I suppose," Laura said.

Bless her, she still didn't get it. "Not shock, more like embarrassment. If you've ever wondered what vampires wear to sleep in their coffins, you are about to find out: nothing!"

"Oh!" Laura paused, but only for a beat. "At least it's summertime."

"Hypothermia isn't a problem," Elizabeth said. "Blood loss is a worry, though. Hope Toby has a good supply." He better have with the lot due to arrive, or the locals would end up anemic.

"If not, I have plenty to donate."

"Adela!" Lizzie felt her jaw sag.

Laura gasped.

"Oh, for pity's sake!" Adela snapped. "It's here, isn't it?" She turned up the dark and almost hidden lane. "You've both picked your vampires. Why grudge me?"

Good point. Except . . . "You know about him, Adela?" Elizabeth had to ask.

"My dear, stop worrying, I know the difference between a Mr. Right and a Mr. Right Now." She slowed. "I think we're here and, yes, you were right about the lack of pajamas."

She pulled to a halt by Toby and Etienne, and all three women piled out of the Hummer.

Adela went straight to Etienne. Laura met Elizabeth's eyes. "I'll look for blankets, or something."

"Something" turned out to be an old down jacket and a threadbare picnic blanket. "At least it will cover him," Laura said. "I'll take them; I'm a nurse."

Elizabeth didn't argue. Adela's revelation had knocked her for a loop but now was not the time to stew over it. Adela was certainly old enough to make up her own mind and appeared to harbor few illusions. Besides, Toby was now carrying a definitely limp-looking Etienne to the Hummer. Worries about Adela could wait.

The faded blanket was wrapped around Etienne's waist like a makeshift kilt. The jacket was zipped up tight and he looked worse than five minutes ago.

"He needs blood urgently," Toby said as he settled him on the floor in the back. "He's bleeding."

Quite profusely, if the stains on the down jacket were anything to go by.

"No problem," Adela said, climbing in beside him.

Now it was Toby's turn to look stunned.

"We've got to get him back before dawn, right?" Elizabeth asked. "Let's get going. Want me to drive?"

"I will."

How like a man!

"Keys are in the ignition," Adela said, pushing up her sleeve and exposing her wrist.

This Elizabeth did not need to watch. Blood was too close to sex in her mind. Audience not required. She climbed in the backseat. Laura got back in beside Toby.

"So, you came after all," Toby said.

"Yes," she replied. "I navigated for Adela."

He accepted that with a nod as he started the engine and reversed back to the road. Toby lived up to his last name.

The road was quiet going back—seemed whatever damage Etienne had done to the FBI vehicles was enough to stop pursuit. The most immediate worry seemed to be to get a battered and bloody Etienne into the house without Nurse Redding noticing.

Chapter 20

If Toby had any complaints about Laura coming along, he kept them to himself. Just as well. It gave her time to wonder if any of her nursing training could be of use helping the injured vampire.

Toby stopped the Hummer a few meters after he turned into the drive. "Wait here a jiffy. I need to take care of Nurse Nosy Parker. She's seen more than enough already." He looked back over his shoulder. "How's Larouselière doing?"

"Much better," a tired voice, with a more pronounced than usual French accent, replied. "Thanks to an angel who saved me."

"You'd better give thanks to Toby and Elizabeth too," Adela replied. "They found you."

"Indeed, I am indebted." And worn out, by the sound of things.

"Hold on, everyone." Toby was out of the car and closing the door. "I'll be back."

He was, within five minutes.

Not five minutes after that, they were in the house and Laura, clutching Toby's keys in her hand, was running upstairs to fetch blood.

She wasn't squeamish. She was a nurse, for goodness' sake, but opening the door of the little refrigerator packed full of blood bags stopped her short, pretty much slammed her with the reality of vampires. This was how Toby fed, when he wasn't tasting off her. She would never, ever take him home for Sunday dinner. They'd never eat scrambled eggs and bacon together on a Sunday morning. Never share cotton candy or popcorn.

Too many "nevers."

She grabbed seven or eight bags—if it wasn't enough, she'd come back for more—wrapped them in a towel and hurried downstairs.

They were in the wine cellar, Etienne on a blanket, propped on Adela's lap, while she and Toby washed the blood off him. He had lacerations all over his head and shoulders, and several bullet wounds, but none looked as bad as she'd expected, from the amount of blood on him earlier.

All three looked up as she came in, and Etienne's eyes all but sparkled. "You brought blood?"

"Yes."

He ripped the first bag open with his teeth and all but aspirated the contents, before reaching out for a second. By the fourth or fifth he was drinking more slowly, and his color was returning. He'd never look ruddy, she presumed, but he no longer had the skin tone of cooked spaghetti. And . . .

She couldn't help staring.

His bullet wounds closed as she watched, and the cuts and lacerations disappeared.

"We heal fast," Toby said quietly. "That's how we are."

"You'd heal like this?" He nodded. "What about the scars on your back?" Long weals of proud flesh she'd hesitated to comment on.

"I had those while still a mortal. They will never go."

That was a talk for another time.

Another glance at Etienne revealed almost no cuts, and the gunshot wounds were just pink blobs. Incredible. Unbelievable. Except she'd seen it with her own eyes, and it scared her.

"I thank you all," Etienne said. "I am . . . revived."

"Can you tell us what happened?" Toby asked.

"I was resting, not asleep, and was aware they were carrying me out but judged it best to stay inside—at least for the moment. However"—he shrugged—"when they set off and started discussing opening my cocoon, I deemed it wisest to depart. Getting out of my cocoon was simple. Battering a hole in the vehicle took effort, hence my wounds."

"What about the bullet wounds?" Adela asked.

"Oh, them!" He brushed them off as less than mosquito bites. Maybe they were to him. "There was some consternation as I broke out. I believe they got a little nervous."

Nervous! Laura laughed. "Sorry, I just had a mental picture of you ejecting out of the back of the van like a speeding bullet and everyone all het up and shooting in all directions."

The thought pleased him no end. "And I must admit, I came out so fast, I hit the windshield of the car behind. They shatter like spiderwebs, you know? Fascinating."

Now it was Toby's turn to snort. "That explains why no one tried to follow you. Not that they were likely to believe the evidence of their own eyes. Mortals have difficulty comprehending anything that doesn't fit their own perception of reality. And a damn good thing too," Toby added, standing and looking in Laura's direction with an odd little quizzical smile. "I think I have a few questions to answer and you, Larouselière, need to rest. You'd better be in fighting trim by tomorrow night."

"Rest your fears, my friend," Etienne replied. "I will fight as I did at the walls of Jerusalem."

Toby raised a dark eyebrow but said nothing.

"What happened at the walls of Jerusalem?" Laura asked as they went upstairs.

"He was killed," Toby replied, "during the First Crusade."

She had to ask, didn't she? "As in the Crusaders and Saladin and Richard the Lionheart?"

"Yes, except Saladin and Richard the Lionheart belong in later Crusades—assuming Etienne died when he claims."

"You think he didn't?"

Toby shrugged. "Who knows? Etienne plays his own game but it's always mystified me that he supposedly died during the siege of Jerusalem at the end of the eleventh century but claims connections to the Knights Templar, and they weren't formed until early into the twelfth century."

"Maybe he joined them as a vampire."

Toby went silent a beat. "By Jove! I never thought of that."

Didn't seem that revolutionary an idea to Laura. "He could have. Might explain their rise to power and influence and some of the subsequent politics." He was looking at her as if she had ferns growing out of her nose. "Mightn't it?"

Toby creased his forehead in thought. "It might indeed, my love. The idea certainly bears close scrutiny, but not now."

She couldn't agree more. She was dead on her feet and had a horrible suspicion she was facing an unpredictable and worrying day. "I think I was actually trying to get some sleep when the Feds so rudely interrupted."

Laura slept with very little nudging on his part. Toby was tempted to stay right beside her but he had a couple things to check up on before Vlad arrived.

Adela was coming up the basement stairs as Toby crossed the hall. "Larouselière's alright?" he asked.

"He will be. I can't get over how fast you vampires heal. He's tired and worn, but not a mark on him."

"You look tired and worn too." No point in commenting Larouselière had obviously taken too much blood. "Better get yourself a good snack before you go to sleep. Take a steak or two from the fridge."

She didn't take to the idea. "No, Toby, after all the ups and downs tonight, I think we all need to be as unobtrusive as possible. No point in inciting that nurse's curiosity any more. I'll last until morning and indulge in a Texas-sized breakfast. Right now, I need sleep."

She needed solid protein too, but she had a good point. "Fair enough. Keep those silver bracelets on. No point in taking any chances." He certainly wasn't.

She went silent and paled even more. "You think he'll come here?"

"No, but you can't be too careful, and on the off chance he were to inveigle someone into admitting him, we need to be protected." He'd made darn sure Laura had them on wrists, ankles and neck. That slender chain had protected her before, but he was taking no risks. Nothing was going to happen to her. "Good thing Elizabeth thought to bring them."

"After her encounter with Laran, she's hardly likely to omit that protection."

True. "And after that ordeal, here we are asking her to do a repeat performance. Hardly seems fair."

"Nothing is 'fair' when dealing with monsters," Adela replied. "We all do what we can. Elizabeth will too. Not just to protect Laura's father from Piet's fate, but she owes Vlad. If he hadn't found her and Heather . . ." She gave a shudder. "Best not think about that."

The possibilities that didn't bear thinking about were mounting. Once Adela went up the wide staircase, Toby headed for the basement. Etienne wouldn't be in deep day sleep yet, and Toby Wise wanted a chat with him.

"The other one?" Larouselière lay, unmoving; his eyes flickered open at Toby's question and his lips moved. "The vampire Roman sent? Yes, he is without doubt dead. I found ashes and charred bones not far from the house." So Vlad had been right. Not that Toby expected otherwise but one always hoped. "And I found a ring. A heavy cold one and keys. A bundle of them. I brought them back with me."

"Where are they?"

"Perhaps on the desk in your study. I put them there before easing into my cocoon to rest. Who knows now, after those Philistines pillaged the place."

"Pillaged" was a bit strong, but Toby wasn't about to argue semantics.

"Thanks, Etienne. I'll have a look." He stepped back. "See you at sunset. No one will bother you here. You have my word."

"*Bon!* If those policemen of yours had exposed me to the light, I would have been compelled to haunt them."

Did expired vampires haunt? Hell if Toby knew! He'd ask Gwyltha or Justin next time he saw them.

Upstairs, in his seriously disordered and denuded study, Toby found the blackened and heat-twisted keys on his desk. Zeke's ring he found on the floor, kicked to the side by some Fed's big foot.

Rubbing it clean on his shirt, Toby recognized the distinctive heavy gold ring. The evidence confirmed Vlad's belief. Zeke was extinguished. Sadness washed over Toby's mind and soul. He'd only known the vampire a few days. He'd irritated Toby with his brash talk and swagger, but the thought he was no more, that there was one less vampire among their scattered fraternity saddened Toby to the core. Zeke had been the first American-born vampire he'd ever known. The only one so far, come to that. He'd been a compatriot by soil as well as blood need and was now no more.

He took a white envelope from his desk drawer, slipped the ring and keys inside and sealed it before placing it back in the drawer. He'd give it to Vlad when he arrived, but meanwhile he needed to check up on the mess Larouselière had left down the road.

Transmuting into bird form got Toby there fast and let him sit around and watch unobserved from his perch on a branch. Interesting. Hadn't been that long but both the car and the van were gone. Towed away, he presumed. There wasn't a trace of glass or taillight fragments or slivers of metal. Nothing, and two agents were carefully dirtying up a gouge in the stone wall.

Hiding any evidence of the incident seemed the order of the day—or rather night. Erase the inexplicable from the record. Not that Toby would complain. If they'd just forget he and Connor Inc. existed he'd be chuffed to the high heavens.

But this was interesting. Very, in fact. And he bet poor old Larouselière's cocoon—as he called it—was right now under intense scrutiny. If it kept them busy, that was great. But if it brought the Feds back down on the household, it was a proper pig's ear.

Now if he could just find somewhere to sic the FBI onto Axel . . . Not a good idea. If the foul creature could annihilate a vampire, the poor old Feds didn't stand a chance.

What a handicap it must be to be mortal!

Elizabeth gazed at the screen. Almost done. Amazing how much you could do online. She had a handicapped-equipped van coming after breakfast, a suite for her father and rooms for the nurses reserved in a resort near Florence, and had left a message with the nursing agency voice mail. She'd already spoken to Nurse Redding, who'd agreed to come in and cover nights. (As if anyone would turn down a few nights, all expenses paid, at a very nice resort.) And Elizabeth counted on the agency to contact a second nurse. It was the best option: Dad would be out of the house and undisturbed by any activity and with him would go the nurses.

No more need to skulk around the house hiding vampires.

What she really wanted was to go there with him. She saw so little of him because she was so far away, it was hard to move him out when she was in the house. But she had to stay. Stay and try to vanquish a second Laran.

That thought gave her shudders. Vanquishing Laran had drained her for weeks. Plus she had had the full power of the Totnes Coven joined with hers, to say nothing of Gwyltha's incredible strength. Okay, Gwyltha had never admitted to helping, just neatly avoided all Elizabeth's hints and cues. A direct question might have worked, but how do you look a two thousand (or more)—year-old vampire in the face—a vampire who claims to eschew all magic and witchcraft—and ask point-blank if they summoned the power of the moon?

A bit late now. Gwyltha was on the other side of the big Pond, but Adela was here. Adela who'd first noticed and then nurtured Elizabeth's growing powers. Together—with the coming horde of vamps—they'd have to do the job. Besides, the full moon was two weeks away. They couldn't wait.

It was a darn good thing Dad would be away. She had this sneaking fear, after talking to Laura, that Axel would come up to the house and create mayhem. Deep in her memory lurked the horrors of Laran's mind rape. She would not ever stand by and let another living creature suffer that horror. She had to summon whatever strength and power she could to destroy him.

Seemed Laura's father was in it up to his ears, an acolyte, impressed or otherwise, of Axel. She felt for her worry and uncertainty, remembering her own hurt as Dad drew away from her into Laran's power and influence. If there was anything she could do to save Granger Fox from her own father's sad end, damn, she'd pull out the stops and do it.

And no doubt she'd have Toby's full support. Elizabeth smiled, remembering Toby's insistence that Laura drape herself in silver chains. Yes, no doubt about it, the aloof Brit was smitten.

Good for him.

And good for Laura; she seemed a sensible, intelligent woman. What Gwyltha, as colony leader, would say about bringing a mortal into all this was another matter entirely, but they could worry about that once Axel was disposed of.

Chapter 21

Someone, something, had intruded while Axel slept. Intruded and disturbed the trespassing vampire's pyre. Axel snarled to the heavens. Who was daring to invade his property, his domain? Granger's pathetic mortal offspring? No, she was too scared to come to the house. Sneaky little phone calls and visits to the newspaper office were about all she dared anymore and, with a bit of luck, after last time, he'd put paid to that. Odd about the silver, though. Without that he really could have terrified her delightfully. Still, these irritating coincidences happened. And coincidence it had to be. If, by an impossible chance, she did suspect his nature, how could she know what silver did to him?

No, it was pure chance. That he could brush off. An invasion of his territory he would not. First the inquisitive vampire and now . . . he sniffed the air and ground around the pyre, following the trail a hundred meters or so until he lost it. The fucking intruder smelled like vampire but apparently could fly.

This was a declaration of war but he, Axel Radcliffe, had survived other battles. He'd be the victor in this one too. But who the stinking hell was daring to invade his territory? Too much had happened in the past few days: his pet's murder, the first invading vampire, the disappearance of the witch from the city jail—after she'd oddly escaped the burning he'd set up—and now a second vampire spy. Why? And where did it all stem from?

It had all started when he had Granger pressure his whiny daughter to comply. Interesting. Was there more to the bitch than he'd imagined?

If that was the case, he was taking care of it right now. Striding back into the house, he found Granger wobbling against the kitchen countertop, attempting to pour a glass of milk. The puny mortal's wrist shook so much he'd spilled more than he had in the glass.

"Time to go!" Axel told him, taking the jug of milk from his hand. "I need to have a little conversation with your useless daughter, and you are inviting me into her house."

"No!" Granger wobbled his head from side to side like one of those bobble-head dolls.

Axel smiled at his pathetic attempt at defiance. "Yes, you are, Granger. If you don't want to see your precious daughter a bloody mess on her carpet, you are going to do exactly what I tell you." That Laura would most likely end up dead either way was a moot point.

As he drove down the lane and onto the main road toward Florence, Axel looked at the passing trees and the woods on either side. A beautiful place to live, and he had no intention of leaving until it suited him. A pity Granger wouldn't last much longer, but just as well. He was getting to be a proper pain but he'd served his purpose: He and his tatty little newspaper had provided a convenient alibi to lurk around and suss out what the frigging hell had happened to his brother vampire and his money. Five, almost six, months was quite long enough to wait. Granger's useless daughter was going to give him access to the house and he'd do the job himself.

"She won't do it," Granger muttered. "She's a good girl."

Axel refused to dignify that comment with a reply. He had no doubts Laura would do whatever he demanded and admit him wherever he chose, if the alternative was to see her father's head ripped off his body before her eyes. Instincts told him Laura knew more than she shared about the house at Devil's Elbow. Question was: Was there any connection between Laura and these pesky vampire spies? Unlikely. What vampire, even a puny one, would waste effort on the whiny, scared Laura Fox? No, they were a separate and incidental problem. One to deal with when his mission was accomplished.

Soon.

Let Granger fret and worry. The anxiety emanating from the man was sweet and powerful. Just what Axel needed to sustain him while they waited for Laura to return from work.

Damn good thing he hadn't relied on Granger to drive. The man was unconscious by the time Axel pulled into the drive beside Laura's miserable little rented duplex. He was going to have to find alternative fodder very soon. The man was on his last legs: his breathing shallow and weak and skin as rosy and blooming as a corpse. Shit! He had to live another day or so. With Granger dead, he'd have no leverage over Laura. Damn the bitch for not being where she should be. Right now, one glance at her precious father and he'd have her eating out of his hand, or rather, offering her veins.

He'd handled this all wrong, should have compelled Laura to him and ignored Granger's pathetic paternal sensibilities.

"Hello! You looking for Laura?"

He was losing his touch if a mortal could creep up on him like that. "Yes." He added a smile for the young woman's benefit as he contemplated how best to use her. "I've got her father in the car." He angled his head toward Granger's slumped form and rather enjoyed the shock in her gray eyes. "I wanted to let her know I'm taking him to the doctor."

"He does look bad," she replied, a furrow between her brows. Odd how mortals showed their emotions so. "You're trying to get hold of her, aren't you?"

Obviously! "Isn't she usually home by now?"

"Yeah." She nodded. "She won't be back this morning, though."

"Oh?" Why the hell not?

"She called me ten minutes ago. That's why I'm over here. I live next door." She indicated the other half of the wretched little building. "She asked me to feed her cat, as she's staying and working a double shift. I told her she needs to watch that. She'll wear herself out, but she said there was a bit of a crisis there and they needed her." She gave a shrug and smiled. "Can't say I blame her. It's all money, isn't it?"

It was all annoyance and frustration!

Still, he was vampire and not to be deflected by mortal plans. "Never mind. If she calls again, or you see her, do please tell her that Axel Radcliffe came by and is taking her father to the doctor." That should get the wind up her nicely.

"Oh, I will. I promise. Do you have her cell phone number?"

She was leaning so close, her fingers resting on the edge of the window. It was a temptation to grab her wrist and bite down. Her blood would be warm and rich, a welcome change from Granger's, but . . . "Yes. I'll call her. I just hoped to see her first."

She nodded, her short curls bouncing around her young and healthy face. "I understand. You do hate to make phone calls that cause worry, don't you?"

Not in the slightest. "Just tell her when you get the chance. Okay?"

He drove off, the woman's oh-so-sincere promises and wishes for Granger's good health accompanying them down the road.

What now?

What now was Granger really did look about to snuff it. That could not be permitted. He pulled into the parking lot of an office building with a prominent FOR RENT sign planted in the front weeds. Perfect. All he needed was a few undisturbed minutes. Wrapping his arm around Granger's skinny shoulders, Axel pulled him to him. Holding him steady, Axel ripped his own wrist open with his fangs and held it to Granger's mouth. "Drink!" Axel ignored the mumbled protests and feeble efforts to break from his grip. "Drink, you bastard," Axel hissed in his ear. "It's more than you deserve, but I need you well and coherent, at least for a few more hours. Swallow, you worm!"

When Granger persisted in his futile attempt at resistance, Axel clamped his fingers on the dratted mortal's nose. As he gasped for air, Axel forced his wrist into his mouth, jamming his jaw open. The man had no option but swallow. After a few minutes, the change was quite gratifying. And the look of total and utter disgust on his face was almost worth the sharing of blood.

"Dear God in heaven!" As if the puny mortal's God was likely to intervene. "What did you make me do, now?"

Axel seldom laughed, but sometimes one was so

entitled to. He snickered. "Shocked, Granger? Horrified? Disgusted? Now, where is your gratitude?"

"Gratitude?" he croaked, his face twisting in an amusing grimace. "You forced me to take your blood!"

Axel shook his head. The ungrateful creature had no appreciation of the favor he'd just received. "And despite your disgust, you enjoyed it, didn't you? Admit it, Granger, you've got a stiffie in your pants." He'd swear the mortal had tears in his eyes. "Oh, Granger. You may not appreciate it, but I did you a big favor. I saved you from kicking the bucket. You should be thanking me." The ungrateful mortal had no understanding of the honor just bestowed on him.

But he would, if Axel permitted him to live that long.

Laura reached out for the cell phone that was insistently chiming "Big Ben." Might as well answer it. Elizabeth was overseeing the packing and loading necessary to take Mr. Connor away for a few days. Adela was sitting with him to keep him calm and Toby, after a quick call to Connor Inc. to make sure the FBI wasn't visiting there yet again, was off to Dark Falls to reconnoiter and, she suspected, to have a look-see around her father's house.

Etienne was sleeping the sleep of the nocturnal undead, so it was left to her to press the little green button.

"Adam, Mr. Roman's assistant, here. Is Wise there?"

"Er . . . not right now. I can give him a message."

"We'll be landing in Eugene in about thirty minutes. We'll need picking up. See him then." And he hung up.

Great! Vampires were definitely better at telling than asking. She'd sort of noticed that before. She could hardly ask Elizabeth to interrupt her preparations, and who knew when Toby would be back.

And the Hummer was still parked outside. All she had to do was find the keys and grab her purse.

"You're going to get them?" Elizabeth asked when queried as to the possible whereabouts of the keys.

"Who else? You're busy. So is Adela. I just hope I recognize them. I've never seen any of them."

"You'll know them on sight. They're vampires. They'll be arrogant, opinionated, think they run the world and have that characteristic pale skin tone."

"Unless they recently snacked on the flight attendants!" And just in case, she'd better carry some blood. She certainly wasn't offering her neck to them.

"Just a minute." Adela stood in the doorway of Mr. Connor's room. She came forward. "You're not sending Laura to meet Vlad and his bunch, surely?"

"It's okay," Laura replied. "Someone has to go, and Toby's not back yet."

"I'll go," Adela said. "Laura can sit with Piet. Better I pick them up. Apart from anything else, I've met Vlad before. First impressions can be a bit unnerving."

She wasn't that helpless, or fragile. "I'll do fine. You're busy here."

"No." Elizabeth shook her head. "Adela's right. Let her go, Laura. You wait here for Toby and hold the fort. He should be back any minute."

"Your daughter is inconveniencing me!" Axel snarled, including Granger and the universe in general in his ire. He grabbed Granger by the neck. "You are going to call her at work and get her to invite us both into that house."

"No, I won't." It came out squeaky and faint. He'd noticed that before when he had Granger by the throat. "I won't let you hurt her!" he gasped out.

Such paternal concern was almost touching. Almost, but not quite. "You will." The man made a futile effort to push Axel's hands away. After watching the mortal's face turn an interesting shade—funny how mortals tended to do that—Axel released him and smiled as he gasped and sputtered for air. Better not strangle him right after resuscitating. "She's going to invite me in, because you will tell her to, Granger."

"No!" he growled out. "You're not getting your hands on her!"

"I'll put my hands and my fangs wherever I choose. It's up to you to persuade her and save me the trouble of coercion, but one way or another she's inviting me into that house." Something he should have done months back. He hoped it wasn't too late. Trouble was, in the past week, affairs at Dark Falls and the damn trespasser had distracted him from his purpose. He'd let details and mortals interfere with his appointed mission.

A mistake he would not make again.

"Call her!"

They were waiting by the entrance to the Eugene airport's one and only luggage carousel. Vlad was unmistakable. How no one recognized him for what he was never ceased to amaze Adela. But maybe that was just as well. She smiled, imagining the consternation on the faces of the happy tourists, if they had even a shimmer of a suspicion that a medieval warlord and his minions stood waiting by a handcart laden with boxes and packing cases.

"My dear Mrs. Whyte." Vlad all but bowed as she approached him. "I hope you are well."

"Thanks to Toby Wise, I am well and safe, but things aren't well."

"No, and my Zeke is destroyed. I come for vengeance, Mrs. Whyte."

The smile belied his tone. She got both messages. "I can't tell you how glad we all are you're here. Toby's good, but I don't think he can handle this alone."

"He no longer has to. I come prepared with two of my finest warriors. This is Adam." He indicated the Hispanic-looking vampire. "And Wilson." Wilson was as dark as Zeke but had a hard, almost scary look in his eyes. "They are my most valued warriors."

By the looks of them, "valued" was a synonym for "ruthless" and "badass." Warriors was as good a description as any. "This your vehicle?" Adam asked. "Okay if we load it up?"

"Please do."

As they hauled up several large boxes and what looked like a rolled-up carpet, or a tent in a heavy nylon bag, Vlad asked, "You are in Mr. Wise's confidence?"

It wasn't really a question. "You might say I dragged him into this. It's a long story. Let's load up and I'll fill you in." She held open the passenger door. Vlad got in with one graceful movement and enthroned himself in the passenger seat, like a general at the head of his army. Not hard to believe he'd once been an autocrat and led armies against the invading Turks.

The other two seated themselves in the back, after stowing the luggage. As she drove off, she noticed none of them wore seat belts. She bit back the reminder of Oregon traffic laws. Being a traffic fatality wasn't a concern for this lot.

"Tell me what's happened," Vlad said. His voice was low and steady but it came out like an order.

Adela changed gear, steered out onto the road, and took a deep breath. "Okay." She told him everything, starting with the chupacabra and events in Dark Falls, touching on Toby's complications with the FBI and ending with Etienne's little adventure last night. The only thing she omitted was Toby's attachment to Laura. The narrative took them halfway to 101.

"You have my Zeke's ring?"

"It's in the house. Toby will give it to you."

He nodded. The silence that followed felt like prayer—if vamps prayed, that was. But why shouldn't they, if they'd prayed as mortals? She'd ask Toby about that. The ones in the back hadn't said a word and didn't until Vlad asked, "Well, Adam and Wilson, what now? This creature, this rogue revenant, this interloper, attacks innocents, commits crimes, uses his power against others and extinguished Zeke. What does he deserve?"

"We surround the house where he lurks, where he destroyed Zeke, and fire it and watch it burn to the . . ."

"No, you won't!" Adela snapped at Wilson, turning to yell at him, then having to look back and right the Hummer before it left the road. "You will not!" She went on, keeping her eyes on the road. "There is a damn good chance Laura's father will be in there with Axel. You're not incinerating him! He's not done you any harm. He's as much Axel's victim as Zeke. Besides, don't you want Axel alive? What use is he to you as a pile of ash?" Her throat tightened, remembering that had been Zeke's end.

Someone in the back, Adam or Wilson, she had no idea who, muttered. "Well, I'll—" but was cut off by a brisk movement from Vlad.

"I want this animal alive if possible, yes. But dead will be acceptable as an alternative to escape."

"You'll get a lot more information out of him alive." Or whatever the nearest vamp equivalent was.

"Indeed we would," Vlad agreed, "but tell me, how does this connection between Axel, the newspaper and this Nurse Fox come to be so significant?"

Trust him to seize on the one detail that wasn't hers to share. "Better get that from Toby."

"Ah!" Amazing how much meaning he packed into one syllable. "She is significant, then?"

Unless Adela was totally misreading every single detail. She slowed going through a tunnel, as she emerged the other side, Vlad was still waiting for a reply. "We should be there soon."

"Your discretion does you honor, Mrs. Whyte. But I admit to curiosity. The ways of Gwyltha's colony always interest me."

She bet they did! Very different from his own, by all Adela had picked up in the past few months. "Elizabeth should be back by early afternoon. She offers her abilities, and I will add mine." Obvious subject change, but what the hell did Vlad expect? For her to blab all about Toby and Laura? To what end?

"Then we have an army: two witches of power and courage, Larouselière's vast knowledge and my henchmen." Odd word but it rather fit the silent duo in the backseat. "We shall best this troublemaker."

"Don't forget Toby. Or Laura. She's got more reason to want Axel gone than any of you."

He acknowledged that with a curt nod. "True, but with the best will in the world, what can a mere mortal do against this monster?"

Not an awful lot, except . . . "She can invite you into their house. I doubt her father would be inclined to extend the necessary invitation."

"You think we should take the battle to him?"

Hell if she knew. "It's a possibility. I doubt Axel will come out at an invitation."

Vlad nodded. "There is still too much I do not know. Once I meet with Wise and Larouselière, we can make our plans."

Adela was about to add something about including Lizzie, Laura and herself in those plans when her cell phone chirped.

Chapter 22

Toby put his face to the wind, spread his wings and headed south. Those FBI sorts would curl their hair if they saw him now, flying down the coast on eagle's wings. Darn good thing they couldn't. With a bit of luck they were still busy pretending last night never happened, while cudgeling their narrow minds over what caused a big hole in the back of the van and a seemingly sealed packing case. They'd certainly been too busy to drop in on Connor Inc. again.

He hoped to Abel that Vlad turned up darn soon and they sorted out this second Radcliffe fast. There was only so long a company could be neglected. Dealing with a vicious and predatory vampire was definitely making the world safer for mortals and ensuring the security of Connor Inc. and its employees, but it wasn't the sort of activity one listed on one's daily planner.

But Axel Radcliffe, Larouselière and Vlad aside, life was pretty damn good. He had Laura and, by Abel, he was keeping her. How, was a bit of a poser, but he would. Gwyltha, as leader of the colony, would no doubt throw all sorts of wobblies at admitting a mortal into the colony, but if push came to shove, he'd ask Vlad for asylum. He was keeping Laura.

Of course, he had to ask her first, but so far she'd given every indication that she didn't find him totally repulsive, and a vampire lived on hope.

By Abel! If eagles had smile muscles, he'd be grinning like a fool in love. As it was, he banked, as the outskirts of Dark Falls came into sight. Staying aloft and taking full advantage of his eagle sight, Toby scanned the small town. Nothing much going on, so presumably no more decapitated bodies. Just townsfolk going about their activities. Made a nice change after yesterday's frenetic activity. Two cruisers and a green van were parked behind the deputy's office. Toby idly wondered how the replacement deputy had fared over Adela's disappearance. Apparently Axel hadn't wreaked vengeance. Yet. And with a bit of luck he would be neutralized before he got around to it.

Toby circled the town once more before heading southwest. It was much easier in daylight. Following a county road, he crossed a stream and veered off over a narrower road that led to Laura's old house.

No one was at home. Not a single heartbeat under the low pitched roof. Of course that said nothing about the Radcliffe chap's absence or presence. A couple of heavy landings on the roof, and swoops into any window of size were pretty much guaranteed to get attention, but nothing and no one stirred. Toby had his assurance the house was empty, and a bit of a headache from dive-bombing a sliding-glass door harder than intended.

Time to snoop.

Didn't take long to find the heap of ashes and bone that had once been Zeke. The young vampire had irritated Toby, but to think of all that zest, attitude and enthusiasm reduced to a pile of dust was untenable. Radcliffe had to be neutralized. Lizzie had done for the other one. With her help and all the power and gizmos Vlad was supposedly bringing, they couldn't fail. Mustn't.

Toby landed on the grass and, sure he was nicely concealed from view, transmogrified back. Talons had their uses but he needed hands for this. He broke open the lock on the tool shed. There had to be a tarp or canvas inside that he could use to shroud Zeke's remains, and hide them somewhere to retrieve later for burial and proper respect. Leaving him to be blown by the winds offended Toby's sense of right.

He was still poking among the rusted lawn mower (no wonder the darn grass was knee-high) and a jumbled assortment of empty petrol cans, rubbish bags and tools, when he heard a car approaching. Damn! No time to transmogrify. Leaving the shed door wide open, Toby took a leap and flattened himself on the roof. Hiding bare-arsed to the sky was not his idea of fun and the shingles did nothing for sensitive parts of his body but . . . He peered over the roof ridge. A car was making its way up the drive—a deputy's cruiser, no less.

Interesting. He flattened himself even more and listened.

"I just don't get why we have to come out here, Bud," one said. "What's so urgent?"

"Mr. Radcliffe needs a report on how things are proceeding."

"They're not going anywhere! We're no closer to finding who did Sam Johnson in, let alone who left Pete Travers halfway to dead, and we're hardly likely find out up here."

"Yes, I must tell him."

"Honest, Bud. You're as bad as Sam was. Why the

heck does this man matter? And, what's more, how come he needs to be in on every investigation?"

Toby wouldn't mind knowing the answer to that one. Sounded like a vampire-imposed compulsion.

"You don't understand, Lewis. It is important we share everything with him, for the good of Dark Falls."

Lewis responded with something very much like a snort as his shoes scrunched on the gravel path and he rapped on the door a couple times. "Granger!" he called. "You in there?"

Toby already knew the answer to that. It would no doubt take the mortal law enforcement a little longer than him to work things out.

Another rap on the door, then the sound of seldom-oiled hinges as the door opened. "Granger? Mr. Radcliffe?"

Mortals had the edge there—what Toby couldn't have learned about Axel from a good look around inside. And were they lucky the house was empty. These mortals had no idea what they were dealing with, or the potential danger if they roused a resting vampire. Especially one of Axel's disposition.

"Anyone home?" Bud called, stepping inside.

Seemed Lewis followed him. Toby glued himself to the roof, listening.

The first comments were disgust at the standard of housekeeping. Coming from cops who, no doubt, even in as small a town as this, had probably seen just about everything, that was quite a statement.

"Sheesh, look at it!" Lewis said. "Imagine a daughter letting her father live like this."

"Hardly her job to come here and clean."

"She should at least look after him. Downright neglect, this is."

"Hell, two able-bodied men should take care of

themselves, and can't see Radcliffe is her responsibility anyway."

"He saved the newspaper and her father's job. She should respect him."

"Who's to say she doesn't? Laura's okay. Even if she did beat me out of the spelling bee in fourth grade. Hell, she lives up in Florence. She can't come down here and cook and clean for her father."

Quite enough speculation about Laura, as far as Toby was concerned. If there was nothing in the house, they'd best be on their way and leave the coast clear for him to transmogrify and return to Devil's Elbow. And ask Laura what a spelling bee was.

On the other hand, while they were out here on supposedly official business, why not let them see what Axel did in his spare time?

The suggestion was easy to plant, even through roof and rafters. One mind, Bud's it turned out, was easy to penetrate. Obviously had taken vampire suggestion before. Minutes later, he was leading Lewis through the overgrown grass that surrounded the house.

"Sheesh, look at this," Bud said. "Hasn't seen a lawn mower in months."

"You don't think Laura should have come back to mow it?"

"Put a sock in it! Nothing much here. Let's go back."

Not yet, another suggestion, quite a gentle one this time, and Bud was headed for the long grass behind the garage, and . . .

"Christ on crutches!"

"Hey, Bud. What is it?" Lewis found out seconds later. "Shit! That's never an animal, not with those long bones."

"What's Granger been doing?"

"What have either of them been doing? And who the fuck is it? We've not had anyone reported missing."

"Better get the crime scene team up here again. Sheesh, we've had more going on here the past three days than in a week in Portland."

Bud called it in. Lewis produced yellow crime-scene tape and Toby wondered if he hadn't been a bit too clever. Now he was stuck on the roof and in no time at all the place would be as buzzing with law enforcement as Main Street had been yesterday. He had to get out. Vlad would be arriving anytime, and sooner or later someone would notice a naked black man plastered to the roof. He waited until the pair of them was occupied draping yellow plastic tape from garage to tree to rusted washing pole and jumped down the front of the house, ran as fast as a vampire's legs could carry him to the nearest clump of trees and transmogrified. Moments later he was soaring north, back to Devil's Elbow and Laura.

But he couldn't help wondering where exactly Granger and Axel were and what in Abel's name they were doing.

Adela reached for the cell phone on the dash and realized that in her haste, she'd picked up Laura's. It chirped incessantly at her. Was it Toby? No. The little screen clearly read "Dad."

She punched the "on" button. "Just a minute, I'm driving." Her voice sounded nothing like Laura's but . . . There was an overlook ahead. She pulled over as she pressed the "mute" button. Putting a finger to her lips, while she half-wondered what happened to mere mortals who told vampires to keep quiet, she pressed on the speaker phone, glad Laura's phone was so like her own model. "Okay, what's the matter? Dad . . ." she added.

"Laura, where are you?"

She'd fooled him! But for how long? "Driving along 101." Was the man so far gone he really didn't remember his daughter's voice?

"Why aren't you home? I have to see you."

"I'm still at work."

"At Devil's Elbow?"

"Err . . . yes!" She was getting a bad feeling about this.

"The big house, up on the cliff? The one you showed me?" Had Laura? Hell if she knew.

"Why not go back home, Dad? I'll come see you when I get off work." Good thinking that. "Is Axel with you?" Might as well know.

"Yes, I am, Laura." Goddess! The menace in the voice sent shivers down Adela's spine. "I'm here and very disappointed how you let your father down. He needs your help. Right now."

"Wait until I get off work."

"No. We're coming to you. You failed to find what I expected. I'm coming to get it. You and a sick old man won't stop me."

He broke the connection.

She glanced at Vlad. He was actually grinning. "How far to Devil's Elbow?"

"About twenty, twenty-five minutes."

"Drive as fast as you can with safety. Don't let speed limits delay you. If you get stopped, I'll take care of it."

Okay for him. But there was no point in arguing. She handed Vlad the phone. "Try to call Laura and warn her."

* * *

The house was eerily quiet once Elizabeth left with her father. The silence and echoing rooms gave Laura the willies. She should have gone with Adela or Elizabeth; anything was better than listening to her footsteps, the tick of the grandfather clock and the sound of the surf below. Surf! That meant open doors or windows! She ran through the house, checking every window and door, closing every one she found open. Why didn't Toby get back?

She was being ridiculous. Adela would be back anytime now. Toby was no doubt already on his way home. Okay. She'd make herself a cup of mint tea. Settle her nerves and they'd all be back before she even finished it.

She walked into the silent kitchen and plugged in the kettle. She was reaching for the tea bags when she heard a thunder of knocks on the front door. No mortal had that sort of strength, to hit hard enough to be heard back here. Toby! She ran across the hall, wondering why he didn't have his key, and froze with her hand grasping the knob.

She stared at the heavy oak door, knowing in her heart it wasn't Toby. "Who's there?" she asked.

"Laura?"

"Dad?" Had he finally broken away from Axel and come for help?

As the hope rose in her, he said, "Let us in, Laura."

That pronoun told her everything.

Sweat ran down her back as cold clawed at her gut. It wasn't meant to happen like this. They were supposed to attack Axel, with a bunch of uber-vampires. But now . . . Just as she considered running, she knew it was useless.

She put a damp hand back on the knob. "Axel, what do you want?"

"Open the door before I break your father's arm!"

If only she'd activated the security system. Not that

she knew the code, and if she had, she already knew what use it would be against Axel.

Her father's scream cut into her panic.

"Open the door or I break the other one."

A horrified calm settled over her. Why not? She was wearing silver. Axel couldn't hurt her and surely it was only minutes before someone came back. Her hand shook as she slid back the bolt.

"Get a move on, Laura, I'm feeling impatient."

"I've got to get the other bolt."

That open, she turned the deadbolt, grasped the knob with a sweaty hand and flung the door open.

She stepped back, fighting the urge to run to her father, who shook and moaned with pain. How far away did she need to be before Axel sensed the silver on her? The long sleeves of Toby's shirt hid the bracelets from sight and perhaps . . .

"Invite me in!"

She could refuse.

Time seemed to stop as Axel reached for Dad's good arm, grasped his shoulder with his other hand and smiled.

"No! No! Not again!" her father screamed.

Defeat ripped that last hope away. "Come on in."

Axel stepped over the threshold, dragging her father with him. Laura backed away.

"Who's in the house?" Axel snapped. "The old man? Nurses? Wise?"

"Mrs. Kyd took her father away on a vacation. I'm the only nurse here."

"And Wise?"

"He went into the office."

"I hope, for his sake, he stays there." And she hoped he got here pronto.

"Dad?" she said. It was an effort not to rush to him, but her best chance lay in not getting close.

"Your father is . . . not too well. I hope you do nothing to endanger him."

"Why would I?"

"Why indeed? Now, be a good little girl. For your daddy's sake." As he spoke, his fingers tightened and her father jerked in pain. "Don't thwart me."

Where were Vlad and the rest of them? "What do you want?"

"Show me where Piet Connor's study is. What I want is there. Should have come here myself in the first place."

He let go of his hold on her father, who collapsed to the floor. "Laura, help me," he croaked, pushing himself up on his good arm and crying out in pain.

The sound ripped her apart. But she had to keep her distance. Lure Axel away from Dad, wait until he was distracted, then run, taking Dad with her.

Chapter 23

The moment Axel looked at her, she knew it wasn't going to be that easy.

"Show me where it is."

"Down the hall, but there's nothing left. The FBI took all the files, computers, everything."

He stepped toward her and leapt back. "Bitch!" he hissed at her. "Think you're so clever, do you? Take them off!"

"No!" Without her silver she had no protection. "I'll show you where the office is, if you insist, but I'm not stupid enough to take my bracelets off."

"You will."

He moved faster than she could follow. She blinked and he was holding her father up by his hair. Dad cried out as Axel reached for his hand. "No," he whimpered. "Please, no!"

With a particularly nasty smile, Axel took her father's good hand in his. "I'm going to count to ten. If you have one particle of silver on you when I finish, I'll break every finger on this hand, then this arm," he paused, just to let it sink in, no doubt. "One!"

She had no choice. All options were off. Unless a

miracle occurred and Toby or someone miraculously appeared, she and Dad were done for.

"Two!"

She unsnapped the first bracelet on her left wrist.

"Drop it on the floor and kick it over to the wall."

She nodded in acquiescence, carefully unclasping the second one, fumbling with the clasp as a wild hope sparked inside her. It was insane but since she and Dad were as good as vamp fodder anyway . . . She closed her right hand over both bracelets and let one drop to the ground, hiding the other in her fist. She made a show of kicking the other way across the room.

"Three!"

"Okay, I'm taking them off!"

She fumbled with the bangle on her right wrist. Hard to do with one finger and a thumb as she concealed the rest in her clenched fist, but she managed, shaking her wrist to let the bangle drop and bounce on the floor.

Axel jumped back, taking Dad with him.

"Four, five, for that little trick!"

"It was a mistake. I never thought it would roll that way!" She stepped forward and kicked it aside. She had one in her hand, and the heaviest, but would it be any use?

"Six!" Axel snapped in reply. "How many more do you have?"

"One on each ankle." And the necklace under her shirt. Not that she could hide it. Axel would sense it if she kept any on. Perhaps her smart-ass idea wasn't so bright after all.

"Get them off! Seven!"

Shit! Her heart raced. Her hands were so sweaty, she had a hard time undoing the anklets but managed, just as Axel said, "Eight!"

"Give me a break! Stop counting a minute and let me see how Dad is, okay?"

"No! You know how he is: in grave danger of losing use of his fingers for good if you delay. Nine!"

"Let me get the necklace off. It's hard to do, when I can't see."

"Nine and a half!"

This was it. She reached inside the neck of Toby's turtleneck, holding back the sob at the thought that if this didn't work, she'd never see him again, and pulled out the heavy chain of zigzag links and pulled it off her neck. Balling that and the chain tight in her hand, she ran toward Axel.

"Ten!" he shouted, as her father screamed and Laura slammed into Axel and shoved the balled-up chains into his open mouth.

Dad's scream was lost in the howl of pain, fury and agony, as Axel reared backward. She grabbed her father and dragged him away from where Axel rolled on the slate floor, writhing in agony as wisps of steam rose from his screaming mouth.

The front door was still open. Her father wailed and cried. She had to get away, get Dad away. She had him out the front door, and his little Honda sat with both doors open, the keys dangling in the ignition.

Ignoring her father's cries and wails, she opened the back door and somehow manhandled him onto the backseat. He screamed as he moved his broken arm. "Sorry, Dad, but this is our only chance."

The screams from the house now rose in one endless cry of agony. Anyone else, she'd have spared a smidgen of pity for. Then came the sound of a crash and a jangle of bells. She didn't have time to worry about the Connors' antique clock. She pushed Dad's feet into the car,

slammed the door, ran around and closed the passenger
door, and leaped into the driver's seat. She started the
engine as Axel staggered to the doorway, emitting one
long howl of pain as smoke poured from his mouth and
his face twisted as if melting. It was the last sight in her
rearview mirror as she did a racing U-turn and sped
down the drive.

Once on the road, she put her foot down, as much as to
put space between them and the horror behind as to
hasten her trip to the nearest emergency room in Florence. She passed cars and trucks, while her father
groaned in the backseat.

Wasn't until she felt Dad hit the back of her seat that
she slowed, just a wee bit. No point in getting them both
killed. Dad wouldn't die from a few broken bones and
she might as well think up a tale to tell the hospital. "I
just rescued him from a violent vampire" might get odd
looks. "Hold on, Dad," she said. "You'll be okay!"

"See that?" Adela asked Vlad. "The car that just
passed us?"

Her passenger raised a dark eyebrow, seemingly little
interested in other traffic on the road.

"It is important?"

"Looked a bit like Laura driving," she replied. "Might
not have been, and it was going fast, but . . ."

"It appeared to be in a great hurry."

"She didn't answer the phone, did she?" Could be a
perfectly good reason for that. She was outside and
didn't hear. In the basement checking on Etienne and
didn't hear. Or driving pell-mell away from the house.
Adela slowed a little.

"No, Mrs. Whyte, hasten! If there is trouble there,

best we arrive as fast as possible." He turned to his warriors. "Prepare what we have."

Having them clambering over the backseat did nothing for her concentration, but Vlad had a point. Even if that had been Laura, their best course was to find out what had sent her racing down the road.

While Vlad's two sidekicks opened boxes and rattled something that sounded like chains, Adela drove on.

They were close, just past the entrance to the state park, another bend or two, and she slowed to turn up the drive.

She couldn't miss the marks in the drive where a car had very recently taken a racing turn on to the road. "I think that was Laura," she told Vlad.

"Let us proceed."

Damn, the man was cold-blooded. Right, perhaps, but what about Laura? What if Axel had been in the car with her, forcing her somewhere?

She heard the scream even before the house came into view. "What is that?" she asked. The sound was unearthly, animal, inhuman, hideous.

Vlad chuckled. She wished he'd share the joke.

"Something up, sir?" one of them in the back asked.

"So it would seem."

Before she'd even stopped the Hummer, all three were out of the car, Adam carrying what looked like a silver blanket, and leaving all the doors wide open. While she pulled on the brake and killed the engine, the screams rose to a crescendo that made her blood curdle, and then stopped.

The silence was almost worse.

"Have no fear, dear Mrs. Whyte." Vlad appeared in the doorway, a rather twisted smile on his face. "My warriors are checking the house, and I would be obliged if you could do me yet another favor."

"Maybe, Vlad." She jumped down and held back the smile. That wasn't a response he was accustomed to. "Tell me what's going on. Anyone hurt?"

Those hadn't been screams of pleasure.

"It would seem," he replied, "that someone attacked before us."

Dear goddess, no! What had happened to Laura? Damn! Why had she left her behind? "Laura?" she asked, running toward the open door. "Is she hurt?" Dead given the silence, and why wasn't Toby back?

An eagle swooped past her and into the house, and just moments later . . . "What the hell is going on, and where's Laura?"

Toby was back. Wobbly after transmogrifying that fast, but it didn't seem to be slowing him down one iota.

Nothing quite as impressive as a naked, irate Toby. Even Adam and Wilson were silent.

"My friend," Vlad began, "do not be so alarmed."

"And why the hell not?" Toby lashed back. "I come back to find Laura gone, her silver bracelets strewn over the floor and this monster"—he punctuated his tirade with a well-aimed kick to said monster's ribs—"here instead." He bent down, hauling Axel up by the silver mesh that enveloped him like a shroud. Maybe it was. "Tell me where she is, you excrement, or I will rip off your balls and cock one by one and shove them through your eyeballs into your demented, twisted brain."

Adela couldn't help noticing the collective wince that rippled over every male still standing.

"My friend"—Vlad finally got his attention by moving at vamp speed to stand on the other side of

Axel—"I sympathize with your anxiety but I fear our prisoner is perhaps unable to reply."

"What the hell are you blithering about, Vlad?"

Vlad cast his two minions a warning glance as they both moved, presumably to knock a little courtesy into Toby. An imperious wave of Vlad's hand had them both stepping back. "Wise," Vlad said, "look at him. I doubt he can do much but scream with that mouth."

At that Adela had to look. "He's right, Toby."

Axel's lower jaw was twisted and misshapen. Screaming must have been quite an accomplishment. Or an indication of the extent of his agony. "What happened to him?" Adela asked. "I've seen him before but he didn't look like that."

Toby dropped the inert body and shoved it away from him with a kick. "Good question. What the frigging hell happened to him?"

"We had better find out," Vlad replied.

"You can find out," Toby replied. "I'm looking for Laura."

He raced through the house. Adela gave up trying to follow at his speed, but she saw enough to notice that the other rooms appeared untouched. Only the wide entry hall looked as though the Cyclops and the Furies had been playing touch football.

Toby returned in minutes, looking more anguished than ever, but he'd paused at some point to put on pants. Good thing too. Not that he wasn't a fine sight to behold. But now was not the time to ogle a fine-looking man. Especially one so obviously claimed by another woman.

"What's going on?" Toby asked, striding across the slate floor.

"We are examining him and . . ." Vlad said. "Look."

Adam had Axel pinned down with a silver rod across

his neck. The vampire was obviously in pain, but no one seemed too concerned about that. Vlad, who appeared to be wearing gloves of what looked like fine silver mesh, pried open the vampire's jaws and shook his head to the side. Reaching in with what looked like a large crochet hook, he pulled out a balled-up length of chain and held it up for Toby's inspection.

Toby reached out and took the chain, holding it up by one end as it unraveled and hung down. A smaller chain fell from it and landed on the floor. Adela picked that up.

"I think it's one Lizzie brought with her," she said. "It's almost the twin of mine."

"It was Laura's," Toby replied. "The last time I saw it, it was around her neck.

"You bastard, you shameless perversion of Father Abel's creation, what the hell have you done to Laura?" As he shouted, he landed a series of kicks to every part of Axel that presented itself. "I wish to Abel I'd put boots on!" he finished as Axel rolled over from a particularly vicious kick.

"Peace, my friend," Vlad said, holding on to Toby's arm with a grip that was just about strong enough to calm him.

"Vlad," Toby replied, his voice tight with grief and anger, "I'll have peace when this filth fries and not before—after what he did to Laura!"

"I believe you are mistaken, my friend. I do not think it is what this mistake of a vampire has done to your Laura, but rather what she has done to him."

"What the Hades are you talking about?"

"Consider, my dear Toby, how do you think that chain came to be in that creature's mouth?"

"He bit her?"

Vlad shook his head. "He bit her with silver on? No, I think not."

"Then what the Hades do you think happened?"

"Possibly—just a conjecture, you understand—she forced it in his mouth?"

"And how did she do that? He's stronger, faster, vicious."

"How, I do not know, but I believe that is what happened. Perhaps he was distracted. However she accomplished it, I sincerely hope she will share the technique with us. Seems like a trick my warriors might find handy one day."

Toby stared at Vlad, mouth open, eyes wide as he absorbed the meaning in Vlad's words. "You think Laura did this to him?"

Vlad shrugged. "Merely a supposition, you understand."

"If she did, where the hell is she?" He was steaming up to panicky again.

"I've been trying to tell you lot," Adela said. "I think we passed her going the opposite direction on our way here. She was driving a red Honda, not her car but . . ."

"Her car is white but if she was fleeing, terrified for her life, she'd have grabbed the closest vehicle. I'm going after her!" Toby raced for the open door. Vlad was even faster, blocking the way. "A moment, my friend. We do not know where she went, and perhaps a pair of shoes and a shirt might draw less attention."

"Alright!"

He was gone in a flash. Adela saw the blur and felt a gust of air as Toby raced upstairs and reappeared almost immediately, dressed this time and with keys in his hand.

"Which way was she going, Adela? South?"

She nodded. "Maybe going to her house?"

"I'll try there first. No, I'll call her cell phone."

"No use. I have it. Picked it up by mistake this morning

but . . . wait a minute." Where were her brains? "I got a call on it. It was her father. He and Axel were on their way here."

"So"—Toby pondered a minute—"she was here. Axel and her father presumably arrived, Axel is still here, her father isn't. He has to be with her."

"And unfortunately we do know how far her father is under Axel's compulsion."

Thanks, Vlad! Get Toby steamed up again, just when he was calming enough to think straight. "Or could be her father is hurt. Or she's hurt," Adela suggested.

That didn't seem to reassure much. "If she was well enough to drive"—Toby shook his head—"she walked or rather ran away from this." He spat at Axel. "She can't be too injured, praise Abel! All I have to do is find her. Adela, what's your cell phone number? Maybe she has yours."

She didn't. Adela's phone jingled from the kitchen.

"Damn! Bet she doesn't have a phone with her. Double damn. Look, Adela, you stay here. I'm going looking for her. Call Elizabeth and tell her what's happened. Call . . ." He shook his head, seemingly unable to think of anyone else to call. "Call me if anything new happens or you hear from Laura."

"I will."

He barely nodded as he darted out the door. Adela looked around at the mess as the sound of Toby's Jaguar faded down the drive.

"Okay." She raised her eyebrows at Vlad. "Want to move that specimen so I can start tidying up? Oh, and anyone need a snack? I know where Toby keeps his blood bags."

Chapter 24

This might not have been the best idea of her career. Laura reached the hospital without ID, driver's license or even a dollar bill. At least Dad had his wallet in his hip pocket. So they had his ID and insurance cards, and she forgave herself for filching a five-dollar bill. She needed coffee.

The rate things were going, they'd be needing lunch and dinner as well.

Once they checked Dad and decided his injuries weren't life-threatening, they clapped a temporary cast on his arm and left him to wait. The arrival of victims from a multicar accident delayed things even longer.

Fair enough Dad wasn't likely to die from broken bones, but listening to him sob softly ripped her apart.

"Why, Laura?" Dad muttered at intervals. "Why? Where's Axel?"

She'd like the answer to that one. Every time the outside door opened, she looked up, dreading the appearance of Axel, bent on revenge. They'd left him writhing on the floor, but Laura suspected she'd only won them time. Every minute they sat here increased the chance he'd follow. She should have gone on to Eugene, but Florence was closer, and closer seemed better.

Now she doubted.

She had to find Toby. Delving in Dad's pocket, she found a handful of change and went in search of a pay phone, but she'd gone only a few meters before her father called out, "Don't leave me, Laura!" She couldn't ignore his plea, so she sat back down, holding his unbroken hand.

When they finally moved him, he begged her to go with him. She couldn't refuse, not when he clutched her hand and kept up his whimpering.

"Oh! Laura? I saw the name 'Fox' but never connected it with you." It was Jane Wallace, one of her nursing school contemporaries.

"Jane, it's Dad." Jane hadn't been a particularly close friend, but any familiar face was welcome. "He's hurt. Look, I need to make a call. Can I leave him in your hands a minute?"

"Of course you can. I'll get him ready for the doctor. See you back here in a minute."

Dad still didn't look happy. "Look, Dad, I knew Jane in nursing school. She's a great nurse. You'll be safe with her. I'll be back as soon as I make a phone call."

She almost ran. She found a pay phone, shoved in the coins with a shaking hand and prayed someone other than Axel was there to pick up.

It wasn't Axel, but an unfamiliar voice answered with, "Connor residence."

"Is Toby there, Toby Wise?"

"No, madam. Could I give him a message?"

"Where is he? I must speak to him."

"Would this be Miss Fox?"

It would! "Yes! Who is this?"

"I'm Adam, one of Mr. Roman's assistants. I'll fetch Mr. Roman."

That meant Vlad. While she paced as far as the short metallic cord permitted, Adela came on the line. "Laura!"

"Adela!" She almost cried with relief. "Where's Toby? Is he okay?"

"Apart from going insane with worry over you, yes. Where are you?"

"Florence Hospital. In the ER."

"Sweet goddess! Are you badly hurt?"

"I'm fine." Using the term loosely. "I'm here because of Dad. Axel broke his arm and some of his fingers. I've been waiting for ages for someone to see him. He's back there right now." She paused to catch her breath and steady herself as the walls swayed around her. "What happened at the house?"

"We were hoping you'd tell us. We came into chaos and a severely wounded vampire rolling around on the floor."

"Axel!"

"Yes, dear."

"I've been scared he'd get up and follow us."

"My dear, Axel isn't going anywhere under his own steam for a very long time. Vlad and his crew have him trussed up like a chicken."

Now she did have to grip the edge of the phone booth for support. All that worry and she and Dad were safe. "You don't know how glad I am to hear that."

"And you don't know how curious everyone is to know how he got in that state. There's been some consternation here. Toby will be vastly relieved to find you safe. He's half out of his mind, picturing you dead, mangled or dismembered. Look here, dear, let me hang up and call him, or better still you call him."

"I came out without my cell. I'm using a pay phone."

"I'll tell him where you are."

"Ms. Fox, the doctor needs to speak to you." Laura turned. It was a nurse. At last Dad was with a doctor!

"I have to go, Adela. Call him and tell him where I am. Please."

"Of course. If I know Toby Wise he'll fly there!"

Laura smiled, knowing Adela wasn't joking.

As she turned after hanging up, the nurse wasn't smiling. "Dr. Hayes needs to speak to you."

"How's Dad? I hated to leave him but I had to call a friend I knew would be worried."

"Your father is up in X-ray."

"I must go up and see him. He's scared and nervous." He didn't know Axel was never coming after them.

"Later, Ms. Fox, after the doctor sees you."

Her attitude rather got up Laura's nose. But the sooner she dealt with this, the sooner she'd be with Dad. And Toby was on his way. She let out a long sigh of relief as she followed the nurse back through the double doors.

"Ms. Fox?" The doctor was young and worried-looking. "I'm Dr. Hayes."

"I'm Laura Fox." She offered her hand but he kept tight hold on his clipboard. "How's my father?"

"That's what I need to talk about. Please come in here." He indicated a small office to the side.

Laura walked in, followed by the doctor and—she was a bit surprised to see—the grim-looking nurse. Where was Jane? With Dad, she hoped.

"Have a seat."

She shook her head. "Just let me know how he is, okay?"

"Sit down, Ms. Fox."

Against her better judgment, she sat. "Well, Doctor?" She had an edge in her voice, but after all she'd gone through so far this morning, she felt she could be excused.

"Ms. Fox, how exactly did your father receive his injuries?"

Laura's mouth went dry, her throat all but closing tight, as the subtext of his question penetrated her mind. She stared at him through a fog of shock, refusing to even look sideways at the nurse seated by the door. How dare he take this attitude after she'd saved her father—and could never tell.

What wouldn't she give for Toby's support right now. She was going to have to manage without.

"How precisely, I don't know. Maybe he can tell you that. He was in shock when I found him, but all he said was he'd fallen."

"And where did you find him?"

She'd gone over this constantly during the long wait. Nothing she said would sound plausible, so she might as well stick to the incredible truth—or the small part of it that could be aired in public. "Doctor, I'm a nurse. When I first saw Dad, I could see his fingers were broken. They were twisted and crooked. He was a bit vague over what happened. Once I realized his arm was broken too, I brought him right here."

Dr. Hayes sat and said nothing. Waiting for more explanation, explanation she could never give. She realized, in a flash of panic, he'd hoped to use her words to convict her. Elder abuse. Granny bashing. The terms raced through her mind. This on top of everything else today just about finished her off. She stood.

"Dr. Hayes, which way is X-ray? I need to see my father."

"He'll be down in a short while." Please, heaven alone knew what Dad might say. She hoped he had enough sense to keep quiet about Axel.

What now? She couldn't just sit out there and wait while the TV overhead droned on and her mind and emotions roiled. What if they gave Dad painkillers and he told them about Axel? Or worse still, told the whole story? The only consolation she could drag up was that no doubt they'd brush the whole thing off as drug-induced hallucinations.

She pushed open the double swing doors to the waiting area and glanced across to the registration desk. "Toby!"

She probably shrieked. She certainly ran, crossing the space in seconds to be wrapped in Toby's strong arms.

"Laura, I was so worried," he said into her hair as he held her tight. There was no warmth in his chest, and no breath in her hair, but he was strength and comfort and right now, she was in desperate need of both.

"How did you get here?" It seemed too good to be true.

"Adela called me as soon as you called her. I was at your house, trying to find you. All I had to do was get here." He pulled back a little and looked down at her. "When I saw the wreck of the house, I more or less freaked out."

"Toby!" She paused to breathe deeply, hoping it would calm her. It didn't much. "It's been a nightmare. Dad's hurt and I've been terrified Axel will walk in any minute and massacre everyone."

"Axel Radcliffe won't be doing much of anything but answer questions for quite some time, assuming his jaw ever heals properly. What did you do to him?"

"Oh, that!" She gave a very deep sigh. "He made me take off my bracelets and necklace by threatening to hurt Dad. I took them off and dropped a couple but balled the rest up in my fist, then ran at him and rammed them down his throat. Don't quite know how I did it, but you could say it was a desperate last-ditch effort." She was shaking as the horror returned.

"I'm in love with Wonder Woman," Toby said and dropped a kiss on her forehead. "Bloody Wonder Woman."

"I don't feel like Wonder Woman right now. More like Mashed by a Mack Truck Woman." She couldn't stop the shudders gripping her inside.

"Laura." Toby rested his hand on her shoulders and met her eyes as she looked up at him. "We'll take care of things. You have nothing more to worry about."

His words washed calm over her, but she knew the last to be wrong. "Toby, there's another crimp in all this." She told him about the last conversation with Dr. Hayes.

Toby went very still for a few seconds. No mortal ever went that still. Did no one else notice? No, everyone was too caught up in their own pain and worries to notice a lone vampire on a green plastic seat. "Laura, he implied you attacked your father?"

Laura nodded. "I can see why. I was really vague about how he was hurt and how I found him, and the injuries to his arm are horrible. It's all swollen and discolored. I wouldn't have believed my story. But what else could I do? The truth would have gotten us both shut up in the psych ward."

He held her close. "Don't worry, love. I'll take care of it."

By Abel, he darn well would! His woman had overcome a vampire, most likely saved her father's life and her own, and was now being harassed by petty mortals. Intolerable! He willed calm on her, soothing reassurance into her frazzled mind. "I'll take care of this, Laura," he repeated. "Come with me. What was the name of that doctor?" he asked as he crossed to the gray-haired clerk manning the reception desk.

"Hayes." She still sounded strung-out. That too he'd take care of, after he dealt with this little crimp.

The clerk looked up at him. Her smile was as stiff as the little plastic tag pinned on her overall. "Can I help you?"

"Yes. I'm Toby Wise, Mr. Fox's son-in-law." He forgave himself the white lie—desperate times merited desperate measures. "I just got Laura's message about her father's accident. I need to see Dr. Hayes."

"He's busy with patients."

"And I need to speak to him about a patient." He didn't have time to argue with her, just looked her right in the eyes. It didn't take much. "Tell Dr. Hayes I must speak to him as soon as he finishes with his next patient. Take us in to wait for him."

He sensed Laura stiffen beside him. He couldn't explain this, not now. She had to trust him.

Abel be praised! She did, following him in to wait in a little cramped office. He nudged her into a chair, taking a position behind her and resting a hand on her shoulder to calm her. "Just let me handle this."

She was too spent and worn to argue, just put her hand over his and nodded.

It seemed they waited an age. It was nine and a half minutes by Toby's watch. Nine and half minutes for him to absorb her worry. She was torn to shreds inside. Understandable, because she wasn't Wonder Woman, but a mortal who'd achieved the next to impossible and now faced suspicion and mistrust.

The door opened. Dr. Hayes was young and weary-looking. A tired mind was easier to influence than an alert one. Toby smiled and offered his hand. "Dr. Hayes? I'm Toby Wise. How is my father-in law?"

The doctor glanced at Laura. "Mr. Fox is your father-in-law?"

Toby nodded. He would be soon—one way or another. "Laura called me as soon as she got the chance. I came right over. How is Mr. Fox?"

"Several broken bones. I've just received the X-rays."

He indicated a large manila envelope. "After seeing them I need to talk to Ms. Fox again, or is it Ms. Wise?"

"Fox," Laura answered, her voice tight.

"Laura uses her own name," Toby added. That much was true, after all.

The doctor nodded. "I see."

Toby didn't let him go on any longer.

"Doctor, having reviewed the X-rays, you see they concur completely with Ms. Fox's account."

The doctor stared.

Before he could open his mouth, Toby repeated the suggestion.

Dr. Hayes nodded. "The X-rays concur completely with Ms. Fox's account."

"There is no suspicion attached to Ms. Fox," Toby said.

Dr. Hayes nodded. "There is no suspicion attached to Ms. Fox."

"She may see her father right away."

"She may see her father right away." The doctor sat down, exhaustion graying his face.

Toby understood. Although the man was tired, it had been a strong mind to penetrate, but it was done. He helped Laura stand. She'd gone pale. One more shock on top of a morning of them. "Okay, my love," he whispered in her ear. "We'll see your father now."

They'd splinted Dad's fingers but he needed surgery for the multiple breaks in his arm. They were keeping him overnight, maybe longer. Worrying, yes, but it made a welcome change to be treated like an anxious daughter instead of a criminal suspect. She owed Toby for that, and he owed her an explanation. She'd seen and heard what had happened with the doctor.

* * *

"Let's see what we can do with this." The crime scene tech hefted the box of samples and nodded to the deputy standing nearby. "Looks like an impromptu cremation but . . ."

"But what?" the deputy asked. With two deputies dead, he was senior officer and very happy the crime scene techs and detectives were taking over.

"Looks like a human body. The long bones would imply that, but bodies don't burn that easily, especially on damp ground. I'm checking grass and soil for combustible materials. Something had to have been used."

"Wonder who it is? With all that's gone on here the last few days, checking missing persons reports hasn't been high on our priorities."

"Yeah," the tech replied. "Proper crime wave you've had going on down this way."

"And now this. It's Granger Fox's house—the editor of the local paper. I'd like to know what he knows. You can hardly burn a body in the backyard and not notice."

"It's a good way off the road, and the nearest house is half a mile away."

True but . . . "Someone should have seen the smoke, surely, and . . ." He looked from the ashes to the garage and tool shed not four feet away. "How come the body burned but nothing else? Surely the garage or one of the overhanging trees would have caught fire?"

"Odd," the tech agreed. "Just like everything else going on around here." He stood, packing his samples away. "Got any suspects in the other two?"

"Not yet, but we will. I'm going down to the newspaper office to go talk to Granger myself. Should be interesting to hear what he has to say."

Chapter 25

Toby finally convinced Laura to leave the waiting room and get something to eat. Mortals needed food and she was pretty vague as to when she'd last eaten. "What did you do to Dr. Hayes?" she asked, looking up from the plate of rather dismal-looking lasagna Toby had insisted on buying. Her father was now in surgery and it was time for her questions.

"Dr. Hayes?" Toby repeated.

"Yes. You did something. Before you intervened, I could almost feel the handcuffs coming, and now we've pretty much had the royal treatment. You did it, but what?" She dug up a forkful of lasagna.

He propped his elbows on the table and rested his chin in his hands. "I changed his mind."

She stopped chewing. "I sort of noticed that myself. How?" She put down her fork. Lasagna could wait.

His dark eyes met hers. He looked worried. Really worried. "It's a skill I have. We have. Vampires. We can influence some mortals' minds."

"Just like that?"

"No, not just like that." He shook his head. Not just a

denial, perhaps more to clear his own mind. "It develops. I've only been able to do it the past thirty years or so."

She didn't have time now to ponder how she really felt about this. Better go by gut. "You change people's minds?"

"Only in dire circumstances or for their safety."

"Have you messed with mine?"

He let out a tight laugh. "Laura, I tried but never had much success. Your mind isn't the sort that bends easily."

Was that a compliment or not? "But you tried, didn't you?" Had he made her fall in love with him? Lasagna curdled in her stomach. "What did you do to mine?"

"I might better ask, what have you done to mine? I've taken risks with you I've never taken in my entire existence. I've never trusted a mortal with what you know about me. All I ever did with your mind was try—unsuccessfully, I might add—to remove a couple of memories."

"What sort of memories?"

"Ones like you seeing me naked when I flew through the window."

Her face burned as her mouth quirked in a smile she just could not hold back. "I'm rather glad you didn't!"

"Yes, well . . . that one I should have removed but forgot at the time and then, well, later we sort of became enmeshed."

She reached and grabbed his hand. "And am I glad we did. I don't know what I'd do without you. This mess is hideous." Without him behind her, she and the rest of Dark Falls, including Adela, would have been Axel's prey.

"Can't disagree, Laura, but I think we're out of the woods now. Vlad and his bunch will take care of Axel, and all you need to do is take care of your father."

She let out a long sigh, as only a mortal could, but

then leaned into him, resting her head on his shoulder. "I can't help feeling it's not going to be that simple."

No longer concerned about her brain being invaded, now she was back worrying about her father. Understandable, if Toby had ever known for sure who his father had been, he might have wondered or worried about him. He'd certainly worried about his mother left behind. Took him years to forget the blank resignation on her face. At the time he'd taken it as not caring but later realized it was the resignation of the powerless.

Enough dwelling on his long-ago sorrows and hurts. His woman, his love, was leaning on him for comfort. To see strong, able, competent Nurse Fox shaking with worry cut Toby to the core. He wrapped his arms around her and whispered, "Your father is in good hands here. Your incredible action and quick thinking saved him from Axel. Vlad has Axel now and trust me, darling, no one escapes from Vlad Tepes's clutches."

She went quiet, while he luxuriated in the simple pleasure of Laura Fox in his arms. He bent down and kissed her hair, inhaling her sweet, womanly scent. In the midst of all this roiling mess, he had Laura. Heck, he might just tell Vlad and his retinue to hoof it off tonight somewhere else so he could make love to Laura all over the house. Whoa! Only a horny vampire imagined making love to a woman who was keyed up with worry, but heck, he was a horny vampire. But for Laura, he could wait until she was ready, which he hoped to Abel would be very, very soon.

"Is Vlad really as bloodthirsty and dangerous as the stories of Dracula make out?"

Good question. "When he was mortal. History speaks for itself. Since then, few dare cross him. But my love, a hint to the wise: He gets a trifle narked over references to Dracula and the mention of Bram Stoker tends to get him agitated."

"And an agitated Vlad is not a safe thing to be around?"

"Not in that way. I doubt he ever loses control, but it's not a good idea to get him wound up. I imagine Axel is learning that right now."

"But why was Vlad so keen to get Axel? Because of the harm he did?"

"Yes and no." She looked up at him at that, a look of puzzlement in her eyes. Toby eased her head back to his shoulder. He loved her closeness and her warmth against him. "To be honest I don't think the fate of a few mortals registers on his radar, but Axel came into Vlad's territory without the courtesy of a request of passage or hospitality—a major insult and affront to Vlad's dignity and position—and most damning of all, Axel drew attention to himself and the town. Not a good idea. We continue to exist by being inconspicuous, by fitting in among mortals. Anything that draws attention is distinctly frowned upon."

Another sigh. Damn! He shouldn't be loading all this on her right now but . . .

"It's like a parallel universe, isn't it?" Laura said. "Vampires living quietly among the rest of us and no one ever noticing."

"It's the best and safest way for all concerned."

"What will Vlad do to Axel?"

Yikes! The one question he dreaded but couldn't evade. She'd been so accepting of vampires so far, but would she accept this? "After he and Etienne get the information from him they want, they'll kill him." He didn't add "slowly." If it came out for certain that Axel had killed Zeke, then Vlad would wreak a very slow and unpleasant revenge.

"I hope they take their own sweet time." Maybe her sensibilities weren't as delicate as he believed. "It isn't just Zeke. Think what Axel did to Dad. I never liked the deputy—but he didn't deserve that. And what about what he tried to do to Adela? If he could be brought to justice he'd get the book thrown at him. Since he can't, I hope Vlad takes his own sweet time and fixes Axel's wagon for good."

Not much doubt of that.

She went quiet, as if that pronouncement had taken the last of her energy. Toby wrapped his arm around her shoulders as she relaxed against him. "I wonder why Axel ever came to Dark Falls?" she murmured, half to herself, and Toby stroked her arm and willed sleep on her. He succeeded but suspected it was her exhaustion as much as his skill.

Sweet Abel, what a woman! A mate to keep for life. Yes, Gwyltha would no doubt have a few things to say, but heck, after accepting Antonia's shifter, a mortal— and a mortal who could best a vicious vampire—was not to be dismissed with an imperious wave of the hand.

Of course, might be good idea to explain the ramifications of the colony to Laura.

Later.

There was plenty of time.

"Where to, sir?" Wilson asked as he and Adam looked down on the trussed-up Axel. The silver netting was wound around him so tightly, it seemed even moving his eyelids appeared an effort. But it was amazing how much emotion a vampire could put into an eyebrow twitch. Adela stepped back. Axel might be wound round with links of silver mesh, but his eyes still flashed the venom she'd faced in the Kountry Kitchen just a day or so ago.

"You know what I want to know?" she said, looking at Vlad and his aides. "Why he picked Dark Falls, and what he has against me?"

"Ah." Vlad let a little smile flit over his narrow mouth. "I believe I can answer the latter, my dear Mrs. Whyte. You are a witch; many of our kind fear witches. Many abhor your kind." The feeling was mutual on both counts.

"That's why? Heck, I used to be more than a trifle leery of vampires, but I never tried killing any."

"He may have suspected your power might be launched against him."

She shook her head. She could say it until she was blue in the face, but vamps would never get it. She owed Vlad, he'd restored her daughter, Heather, and Elizabeth to her, protected them when they were in dire straits, but he'd never understand The Way.

Probably just as well. Combine vampire strength and a witch's wisdom and the rest of the human race would be left behind in the dust.

"We will find answers to your questions, and to ours," Vlad assured her. "Where do you think our host, Toby, would wish us to examine this creature?"

Not on the nice Oriental rug, that was for sure. "How about down in the basement? Avoid the wine cellar, as Etienne is sleeping there, but anywhere else. Shift what you need to and help yourself."

"Ah!" A light appeared in Adam's dark eyes. "Basement. Perhaps a workshop? Tools?"

Yikes! A little woodwork and handicrafts was not what he had in mind. "I doubt it. Piet was never the do-it-yourself sort."

"Unnecessary!" Vlad barked—it was the only word

for his sharp reply. "Look in the leather bag in the back of the Hummer. That has everything you will need."

Adela did not want to look in that bag. Ever. The deep-seated part of her soul niggled that she should stop this, that they were planning on torture or at the very least strong-arm tactics and she, as an ethical witch, should step in and object. The vindictive streak that reared up at the thought of Axel insisted he was getting his due. The rational part pointed out to her emotional side that there was no way she could stop three vampires—four in a few hours when Etienne awoke, and heck, five if Toby ever got back. Which, given the speed he hung up after learning where Laura was, was not to be guaranteed.

"What are you going to do to Axel?" she asked Vlad and almost wished she hadn't.

A look of cold ferocity darkened his eyes. Not hard to picture the medieval warlord impaling his enemies or hammering hats into the skulls of those who offered insult. Adela looked him back in the eye and raised her eyebrows. Tapping her fingers impatiently would be overkill, and possibly fatal, so she clenched her fist.

"My dear Mrs. Whyte," Vlad replied with a little bow but scant lessening of his expression. "We will ask whence he came and why." Simple enough but . . . "We must know this. I cannot tolerate any vampire entering my domain and causing such havoc."

Good point. Better not point out Oregon was part of the U.S. of A and not a transatlantic outpost of Wallachia.

"Okay, Vlad." She tried not to sigh but failed miserably. "I know."

Adam and Wilson carried the next best thing to an inert Axel down to the basement, Wilson nipping back up to bring in the bag of necessaries from the Hummer.

Adela went into the kitchen, her footsteps echoing on the tiled floor. The place was quiet as a tomb. Even when she'd been alone with Piet at night, there had been life in the house. Now . . . it was just her and four dead men.

And on that note, she put on the kettle and hoped to the heavens above that Lizzie would get back soon. It wasn't that far—a whole lot closer than Eugene, but wishing wouldn't get her back.

Might as well make a cup of mint tea and try to calm herself. She was waiting for the kettle to boil and debating whether to burn a few purifying herbs and set a spell of serenity around the house, when she heard an engine approach up the drive.

Lizzie! Adela ran out the side door and down the drive, but it wasn't Lizzie, it was a dark green sheriff's cruiser. Wild horrors tumbled through Adela's mind. Accident? Something happened to Piet? The van tumbled off the road down the cliff? Something with Toby and Laura? She had been at the hospital, after all. Adela's heart raced and her mouth went dry as she watched the car come to a stop on the side of the drive.

Damn! Had she shut the front door? Last thing they needed was the law seeing the shambles in the front hall. "Officer!" she called and waved as he opened his door. She stepped forward into the drive so he couldn't miss her. "Can I help you?" Darn, there were two of them, both striding toward her.

"Good afternoon, ma'am," the first one said. Sheesh, was it afternoon already? Coping with vampires certainly took up the day.

"Good afternoon," she replied.

"We're looking for a Laura Fox," the second one said. "I understand she works here."

"Yes, she does. She's one of the night nurses who takes care of Mr. Connor." What was happening?

"She's not here now?" It was the taller one.

"No."

"Would you know where she is?" They took turns like Click and Clack.

What in the name of the goddess, was the matter? Still, might as well tell the truth; after all, one shouldn't lie to a policeman. "She's in the hospital. In Florence." That got a reaction. Both stared at her, then at each other and back to her.

"An accident?" Number Two asked.

"I think so. She called a few hours ago. She was taking her father there. He'd been hurt. I'm not sure of the details." And was about to split if she didn't find out.

"I see," said Deputy Number One, sounding as if he didn't really at all. "Do you have any idea of the nature of the accident?"

"No. I never thought to ask. Didn't seem that tactful. She was obviously worried. I told her to call me if she needed anything."

Number Two looked as if he only half-believed her. Well, it was only about a fifth of the truth but she drew the line at saying she'd been busy taking care of vampires all morning and had all but forgotten about Laura.

"Something the matter, ma'am?" Number One asked.

Other than blushing because she was concealing information from the law? "No. I wish I could help you more. I'm afraid she won't be here tonight. Mr. Connor, her patient, is away for a few days."

"He left, ma'am?" Number Two chimed in.

If it was any business of theirs . . . "His daughter is visiting and took him off for a short vacation."

"And you'd be?"

"I'm Adela Whyte, here to hold the fort." She was not going into her relationship with Piet and she was not inviting them in. Too much going on inside the house. Thank heaven there was only the Hummer parked out front.

"Well, ma'am, if you'd just let your employer know we were here looking for Ms. Fox and if she comes by, please have her call us."

She didn't correct the error; let them think she was a housekeeper. Servants were quickly forgotten. "I'll certainly pass the word on."

She watched them walk back to the cruiser and drive away. Once they were gone, she grabbed her phone from her bag and punched in Toby's number. No reply. Darn! He must have turned it off in the hospital. Adela left voice mail for him to call her.

She told herself one or the other of them would call back soon. She so hoped. Adela couldn't rid herself of the notion that worry loomed all around, and it wasn't just from the vampires in the basement.

Chapter 26

Toby wasn't used to the feeling of tightness in his chest, the gnawing anxiety, or the rush of contentment whenever he looked down at Laura sleeping in his arms. He wasn't used to emotions like this. It was so . . . mortal!

Not that he'd complain. He welcomed every single complication Laura brought to his existence but he'd be a total fool—and a fool Toby Wise was not—if he ignored the snags piling up ahead of them. He bent down and kissed the top of Laura's head, luxuriating in the sensation of her soft hair against his face and relishing the wondrous mortal female scent of her. And therein lay the rub.

Laura was mortal.

He'd sigh if he could. Not that that would help one iota, but it seemed mortals found it a great release. Had he in his mortal days? Darned if he could remember. As if it mattered! What mattered was finding a way to keep Laura as she was: mortal and wonderful and his love.

What the heck! Although defiance to the ways and mores of the colony went against the grain, Oregon was a long way from England. What happened between Laura and himself was no concern of Gwyltha's. He'd already revealed his nature to Laura. Too late for Gwyltha's taboos and prohibitions. And any suggestion that Laura posited a danger to the colony and their existence was ludicrous. Hell! Hadn't she protected them all by vanquishing Axel Radcliffe?

He had to smile. His woman was a true fighter, a wonder and a prize above all others. He was keeping her come hell or high water. He'd settle it with Gwyltha somehow.

And hope Laura felt as he did. She said she loved him, but could she accept that he'd never be able to give her children? That he'd never age? As the years passed their physical differences would become more and more apparent.

No point in borrowing trouble. Together they would cross those bridges. Somehow. Kit and Justin had. Yes, by bringing the women they loved over to the vampire life. That was no solution to Toby. He couldn't wish violence and death on Laura, and above all he wanted her mortal. It was the warmth and life in her that so attracted him.

He wanted her just as she was.

"Ms. Fox?" A weary-looking doctor in a rumpled white coat stood in the doorway. He gave Toby a nod. "She's sleeping?"

"I'll wake her."

A gentle nudge did it. She yawned and opened her eyes. "What happened? Dad?"

The doctor crossed the room and took the chair on the other side of her. "The surgery went well, Ms. Fox. He'll need physical therapy but in time he should regain all use of his arm. A couple of the fingers might remain stiff, but with luck he'll get back most of the use in them. He's lucky you brought him in as fast as you did."

"He'll be okay, then?"

"Don't see why not. He's coming out of recovery in a

little while. You can go in and see him when he does, but be warned he's still very groggy."

She was on her feet before he finished speaking. "Thank you!" She wasn't exactly steady on her pins. Stiff from sleeping in a plastic chair, no doubt, but Toby reached out and steadied her as he stood beside her.

"Let's go and see him. Then you need to go home and rest."

The doctor nodded. "Good idea. He'll be sleeping most of the rest of the day, I expect, and, barring complications, we'll discharge him in the morning."

And so the morning would bring another wrinkle. Another bridge to cross. Later. Right now, Laura was the one who mattered.

Groggy was not the word for Granger Fox as Laura sat down on the wobbly chair by his bed. He barely registered Toby's presence, which all in all was probably a lucky break. Sometime soon Toby was going to have to ask the man for his consent to marry his daughter. Later. Much later, when the current coil was all straightened out. Meanwhile, Toby stood in the corner while Laura hugged her father and shed a few tears of relief. "Dad, I was so worried for you."

"I worried for you, Laura. He wanted to harm you, Axel did."

"But he didn't succeed, and you're going to be okay. When you get out of here, I'm taking you home and taking time off to look after you."

"No need, Laura. You have your own life."

"Think I'm hiring another nurse to take care of my father? No way!"

He went quiet a few minutes. "You're a good girl, Laura. Always have been. Axel wanted to hurt you. Needed that information. You made him angry."

Granger closed his eyes as if the efforts of thought and speech were too much.

"It doesn't matter now, Dad. He can't hurt either of us, or anyone. Forget he existed."

"What happened? He won't give up."

"He's given up, Dad. I'll tell you the whole story later. Right now, you rest and I'll be back in the morning." She stood and turned to smile at Toby.

He opened the door for her and together they walked down the long corridor out into the afternoon sun.

"I ought to go to the house and tidy it up for Dad," she said. "It was a horrid mess last time I was there."

"Why worry about it? You need rest more than scrubbing and washing. Let's go back to your place." Much less likely to be disturbed than at Devil's Elbow. "You bring your father up to the house in the morning. Much more space there, and everyone should be gone by then."

"You really think so?"

"I hope so. If not, your father's unlikely to be venturing into the basement with a cast from wrist to shoulder. We'll manage."

"Dad can't just move in."

"Why not? The house is big enough, and that way I'll have you close. If it meant keeping you handy, I'd invite a herd of elephants into the house. One sick man I think we can handle without a ripple."

She grasped his hand and meshed her fingers with his. "You make it sound so simple, Toby."

"I'm a vampire. I make things simple." He hoped.

Her chuckle was a joy to hear. "I think you also complicate them."

"That too."

"I was so worried about him, but we're not out of the

woods yet, are we? Axel is still around. Will they really kill him?"

"Eventually."

She went quiet at that. "I don't think I want to know about that."

"What you want right now is proper rest. A doze on a wobbly plastic chair doesn't count."

"What I really want is you, Toby."

Hell! He wasn't about to argue with that. "Let's get somewhere soon, then."

"I'll race you!"

"Who said anything about racing? I'll drive you."

"I'm not leaving Dad's car here. I'll drive it. You follow me."

He'd follow her anywhere. A few miles down the road was nothing. He kept the little red car in view every inch of the way, pulling in right behind her when she stopped in the narrow drive beside her house. He beat her out of the car, opening her door for her before she'd barely cut the engine.

Laura looked up at him, one eyebrow raised. "Showing off your vampire speed?"

"Don't need to. That's no great shakes but . . ." He had a hard time holding back a grin. "Once we're inside, then I do aim to impress you."

She tilted her head, a sparkle in her eyes. "Good! I'm in the mood to be impressed." She stood and stepped closer. "How about it?" Her lips parted, her breath caressing his lips as he brushed his mouth over hers.

She wanted him and he was delighted to oblige. In the aftermath of her stress and worry came a wild relaxation, and her own needs rose to the fore. He couldn't be happier. He pressed his mouth on hers as her tongue found his, her desire only too apparent. He was darn well not going to disappoint her. Cupping the back of her head with his hand, he deepened the kiss, losing himself in her life and warmth. She was wondrous, alive, vibrant, and wanted him. He, who'd seduced so often, was now being taken, and frankly the sensation sent his mind spinning. If they weren't careful he'd have her here and now on the driveway. He should stop but how could he end this kiss? Her lips pressed on his, his tongue caressed hers, and between them they were caught in a wild need, a sweet desire and deep, loving lust.

"Laura! Sorry but . . ."

Shit! He kept the sentiment under his breath as he turned to the speaker and kept a tight hold on Laura. A fair-haired young woman, about Laura's age, stood on the lawn a few yards away.

She blushed. "Sorry to bother you but, Laura . . ."

"Yes, Jenny?" Laura stepped away. He wanted to yank her right back where she belonged but restrained himself. He was vampire, after all. He did have some control, didn't he? "Something the matter?"

"Not really. Well, perhaps. Did your father ever find you?" He knew Laura so well, he sensed her tension. Heck, he could hear her sudden intake of breath and her heart race. "Dad? You've seen him? Today?"

"This morning. He came by with another man. Strange he was . . ." She broke off and eyed the car behind them "Silly. You must have found him. You're driving his car."

"Yes, I brought it back. He was hurt. Had an accident. He's in the hospital."

Jenny covered her mouth with her fingers. "Oh, dear. Is it serious?"

Laura shook her head. "They're talking of discharging him tomorrow. A broken arm."

"What about the other man, the one who was with him? Was he hurt?"

Toby also caught Laura's laudable effort to restrain the smile. "He wasn't hurt with Dad, but tell me, when were they here?" Worry had crept into her voice.

"First thing this morning, just after you called and asked me to feed Hercules. I remembered your dad from when he helped you move in, but the other one . . ." She let out a sigh. "He's freaky."

That was one way to describe the vermin. "He didn't bother you, did he?" Toby asked, looking at the woman carefully for signs of taint.

"Other than giving me the heebie-jeebies, no. Got real snitty when you weren't home, Laura, but that's all. They left right afterward. Wasn't anything important, was it? I thought about calling you, but, heck, you were at work and . . ." She shrugged and gave a little smile.

"Just a minor panic," Laura replied. "It's all taken care of."

"Glad to hear that." She looked at Toby, curiosity in her eyes. "Hi, sorry to interrupt. I'm Jenny Carr." She held out her hand.

He grasped it. "Toby Wise. How do you do?"

"Don't blame you for not wanting to introduce him, Laura. He's a keeper. Have fun, you two. Think of me, cleaning the bathroom on my afternoon off!" With a wave, she turned and went back into the house next door.

"Do you think," Laura said as she opened her door and closed it behind them, "that Axel's coming here poses any sort of problem?"

"How could it? He's neutralized. Besides, this might even work to your advantage. When questions get asked about his disappearance, as they no doubt will, he came by here, found you at work, and dropped off your father."

"Then how come I'm driving Dad's car? What did Axel do? Fly?" She did grin at that. "Can he fly?"

"Vlad will find out soon, if he hasn't already."

"Should we be back there instead of here?"

"Definitely not. We couldn't make love with such abandon knowing that lot were underfoot."

She hugged him, squashing her lovely breasts against his chest. Darn, he wanted her skin to skin. Fast. He slipped his hand under her shirt.

"Just a minute!" She pulled back. "Before my brain gets utterly fogged out with lust and hormones, what about the car? Axel was driving it. Now I have it. What happened?"

"You dropped him off somewhere, on the way to the hospital." He thought a minute. "At the bus stop. He wanted to get back to the newspaper office."

That apparently was wildly humorous. "Toby, have you tried getting a bus around here? This isn't New York or London."

"Alright, then . . ." He thought. Obviously he was going to have to solve this one. Fast. "Simple. After he found you, he told you to drop him somewhere, as he was going to pick up a taxi or get a lift into Dark Falls. We'll think up the details later."

"Okay." Her smile proved it was.

"For the next couple of hours, Axel, Vlad, even your poor father, don't exist. Just you and me and . . ." He looked around. "Where's the bedroom?" He drew the line at loving her on the twin rocking chairs, although the hairy-looking rug had possibilities.

"Let me show you, but first we're stopping by the shower. I want to lather you up!"

Get him in a lather, more like, given the glint in her

eye. Nothing could please him more. "By all means, my love, but I get to undress you first."

"Okay!" She took a half step back and grinned, her hands on her hips. "Go for it!"

He went for it, or rather went for Laura. He was vampire. She knew it. Why dillydally? Both hands slipped under her shirt and had it off in seconds. Her bra followed fast. She let out a little gasp. Alright, maybe he was going a bit fast but darn it, he was in need, and judging by the stiff peaks of her luscious nipples, she was in the same state.

How could any man or vampire ask more than to have the object of his desire lusting in return? He was grinning as he lifted her by her waist, ignoring her gasp of shock as he held her over his head. He had her safe and secure, and she knew it. He forestalled any possible complaints by licking the tip of one nipple, then the other. Her murmur of pleasure was just what he had in mind, and to make quite clear how he meant to go on, he closed his lips over her left nipple and drew it into his mouth, teasing it with his tongue until she let out a lovely sigh of contentment. Since she appeared to enjoy it so much, he switched to her right nipple.

Her sigh of satisfaction was a joy to hear. He wanted more. He wanted her moaning and crying out and shouting for him. She would. Still holding her aloft, he carried her across the room, ducking as he passed through the doorway. The last thing he intended was to knock her out. He wanted her very, very much aware of everything he planned.

The doorway led to her bedroom. Very nice, but hadn't she suggested a shower first? He looked around. The bathroom door was ajar and he turned toward it.

"Are you keeping me up here in the air all afternoon?" Laura asked.

"No!" He crossed the room in seconds and set her on her feet.

"Whee!" She brushed her hair back off her face. "You move so fast it makes me dizzy."

"Complaining?"

"Not in the least, apart from the fact you're still dressed and I'm half naked."

"I'd rather you were completely naked."

"My turn!" She reached forward and, as if to make some sort of point, unbuttoned his shirt. Slowly. Running her hands over the cotton fabric between slipping each button, and sliding her fingers inside his trouser waist to ease out his shirt centimeter by centimeter. She might not do vampire speed, but she knew how to set his body afire. By the time she had the last button undone and his shirt open, he was ready to sling her over his shoulder and turn on the taps. But they were both still half-dressed, and he, at least, had nothing else to wear. "What's on your mind, mortal?"

"You." She snickered. "And wild vampire sex."

"Sounds utterly delightful."

"Is that a promise?" She cocked her head to one side and let her finger slide inside his waistband.

"Ease that hand a little lower and find out for yourself."

He hadn't actually meant inside his trousers. But who'd be fool enough to complain? One hand unbuckled and unbuttoned and the other was inside his Y-fronts. Holding him.

Sweet Abel! Toby gritted his teeth as her fingers closed over his cock. If he hadn't been hard before, he would be now! Not that he wasn't in that state most of the time around Laura. As each soft fingertip stroked his cock, he decided to repay the compliment and cupped her breasts. One in each hand. They were luscious, wondrous and incredible, just the right size to fill his hands and perfect in every way. He rubbed her nipples with the pads of his thumbs. It almost distracted her from her caress inside his trousers, but not quite. This was fun but what he had in mind was even better.

"Hold on a tick." Was all it took to unsnap her blue jeans and lift her out of them. She looked surprised, letting out a little cry as he set her on the lid of the loo and yanked off her shoes and socks, then lifted her and whisked off her panties.

Laura naked was a distinct improvement. Still holding her by the waist, he reached into the shower and turned on the water. Give it a minute or two to warm up and he'd have her wet and soapy.

"How come you're still half dressed?" she asked.

"Must be the woman I love is sleeping on the job."

"Sleeping! I don't think there will be much of that this afternoon."

Good point. "Oh, I hope not!"

He stepped out of his trousers, kicking off his shoes and pulling off socks and underwear faster than her mortal eyes could follow. Testing the water, and adjusting it to a comfortable temperature for a mortal, he lifted her with one arm and pulled her under the spray with him. "Soap?" he asked.

"Right here." She reached for the cake of soap and held it under the spray, a soft lavender scent filling the shower stall as she soaped up her hands.

"Give it to me."

"No! My turn first. I'm going to lather you all over."

Lather him up, more like! What a delightful prospect. "Very well, if you insist." He leaned back against the tile, saluted her twice with his cock, just for luck, and waited.

Laura licked her lips. Couldn't help it. She had Toby

naked, in her shower, and he was all hers. After one of
the roughest days of her life, she was ready for some
nice hot sex and so it appeared was Toby.

She was half tempted to turn off the water, yank him
out and have her wicked will of him on the bath mat, but
on reflection, a nice session of foreplay seemed a marvelous idea.

"I'm waiting, mortal," he said, his voice smooth and
even, even if his cock looked ready to go wild.

"I'm getting ready, vampire. Hold your horses."

"I'd rather hold your breasts!"

"In a minute." After she had her fun. She took her
time rubbing the soap between her hands, then over her
breasts and belly. She did need a good shower, as it happened, and he seemed to enjoy watching, at least if the
state of his splendid cock was anything to go by. But she
couldn't tease him, and herself, forever.

Stepping closer, and grabbing her sponge, she soaped
it up with scented bubbles and slowly brushed it over his
chest. The result was every bit as good as she'd hoped
for. He smiled, his dark eyes glinting with desire. She
took her time, slowly and carefully lathering up every
inch of his dark chest, taking full opportunity to admire
his lovely body, strong and firm and dark as bitter
chocolate. She worked on down his belly and legs, deliberately skipping his cock. When she got down to his
knees, he let out a little growl.

She got the message. And ignored it, while she washed
his ankles and every single toe. Then, because she could
stand the wait no longer, she knelt and covered his cock
with scented bubbles, easing his foreskin back and forward before soaping his balls very, very thoroughly.

"How about you turn around? I bet your back needs
a good scrub."

"Scrub fast, mortal! It'll be your turn next."

She took that to heart and whisked over his back, but she did succumb to the temptation to make the best of his lovely butt. If they had butt contests, Toby would beat out every man on the planet. His was truly a sight to ogle. And his thighs weren't half bad either. A mortal life of physical labor had definitely given him a body worth preserving.

She'd just about covered every inch of him, short of his head and his face, and was about to turn him again and reach for the shampoo, when he took over, spinning around, yanking the soap and sponge out of her hands and then pinning her face to the tile with a hand on her shoulder, while he had his turn.

Not that she was about to complain. His touch was magic, sending wild thrills through her as he stroked the sponge down her back. She was sighing as he covered the backs of her legs and butt. Her eyes closed to shut out everything but the sensation of his hands on her skin. She was in need, whimpering as he slowly soaped the back of her thighs, and yelping with surprise when he kissed her butt!

"Keep still!" he said, as he angled the spray to rinse her off.

Keep still? She could hardly move, the way he held her. She was suddenly aware of his strength. Of what she was playing with. A vampire. "You're strong, aren't you?" Stupid question, but an odd worry snatched at her thoughts.

He turned her around to face him and tilted her chin up, fixing her with his eyes. "Yes, Laura, I am. Stronger by far than I've let you see, but I promise you, I will never hurt you. I love you. I never thought I could feel this way about a mortal, but I do. Will you stay with me, Laura?"

Her mouth went dry. "Toby, I love you. But how can we? I mean, you're going to live forever and . . . I won't."

"True, but we've a good many years between us before you have to worry about your old age. Does it bother you that I'll always be young, virile and want you?"

Put that way . . . "No, I just think it might cause difficulties."

"We'll cope with them when we meet them. Now, that's agreed on . . . let's continue our conversation."

Had they agreed? Apparently. She was in no mood to argue, not when his hand cupped between her legs and his fingers opened her. She was wet and slick, had been since before they walked in the house, and as his finger entered her, she groaned. "Oh, Toby!"

"Yes, my love." A second finger, then a third came in deep. It wasn't the same as his cock, but right now she'd not complain. His fingers curled and stroked inside her, her body rocking and her legs wobbling so much, she'd have fallen if his other hand wasn't holding her firm against the wall. Wild rushes of sensation raced from her pussy to swell through her body. She was gasping, as her arousal grew. "Happy?" he asked.

Her reply was to throw her head back and angle her hips to bring his fingers deeper. He responded by stroking her clit with his thumb, tiny soft circles that magnified the pleasure soaking her mind. She felt herself climbing, peaking toward her climax. She was crying out now, gasping his name and groaning her pleasure. She was being pulled, drawn up into a spiral of pleasure, as sensation raced though her body and her mind soared. Steadily he kept up the sweet rhythm, fingers pumping as his thumb stroked her to orgasm. When she came, she screamed his name and would have collapsed into a heap on the tile, but he held her up, pulling her against his body so his erection pressed into her belly, as the last ripples of her climax eased and slowed.

"I love you so," he whispered, as he turned and held he under the warm spray.

She was still light-headed and weak-kneed when he lifted her out of the shower and wrapped a towel around her. "That was incredible," she said between gasps. Her body sang deep inside with the sweet pleasure of her climax still swelling. "But what about you?"

"What about me?" he asked, grinning.

"Well"—she stroked the side of his cock—"seems you need a little attention."

"More than a little. I intend to take you. All of you."

"I'd rather like all of you, deep inside me." She wrapped her fingers around his erection, strength and energy returning in a rush at the prospect of more lovemaking.

"Come on, then." He took her hand. "Let's find your bed."

Chapter 27

It wasn't that Laura objected to being swept up in Toby's arms. She suspected she was too wobbly and limp from the climax to walk very far under her own steam, but the speed he moved left her dizzy. She'd better get used to it. Getting accustomed to a vampire lover and a vampire who loved her hadn't been a hardship so far. In fact . . .

She let out a gasp as he lay her on the bed, on the sheets, no less, when she hadn't even noticed him pull back the covers.

The mattress gave as he climbed on the bed with her, and then her mind all but blanked out as he spread her legs and put his mouth on her pussy.

"It's too much!" She managed to gasp with supreme effort. She'd not yet recovered from her climax and his tongue on her sensitized flesh had her all but reeling.

"No," he insisted. "Not at all. That was just a prologue."

He blatantly ignored her whimpers of pleasure and her groans of bliss. She was lost in sensation. Her entire being focused on his mouth between her legs and the searing trails of pleasure that wrapped her mind and fuddled her reason. It was too much, far, far too much, and she never, ever wanted him to stop. Caught up in the wonder in her body, she was crying out with joy as he moved. One second he was caressing her with his lips and tongue, the next, he was kneeling between her thighs, his hands on her hips, and was deep inside her.

Her cry became a scream of anticipation and a series of screams and yells, as he drove in and out with a loving force that took her higher and higher. She was climbing, soaring, leaping as if ascending to the heavens, caught in a great spiral of joy. He leaned forward, his lips finding the pulse at the base of her neck. She wanted his bite. Longed for it. Needed it. She barely felt it in the wildness of her arousal, but the instant his fangs pierced her skin, she came again, with a force and intensity that left her sweaty and shaking as he pounded, deeper than ever and climaxed himself.

She was limp on the bed, he was poised above her, still hard inside her, as her inner muscles throbbed and her clit pulsed with pleasure.

Sated was not the word. Pleasured was way too inadequate. Language failed utterly to describe her feelings. She opened her eyes and smiled up at him. "Oh, Toby!" She wanted to say more, but her brain just couldn't shape the words.

He kissed her, staying deep inside her as his erection softened. "We'll work it all out, Laura. Promise."

Why not? At that moment in time, anything was possible. Speaking was still too much effort. She settled for kissing instead.

Toby broke the kiss as he slipped out of her, stretching beside her on the bed and pulling the covers over her. "Take a doze, love. I'll wake you."

No way! Who'd sleep when they had the option of snuggling up to the most magnificent man in the world?

She rolled on her side—she could just about summon the energy for that much activity—and leaned up on her elbow. "I'd rather snuggle up with a vampire." The incongruity of that struck her and she burst out laughing.

"Find me amusing, do you, mortal?" He reached out and stroked the top of her breast. "Need further demonstration of my serious intent?"

Not if she hoped to walk anytime in the next twenty-four hours. "You convinced me there, Toby. It was the thought of snuggling with a vampire that tickled my funny bone. Your public image isn't exactly cuddly."

"Just as well. If vamps were perceived as soft and cuddly everyone would want one."

"And there wouldn't be enough to go around." She dropped a kiss on his shoulder. "And I, for one, have no intention of sharing."

"Good thing too, mortal!" As if to prove his point, he rolled her on her back and leaned over her. "You're mine."

"And you're mine, Toby Wise." She avoided simpering—just. She felt light-headed and silly and immensely happy. Once they walked out the front door, they'd have to consider the entwined worries of her father and Axel, but meanwhile, only Laura and Toby existed, caught in a great bubble of love and that, for now, protected them from a passel of concerns.

"Fancy a trip to England?" he asked.

She would but . . . "Why? I thought you planned on staying here?"

"I do. On my native land, I'm stronger, faster and won't give that up in a hurry. But over in the U.K. we can get married without all that nonsense about blood tests."

"Don't need them here in Oregon. You're living in the past, Toby Wise."

"Serious?"

"You bet! Are you?" Seemed too much and too sudden.

"Very much. I know this is fast. But I want you, Laura, for the rest of your life."

She couldn't miss the implications of his choice of pronoun there. She eased from under him and sat up. Easier to think that way. "Is it going to be that straight-forward? Really?"

His hesitation answered that one. Perhaps. "No." She should have known. "But there's nothing we can't work out. Yes, it will be tricky with my colony."

"Colony?"

"My colony, my family, my blood kin, if you like. The group of vampires, which included the one who made me. We are all linked by blood connections. We have our code, and that code prohibits long-term associa-tion with mortals. For everyone's protection. But it has happened. Jude, one of us, left the colony for several years after he fell in love with an air raid warden during the Second World War. He stayed with her until she died, and recently rejoined us."

"So it's like exile or shunning?" Could she ask that of Toby?

"In name, yes. In theory, no. I kept contact with him; so did some of the others. Some members observed it more rigidly than the rest of us."

"But to cut yourself off from everyone?"

"I'm pretty much cut off here on the Left Coast as it is. I won't be a solitary. Vlad will give me, us, mem-bership in his colony."

"You're sure?"

"I asked him. And now after what you did to Axel, you'll be the talk of half the colonies in the civilized world."

She had the suspicion that might be a two-edged sword. If vampires wanted to stay unobtrusive, it also made sense for mortals not to get too much in vamps' faces. "How about we just stay quietly in Oregon?"

"Nothing, my love, could please me more."

She snuggled next to him. If only they could stay in this bed forever and let the world spin. Unfortunately . . .

"I should go back and check on Dad, and shouldn't we see what's happening at Devil's Elbow?"

"Yes." He sounded as reluctant as she felt. "We should."

"Ride in my car," Toby said, as Laura stepped out of the house. "Better not drive any more without a license."

Good point but . . . "What about Dad's car?"

"Leave it here. We can pick it up later. He won't be driving for a while." And her little Toyota was still sitting by the kitchen door at Devil's Elbow.

Laura wasn't too thrilled to be returning to Devil's Elbow. Just thinking of Axel dragging her father into the house and leering over her made her shudder. But she might as well suck it up and get over it. After all, she had a vampire by her side.

"Toby," she said, as they passed through the center of Florence and headed up the coast. "I need to get my story straight about how Dad got hurt."

"Yes," he agreed. "This is one instance where the truth will not suffice. But do you think many people will ask, once you get him home?"

"Toby, let me tell you one thing. Appear in public in a cast and total strangers ask personal questions. I broke my leg when I was in nursing school. I wanted to carry a placard: 'Fell down a flight of stairs. No, I was not drunk. The black eye came from hitting the wall.'"

"It was that bad?"

"Yes! Honest, you will not believe the way people ask

for details that are none of their business. With Dad being in the newspaper, I bet it will be ten tines worse. So"—she paused—"we need a story that is believable and stands up to scrutiny. How about this? It'll need Dad's cooperation but I think I can get him to see reason."

"Go on."

"I was at work, tidying up after Elizabeth left with her father, and on the point of leaving to come home. Dad drives up. Alone. He's in shock and pain. I can't understand how he even drove with his obvious injuries—he has to have been running on shock and adrenaline. I took him immediately to the hospital. He is so traumatized by whatever happened, he has no memory of it."

"Might work." He glanced from the road. "Pretty good, in fact. Ever thought of writing fiction for a living?"

"No thanks. My life right now is quite enough!"

"How do you account for your neighbor seeing your father with Axel not an hour earlier?"

"We don't. She saw him, yes, but since Dad has lost him memory from shock, he has no idea what happened. I'll really have to work to convince Dad to 'forget' but it could work."

"I can help. I can make him forget."

"What do you mean?" Uneasy was not the word for her reaction. "How?"

"It's something we vampires can do. Remove memories from mortals." Yes, already knew. "It's tricky, messing with mortal minds but necessary sometimes. I need to do it soon, though."

Yes, he'd told her, or as good as. The thought still freaked her out, but it was the best solution. "How about now?"

He turned the car around. "We'll just pop in. We'll say you want to check on him. Then we have to get back to the house. It's getting late, and Etienne will be waiting. I want to know what the hell is going on there."

It was almost shockingly easy. Dad was drowsy, still groggy from the anesthetic, but he recognized her and half-focused his eyes on Toby. "Who's that?"

"A good friend. You'll see him again tomorrow, when we pick you up."

That satisfied him and he shut his eyes, opening them to say, "He wants to hurt you, Laura. Don't let him!" Laura wanted to tell him, Axel never would hurt anyone again, but instead, as Dad drifted off into the drugged fuzziness, she looked at Toby. She was not in the least sure about this, but it was the best choice. Dad's "forgetfulness" could be ascribed to shock and drugs. Better than having him blow the story.

She stepped back, dropping his hand when Toby signaled her, and watched. Toby leaned over him and rested his hand on Dad's forehead for a few moments and then stood up and smiled at her. "It's done."

Just like that. "Sure?"

"Yes. He has no memory after leaving your house until he arrived at the hospital. I think everything is now taken care of."

She kissed her father's forehead. His eyes flickered open. "I'll be back in the morning, Dad, and we'll take you home."

It was going to be all right.

Two deputies waiting by the nurse's station changed her mind.

"Ms. Fox?"

"Yes." She could hardly deny it, and maybe it was merely routine.

"Do you have a minute?"

Could you tell a cop no? "Sure."

They gave Toby a questioning look.

"Toby Wise," he said, holding out his hand. "I just drove Laura in to see her father, and now I'm taking her to get something to eat and a rest. It's been a rather upsetting day."

"I'm sure it has, sir. Just a couple of questions for Ms. Fox and you'll be on your way." He looked back at Laura. "Do you know where we could contact your father's business partner, Axel Radcliffe?"

Dear heaven! She was going to have to lie to a policeman. She swallowed. "Axel?"

"Yes, we've been trying to find him."

"You've tried the newspaper office and the house?"

"The *Dark Falls Weekly News*?" She nodded. "No one there, and it was because of what we found at the house that we came here."

What now? What had they found? "There's trouble at Dad's house?"

"We found human remains there this morning, ma'am."

She'd have collapsed in a heap on the floor, if Toby hadn't caught her. As it was, she had a hard time focusing. The hallway went blurry and voices seemed distant. "What?" One word took a tremendous effort. "Whose?" At that she was very glad to sit on the chair someone had grabbed.

"That's a bit of a shock, Officer, at the end of a very stressful day." Bless Toby for that. Gave her at least a breathspace to think. Not that it was long enough. She took a couple very deep breaths. "Are you alright, Laura?" he asked.

"I will be." She hoped. "Just a shock." She looked the

officer in the eye. No point in acting guilty or worried. "You found a body in Dad's yard?"

"Human remains, ma'am. We're checking on all missing persons in the area, and were hoping to talk to Mr. Fox, but he seems very confused. He did mention the other owner of the newspaper, Axel Radcliffe, and we have been unable to find him."

Deep breath and pause to give the impression of worried thought. "He lives with Dad, they share the house. He should be there or at the office." A bit of fudging, but the truth. Axel should be there. He just wasn't right now.

"I see." He most certainly did not. "We'll find him." Not if Dracula himself had anything to do with it.

"Can you give us a number where we can contact you if we need?"

It was the other one. She gave him her cell number. "I'll be back in the morning. I think they're discharging Dad then."

"So we understand." Number One again this time. "Would you happen to know Mr. Radcliffe's car make and license-plate number?"

"He didn't have one. He used Dad's car if he drove." They were no doubt getting a very skewed idea of Dad's relationship with Axel. Or were they? Hell if she knew.

"Do you know where your father's car is?"

That was easy. "Parked in my driveway." She gave a brief explanation. The image of Dad driving to her injured, in shock and in panic, caught their interest.

"Mind if we check the car out?"

She did but could hardly refuse, and what was there to find? Axel's fingerprints? Did vampires have fingerprints? "Fine, but I don't have the key with me."

They didn't appear to find that a problem. "We'll let

you know if we need to take it into the lab," the first one said. She nodded. How much more?

"Officers," Toby said, "Laura's worn out. The rest of your questions can surely wait until tomorrow."

She wasn't sure if it was vampire mind control or not. And didn't much care. Whatever it was, it worked. Fifteen minutes later they were driving out of the parking lot.

"I'm afraid," Toby said, "this new twist is my fault."

"What?" It wasn't quite a scream. She was too weary to put her full force behind it. "What do you mean? Whose is the body they found?"

"It's not a body. It's a pile of ashes and disintegrating bones. It's Zeke's remains."

Zeke! The young, rather mouthy vampire. The one she'd first overheard talking to Toby. The one Vlad insisted had died. "Axel killed him." Her mouth went dry and her stomach clenched.

"So it would seem. Extinguished is the word we usually use. You can really only die once."

"How did you die?" Big change of tack, but . . .

He seemed equally surprised and went so quiet, Laura thought he'd never answer. "I was twenty-six. I'd been in England nearly six years, first working on the Liverpool docks, then, after I learned to read and write, I was promoted to clerk in a shipping office and later transferred to London. A few weeks later, I contracted measles and it killed me. The company owner, a man who'd become my mentor, transformed me. I had no idea he was a vampire, or what the life entailed. When I awoke from death, I was astounded. Took me awhile to come to terms with my altered state, but given the alternative, I learned to appreciate the extension of my mortal life."

"Who was your mentor?" Maybe she shouldn't ask

those questions but heck, she already knew there were
vampires on both sides of the Atlantic.

"His name was Augustus Leatherbarrow. A good friend
and a brave one. He died in the blitz. We can survive a lot
but not being blown to pieces." Toby went quiet, obviously
remembering.

"How do you think Axel killed—extinguished—
Zeke?"

"I don't know. Staked him, maybe. It does work on
some vampires. Vlad has never told me his weaknesses,
and I'd never dream of asking. One doesn't ask that sort
of thing."

"Why did you say this mess with Zeke's remains was
your fault? It can't be."

He slowed as they went through a tunnel. "It can be
and is." He told her what he'd done that morning. "I
thought it would get the cops looking in Axel's direction. It never occurred to me it would drag your father
in too. My temper and desire to get at Axel rather
snuffed out my common sense."

She wouldn't argue there but . . . "It's done now.
Might as well figure out how to deal with it and deal
with Axel."

"Vlad will take care of that."

Chapter 28

"Am I glad you got back." Adela set a mug of mint tea in front of Lizzie and pushed a jar of honey in her direction. "I thought getting arrested was stressful; that pales in comparison with today. And it's nowhere near over yet."

Elizabeth stirred a generous spoonful of honey into her tea. "That bad, eh?" She lifted the cup to her lips, watching Adela over the rim. She did look stressed. Most unlike her, but the past few days had been insane.

"Lizzie, love, it has been a nightmare."

It took Adela a good fifteen minutes to cover the entire saga. Elizabeth's tea went cold, but she swigged the lot down anyway. Her throat was tight and dry by the time Adela finished.

"It's incredible." Darn, she needed days to sort all this out. "Okay, so they have Axel downstairs, working him over." She couldn't hold back the shudder at the implications there, but she'd incinerated Laran, so she wasn't really in a position to be squeamish. "You're telling me Laura felled Axel?" Almost impossible. It had taken all her power and that of an entire coven to overcome Laran.

"By an incredible slice of luck, no doubt fueled by

fear, anger at his treatment of her father, and some very fine-quality silver, according to Toby."

"And he's still with Laura?"

"And will be permanently, I suspect. Our stalwart Toby is smitten."

"They certainly picked their time. Her father hurt, the Feds breathing down his neck, and the place overrun with Vlad's posse all bent on revenge."

"Don't forget the local law enforcement coming a-calling. And talking of that, I do need to get back down to Dark Falls and take care of the rest of the insurance business for Gertrude. Why is it, wherever vampires go, things happen?"

She'd treat that as rhetorical. "Makes life interesting. But thank heaven I got Dad away. All that crashing and fighting and tossing of furniture would have done him in."

"Talking of that, dear, we really should finish tidying up. I can't say how glad I was I headed the deputy off before he went toward the front door. If anyone sees that mess, I don't think we can pass it off as the aftermath of an afternoon of high jinks."

Adela wasn't kidding. It was a hideous mess. The old grandfather clock she remembered from her childhood lay on its side, the glass smashed and the pendulum hanging out of the open door. Chairs and tables were tossed around like old clothes in a rummage sale. Pictures hung awry or lay smashed on the floor, and a beautiful craftsman pottery bowl lay in shards on the slate floor.

"So this is what happens when a vamp's on the rampage." Or rather a vicious one on the rampage. She couldn't picture Tom, or any of his colony, countenancing such wholesale destruction. "It's going to take all afternoon to clean this up." Might as well start here and now.

Elizabeth righted the overturned furniture while

Adela swept. Or rather she swept until Elizabeth picked up the fallen grandfather clock. "Sweet goddess!" Adela stared, eyes wide, mouth gaping. "Heather said she was stronger now, but . . ."

"Yes." Lizzie hefted the clock upright and brushed her hands together. "Comes in handy at times."

"Might get you attention you don't need."

Adela always worried so. "I know better than to go around lifting Mack trucks with one hand."

"Yes." Adela sighed. "I know you do. Just unnerved me seeing you do that. I know only too well what happened to you and Heather, but sometimes the reality slaps me between the eyes."

"But we're still nice ghouls."

Adela groaned. "If I had a dollar for every time I've heard that hackneyed pun . . ." She broke off. "Etienne's awake. Early." Elizabeth froze. Adela sensed when a vampire awoke. Of course, she'd given him her blood. "Don't look so horrified, dear. I might be your step-mother and way over fifty but I'm still a breathing woman, you know."

"I wasn't criticizing. Didn't mean to, I was just a bit . . ."

"Shocked I've hooked up with a younger man?"

"He isn't really."

"He was thirty-four when he died."

"Are you serious?"

"About Etienne or about his age?"

Elizabeth needed to sit down for this and there wasn't a single undamaged chair in the hall. She wasn't going to be able to sit. "About a relationship with him."

It was the same old chuckle. That was something. And the hug felt the same. "Lizzie, get over it. Didn't I make it clear last night? I'm not planning an eternity with him. He's pleasant company, he needed blood and to be blunt, he's attractive. I've overcome my aversion to vampires—to the point of being curious."

Shock upon shock, but Adela was a single, consenting adult. "You know about him? His reputation?"

"Of being a bloodsucking Lothario? Yes, dear." She paused to hug Lizzie close. "Don't worry about me. Think of him as my 'Mr. Right Now.'"

The laugh burst out. She should have trusted Adela's sense but . . . "You do know about him and Antonia?"

"Seeing her obvious love for her Michael during your double wedding last fall, I'd say she got over Etienne quite nicely."

True. She half-suspected Antonia had forgotten the existence of a certain Chevalier Larouselière.

"Still worried about me?" There was just the slightest edge in Adela's voice. Irked? Irritated?

"No. Perhaps I should be worried about Etienne."

Nothing like a good laugh to ease the tension. "Yes, dear. Definitely. Though I must admit, I got the impression he felt it was a trifle risky to be snacking off a witch."

"Gave him a thrill, did it?"

"Certainly gave me one. Honestly, dear, if I wondered what you saw in Tom, I really understand now." This was not a conversation she really needed right now. Or ever!

"Take care, that's all, Adela." Sheesh, she did so not need to be giving her stepmother relationship advice.

"After all we've gone through the past couple days, Etienne seems like a cuddly bunny."

"More like a Monty Python Killer Rabbit!" "Bunny" just didn't fit Etienne Larouselière.

"A bunny with fangs?" Adela grinned. "Yes, I think that might well describe him. Don't worry, dear. I've a tight hold on my heart but I must admit, the encounters have been most . . . gratifying!"

Lizzie couldn't argue there. She'd gone and married a vampire and knew all about "gratification." They finished straightening the front hall as best they could. The gouges in the wall and the chipped paint would have to wait.

"I'm ready for another cup of tea," Adela said, "and I think you need a few steaks or a couple of chickens. Something tells me we might not get much sleep tonight."

Something told Lizzie Adela was spot on.

"This new mess is all my doing." Toby scowled at the road ahead as they steered north toward Devil's Elbow. "Never thought it would drag you and your father in too."

She bit back the comment that her father would obviously be implicated at the discovery of human remains in his backyard. "With everything else that's happened today, suspicion of complicity in murder seems negligible." A bit tart, but darn, it had been, to put it mildly, a stressful day.

"We'll sort it out, love." He reached across and squeezed her hand. "A promise."

The royal "we"? Or did he mean himself and the rest of the vampires currently congregating hereabouts. She was more than curious what this twenty-first-century Dracula was like. Judging from poor Zeke, not quite what Hollywood depicted. "There's a lot to sort out: Dad, Axel, the FBI . . ." Sheesh!

He actually chuckled. "We're vampires, Laura."

Right! Wasn't that part of every problem they were facing right now? She let out a long sigh and leaned back in the seat. Not much she could do about anything right now. Dad was her big worry. She'd save her energy for him and let Toby and the rest of them cope with bloodsucking villains and government investigations.

Her quiet left Toby uneasy. She'd been spot on. They did have a collection of problems piling up. Still, Granger Fox was her first concern and he'd make it his. Vlad could take care of all the Axel complications, and as for the damn Federal Bureau of Irritation, they came last.

He hoped they gave him time to explain the mysterious exploding packing case. That they hadn't come beating down his door already was a miracle. Despite his reassurances to everyone earlier, he was worried about how to explain that away. He could hardly mind-sweep half a dozen agents' brains. He was still pondering that when he turned into the driveway and headed for the house.

Laura stared at the smashed clock and the damaged furniture. "What happened?" It had not been that bad when she ran out with Dad. Had it?

"You left behind a severely wounded vampire," Toby pointed out, "no doubt in the throes of agony he moved around a bit."

No doubt. "Where is he now?" Despite all Toby's assurances, she'd been half-terrified he'd still be lying in wait for her.

"Down in the basement, getting worked over by Vlad and his henchmen and with a little bit of help from Etienne," Adela said. "I don't think he'll make any more trouble for anyone."

"The basement, you said?" Toby asked with obvious anticipation. "Better go down and see how things are going." He gave her hand a squeeze. "Shan't be long. Adela and Elizabeth will keep you company, okay?"

Since her yea or nay was obviously irrelevant, Laura just nodded and stared after him as he nipped down the hallway toward the stairs.

"You look as though you need a nice cup of tea," Adela said.

A stiff drink sounded more like it but since Laura suspected she still had need of all her wits for a few hours, she nodded. "Thanks. It has been a rough day."

Adela put on the kettle and gathered mugs and tea bags while Elizabeth produced a bottle of rum. "Want a tot in your tea? You look as though you could use it."

Rum had never been her tipple of choice but . . . "Just a small one. Much more and I'll be out for the count."

"You are not passing out on us until we know what really happened to Axel and how your father is," Adela said.

She told them what had happened with Axel. "Bloody brilliant and inspired" was Elizabeth's comment.

And her flight with Dad to the ER. "You must have been petrified," Adela said. "He's going to be okay, isn't he?"

Laura was about to embark on her worries regarding the sheriff's department and Zeke's pyre when Toby, Etienne and three unfamiliar vampires appeared in the doorway. Triumphant was too mild a word to describe the expressions on their faces.

"Success?" Adela asked, looking up and meeting Etienne's eye. He smiled and inclined his head.

"Indeed," replied a tall, dark-haired, dark-eyed vampire. Just that one word carried authority and assurance that left Laura in no doubt this had to be Mr. Roman, the reputed Vlad Tepes. "Thanks to the assistance of my valued friend, Larouselière, we have an abundance of invaluable knowledge." His dark eyes fixed on Laura. Something inside her tightened and didn't relax even when he smiled and inclined his head. "You must be the courageous Miss Fox." Sheesh, he actually bowed, as did the two unfamiliar vampires standing behind him. "Madame, I applaud and admire your courage. I am honored to have met you. I am Vlad Tepes." He indicated the two behind him with an imperious wave. "My subordinates Adam and Wilson."

"Honored," they echoed in chorus and bowed again.

Her face burned. This really was getting over the top. "I just stopped him as I was afraid he was going to hurt Dad even more. I was terrified at the time."

Toby was now at her elbow. This moving fast was more than unnerving but his closeness reassured her. Between vamps and witches and ghouls, she was the lone plain, ordinary mortal here.

"That, my love, is most people's definition of courage."

Maybe, but . . .

"Indeed, Miss Fox." It was Vlad again, inclining his head. "I have faced many foes, both before and after my rebirth. Always one has fear facing a powerful enemy. The courageous surmount that fear. You, lady, are courageous."

She was not about to argue with Dracula! She forced a smile and inclined her head in return. It felt odd but somehow seemed appropriate. From the odd reading she'd done here and there, she was, after all, looking a medieval warlord in the face. Toby's hand on her shoulder was more than welcome, though.

"I have been remiss," Toby said, his voice low and firm, the accent coming over clear as morning. "This is Laura Fox, the defeater of the renegade Axel Radcliffe, and she is mine."

Sheesh, she might as well tattoo it on her forehead! Property of Toby Wise.

Adela coughed. "Now that's all settled, what exactly did you learn from that Axel creature?"

Chapter 29

Three pairs of female eyes scanned the assembled vamps. If Vlad and his lot thought they could walk away from this one, they were dead wrong. Literally!

"Yes," Laura said, trying not to sound snippy. The vampires did outnumber them, after all. "I really, really would like to know that. Given the trouble Axel has caused hereabouts, it would be good to know why exactly he picked Dark Falls."

"That," Etienne said, with a flourish of his perfectly manicured hand, "was one of my first inquiries."

The way he said "inquiries" pretty much implied he'd not sat down beside Axel and said "please."

"One of many?" Elizabeth asked. "Why don't you all sit down and tell us everything?"

"Very good idea," Adela added. "There's a few answers I'd like to hear."

Etienne accepted the invitation, seating himself next to Adela. Laura had no time to consider any implications there, as Toby swung a chair around and wedged it between her and Elizabeth. "Keep that place for me," he said. "I'll get some more chairs." Vlad took the remaining spare one and the two attendants stood behind him until Toby returned in minutes swinging two heavy oak chairs as if they were folding lawn chairs.

Vlad's silent shadows sat down. Toby slid between her and Elizabeth, sitting so close his knee rubbed Laura's. Nice but definitely a distraction, and right now she needed to concentrate. She was not about to miss a word.

"Okay, Etienne," Adela said. "Sing."

The *Godfather* terminology was obviously lost on him.

"Spill the beans!" Toby added. Not much of a clarification.

"Tell us," Elizabeth said. "Why pick Oregon? And this end of it, in particular?"

"Yes." Laura decided to add her two cents. "What's the big attraction of Dark Falls?"

"Ah!" Etienne smiled, leaned back in his chair and nodded. "It has been interesting." And if he didn't share the how and why in the next twenty seconds, he'd have three irate women at his throat.

"And?" Adela asked, a testy edge in her voice.

"This Axel and another, Laran"—seemed everyone else recognized that name. What was she missing?— "are members of an ancient nest in El Salvador. Seems about twenty, twenty-five years ago, they were expelled, abjured, cast out, call it what you will, Laran for using mortals in ways prohibited by their laws." A shocked gasp and quick intake of breath came from Elizabeth's end of the table. "And Axel for what they considered an even more heinous offense: creating familiars."

"The chupacabra!" Adela burst out.

"Several of them, I gather. Seems he delighted in the fear, chaos and destruction his 'pets' spread across the landscape. He and Laran met up from time to time, sometimes operating together, but constantly moving on as local nests and colonies became aware of their presence. They spent several years in Mexico and set up a profitable drug ring before having to move on. Seems Laran reached this area first, found it free of other vampires and established himself, passing on word to Axel a couple of years later."

"So they planned to set up shop here?" Lizzie asked.

"More, I think, they wanted an empire. Laran had the money by his control of your father's business. Axel moved in and was intending to control the press and the local law. He intended to buy up more newspapers, even radio and TV stations and he gained control of the deputy. They were all set, until Laran disappeared so mysteriously last year."

"Right." Elizabeth spoke between clenched teeth and tight lips.

There had to be another story there.

Whatever it was, it got a smile and a nod of acknowledgment from Etienne. "Indeed, Madame Goule. You caused that debased creature much distress and mystification."

"Good!" She sounded delighted. "Anything to foil their nasty designs." She turned and grinned at Laura. "Just think, I did in Laran, you fixed up Axel. I bet it sticks in their craw to be bested by girls."

"And Laura really did stick it in his craw," Adela added with a very dry chuckle.

Laura didn't even try to hold back the grin. She had, hadn't she? Toby's hand on her shoulder just added to her pride. She might have acted out of fear, but Vlad accepted it as courage, and so, it seemed, did the lot of them, even Vlad's silent henchmen.

"So," Laura said, "these two wanted to set up a little fief and distribute drugs."

Vlad took over here. "So it would seem. Mrs. Kyd's

elimination of Laran disrupted plans. Axle hoped to continue alone, but it seems Laran had the money."

"The money laundering!" Laura said.

He nodded. "Yes. Without capital, Axel was stymied. That, we learned, was why he sent the FBI after my friend Toby Wise and you, lady, to investigate affairs here." She couldn't help the blush at that; only Toby knew about her poking and prying. Now everyone did. Not that they seemed the least bothered. "He hoped with enough investigation, information would become public and he would be able to discover the money—or at least some of it."

"The bastard sicced them on me," Toby muttered. "All that trouble and disruption was his fault."

"Seem he excelled at trouble and disruption," Laura said. "What about the mess in Dark Falls too? He was behind all that, wasn't he? Adela's house being burned, the deputy's death, accusing Adela."

"Indeed he was," Vlad went on. "He feared my friend Mrs. Whyte because he knew her power could possibly destroy him. The first deputy's death was from anger. He believed the man had killed his familiar. The second because you, my dear Mrs. Whyte, had evaded his clutches."

"The first one was me." Toby's voice was low with regret. "The damn thing attacked me. That deputy was a poor specimen of humanity but didn't deserve to die for it."

"He was that creature's servant," Etienne said. "He intended harm to Adela."

Good point, but hadn't that been under Axel's influence? Besides . . . "So, we know he was intent on harm and hurt all around. What's going to happen to him now?"

"He killed my Zeke," Vlad replied in a voice that sounded as if it had pronounced judgment on thousands over the years. "He will pay for that. When I leave, he comes with me. He will never again cause trouble or upset in my territory."

She was not asking details of how Axel would pay. She did not want to know. But . . .

"It's not quite settled yet, Vlad," Toby said.

A dark eyebrow lifted. "Indeed?'

"Yes, indeed!" The lion's share of this mess was because of Axel and Zeke. They were not skipping off, leaving Toby and Dad to carry the can. "Zeke's remains were found by the police. Right now they are investigating it as murder. Since the remains were found in Dad's backyard, he seems to be a prime suspect."

Toby flinched beside her, gripping her hand. "Sorry about that!"

"Hardly your fault. You didn't off poor Zeke." She looked back at Vlad. "I'm afraid Dad will get blamed. Especially after Axel disappears mysteriously too."

Vlad acknowledged her words with a slow nod and went silent for several seconds. He turned to the vamp on his right. "Adam?"

The man—okay, vamp—looked up, his mind visibly clicking into gear. "Sir, you planned on retrieving Zeke's remains if at all possible. Let us make sure we do. That way we'll remove any evidence and bring Zeke home."

"I bet they have police tape all over the place," Laura said. The look all five vamps gave her clearly showed how vast a consideration that was.

"I'll come with you, Vlad," Toby said. "I want this all taken care of for Laura's peace of mind."

Vlad gave her another bow from the neck. "Indeed it will be, lady. No mere law enforcement individuals will be permitted to cause you or your family distress."

"While we're on the subject of law enforcement

individuals," Adela said, "what about the FBI van that Etienne damaged? They're not going to forget that in a hurry."

Did Vlad practice that eyebrow lift in front of a mirror? No, he couldn't! The little wry smile was a nice extra touch too. Vamps certainly had style. "Mon ami, Larouselière, what is this?"

Yet another explanation needed. Vlad actually let out a dry laugh at the mention of Etienne ejecting from the rear of an FBI van. "Indeed, my friends, life is not uneventful here on the Left Coast."

A bit of dull and boring would be welcome, once in a while. "They might drop the investigation against Connor Inc. as to Axel's accusations, but how can they ignore a whacking great hole in the back of a van?" Laura asked.

"We will take care of all," Vlad stated, leaving Laura in little doubt of the origins of the royal "we." "Is there anything else?"

She hadn't done laundry for several days but suspected the Lord of Wallachia and his minions didn't do ironing.

"We had best start as soon as we can," Etienne said. "The night wears on."

Not that it was a problem for the rest of them. "First we recover my Zeke." Vlad stood, his shadows stepping back as he rose. "Wise, Larouselière, are you with me?"

"Indeed!"

"Bien sûr!"

Standing simultaneously, they spoke together, sounding disturbingly like teenagers ready to party.

Darn this! Laura stood too. "So am I!"

That certainly got attention. The two minions glanced

at Vlad. Etienne gave her a short bow, and Toby squeezed her hand. "We might not be driving, my love."

Oh! She'd forgotten about the flying or running at vamp speed options. "Are you?"

"In any case," Vlad replied, "with respect, lady, it is safer for all if you remain here." He went on before she even had a chance to open her mouth. "As you pointed out, our actions will contravene the law. If we are discovered, we can leave by our own power." He left the rest unsaid.

It was perfectly true and it pissed her off to no end. She looked at Toby. If they were disturbed, he'd stay by her and get nabbed himself. "How are you going to bring back Zeke's remains?"

"I have an urn. Adam and Wilson will bear it there and back. We can run faster than mortal eye can follow."

"You'll remove every last trace?" Sheesh, she was interrogating Dracula, but darn it, Dad's reputation, maybe freedom, were in the balance here.

"Trust us, lady."

She was going to have to. "Be careful and don't get caught." They were all far too polite to smile at that.

They were also gone within five minutes. Toby stayed just long enough to give her a kiss, then stepped out the back door and disappeared into the night. The others were waiting for him. Laura couldn't miss Etienne's tender farewell to Adela. Seemed she wasn't the only one losing her heart to a dead man.

"We need to focus our energy," Adela said, as she closed the outside door.

"Yes," Lizzie replied. "Will you join with us, Laura?"

Would she? They were inviting her to participate in some witchy rite. It was on the tip of her tongue to say she was Methodist, but the words stayed unsaid.

Heck, she was sleeping with a vampire. Might as well join forces with witches. She couldn't remember any Methodist prayers for success of vampire ventures, and prayer might be a good idea. "I'm not sure what to do."

"Bring an open heart. That's what's needed," Adela told her. "Elizabeth is right. We need to send positive energy their way."

So ten minutes later, Laura was sitting cross-legged on the terrace, inside a sacred circle watching a wisp of sweet-scented smoke rise from a small brass dish. Lizzie and Adela had been right, concentrating on the smoke did focus her thoughts, which were on Toby, Toby and Toby.

Tampering with evidence sounded downright risky, forget illegal and unethical, but if left alone, it could implicate, if not condemn, her father. Toby had to succeed.

To run through the night was always exhilarating. To do so in the company of four fellow vamps? Mortal words were pathetically inadequate. Who needed them when one had the wind in one's face? Landmarks, buildings and trees rushed past as Toby led them toward Dark Falls. He followed the coastal road at first, then south of the turnoff for Florence, he headed southeast, eventually turning off to skirt Dark Falls itself and head for Granger's house close to Wyatt's Bend.

He'd half-expected a watching cop car at the end of the drive, but either the local force was too stretched thin—it had taken a couple losses, after all—or with everything else going on, a bunch of unidentified human remains in a remote house was just not high on their priorities. Whatever, it was a clear indication that luck was on their side, at least in this.

He led Etienne, Vlad, Adam and Wilson around the side of the house, and they paused in silence at Zeke's pyre. Laura had been right about the yellow crime scene tape that was looped from shed to tree to old clothesline post. "He'd been staked," Toby said. "I saw it clearly. Right through the chest. The police must have taken them." Evidence, he supposed. Pity that, they needed destroying too.

"How many stakes?" Vlad asked.

"Three." As far as he remembered.

"Must have missed his heart the first couple times," Wilson said and earned a sharp look from Vlad.

So, that was how to destroy one of Vlad's get. Not that Toby actually anticipated ever needing the information.

"Adam!"

Adam jumped forward at Vlad's word. "Sir?" Toby half-expected him to salute. Vlad nodded and he placed the box he'd carried on the ground and lifted off the lid. It was a matter of minutes to scoop up the last undead remains of Zeke Randolph and seal them up in the wooden casket.

Unfortunately there was still the matter of the fine ash residue scattered over the grass and the trampled ground. As tactfully as he could, Toby pointed this out to Vlad.

"Have no worry, my friend," he replied, sounding almost amused. "That I have considered. There will be nothing to implicate your lady's father. Nothing will remain." He looked at his two aides and glanced in Etienne's direction. "Spare me a little time."

The leap up onto the roof wasn't that spectacular. Toby or any one of them could easily have done the same. But what followed certainly underscored the old bloodsucker's power and abilities.

Standing on the ridge, he raised his arms and looked

up at the clear night sky. Praying to some long-ago god? Calling on the heavens for vengeance? Not exactly. He chanted a string of words, in a guttural language Toby didn't recognize. He finished. For a second or two the night silence returned, then a great flash of lightning was followed by a clap of thunder and the heavens opened. A great curtain of rain poured on them, as Vlad resumed his chant. Thank Abel for vamp hearing. The words were barely audible over the noise of the violent storm, but Vlad's intentions were clear: The rain flowed off the roof and soaked the ground.

For ten, fifteen minutes, he kept up the chant, thunder clapped, lightning flashed and the rain poured down on the now-sodden ground and a veritable flood carried away the last remains of Zeke, and any possible traces of evidence.

"Satisfied, my friend?" Vlad asked after he ended his chant and jumped back to the ground.

"Utterly, Vlad. Can't wait to tell Laura. That's a terrific load off her mind."

"A woman of her courage and resources does not deserve to be pestered by petty mortal bureaucrats."

Harsh words toward the force of law. But Vlad had ever been his own law and power. "She will be obliged."

Which no doubt was exactly what the old vampire had in mind. He was not likely to forget they were both residing in his territory. They'd better remember that too. "We'd best get back."

Why hang around ankle-deep in wet grass when he had a warm Laura back at Devil's Elbow to welcome him home?

Chapter 30

"Everything alright?" Toby asked. He tossed the suit-case into the trunk and opened the door as Laura got back in the car.

"Sort of. I got clothes and toiletries for Dad." And was eternally thankful Toby hadn't come into the house and seen the squalor. She'd stifled the guilt at not having come in to clean. Heck, she'd spent all her junior high and high school years cooking and cleaning for Dad. But it had shocked her how horrible the house looked. The cop who'd checked her ID and followed her into the house hadn't turned a hair, but presumably cops saw as bad or worse on a regular basis. "Did get a peep at the kitchen when I went in to check the fridge." And nasty that had been too. "It rained here last night, all right. The backyard is a quagmire. The yellow tape was hanging in tatters, and I swear there can't be a trace of Zeke left."

"Vlad carried away all he could. The storm was a complimentary extra," Toby said. "Never seen anything like it in my life. Doubt even Gwyltha could do that."

Gwyltha, the leader of the colony. Toby had explained that much: a Druid priestess turned vampire. Laura was quite content to hear she seldom left Britain. She'd had

enough vampires to last her awhile. Toby excepted, that
is. "What did you and Adela find out? All I got from the
deputy was they were investigating a possible crime and
would I please give him an address and phone number
where Dad and I could be contacted."

Adela laughed. "Toby hit pay dirt. If you want to
learn anything, talk to a reporter."

Toby grinned at her. "True. That Channel 43 chap was
downright chatty. Of course, he did want me to be interviewed, or better still you, but I declined for both of us."
God bless Toby for that! "Still," he went on as he started
the car and backed down the drive, giving a cheery wave
to the TV crew as they passed them, "seems there's been
a spate of odd incidents in Dark Falls the past couple of
days, so the FBI have sent in a special investigation
team. All very hush-hush but apparently the town is
crawling with Feds."

"We've got to see this!"

"Hell, no!"

She stared, couldn't help it. Toby seldom swore and
never directly at her. "Of course I am. We are. Adela
needs to go downtown to the town hall anyway."

"Laura, see reason! I'm taking you straight to the hospital to pick up your father."

Deep breath needed here. Two, in fact. "Toby, please understand. I need to know what's going on, for Dad's sake."

"She's right, Toby, and you know it in your heart."
Thank you, Adela!

"Are you women loony? Adela, you've been burned
out of your house and arrested. Laura, haven't you seen
enough?"

"Yes, drop me off at my house and I'll get my own car."

"Father Abel, give me strength!"

"He's already done that," Adela piped up again from

the backseat, "in abundance. It's patience you should be asking for!"

Vamps didn't exactly splutter, but the noise that burst from Toby was a pretty close approximation. "We are not going anywhere other than the hospital to pick up your father and then home. Adela, you too! Forget doing anything else here. This place is giving me the willies! We know there's nothing left here to implicate Laura's father in anything. We're getting out while the going is good."

"I do need to get that form notarized," Adela said. "I promised Gertrude. It's why I tagged along, after all."

"There are notaries all over Oregon! I bet there are half a dozen in the office. We'll go by there."

Spitting nails wasn't quite it. But it was getting close.

"Look, Toby . . ." Laura began as he started the car and began to back down the drive.

She never finished.

A scream and a gunshot echoed from somewhere behind the house. While Laura froze, wondering what the heck had happened, a small gray figure dashed from the shrubbery and raced, on all fours, across the unmown grass.

"Not again!" Adela yelped from the backseat.

"Stay in the car!" Toby snapped, as he yanked on the brake and got out, slamming the door shut.

Laura had her hand on the door handle ready to ignore him but instead stared. It all happened so fast. She knew about vampire speed but this had both of them gasping. As the creature rushed at Toby, Adela gasped. "It's another one! A chupacabra!" The whole scene blurred. Toby moved, the creature sailed through the air and hit the front of the car with a resounding thud. The cop, who'd followed her through the house earlier, ran forward, gun drawn, with the second one following. He was much slower and covered in blood, his shirt hanging in shreds from his shoulders.

Adela was out of the car. Laura was right behind.

"Get back, ma'am. Sir!" the first cop said.

"I don't believe it will do any more harm, Officer," Toby said, a touch of dryness in his tone.

They all stood in a ring around the crumpled, inert creature. It was a lot smaller than Laura had expected from Adela and Toby's descriptions, but its blood-covered claws were nasty enough for a creature twice its size.

"What the frigging hell is that?"

Everyone treated the cameraman's question as rhetorical.

"You put that away!" the deputy said, nudging the camera away. "You'll get your pictures later. Right now we need backup and medical help."

"Okay." He lowered the camera but kept it ready. Probably sensed he was missing the shot of his career. And just as well he was.

Laura stepped forward, ignoring the deputy's glares and peered at the creature. "Is it like the other one?"

"Smaller," Adela said, not stepping any nearer.

"Yeah," the bleeding deputy agreed. "I saw the other one in Sam Johnson's cruiser. What happened to this one?" He gave Toby a very curious glance.

"I think it ran into the front of the car. Luckily the impact seems to have knocked it out."

"More than that." The deputy got his courage up and bent over it. "Looks as though you killed it." He looked up. "I think, sir, you'd better come and make a statement.

So they ended up in Dark Falls against all Toby's better judgment. A dark-suited plainclothes agent interviewed them separately in the deputy's office—now smelling of very new paint. Their agreed story was simple enough: The chupacabra hit the front of the car as they backed out. There was no one to contradict their story. And since no one quite knew what to make of it, they were soon let go, with strong warnings not to gossip about what had happened.

"As if the whole town won't be talking about it non-stop," Laura said.

"But we won't be here to listen," Toby replied.

Darn good idea. Even Adela seemed more than happy to turn around and leave Dark Falls behind. No one said another word about a notary.

"You're late!" Dad said, as she and Toby walked into the room.

"Sorry, Dad. We went by the house to pick up some clothes for you and got delayed." Might was well sound cheery and casual.

Didn't work. "Axel bothered you? He's after you, Laura. Stay away from him."

"No sign of him, Dad. In fact the cops are looking for him. He seems to have . . . er . . . disappeared."

Her father frowned. "He meant to hurt you."

Right there. "I'm fine, Dad. And so will you be. Something tells me Axel won't be bothering either of us anymore."

He shook his head as if clearing his thoughts and then looked up at Toby. "And who are you?"

"This is Toby Wise, Dad, a good friend. I'm taking you to his house for a few days. I'll be there to look after you."

"Indeed?" He looked from Toby to her and back again. "Feeling ultrahospitable to an injured man, are you?" he asked. "Or might you have some sort of ulterior motive?

You work for Connor Inc., right?" Darn, he was still on about Axel's obsession.

Toby looked him in the eyes. "Indeed I do, sir, and my motives are definitely ulterior. I'm hoping to soften you up with comfortable living and get you to agree to let me marry Laura."

Dad stared, then laughed out loud, the first time she'd heard him laugh in ages. "You do, do you? As if she'd give two pins over my consent or otherwise. Stubborn girl, she is, like her mother." He let out a sigh. Had been months since he'd mentioned Mom too. Maybe he was slowly coming free of Axel's influence. He looked her way and raised an eyebrow. "So," he said, "is that why you stalled over getting the information Axel wanted?"

"Pretty much." It was the truth . . . just not all of it. And all of it she would never tell him.

But he smiled. At both of them. "Get me out of here. I suppose you'll want me to give you away . . ."

"Yes, please, Dad!"

It couldn't be that simple, could it?

It was.

Well, almost.

There were weeks of driving Dad back and forth to physical therapy and to and from the newspaper office. Toby helped by finding a couple of journalism students to work part time and take up a lot of the slack, and somehow the paper came out every week on schedule. Once Dad's casts came off and Laura had invested in a cleaning service, he moved back to Dark Falls.

In order to save money, and make the vampire she loved supremely happy, Laura gave up the lease on her house in Florence. It was easier with Dad living at

Devil's Elbow, after all, and once he moved out it was wonderful to be alone with Toby. Elizabeth returned to England and her Tom, and Adela left to visit her daughter, Heather, in Ohio, until she could get back to her own house in Chicago and Toby and Laura shared the vast house with Piet.

Two months after the hideous dram of Axel, life seemed wondrously quiet and utterly lovely. Toby had had a couple of visits from agents Bright and Healy but it seemed they were more intent on finding Axel than investigating Connor Inc. When Laura asked if they'd inquired about Etienne's exploding cocoon—it was hardly the sort of thing they'd forget, after all—Toby grinned and told her not to worry, they were utterly satisfied. Seemed they believed it was some sort of sabotage aimed at Connor Inc., the shipping manifest naming some dummy company in the Turks and Caicos that had suddenly disbanded. Toby and Etienne had to be in collusion there. The last she heard of Etienne was when she received a package containing an exquisite antique silver chain, "To replace the one that was lost." Nice of him. She hoped she never needed it for anything more than hanging around her neck.

And just when life didn't seem it could get any better, a certain September Saturday dawned. With just her father to give her away and Kit and Dixie, Toby's friends from Ohio, as witnesses, Laura and Toby were married on the terrace of the house at Devil's Elbow.

Not quite four feet from the study window he'd flown through, naked, a few months earlier.

If you loved this Rosemary Laurey book,
then you won't want to miss
any of her other fabulous vampire stories
from Zebra Books!
Following is a sneak peek . . .

KISS ME FOREVER/LOVE ME FOREVER

He's hot. He's sexy. He's romantic. He's immortal.

If there is one thing Dixie LePage does not need in her life, it's complications. And the man sitting across the table from her in a crowded English pub, the one offering to buy the library of her inherited estate in a small English village, is a major complication. For starters, there's the broad shoulders. The slightly amused smirk. That smoldering look that makes it impossible to concentrate. And that infuriating, old-fashioned, and well, okay, incredibly appealing sense of chivalry. No doubt about it, the guy is hot and sexy. Of course, there is one wee little problem: He claims to be a vampire named Christopher Marlowe, as in *The* Christopher Marlowe, famous playwright, contemporary of William Shakespeare. Right. Amend that to hot, sexy, and totally insane. Please don't see "any more complications." So why can't Dixie seem to resist the warmth of Christopher's charm, the protective feel of his strong hands, or the tempting pull of his full mouth when the sun goes down . . . ?

This time he didn't offer to walk her home. He didn't need to. There was no moon, but Christopher had no problem finding the path. She stumbled on a root, but he reached out and caught her. After that, it made sense to hold his hand and follow him across the green. It also made for distraction and wild imaginings. Her fingers felt warm against his, his handclasp firm and sure. How would his fingers feel on her neck, her shoulders, her . . . ? *Enough.* She didn't want *any* involvement. She'd come here to catch her breath and find peace of mind. Not lose it.

"No visitors tonight," he said as they stood on the gravel drive looking up at the house.

"With my new locks, they'd have to be desperate to keep trying."

"Maybe they are. . . ." He whispered it, as if talking to himself.

She walked up to the door, key in hand. He came with her. Did he expect to be asked in? He'd be disappointed. She wasn't ready for that. Wasn't likely to be, either.

His hand tightened around hers. Her heart tightened inside her chest. "Dixie, make sure you double-check every lock and the windows."

"Worried about me?"

"Why wouldn't I be? Someone's up to no good."

"Offering to come in and protect me from ill wishers?"

"No." It came out a hoarse cry.

His hand closed on hers. She clenched back. She

didn't want him to go. For two cents she would ask him in. No, she wouldn't! Why not? Because she wasn't stupid. Light-headed from the Guinness and the night air, she turned to face him. "Christopher," she whispered, "I will be all right."

"I know. No one will bother you tonight."

"Good night, and thanks for the company." She kissed him.

Rather than the cheek she'd intended, she found his lips and stayed there. Warm, smooth and moist, his mouth opened and hers followed. She had to stand on tiptoe. She'd have climbed the wall for this. His lips tasted of wine and moonlight and his mouth offered passion and heat. She heard a groan like an echo in the night and reached around his neck as his hands framed her head.

His hands seared trails of sensation through her hair and his tongue half-scrambled her brain. She wanted more. She wanted everything he had. She wanted the night, the world, and the morning and she found them here among the overgrown roses and the ankle-deep grass. Her heart raced. Her breathing quickened as if trying to outrace her heart. She felt heat and need and want and satiation. When he pulled back, she gasped for air. The pulse in her neck throbbing and her body screaming for more.

"You don't know what you're doing," a hoarse, ragged whisper warned as his arms locked behind her back.

BE MINE FOREVER

Just for the thrall of it . . .

Six months ago, Angela Ryan woke up from a mysterious attack with no memory, no ID, and no idea why what had once been girlish about her suddenly seemed . . . ghoulish. Being rescued by a clan of vampires is strange enough, but nothing compared to the fact that one of them is the kind of man she's always fantasized about. Tom Kyd has smoldering eyes, a sculpted body, and supernatural staying power. True, Tom is sure he knows best about everything, including how to figure out who she was before her life turned into an episode of *Dark Shadows*. But when his kisses are so dark, so sinful, and so damn good, Angela is tempted to say yes to whatever he wants . . .

"Are we going to stand here all day, scowling at each other?"

"I hope not."

Her mood wasn't helping by the utter certainty that if he chose, he could will her to do whatever he wanted.

To her utter surprise, he stepped aside, just as someone knocked on the door. "Who is it?" Tom asked.

"Porter, sir. With luggage from the other room."

Tom met her eyes and said nothing. It was up to her. She'd missed him. She was glad he'd come. She wanted him so much it hurt. And he was driving her batty.

"Sir?" the voice repeated.

As Tom stepped aside, Angela grabbed the doorknob. "Come in, and thanks."

The porter set up a luggage rack and swung Stella's borrowed canvas bag beside Tom's leather case. Out of the corner of her eye, she saw Tom's hand go to his trouser pocket. "Just a minute," she said, reaching for her bag on the bed. She pulled out a £2 coin and gave it to the porter. "Thank you so much."

Angela shut the door behind his exhortations to call reception if there was anything they needed. Since peace of mind and restoration of lost memories seemed a bit beyond the capabilities of a provincial hotel, she doubted she'd call.

Door closed, she turned to continue her face-off with Tom. He wasn't there. Water was running in the bathroom.

It would be so easy to grab her bag and go. She had

money and credit cards, and a ten-minute walk to the station. But she wasn't going anywhere. Not until she found out something about this defunct Mariposa company, and spoke to Meg again, and sorted things out with Tom. Did she want to spend the night with him? Yes . . . No . . . Oh hell!

"What are you doing?" Stupid question if ever there was one. He was filling the tub, and must have used every complimentary bottle of bath oil. The room smelled like a summer garden in July.

"After that damp walk, how about a nice, warm bath? If I get your clothes off, I'll have a chance at seducing you."

"Tell it like it is, eh?"

"Thought you wouldn't welcome prevarication."

"Why does just about everything you say and do drive me crazy?"

"Haven't we had this conversation before?"

Yes, and got nowhere.

Tom bent to run his hand through the rising bubbles. Satisfied the temperature was to his liking, he started unbuttoning his shirt.

"Taking a lot for granted, aren't you?"

He gave a little shrug, the vampire equivalent of an exasperated sigh. "Maybe. Either way I need a wash after driving down. Would be nice if you'd join me."

"If you hadn't noticed, two minutes ago we were having an argument." She had a hard time keeping her eyes off his chest, and his one visible nipple.

"I had noticed, but making up with wild sex after an argument is a time-honored mortal tradition." His mouth turned up a little at the corners. "We could pretend we were mortals."

KEEP ME FOREVER

Some guys are real animals . . .

Antonia Stonewright isn't about to change her view on love. A sexy mortal companion is fine every now and then, but a soul mate? A partner for life? Please. She was burned once, and hundreds of years haven't healed the wounds. But reclusive potter Michael Langton is . . . different. His gorgeous wares are perfect for her new art gallery—and his gorgeous body is perfect for her. She can't get enough of his toned muscles or his amazing, dark eyes. Their nights together make them both purr with pleasure—except in Michael's case, purring comes naturally. So much for finding a regular boyfriend.

Antonia has a truly sexy beast on her hands . . .

She'd tried. She really had. She was vampire and not susceptible to mortals no matter how bedworthy and delicious, but heading her van toward Bringham, she acknowledged the truth. She hungered for Michael Langton, and the best way to appease a hunger was to sate it.

Halfway there, she pulled over in a car park beside an olde worlde tea shop and asked herself what exactly she was doing.

Easy one that—running after a mortal. But what a mortal! In centuries, she'd never felt this way about anyone. Apart from the confusion and the bewilderment, it was an experience to savor. She grinned and chuckled aloud. Just as well there was no one around to see her. She turned on the ignition and headed for the common, and the man she couldn't get out of her mind.

He wasn't home!

Alright. She had no right to expect him to be twiddling his thumbs waiting for her. But a vamp could dream, couldn't she? The place was empty and had been for some hours. There was warmth from the kiln shed, but that was that.

Or was it?

It was broad daylight, and she was not standing in shadow. But at her age and on her native soil, why the sense of uncertainty? That was the wrong word. The air was alive, or rather, nearby there was a shifting of power. It had been centuries since she'd been aware of a change of nature. Old magic was stirring. Power was in the woods and the ground under her feet. That was what she'd sensed last night but not recognized.

Magic power. How and why?

Were those witches gathering more power than they'd ever imagined? No. This was not mortal magic. This was ancient power. She sensed it, and then it was gone. Like the passing scent of blossom on a breeze. Now there was nothing. Nothing at all.

She gave a grim smile. Michael Langton was playing with danger. Or perhaps danger was playing with him.

She spun around as she sensed life behind her, and there he was, just emerging from the woods. "You came back then."

Perceptive of him! Oh, she was getting snappy. "I don't have your phone number."

He raised an eyebrow and grinned. "How remiss of me. Good thing you knew where to find me."

Now he was getting on her nerves. "I wanted to talk to you."

"Talk?" She was tempted to turn on her heel at his arrogant, self-assured macho grin.

She didn't. Abel alone knew why not. But she was not retreating. She was vampire. Powerful. Strong, and, darn it, she was in dire physical need and tempted to throw a glamour over him and drag him indoors—or better still, not even bother with the last step. Nothing wrong with alfresco sex. "We need to talk about what you have and what I want." Abel take her! Had she actually said that?

Yes! He raised a sandy eyebrow as he took a step closer. "Vases and slipware dishes, I presume?"

It was the realization his feet were bare that did her in. This man walked the woods in bare feet! Feet she wanted, no needed, to feel against her legs. "No. Not slipware dishes or vases. I left too early last night."

His eyes gleamed. Both eyebrows lifted. "I did ask you to stay."

"My mistake."

"And mine for letting you go." Michael stepped forward. Why had he been such a fool? He should have stopped her leaving, tied her to the bed, kept her. She'd been on his mind all day, distracting him. This wild woman who joked about being a vampire! Siren more like. Soaking into his reason, leaving him obsessed with her. "I followed you home."

"I know."

"Where did you go?"

"Home—I know a fast way."

Damn the van! He should have followed her in puma shape. "I'll remember that next time. But since you are here." He reached out and closed his hand over hers. She was so cool, but he'd have her warm and aroused before long. He could smell the need on her. This was utterly foolish. Detachment had been his path to survival all these years. But what the hell? He meshed his fingers with hers and moved in, sweeping her up in his arms and heading for the door. He nudged it open with his knee and carried her inside.

She made not the slightest protest.

And here's a preview of Rosemary Laurey's
next novel, coming from Zebra
in November 2007.

September 1940
Flying over Southeast England

By Fritz Lantz's reckoning they were twenty minutes from the first drop.

They'd been lucky so far: visibility clear and, miraculously, no ack ack or searchlights looking their way. Not long now and he'd be unloading his odd passengers and heading back to France and breakfast in the *verwirrung*.

"How about our cargo?" Fritz asked Dieter, his radio operator.

"A rum lot!"

That point they agreed on. "I'll be glad when we turf them out and get back home. They give me the willies." Come to that the whole mission seemed off a bit. Dropping spies and saboteurs was nothing unusual, and Fritz hoped every single one of them gave the Tommies a run for their money. It would be a long time before Fritz Lantz forgot the bombs the damned Brits rained down on Berlin. But these four he was carrying over the channel put the wind up him so much he almost felt sorry for the enemy. He was still puzzling over his orders: No observing when they jumped. Dieter was to open the doors and return to the cockpit and give the signal from there. He was to close the jump doors ten minutes after the last one had left and not before. Then they were to head right home. The last bit wouldn't be hard to follow.

"Never had a drop like this in my life," Dieter said, shaking his head. "As good as snapped my head off when I tried to explain how to put on the parachutes. Serve them damn right if they don't open for them!"

"Almost there," Fritz replied. "Better go back and latch open the cargo door and let's unload them."

The drop orders were straightforward enough: four points, five to ten kilometers apart, in a rough circle. Some town was getting a foretaste of the invasion. It was war after all.

"Want to know something?" Dieter said, a while later, as he returned from latching the cargo door, after the drop. "They dumped their parachutes on the floor. Never took them!"

"Don't talk rot! They switched with the spares."

Dieter shook his head. "No, they didn't. Our scary boys jumped without."

He had to be kidding, or hadn't counted the parachutes properly. "They won't give the Tommies much trouble will they?" Dieter did have a screw loose if he believed that, but hell, it would make a good story over a pilsner when they got back.

Five miles beyond Beachy Head, the engine sputtered and died. Fritz stared horrified at the fuel gauge. He'd left with more than enough to get back but now it was empty.

"Bail out!" he called to Dieter, as he unbuckled his own harness.

They both made it out seconds before the plane plummeted down toward the channel but, according to special arrangements of the German High Command, their parachutes failed to open. Dieter and Fritz followed their Focke to a watery grave.

* * *

After jumping, the four vampires glided down toward their designated landings. Well-briefed and with land support waiting, they were more than ready to do their share of preparing the way for the coming invasion.

Gerhardt Eiche, Wilhelm Bloch, and Hans Wiess landed safely and each headed for their appointed rendezvous. Paul Schmidt was less fortunate, by mischance, unexpected wind, or inaccurate coordinates, he missed the clear acreage around Crockett's pig farm, with the potential for restorative warm blood of both humans and animals, and crashed into the ancient cluster of oaks on Fletchers Hill, impaling himself on the uppermost branches of a tree, hitting his head on the trunk of another and mercifully cutting off sense and pain before crashing to Earth.

He recovered not long before dawn. Weak from the wood poison in his system, he struggled to free his flesh of the splinters and bark. As dawn rose, his remaining strength waned. Without blood he would expire before nightfall, his mission unfulfilled. Despair washed over him at the prospect of failing his blood oath. His country needed him. Needed all of them, and he had failed. He would die on this cursed English soil.

Hours later, he heard an engine approach and stop. A car meant a mortal driver, maybe even passengers. He was saved. He'd have his first feeding of English blood and strike a blow to the enemy.

Alice Doyle was exhausted. Staying up half the night to deliver twins will do that to you. The elation and adrenaline of her first set of twins had carried her this far home, but as she turned into the lane that crossed Fletchers Hill, weariness set in. It had been a good night's work though. She wouldn't easily forget the rejoicing in the Watson farmhouse and Melanie's happiness through her fatigue as she breastfed her lusty sons.

"A fine brace of boys. Gives one hope for the future, doesn't it, Doctor?" Roger Watson said as he smiled at his grandsons. "If only Peter were here to see them." The Watsons' only son, Peter, was somewhere in Norfolk with the army and Alice couldn't help but worry how Melanie, a Londoner born and bred, would fare with her in-laws in a farm as remote as you could find in Surrey.

Still, Farmer Watson was right: whatever the politicians did or however many bombs fell, life went on.

The numerous cups of tea she'd consumed through the night were having their effect and she still had several miles to go over bumpy country roads. She pulled over to the verge and got out. Other traffic was unlikely out here. Few locals enjoyed the supply of petrol allocated to doctors. Even so, Alice climbed over the gate and ventured into the woods for a bit of privacy.

She was straightening her clothes when she realized she was not alone. Darn! A bit late to be worrying about modesty. Deeper in the woods, someone crawled toward her. Assuming injuries, Alice called, "I'm coming. I'm a doctor."

It was a stranger. One of the workers from the hush-hush munitions camp up on the heath, perhaps? What in heaven's name was he doing rolling on the damp ground? As Alice bent over him, he looked up at her with glazed eyes. Drunk perhaps? But she didn't smell anything on his breath.

"What happened?" as she spoke, she saw the stains on his sleeve. Blood loss might well account for his weakness. She looked more closely at him and gasped. Part of the branch of a tree was embedded in his upper arm. How in heaven's name? Had to be drunk. If there wasn't enough to do, she had to cope with boozers who impaled themselves on trees. Seemed that was his only injury. No bleeding from the mouth or nose. Heartbeat was abnormally slow but steady, his breathing shallow and his skin cold to the touch. Shock and exposure would explain all that. Best get him out of the damp.

"Look," she said, trying her utmost to keep the fatigue out of her voice. "I'm going to help you up. I need you to walk to my car. I've my bag here and I'll have a look at your arm. Then I'll take you down to my surgery in Brytewood and call an ambulance."

The odd, glazed eyes seemed to focus. "Thanks," he croaked.

"What's your name?"

He had to think about that one. Definitely recovering from a wild night. "Smith." Really? Aiming for anonymity perhaps?

"Paul Smith."

Alice got behind him and propped up his shoulders until he was sitting. "Come along, Mr. Smith," she told him. "I'm going to give you a boost and you have to stand. I can't carry you."

They succeeded on the second go and made slow progress toward her car, Alice supporting Mr. Smith on his good side. He was a lot lighter than anticipated as he slowly staggered toward the road. He supported himself against the hedge as Alice opened and closed the gate, but once they emerged from the shade into the thin afternoon sun, he collapsed.

Thank heaven for her father's old shooting brake. She got her patient into the back so he was lying against the sack of potatoes the Watsons had insisted she take with her.

"Mr. Smith, I'm going to examine your arm. I'm afraid I'll have to cut your shirtsleeve."

Taking the nod as agreement, Alice snipped off the sleeve. The shirt was good for nothing but rags anyway. Her first observation had been right: several chunks of fresh wood had penetrated the flesh of his upper arm. "How did you do this, then?" she asked as she opened her bag and reached for sterile swabs and astringent.

She cried out as he grabbed her free hand in a viselike grip and bit her wrist.

He was more than drunk. He was insane! Alice tried to push him away but he held on, digging his teeth into her flesh. She finally grabbed his nose until he gasped for breath and released her.

"Behave yourself! I'm a doctor! I'm here to help . . ." She broke off when it was obvious he'd passed out.